Noah, Noah

Paul Wilson was born in 1960. He is also the author of *The Fall from Grace of Harry Angel*, *Days of Good Hope* and *Do White Whales Sing at the Edge of the World?*, winner of the 1997 Portico Prize for Literature. He lives in Blackburn, Lancashire, where he works in the field of learning disability.

Also by Paul Wilson

The Fall from Grace of Harry Angel
Days of Good Hope
Do White Whales Sing at the Edge of the World?

Noah, Noah

PAUL WILSON

Granta Books
London

Granta Publications, 2/3 Hanover Yard, London N1 8BE

First published in Great Britain by Granta Books 1999
This edition published by Granta Books 2000

Copyright © 1999 by Paul Wilson

A CIP catalogue record for this book
is available from the British Library.

1 3 5 7 9 10 8 6 4 2

Printed and bound in Great Britain
by Mackays of Chatham plc

Contents

Acknowledgements

Thanks to Kathleen and Phil Calvey, Bev French, Steve Lee and Fred Cumpstey for their help in researching various parts of this book.

This is the book I never read
These are the words I never said
This is the path I'll never tread
These are the dreams I'll dream instead.

– Annie Lennox

1

Noah

He was always arriving, always stepping down from the train. It was always the same man. Noah Brindle pictured him often. Women had caught Noah as a boy staring at nothing, had chivvied him on impatiently. Sometimes he was picturing the man arriving on the train, but he never said.

Noah Brindle had fine blue eyes and a long body that he carried inelegantly like a dead weight. Sometimes he sang awkward words slowly in rhythm – a reminder of the childhood stutter he had beaten. He wore clothes that struggled with his bigness – long arms, heavy shoulders, a lack of definition; things hung on him. He watched the news each evening, anxious about the fall of foreign governments; he shopped for bread, coffee, ice cream, late at night in supermarkets; he listened well to people; he watched old films on TV when sleep evaded him and he couldn't settle to read. He coveted the titles of books he'd read, the poetry they sometimes held in half a dozen words or less, saying what a life had been. *Great Expectations*, *One Hundred Years of Solitude*, *The Book of Laughter and Forgetting*, *The Great Gatsby*. He wondered what his own life would be called. Would half a dozen words embrace him?

Noah was fifty-one years old. His best feature? A kind of stamina, a kind of staying-at-the-wheel. He thought of himself as settled; the way a landslide was settled, once everything had fallen and afterwards lay still. Staring into space sometimes, Noah still pictured the man in a dress suit with a white dinner jacket, stepping down from a train arriving from the anonymous Lancashire hills. The man was always arriving. But Noah had never known anyone to tell.

He had tried to write it down. Noah liked the way that words could wrestle with him like playful giants, leaving him weary and exultant from the effort. He played with sentences on bits of paper, envelopes, the backs of invoices. He didn't understand this need to write. He didn't understand the world. He couldn't shape it as other people seemed to do. He couldn't explain away the world as this or that.

Mr George was the kind of man, Noah wrote one night in the margin of a gas bill, *for whom the accomplishing of big deeds seemed inevitable*. He sat looking at what he had written.

Noah had thought about telling Elly Pascoe. Instead, having shrunk from the prospect, he'd admitted something easier – that every couple of months he was prone to ear infections which made him queasy. She had no sympathy when he said he hadn't been to the doctor.

Elly Pascoe was his one unequivocal friend. She ran the Sandwich Box over the road from Noah Brindle's community centre, his place of work for more than twenty years. Noah went across the street to eat there at lunchtimes. She always called him by his surname (she always had – something about his caution, the things he kept from her) and sometimes she kept the table at the back free for him around noon. Five feet and slight, Elly Pascoe seemed to Noah to be frightened of nothing, as though things she had once weathered had tempered her. She was somewhere in her thirties, her hair cropped short for convenience and her girl's curious eyes following him boldly. He had started to imagine her body underneath the Sandwich Box apron. Guiltily he found it easy, like a trick a dog might learn and perfect – her flesh emblazoned stubbornly in his head. He wondered if lust always came first, like a flag waved at a dumb animal signalling other things that might follow. Noah had watched for suitors, but Elly Pascoe, seemingly self-contained, didn't suffer fools gladly and most would-be suitors, reminding her of the departed Neville, seemed like fools to her.

Elly Pascoe lived with her son, Josh, who was fifteen and finding the going tough. The two of them lived above the shop on Lowell's high street, where the road started its slide into the town's St Silas district. She had bought the Sandwich Box three years ago on a mortgage after her divorce came through. It had been a hard time and Noah Brindle had seemed to be around whenever she wanted to shout things out of her system – ran the place himself for a few days while she took some time away alone. Neville, her ex-husband, was on the police force in Lowell and had Josh Saturdays and Sundays, shifts permitting. Elly's version was that Neville and the boy worked their way through at least half a dozen videos from the video hire counter at Spar each weekend.

'He comes back pale and blinking hard like he's been underground for two days,' she had complained to Noah.

Twice a week, once when Josh was out at the Lowell youth theatre (he liked helping with the technical stuff, the staging and the lighting – things that didn't require him to *say* much) and once on Saturdays when he was with his dad, Elly Pascoe cleaned out the shop and went to do the housewives' shift on the tills at Asda. She spent the money on the counsellor she'd been going to for the past three years.

Noah had asked her why she had started going to a counsellor.

'That's my business, Brindle,' she had told him, slicing finger teacakes three at a time with a fourteen-inch bread knife behind the counter. 'You ever catch me asking where you buy those lumpy sweaters, or get that haircut?' She'd seemed not to mind, though, that he had asked.

'You didn't have to pay all that money just to talk to someone,' he'd said. 'You could have talked to me.'

'What would you know,' Elly Pascoe had told him, 'you're a man.'

In the orphanage, it had been the practice for the staff to choose first names for infants who arrived unchristened. Because Noah's orphanage was a Christian-based institution, it was inevitable, perhaps, that the choice of names was biblical. Thus, 'Noah' hardly seemed extraordinary at all, even in the depths of East Lancashire, since as he was growing up he was surrounded by, amongst others, a Jacob, a Jonah, an Abraham and a Rachel. It was as though the biblical stories to which these orphans were attached served as a substitute for the personal histories which fed and nourished other children.

I am Noah, he would think. Fine. One day, perhaps, I will command a boat or save people from a rising flood.

Occasionally, an orphan would have no birth certificate and no hospital record of who the mother was. This might happen if the mother was an unmarried mill girl and the birth had perhaps been clandestine. Then, the staff at the orphanage would have to find a surname for the child as well. The practice was to choose a local place-name as the child's surname; perhaps the idea was to provide an anchor for the child who had been cast free not just of any relationship with his natural parents but even of knowing their names. So, there was a Clitheroe and a Whalley and a Standish and so on; and Noah was a Brindle. Fine, Noah thought – maybe the rising flood will be in Lancashire. It was a version of the world that, all these years, had held him safe.

The Mustard Seed Centre had formerly been the old St Silas Church. Already derelict, it had been bought from the Diocese twenty-five years ago by the Dounleavey Trust for whom Noah worked, and to whom he had given half his life – the better part of it. The Trust was a Lancashire charity, founded by a philanthropic cotton magnate with the stated aim of promoting the social welfare of the working classes in the mill towns of the Rossendale Valley.

The Dounleavey Trust was listed in the Charities Aid Foundation Directory as: assets £160,000; annual grants £7,000; applications – East Lancashire. It had suffered a brief notoriety beyond the valley two years before when the ageing trustees had appointed a development manager with a business background. The new man had come with references from City firms. Elly Pascoe, who met him briefly once, had christened him the Sundance Kid. He had spent some time (successfully) gambling the Trust's assets in high-risk, high-return investments, without any kind of auditing checks or balances, and salting a percentage of the proceeds away for himself. He had left the country twenty-four hours before the accountants called in the police, having found £272,000 switched unaccountably to an already emptied offshore bank account.

The former church remained in need of renovation. The roof leaked, the belfry was a safety risk and the building had its fire certificate refused twice, requiring work which, in truth, the Dounleavey Trust could ill afford but which Noah brokered at committee meetings. The work of the Mustard Seed wasn't finished, Noah had argued. This was not the time to shut the place down. What about the kids on the St Silas estate? What about the food co-op and the other groups who used the centre? Lowell *needed* the centre. But other liabilities emerged, other pots the Sundance Kid had dabbled in. The prospect of the Trust being wound up and put into receivership by the Charities Commission, and the danger of the ageing trustees being held personally liable for the remaining debts, hung over them. The decision to sell the Mustard Seed was finally taken on the advice of the lawyers and the accountants. In the letter he received confirming that his contract could not be renewed at the end of the year, Noah was told that it was a matter of survival.

Things Fall Apart was the title that hummed in Noah Brindle now, as his own life stuttered to a standstill. The For Sale sign went up. The trustees gave him six months to round things off.

For now, the work went on. Inside the Mustard Seed Centre, the main hall, long since stripped of its pews, continued as a kind of community hall; the vestry was a meeting room; the altar space was split into an interview room and storage for toys and tables; the flagged crypt beneath served as a basement storeroom for unwanted furniture which was collected around the town by the legendary Tipper Gill in a battered ex-Norweb

Transit, and ferried back to the Mustard Seed. There it was stored until it was allocated according to need, more often than not to tenants of the St Silas estate.

The meetings of the St Silas tenants group, set up some years ago by Noah, were still held in the building; its members – all women – ran rumbustious committee meetings once a month and afterwards got drunk in relief and celebration when the books for the St Silas food co-operative (which also operated from the building) still somehow balanced. The railinged yard, behind the former church, had two basketball hoops propped centre stage like flagpoles. Noah had written to the Council eighteen months ago asking for a grant for the roof to be repaired, having been refused funds by the trustees. Four months later, he got a letter back saying that he could have a basketball court marked out in the yard as part of the Council's Basketball Development Strategy. Noah had taken what he was offered; it seemed from experience to be how the Council worked.

The Mustard Seed Centre also ran a couple of junior football teams, and a youth club which still met once a week. The kids liked the flaking plaster statues of the saints hoisted high up in alcoves on the walls of the main hall (taking regular aim at them with tennis balls smuggled into the building) and the way that their shouts into the grilles of the redundant Victorian heating pipes smacked like billiard balls from one part of the building to another: 'FUCK, FUCK, FUCK. MORAG GILL SHAGS DONKEYS.'

In winter, the rooms in the old church relied on mobile heaters to keep them warm enough for the toddlers, and for the classes which ran there – pottery, keep fit, writing; for someone from the Citizens' Advice in Haslingden who came across once a week to talk about welfare rights in the interview room; for the alcohol support group which met on Mondays after the youth club, whose members had by then dispersed to the park with their bottles of premium-strength lager in a kind of eerie evening symmetry.

The writing group was one that Noah ran. It had started as a simple English class. Most of the women joined originally because they wanted help to fill in forms, and they came to the class for a week, sometimes two. When the forms were done, the women shrank back to the edges of the town that was big enough to swallow them for a month or so before Noah saw them again on the high street, or in the launderette, or beyond the railings of the infant school yard at half-past three.

The ones who stayed around – Morag Gill and Dorothy, Theresa who looked after her senile mum, Linde Wzinska who cleaned the centre, and Olwen Sudders who couldn't hear or speak – became, over the years, the nucleus of the tenants group for the St Silas estate, dealing in wholesale fresh fruit and veg on Thursdays and in estate business the rest of the week – with repairs backlogs for the houses infected by damp and woodwork problems, kids causing trouble, and difficulties with the police. The correspondence was always much the same: the police would have noted the tenants' comments (Morag Gill kept a file of the 'incident receipts' posted to them in accordance with the new police customer-relations practice) and the Housing Department based further up the valley would report, in response to whatever a tenant's complaint was, that the routine-repairs budget for that quarter was already spent. But they persisted.

More stamina, Noah thought to himself; more staying-at-the-wheel. And sometimes he dreamed of the man arriving through the hills on a train – the man in the dress suit with the white dinner jacket – as if something here was being augured.

2

Mr George

Mr George was the kind of man for whom the founding of an orphanage, the accomplishing of big deeds, seemed inevitable. There is an old photograph of Mr George supervising the opening of the orphanage. In the photograph, he wears the same white dinner jacket in which he had made his implausible entrance into the life of the town and to which, over the years, he had become so attached.

'I came to Lancashire,' he would say, 'suitably dressed for an *occasion*.'

The children competed to tell the story of the young Mr George's arrival in the town.

'He came with eleven shillings in his pocket,' they would say.

'Yes, eleven shillings, and he was twenty-two.'

'And he came dressed for the occasion.'

They practised versions of it for each other in the long dormitory, lying in their beds at night, imagining the arrival which Mr George had himself recalled many times. After all, to picture a tall, pale young man stepping down from a train is a fine opening, from which other things – easily remembered things – might seem to follow.

Each time the inspectors came round, Mr George's orphans would see it as an opportunity to have their knowledge of the orphanage's founding tested. It was an eagerly anticipated routine for them to be asked and each year they all chipped in, anxious to share in the telling, all wanting to start at the point where Mr George first arrived in the town.

'He came on a train,' Goose, bigger than the others, would yell.

'A *steam* train,' Walter would correct him.

'With a white dinner jacket on, even though he wasn't coming to dinner.'

'And he came to work in Lancashire as a carpenter,' Megan would explain.

'A joiner,' Walter would say.

'A carpenter's what Jesus was, so Mr George should be called the same.'

And so it went on, following the familiar lines of the story they knew by heart, until the inspectors, anxious to keep to the schedule, moved on to a review of last year's accounts. But by that time everyone would have confirmed again that Mr George had arrived in the town at the age of twenty-two, with a carnation in his buttonhole, and with snow beginning to feather the ground as he walked out of the station, wearing that implausible white dinner jacket as though he was a late-arrival for the Mayor's Ball being held in the town that evening. He had eleven shillings in his pocket, the skills of a carpenter in his head, and a life stretching ahead of him.

3

Keeping Vigil

It was only just gone five when Noah was woken. Telephone calls in the night were not new to him. They had the feel of being thrown from a moving horse; there was the same disorientation, the sense of waiting for the remarkable flight to end, and for the sudden smack of reality.

It was usually the same phone call that woke Noah. Every so often, part-way through the night, his phone would ring. He would struggle to come to and fight his way upright, reaching for the receiver.

'Yes?' he said the first time it had happened.

There had been no answer.

'Hello? Who's there?'

A man's voice, distracted, had said, 'Can I speak to Joan?'

'Joan?'

'I need to talk to Joan.' The man's voice was anxious.

'There's no Joan here.'

The man had begun to plead. 'Please,' he had said. 'You have to let me talk to her.'

'To Joan?'

'Yes.'

'But there isn't a Joan living here.'

11

'No Joan?'

'No.'

'Who is this?'

'Noah.'

The man had paused. 'I'm sorry,' he'd said. 'I must have got the wrong number. I'm sorry. I didn't mean to wake you. I'm really sorry.' And he put the phone down.

Noah had told Elly Pascoe about the phone call.

'You know a Joan?' she'd asked.

He didn't know anyone of that name.

Some weeks later, the man had rung again. Again it was the middle of the night. Noah, pulled fast from some astonishing dream, struggled to explain again that he lived on his own. He said there was no one else there. He said he thought the man had got the number wrong, just got one of the digits out of sequence or something. The man seemed in a hurry this time. He didn't seem to hear Noah.

'I just need to talk to Joan,' he said. 'I've left it too long as it is. Is Joan there?'

Noah explained again.

The man apologized again. He rang off. He said he wouldn't bother Noah again.

But every so often – perhaps after weeks, or months – the phone would ring in the night and it would be him.

'Is Joan there?' the voice would say. Sometimes it would be calm, matter of fact, sometimes remorseful. Sometimes it sounded to Noah as though the man had been drinking, or crying. Noah would try to explain that they had spoken before. He would say that this was a regular mistake. He would tell the man his own name in confirmation of this. But the man always needed to be convinced. His anxiety made him sceptical. He seemed to feel that Noah was holding something back. After a while, if the man was still not convinced, Noah would give up. 'There isn't a Joan here – you should know that by now.' And he would put the phone down. And then lie awake, wondering about the man.

And so when the phone rang close by Noah in the middle of the night, stirring him, he was surprised to hear a woman's voice.

'Is dat Noah?'

'Linde?' Even at that hour, Noah could make out Linde Wzinska's Polish vowels.

'Is Linde, yes. I hope I don't wake you.'

Linde Wzinska worked part-time for Noah as caretaker for the Mustard Seed Centre.

Noah stared at his watch while his vision cleared. It was five something.

'I thought you want to know. It's thuh deaf woman.'

'Olwen?'

'They think she was attacked in the night. By a man. By thuh prowler that's been around. They can't make her say any-thing at the hospital. I mean *write* anything. I say to them I know a good man who can help with her.'

Linde, a notoriously early riser, had found Olwen Sudders down by the river. She was bothered by the arthritis in her fingers and her feet, but she also had an extra reason to get up early. After her house had been broken into the second time, she'd bought herself an Alsatian puppy – a sloppy, slapdash eight-week-old creature with paws like blacksmiths' fists – which grew as high as her hip within a year and which she called Herman. She had to be out of bed by four o'clock to walk Herman down past Tipper Gill's football field at the bottom of the estate and on to the towpath. Without the worry of Herman's size and lack of restraint frightening people, she ran the dog off the leash for the hour it needed to burn up its furious energy chasing a tennis ball. That was how Linde had come to find Olwen Sudders so early in the morning.

Olwen was shivering. She wouldn't move at first when Linde indicated that she would walk her back home. She seemed frightened of Herman who was sniffing her. 'He's a stupid dog,' Linde liked to say to Noah, 'but he won't do nothing. You know dat, Noah. He just like a man, he like to stick his nose into things. He just so big he scares people.'

Olwen Sudders wouldn't tell Linde what the matter was. She wouldn't write anything down on the notepad that she always carried with her and she wouldn't go home. In the end, Linde borrowed the pad herself and wrote down 'Mustard Seed' and left Olwen Sudders there while she returned home to collect her keys for the centre. She came back and the two of them walked up through the estate, and Linde unlocked the Mustard Seed. She made a cup of tea and Olwen Sudders sat by the window of Noah Brindle's office, looking out on to the yard with its basketball court and hoops, cradling the cup of tea. Linde noticed that Olwen Sudders was still shivering. That was when she saw the blood and when she decided to take Olwen to the hospital in a taxi, using money from the petty cash. She said to Noah that she hoped it was all right about the money. She said the woman was just shaking all the time, poor cow.

Noah reached the hospital at about seven. Olwen Sudders was

still in casualty. She had been put in a sideroom on her own with a view of the hills further up the valley. Noah walked past the open-plan bays of the casualty department. At the far end, he stood watching her through the glass. The nurse said, 'We had to put her in here. She started screaming.'

The police had been up but they couldn't get anything out of Olwen Sudders. Neville Pascoe and his partner had hung around waiting for Noah to arrive because there was no one else there who could sign, but they had gone shortly before seven on the promise of breakfast in the staff canteen. They'd said they'd be back later. Noah scribbled out the address and number of the Mustard Seed for the nurse and said if the police still couldn't get anything out of Olwen Sudders they could ring him. Then Noah went into the room.

Olwen Sudders was standing with her back to him, looking out of the window. He crossed the room and stood beside her. Her hands were clenched by her sides, white. Her hair was pushed back in tufts. She looked round at him.

Noah signed, 'Hello.'

She took a step into the space between them. Noah signed, 'How are you?'

She shook her head, looked away. It could have been 'Bad', or 'I don't know', or that she wasn't saying.

Her face was rigid, ready to break. Then suddenly she was hitting his chest with her palms. She struck his lip. He caught one of her arms as she struck blows at his head, then released it. As suddenly as she had begun, she stopped. She was panting. Then she began to cry. She fell against him. Noah held her while she sobbed, making no sound, until it was all out of her.

*

15

Noah was watching Elly Pascoe behind the counter. She tore strips from an iceberg lettuce, sliced a beef tomato with an impossibly sharp vegetable knife that, guided by her fingers, slipped soundlessly through the flesh. Outside, cars drove by through the town. People passed the window. Elly turned the bacon on the griddle with a pair of tongs, flipped the egg. Noah found he was watching her rather than the food, even though he had not eaten breakfast and had been up what seemed half the night after the phone call and the drive up to the hospital.

'So how'd you get involved?' she said.

'I got a phone call.'

'Is she in the hospital?'

Noah nodded.

'The deaf and dumb one? From the estate?'

'Olwen Sudders.'

'Bastard,' she said. 'I hope they get him. How is she?'

'Still in shock, I think. Your Neville and his colleague haven't been able to get anything out of her.'

'He's not my Neville.'

'I'll go up again after tea to see how she's doing.'

'How come it's always you, Brindle?' She turned back to the griddle and scooped his two rashers of bacon into the teacake. She poked dismissively at the bacon. 'Brown sauce or mustard?'

She grimaced as she looked at it.

'Both.'

Elly Pascoe had turned vegetarian six months after she started her therapy.

'My counsellor says I should start to make some positive de-cisions,' she had told Noah, 'instead of waiting for things to happen to me. She says it's a way of showing I'm learning to like

16

myself. I said what sort of things. She said like taking up a musical instrument or trekking in Tibet. I said, "So are you going to come and run the business for me while I'm busy doing this stuff?"'

A week later she had turned vegetarian. She'd seen a programme on Channel Four. 'It's something I'm doing for me,' she had told Noah.

She bought a poster that said 'Meat is Murder' and put it up in the shop.

'You want to know what they do to factory chickens to get them to their optimum size in twelve weeks, Brindle?'

Noah said he didn't. 'What does your counsellor think about you becoming a vegetarian?' he asked her.

'She's worried about my profit margin,' Elly told him. 'I said who better to work on people's ignorance about the meat industry. Besides, I didn't think it was going to affect my chances of moving into the forty per cent income-tax bracket one way or the other.'

She carried on turning out sandwiches with ham and chicken and sliced beef for the dinnertime trade in Lowell, and cooking bacon and sausages for the all-day breakfasts, but she expanded her range of vegetarian options and made a conscious effort to be friendlier with people buying cheese and chutney than those wanting cooked tongue.

Noah had found himself edging towards more meatless options until one day she sussed him.

'You're a tokenist, Brindle,' she announced, victorious, as if she'd found some crucial flaw in his character. Since then, he had returned to his standard sausage-and-egg barms or chicken with sweetcorn relish.

*

Elly Pascoe passed him the teacake on a plate and the mug of tea he'd ordered and rang the price up on the till.

'You in a rush today?' she asked as she took his money.

He shook his head. 'I said I'd be back for Tipper at one. A couple of errands on the estate this afternoon.'

'You have the time to sit down?'

'Why?'

'You mind company?'

She meant her son. Josh was already sitting at the back table. 'No school today?'

'He said he felt sick,' she said. She gave a shrug. 'I said he could stop off if he did some revision.'

Noah took his plate and mug and went across to Josh's table. The Sandwich Box was mostly takeaway service, but Elly kept half a dozen tables set for sit-down pie and peas, and all-day breakfasts. It was mostly pensioners who came in to sit. Sometimes she had workmen in for fry-ups. Most of her trade was sandwiches and pies for shop workers, and students from the secondary school.

'Hiya, Josh.'

The boy looked up but didn't answer. He was playing with a plastic fork from the counter, concentrating intently on it. Josh's complexion had soured over the last six months and was pockmarked with blemishes now, the outward sign of his inward transition from boy to youth. He fidgeted a lot. Elly worried about him; they didn't talk like they used to. Noah had tried to get him involved in the Mustard Seed in some way but the boy wouldn't take him on. Sometimes he would barely acknowledge Noah, drifting in and out of his own private world. At other times, Josh would talk and talk in an edgy, imprecise way, as if internal words were swilling in his head, distracting him from the ones he was trying to release in speech.

'Revision going well, Josh?'

'Suppose.'

'Feeling rough?'

The boy didn't seem to hear the follow-up question. He went back to twiddling the fork. He had a couple of closed exercise books on the table. Noah ate his dinner, sometimes watching the boy, sometimes not. Josh remained engrossed in the movement of the fork in his hand. When he began talking, he was still looking hard at the fork, not at Noah.

'Can I ask you something?'

'Sure,' Noah said, trying to seem unconcerned.

'You ever get, like, interference when you're thinking things?' the boy said. He was turning the fork in his hand.

'How do you mean?'

'Damien has this thing he reckons that could explain it.'

'Damien at school?'

'Damien reckons aliens could be controlling us.'

Noah swigged his tea. 'Uh-huh?'

'They could be using us as puppets. He says how do we know they're not. I mean, you wouldn't know, would you, if you were being controlled? If your thoughts weren't your own. If sometimes you were being made to think them from the out-side.'

'Does it worry Damien? It doesn't seem all that likely.'

'Well, that's exactly what I mean. They could be controlling you to say something like that, in order to throw me off the scent because I've begun to suss them out. They could be choosing our words for us – what we do, everything. They could be using us, all the time. In a big experiment. To make us think things.'

'Is that what you believe, Josh?'

The sound of his own name made the boy look up from the table and pause for a minute.

'I don't know.'

'You feel like *you're* being made to think things?'

Josh was twisting the fork. He bent it tighter. It held. Then snapped. *Plick*. He looked down at its two separate pieces, surprised, and then, briefly, at Noah.

'I have to go,' he said. 'I have to revise. Mum says.'

He picked up the books and walked towards the door through to the kitchen and the back stairs, head down, a little hunched, looking at the floor.

After a while, Elly came out front to clear the table. 'How's the man from Mars?' she asked.

'Worried,' Noah said.

'Maybe getting taken by aliens is going to be his best bet,' she said. 'No one else is going to be interested in him at this rate.'

'What's your counsellor say about it?'

'Nothing,' she said. 'It's *my* time when I go to see her, not Josh's. Not that it's anybody's business *what* I talk about.'

She cleared the next table, went through to the back, then returned, not yet finished.

'You know he got another detention slip this week? That's four this term for not handing homework in after reminders. I pin him down about it and he just says he keeps forgetting it. He says it's no big deal. It just doesn't bother him any more. At one time he'd have been horror-stricken to have got a detention. Now, it's like it's nothing.'

She was not defeated, only vexed; only airing her frustrations with the safe Noah Brindle.

'Have you talked to him about this stuff?' Noah said.

'I don't speak Martian.'

'You think Josh wants to talk?'

'Believe me, he doesn't.'

'Maybe he just doesn't know how at the moment. I wouldn't worry.'

'You were born fifty, Brindle – how do you know about fifteen? If I want to worry about him, you let me worry. And eat up – your charred flesh is going cold.'

She rattled some pans stacking them back behind the counter. She served the elderly couple who had just come in. Noah finished his teacake, then carried his plate and mug back to the counter.

'You know your problem, Brindle?' she said. She had been waiting for him so she could finish. 'You don't have anyone to worry about. I mean really worry. When the centre closes down, you'll move on, find somewhere else that needs you. You'll always be up there trying to cure the ills of the world while the rest of us are down here scrapping on the ground.'

She wasn't angry about this. Noah Brindle drove her mad and he kept her sane. As for Noah, he'd heard the speech before. The first time was after she had caught Neville sleeping around. It had been resurrected a few times since then. Noah knew it would pass.

'Brindle!' she said when he got to the door on his way out. He had been dabbing at the swelling under his eye. He turned his loose-knit bulk round to face her.

'Have you been *fighting*?'

The schoolboy in him shrugged.

It was ten minutes' walk for Noah from the high street down to the St Silas estate. The blocks of maisonettes were down at the bottom, overlooking Tipper Gill's football pitch. The door to the girl's top-floor maisonette flat had been left ajar. The flat next door, like almost half of the maisonette flats, was boarded up, though there seemed to Noah to be noises coming from inside as he waited for someone to answer the door.

A couple of times a week, Noah made visits round the valley on behalf of the Trust. As well as the furniture service operating from the crypt of the Mustard Seed, the Trust ran a scheme providing free holidays for families on benefit. Out of high season, the Trust rented a damp chalet in a holiday camp on the coast. The camp had seen better days, but the competition for places remained fierce. People applied in writing, explaining why they *needed* a Trust holiday. Noah's task was to interview families who had written to the Trust. Sometimes the people he went to see had applied for a holiday; sometimes it was for some household item – usually a television if the original one had blown up or been stolen – or baby items: a high chair, a crib, or a pram. Noah visited those making the request, setting out the necessary arrangements if things seemed in order, ruling out applicants if he suspected a con, and prepared a report for the next meeting of the trustees.

Noah knocked twice more on the open door, but there was still no answer from the girl he was looking for. She'd lived on the St Silas estate for a few years and Noah had seen her fleetingly around the town in the man's parka that she wore, pushing a child in a buggy. Her name was Quigley. Her son was the boy who everyone knew had gone missing for two days last summer. He had eventually been found wandering in his underpants up by the reservoir above the town.

'Hello? Melanie?'

There was still no answer from inside the flat. Noah pushed at the door and went inside.

She was sitting on a settee in the living room. A child lay across her lap, asleep. There was a TV on the floor in the corner. Apart from that, the room was empty. The four walls had been painted white unevenly over chipboard. There were no curtains. There were no pictures. There was no clock. Apart from the settee and the TV there was nothing else in the room.

'Hello?' Noah said, imagining the girl might be asleep. Her back was towards him and she hadn't turned round to see who had come in. Noah moved slowly round the room. The window was open, and it was cold.

She waited for him to reach her. When he came into view, she said simply, 'He's asleep.'

'Do you want him lifting so you can get up?'

'No, he'll wake.' She was definite.

'Is he hard work?'

'He doesn't sleep,' she said. Her face was bleached with tiredness.

'It says on the form that it's a holiday you are applying for,' Noah said.

'Someone said you could get us a holiday.'

'It's not for furniture, then?'

'I had furniture. He breaks stuff – hurts himself. He doesn't sleep much. It's not his fault. I used to go mad when he drew stuff all the time on the walls. Crayons and stuff. Now I just let him and I paint over it when I've had enough of it.'

Noah took some details and went through the procedure with her. He explained how the paperwork had to go back to the Trust for committee approval. If they agreed, then there would be a letter of confirmation. She nodded. She didn't ask about her chances of getting it.

'Does he go to nursery?' Noah asked her.

'He won't play much with other kids. He prefers it with me.'

'Is there anyone else to help with him?'

'My brother.'

'Does he help you much?'

'Sometimes.'

Noah nodded. 'Nursery would give you a break for a bit if nothing else,' he said. 'I could have a word with the Social Services place on Cumpstey Street.'

'I had enough of them lot after he went missing.'

'Wouldn't it be a bit of a help?'

'We're all right.'

The girl turned away. The child wriggled on the girl's lap. She froze. The child, reluctantly, settled again into a doze.

'You can go now,' she said. 'He'll be waking soon.'

'Are you cold?' Noah asked.

'There's a coat hung up in the hall.'

Before he went, Noah put the coat round her shoulders. She didn't look round as he left the room.

4

Almost Dounleavey

The train was the branch-line train from Preston, and there were few passengers on board. There were two people in the final carriage. One of them was Mr George. He was in his workaday suit – his only suit – and an inexpensive overcoat to keep out the chill. In the pocket of his jacket he carried eleven shillings; enough for a week's lodgings and provisions while he looked for work; enough to start a life on. The other was a man named Dounleavey. He was ten years older, about the same height as the younger man and just a little stockier.

Dounleavey was looking around the compartment. There was a sign saying 'No Smoking' but Dounleavey was smoking a small cigar. He seemed to be searching for some elusive thought, as if expecting it to be floating up above him amidst the cigar smoke. Dounleavey carried no luggage as far as the younger man could see, and he was wearing a dress suit with an expensive-looking white dinner jacket and a white cummerbund. Mr George imagined that Dounleavey was heading for some lavish party, although in truth Dounleavey had a kind of after-the-party look about him. The white jacket, although still spotless, had the creases to suggest that he had already worn it for a night and a day; the carnation he wore in his buttonhole, though beautifully cut, was a little dry. In addition, his wing-collared shirt was open at the neck. His trousers had the ribbon-ribbed seam of a dress suit. His shoes were highly polished. He reeked unaffectedly of power, the kind that money brought, the kind that let Dounleavey smoke his cigar with impunity without it being a challenge or a dare of some kind, the kind that simply meant some rules did not apply to him.

Finally Dounleavey seemed to notice that there was someone else in the compartment.

'Dounleavey,' he said casually by way of introduction.

'Oh, right, yes,' said Mr George. 'I'm George.'

Dounleavey moved the cigar from his right hand to his left. 'Pleased to meet you, Mr George.'

'Littlejohn,' the younger man said, 'George Littlejohn.'

They shook hands. The train rattled on through the countryside.

'Where are you getting off?' Dounleavey asked.

'Blackburn.'

'You live there?'

'I hope to.'

'No one knows you there?'

The younger man shook his head as Dounleavey looked thoughtful.

'I'm going to ask you a question,' Dounleavey said eventually. 'I would like to conduct an exchange. If you will let me continue my journey in your overcoat and journeyman's suit, I will, in return, offer you the dress suit I am wearing. For this service, I would pay you. You must use your judgement in deciding whether to accept my offer. I do, after all, find myself, in a manner of speaking, in your hands.'

Dounleavey seemed to find it amusing to have a part of his destiny, however small, in someone else's hands.

'What about my case?' Mr George asked. 'My work clothes are in there.'

Dounleavey glanced up at the lined cardboard case above them in the rack.

'I would take the case with me, and return it to you, unopened, first thing tomorrow if you tell me where you will be staying.'

The younger man hesitated.

Dounleavey nodded his head. 'You're right to hesitate of course,' he said. 'That's good. You wonder about my motives. You have noted that I have offered you money, and you are alarmed about any possibly dubious aspect of the exchange.'

It *was* true. Mr George *was* worried about any possible dishonesty or deception, so strange and unexpected was the request.

'Here is my card as proof of my good intent,' Dounleavey said. And he handed the young man a business card. Mr George, curious, read it. The card said simply 'c. b. dounleavey'. Nothing else. No company name. No address offering some kind of guarantee. Yet its simplicity was somehow reassuring and became the clinching argument in persuading Mr George to agree to the proposal.

C. B. Dounleavey had arranged for his chauffeur to meet him as usual at the railway station. But at Preston he had received a message from his chauffeur that the Rolls-Royce had broken down, and that Dounleavey would have to make other arrangements for his journey home.

'On any other night,' Dounleavey told the younger man, 'I would be happy to simply hire a cab at the station.'

'Why not tonight?' the younger man asked.

'Because tonight is the night of the Mayor's Ball. As ever, I have sent apologies. I do not attend . . . functions. It isn't my way.'

'Couldn't I just arrange for a vehicle to meet you at the station entrance?' Mr George said. 'You could climb in before you were seen by anyone.'

'No,' Dounleavey said. 'The driver would undoubtedly suspect. He would see me dressed like this. They all talk together on the cab stand, I know. They are all, particularly tonight, expecting me. The driver would assume, quite reasonably, that here was C. B. Dounleavey arriving for the Mayor's Ball. Not to go if I were recognized would be unpardonable. And even if the driver said nothing, the May Week fair will have arrived in the town, and there will already be a crowd watching them set up in the town square. The driver would struggle to get through; people would see me, peering through the window, and guess my identity.'

'If you declined the invitation,' the younger man asked, 'how can you be so sure they are expecting you?'

'Because I'm the guest of honour,' Dounleavey said. 'I'm always the guest of honour. They never give up. They all want my money, or to be seen with me. They all want some of the Dounleavey magic to rub off on them. They all want *saving*.'

He said it matter-of-factly, neither angry nor sad in his apparent rejection of the town towards which the two of them were travelling, the town which the younger man had never seen.

'They think that if I wanted to I could save all the mills from shutting down. They think I could end the Depression itself if I chose.'

'And could you?'

Dounleavey shrugged wearily, as if he wasn't sure whether he could or he couldn't.

Within a few minutes the two men had exchanged clothes and resumed their seats in the compartment. The train clattered onwards. 'Come far?' Dounleavey asked, adjusting to the roughness of the cheap suit and coat.

'From Annan. It's a small place, north, in the Borders.'

'What is the purpose of your journey?' Dounleavey was still wreathed in cigar smoke. Somehow, he was still clearly Dounleavey, with all that this seemed to entail.

'I've come to make a life for myself in Lancashire,' Mr George said.

'What will you do in the town?'

For a moment, Mr George thought the man was about to make him an offer that would make him rich. But the moment passed; the offer was never made.

'I have a trade. I was apprenticed as a joiner.'

'And now it's time to strike out on your own?' Dounleavey asked.

The younger man nodded.

'What else do you have to help you make your way in the world?' he asked.

The younger man paused, then said after a moment, 'I can do conjuring tricks. They were things I learned as a way of keeping the children quiet in Sunday school class.'

'You taught Sunday school?'

The young man nodded.

'Show me what you do,' Dounleavey said.

Mr George made a shilling disappear, then reappear from behind Dounleavey's ear. It was a sleight of hand – holding the shilling trapped behind his index and second fingers and dropping it through into his palm at just the right moment as though it had fallen from his ear.

Dounleavey looked closely at the younger man's hands, into his face, then back at the hands, apparently trying to fathom how the trick was done.

'What else?' he asked finally. 'What else do you have?'

The younger man thought for a moment. 'I have my faith,' he said finally. 'I hope to find a suitable place of worship in the town once I've found work.'

'No, not that,' Dounleavey said. 'What else do you have that will help you get by with men?'

'*That* will help me,' the younger man said. 'Does faith not help you?'

'I have no faith,' Dounleavey said, 'in God or men.'

'You must owe an allegiance to someone, or something,' the younger man said.

'To cigars,' Dounleavey said. 'To blackjack, and to nights on board ship with good company.'

'No,' the younger man dared to say, 'to something more than that, I'm sure.'

The train began to slow down. Ahead, the lights of the town were visible to the young man and the sound of the town trams could be heard above that of the train. The place seemed organized and well lit; the mill chimneys stood like flagpoles in every neighbourhood. It was then that it occurred to Mr George that he didn't have an address to which Dounleavey could have his case and his clothes returned. He said this, and Dounleavey took a small address book from his breast pocket. The notepaper, like the leather cover of the notebook itself, was embossed with a distinctive family crest: a bear and a unicorn flanking a crown, each animal holding a scroll. Dounleavey wrote down the name of a person – known to his chauffeur, he said – who ran clean lodgings in the town. They would be inexpensive enough, he said; he would have the young man's things returned there. He tore out the page and passed it to Mr George who kept it in his hand, ready to ask for directions when he left the station – and then Dounleavey did something that struck the younger man as extraordinary. He reached for Mr George's arm and, for whatever reason and with an unexpected urgency, said to him, 'Don't be like all those men who are sheep and nothing more. Make something of yourself. Do everything you need to. Leave no unfinished business in your life. You'll promise me?'

Wordlessly, Mr George nodded, knowing it was a commandment he would always have to keep. Then, just as suddenly, as the train juddered to a halt inside the station, Dounleavey released his arm, and his previous languorous mood returned. The two men followed the few other passengers down the passageway towards the ticket office and, as they approached the guard to hand over their tickets, the younger man felt Dounleavey lean close behind him and whisper, 'Leave no unfinished business, Mr George!'

Dounleavey was right – the May Week fair had arrived.

Beneath them, on the far side of the cobbled town square, the fair people had started to set up their stalls and rides in front of the Town Hall.

The fair was not due to open until the morning and the fairmen were still setting up, but a good-sized crowd was milling around, watching the transformation of the square into the fairground it became once a year.

*

The May Week fair in Blackburn was a composite of three or four smaller travelling fairs which toured the North of England and joined together in the larger towns. The people who ran the fairs all seemed to know each other, and they all seemed to be the same *kind* of people. By and large they were darker skinned than the town people, and they spoke with lilting accents that seemed to be a mixture of Cornish and Irish. The weavers referred to them as gypsies, though whether they were real gypsies no one knew for sure.

Some of the stalls were already set up and had the candy-striped canvas covers of their awnings fastened close. Others were still skeletons as men worked to assemble them before night fell. Primitive generators belly-growled; lines of coloured lights, strung across the fringes of tents, served to advertise the impending opening of the fair; an assortment of animals connected with the fair – canaries and mice and finches for prizes, parrots for entertainment, donkeys for donkey rides, two chimpanzees, a dancing bear, and a mêlée of assorted dogs – scratched and snuffled and yelped from cages and caravans; music clanked and clanged from barrow organs and piano rolls. The man who owned the bear had music playing from his piano-roll machine. The bear shifted from side to side with a small top hat perched on its head. Now and then – without changing its single, vacant, bear expression – the animal lifted the hat off its head and placed it on the ground for people to throw coins into.

The weavers had only come to *look* at the fair, as they did each year – to walk round and round, watching the fair people set up. They came to see the colours, the lights, the way the showmen – deliberate and dexterous – constructed the apparatus of the fair-ground. They came to see if this year's fair was how they

remembered it from last year, and all the years which had preceded it in an uncomplicated thread back to their childhoods.
They came because the Depression, which had shut half the mills
in the town and put the rest on short time or half pay, had put
their lives on hold, and anything that offered movement and life
and music, no matter how fleetingly, seemed a touch miraculous. They came – even on the night before the fair could open –
because the fair was exotic and would soon move on, leaving
behind the grey town that had swallowed up their own lives.

Mr George stood on the top of the ramp, taking in the scene,
seeing at the far side of the square the Town Hall – set like an
elaborate and enormous wedding cake – where, as Dounleavey
had pointed out, the Mayor's Ball was shortly to get under way
to celebrate the start of the town's new mayoral year. Mr
George pushed his hands into the pockets of the black dress-
suit trousers in an effort to shut out the cold. The white jacket
wasn't a perfect fit – its shoulders were a little wide – and with
only this for warmth he held his head up to stop the snow and
the chill from blowing down his back. It was then that he
noticed people looking at him. It was then that he heard someone say, 'Dounleavey! It's Dounleavey! He's come!'

'It can't be Dounleavey.'

'It must be. Who else could it be?'

'He's coming to the Mayor's Ball.'

'He's come to save the mills.'

Mr George looked around but Dounleavey himself had
slipped quietly away and was nowhere to be seen. It was only
then that the young man realized that the townspeople had
never seen Dounleavey. They were looking at the tall, pale man
dressed expensively for dinner, with the confidence to come
without a tie and with a brilliant, dying carnation in his

buttonhole, at the man whose head was raised, apparently taking in everything around him, and whose hands were slipped nonchalantly into the pockets of his dress suit; they were weighing up a man who even *smelled* of authority since Dounleavey's cigar smoke still clung stubbornly to him.

'It can't be Dounleavey. He's too young.'

'It must be. He's come to the Mayor's Ball.'

'Dounleavey must be older than that.'

Mr George made his way across the town square as people continued to wonder whether or not the young man was *too* young to be Dounleavey, and why his jacket did not *quite* fit him as neatly as it should have, and whether his shoes were perhaps too worn for this to be Dounleavey returning from a three-day poker game or some party on the yacht he kept anchored on Lake Windermere.

It was then that Mr George saw the child, dodging between the ranks of people and stalls, being chased by three older boys. The boys caught up with him two or three times and dragged him to the floor, pushing and shoving him while trying to drag something out of his fiercely clenched fist, but no matter what they did he wouldn't relent and let go. Each time he would wriggle free and flee across the cobbles, darting between the flanks of weavers, only to be caught again by the older boys who could outrun him and seemed more co-ordinated than him. He escaped one final time and seemed, at last, to have lost them. He snaked away through groups of people, looking back all the time to make sure he hadn't been spotted, looking round, glancing right and left. Suddenly, close by him, there was a shout of recognition. The boy spun away, looking to his right, running head down – and didn't see the tram sliding in from his left, grinding slowly into the terminus behind him.

The tram, its brakes screaming, struck the boy a glancing blow that toppled him as it shuddered to a halt. The boy bounced up from the collision ('As you might imagine a cat would do,' Mr George would often recall), and landed on his feet. Stunned, the boy darted blindly away from the tram, catapulting straight into a tall young man wearing a white dinner jacket.

'We each held on to the other to prevent ourselves from falling,' Mr George would say, 'both of us stunned by the impact of our small collision, each holding the other captive.'

The tram which had screeched to a standstill held them in the full beam of its main lamp. The pursuing boys arrived helter-skelter through the crowd, ready to make a grab for the smaller boy to give him his beating, shouting that he was a thief, but the sight of the white jacket made them hesitate. Everyone in the crowd, who up until then had been egging the boys on or simply laughing at the chase, seemed to hesitate as well. Mr George felt time slowing down; and in that moment of hesitation he could hear a voice distinctly saying, '*Leave no unfinished business.*' He heard the words quite clearly, and felt as if he knew, for the first time, what was expected of him, as though he were casting off a weight.

'He stole summat from us,' one of the boys said. 'He's just doolally is Goose. Give him here, mister.'

'You know these boys?' Mr George asked.

The boy nodded.

'Your name is Goose?'

He nodded again.

'Don't you talk, Goose?'

'Told you, mister,' the big boy said. 'He's doolally is Goose. My da says he's simple.'

Goose blew a raspberry. The older boy swung a clumsy arm

at him. Mr George reached out and caught the boy's arm an instant before it would have struck Goose. He noticed that Goose hadn't even attempted to duck the blow. He was just standing there, still glaring at the bigger boys, clutching in his fist whatever it was he had stolen.

'You stole from these boys?' Mr George asked Goose.

Goose nodded and grinned. Up close, Mr George guessed that the boy was perhaps six years old. His nose was bleeding a little, and his red hair was tousled. His belly was showing below his jumper and above a baggy pair of shorts. Mr George suspected that the boy had little co-ordination even without his ill-fitting clogs. Goose stood looking at his pursuers, still defiant. They were clearly used to chasing him, and he was clearly used to being caught.

'What did you take?'

'He stole a jewel off us,' the oldest boy said.

'A jewel?'

Goose said nothing.

'What kind of jewel, Goose?'

'Expensive one,' the bigger boy said.

'You found it in one of the sideshow tents, maybe?' Mr George asked the oldest boy.

'We didn't nick it,' the boy said. 'One of the gypos gave it us. Worth a lot. The gypo said so.'

'How much, would you say?' Mr George asked.

'A fortune. He's a thief. He should give it back or we'll paste him. We'll paste him anyway.'

'So how much is it worth?' Mr George persisted.

Mr George would say a hundred times afterwards that he knew even before the boy answered what the reply was going to be.

'A shilling,' the boy said.

Mr George reached slowly across to him, seemed to fumble in his ear and pulled something out, holding it up in his huge hand for the boy to take as compensation. It was a shilling. Mr George slid the coin into the boy's pocket.

'You feel the shilling there?' Mr George asked him. The boy nodded, looking round, grinning.

Mr George patted the shilling in the boy's pocket as if for confirmation. 'Now go, and leave Goose alone; I'll be watching out for you.'

'It was *the* shilling,' Mr George would tell the orphans in the years to come, producing a shilling from his pocket whenever he did so. It was the same shilling, he liked to say, that he had magically produced from Dounleavey's ear. But on the night he performed the trick in the town square nobody knew about him meeting Dounleavey on the train. Nobody knew who the young man was, and yet, after that night, everyone seemed to recognize his face.

'There goes Mr George,' they'd say when they saw him about his business in the town, and they'd think of him as the man who was almost Dounleavey.

5

Falling Short

Tipper Gill leaned into each short stride, pushing, as if a cross-breeze was always – just – against him, and always would be.

For a man who seemed to interest the police in Lowell so much, Tipper Gill had always struck Noah as being so amenable, so untroubled. He scurried about the town with his permanent stubble and a grin that showed up nine or ten teeth spread around a mouth of firm, hard gum, scouring the horizon with his one good eye and his one lazy one to a timetable of his own making.

Everyone liked Tipper. He chatted up most of the women on the St Silas estate. He sorted men easily into one of two kinds: those who were no threat and whom he could entertain; and those who could do him damage and to whom he therefore pledged allegiance.

Noah knew that Tipper Gill moved in that grey area between taking short cuts and breaking the law. He had speculated that sometimes it made all the difference to a man like Tipper – not because of the money or the goods it yielded but because of the way it seemed to keep men like Tipper *alive*. Noah's only compromise in the matter of Tipper Gill, in all the years he'd known him, was to be careful not to put too much temptation his way. Noah had never given Tipper a key to the Mustard Seed's office, even though other volunteers (including Tipper's wife Morag) had keys. Tipper never mentioned it. He seemed content with the arrangement. Tipper seemed to grasp that he was not sufficiently reliable. He always seemed, Noah thought, to understand.

The passion of Tipper's life was football. Running his stable of teams on the estate with Barry Catlin was the only long-term work he had ever done. He had never been *paid* to work until Noah began to offer him sessional fees from his own budget and to pay him cash for driving the van used by the food co-operative and the furniture exchange.

Football was what Tipper talked about mostly. He especially loved talking to Noah about it because Tipper's team, Manchester United, like Noah's, had died once – in a plane crash on the way back from a European Cup match. It had intrigued Tipper that Noah was an Accrington Stanley man, because Stanley weren't even a professional team any more. Noah's support for them had begun in the orphanage when he was a boy, but Stanley hadn't played in the Football League since 1962 when, anchored at the bottom of the Fourth Division, they had folded part-way through the season with mounting debts.

'What was it like?' Tipper would ask Noah about seeing his football team fold like that.

'It was like sliding off the edge of the world,' Noah would say, and the two of them would sit in silence after that, contemplating how such things could be.

The kids who played football for Tipper's teams all liked him. They humoured him as if he was the child. Generally, they behaved themselves around Tipper in a way that they didn't with Barry Catlin. Boys of that age could smell weakness, and they smelled it in Barry. Most of the time, it seemed to Noah, they had Barry dangling. They seemed to know, on the other hand, that Tipper Gill had no such fault line. They knew he had served two short prison sentences ('for being in the wrong place at the wrong time, Noah, that was all'). They imagined there must be another side to Tipper, but they had never seen it. They only ever saw that blind-side smile of his with all that gum, the smile that suggested Tipper somehow knew life's secret and that, invisibly, it was connected to the red football shirt he wore and sometimes slept in.

But this wasn't the main reason Tipper was able to handle the kids. His chief tool of discipline was the respect the St Silas kids had for him because everyone knew Tipper Gill had once eaten a live frog.

The frog had been a bet. Tipper was still playing football in those days, not just running teams. Football had been the one thing Tipper had wanted to be good at, but his bad eye was an obstacle he never fully overcame, and so – like Noah's football team – Tipper slipped down the rungs until he hit the bottom.

Tipper was playing for the St Silas senior team which he himself had founded. The match was in the local Sunday league, on the pitch he himself had laid and nurtured on the no-man's land at the bottom of the estate. Tipper (wearing his lucky number 7 shirt) had swept an opponent across the touch-line and into the pile of half-time lager cans and then stood grinning all the way through the ensuing row until he had been floored by a right hook. Both men had been dismissed by the referee. To pass the time while they watched the rest of the game on the sidelines, Tipper had bet the opposition player a

fiver that the man daren't eat a frog. Frogs were always plenti-
ful down by the river's edge in the wet spring months, and
there was usually the odd specimen which had climbed up on to
the field and been squashed by some footballer's boot or bag.
The opposition player, on his hands and knees, had found a
dead one – barely more than a froglet – and, blanching, finally
managed to swallow it. Whereupon Tipper, not having any
money, had to offer to eat one of his own to square the bet.

'You have to eat a live one,' the opposition player said, knowing he had Tipper over a barrel. 'A *grown* one.'

By this time the football game out on the pitch had come to
a standstill as more and more of the players were becoming distracted by the proceedings. They saw Tipper push through the
hedge and down on to the path, then wade out into the river.
They saw him plunge his head under the water until only his
muddied football shorts – and then nothing at all of him – were
visible. Tipper Gill had vanished.

Everybody was watching – even the referee. The game had
been forgotten. They waited. Until suddenly Tipper emerged
through a sluice of black water, arms raised, triumphant, grinning his gummy grin. Clutched in one fist was a struggling
frog. The two teams cheered – and Tipper Gill, drenched and
muddied, and pinching the creature's head between thumb and
forefinger until something popped, ate the frog in three bites
and then let out a huge rasping belch.

Whenever any of the kids got restless, Tipper would sum-
mon a belch from the pit of his stomach (a stomach that was
growing yearly on his small frame since he'd hung up his
boots), and everyone would remember what he'd done to the
frog and that would be enough for order to be restored.

*

41

Evening settled on Lowell. Some boys were playing football in the yard of the Mustard Seed. Noah heard the thup thup of the ball outside and a few desultory cries. The game, after an hour, was old and almost dying; no one was chasing back when possession was lost. The shops along the high street, beyond the fence, were shut, except for the off-licence and the video hire shop. The Sandwich Box which Noah could see across the road was swept and blinded, locked up for the night. Elly Pascoe was working her shift at Asda on the edge of town, processing other men's bread and coffee and ice cream in her checkout uniform. Did she scowl at the purchasers of the fresh-wrapped chickens as she slid them across the blinking eye of the bar-code scan? Did she smile for the fettuccine and the pasta quills?

Noah often stayed on at the centre in the evening. It was, he thought, a time when the centre felt like some last vessel afloat in a sea of lost lives. Evening was the time of day when people chose to come if they wanted to talk, if they wanted Noah – somebody – to listen.

Noah was a fine listener. He gave people the chance to tell versions of their lives that were complete and understandable. It was mostly the women who came. He let them talk; he let them find endings of their own to what they had to say.

Sometimes – not often – when she had finished telling him her own story, a woman would ask Noah, 'Where did *you* come from? What's your story, Noah?' But he would make different stories up or simply shrug, in a vague and non-committal way. Small wells of intimacy sprang up in between the words, in looks and sudden glances. Maybe that was why Noah kept some things to himself. He was wary of what people might see, of what might somehow be lost or misappropriated in the translation of the thing. Noah put this down to being an orphan. He had a sense that not all of him had been traded with the world – that a part of him had been kept utterly private and to himself. It was from this part of him, he knew, that his impulse to write came. He wondered if all writers were kinds of orphans.

Noah himself told gentle, meandering stories that led people away from him. He told them to the kids in the youth club, and those in the football teams that Tipper Gill and Barry Catlin ran. He told the kids, for example, that in the 1930s Blackburn Rovers let one of the club's programme sellers (who sold programmes outside the ground) bring a bear along to their matches. The bear had previously belonged to one of the travelling funfairs which traditionally, during the summer months, pitched camp in the Lancashire cotton towns. This was a bear which had become too old to perform any more. No one knew how the programme seller had come to own the bear. It seemed unlikely that he had bought it. They liked to think that he'd known someone who worked on the funfair and had agreed to take the bear off their hands when it couldn't earn its way. The programme seller was said to be a former Rovers player, fallen on hard times, though Noah couldn't remember his name. He had a smallholding where he was able to keep the bear during the week. His wife had died and he was not in the best of health. That was why the club gave him a job selling programmes; that was why they put up with the bear on match days.

Immediately before each match, Noah said, the bear (which was muzzled and leashed) would be paraded by its owner – who by now had finished selling his programmes and had made his way into the ground to watch the match. The bear became a kind of unofficial mascot. Sometimes it would perform a small bow for the crowd; other times, it would stop and look round at the goalposts, raising its paws and putting them in front of its eyes, as if in mock disbelief, pretending to have seen an open goal missed or a penalty blasted wide, and the crowd would clap in appreciation. As the bear passed by, sometimes on four legs, sometimes on two, people would lean over and try to adorn it with blue and white Rovers scarves and tam-o'-shanters. The bear didn't seem to mind. It was quite tame, or at least old. After a full circuit, the bear would be laden with Rovers colours and its owner would lead it on to the edge of the pitch, where it would take another bow to rapturous applause. The two of them would then leave the pitch and take their place for the match at the front of the Nuttall Street terrace. From there, the man would watch the game and the bear, cocooned in the collection of scarves and hats, would go to sleep down by the low wall that ran round the perimeter of the pitch.

'But it all ended when the club's directors got involved,' Noah would say sadly to the kids, shaking his head as if wondering whether to go on or not.

'Why?' the kids would ask. 'What happened to the bear? Fucksake, Noah, what happened?' And Tipper Gill, if he was close enough, would give the lad who'd sworn a smack across the head.

'Bloody watch it,' Tipper would say, and then to Noah, 'Sorry, Noah. Sorry. Go on, go on.'

And Noah would continue. He would tell them about the complaint that the club received. He would tell them how someone had protested that the bear was getting into the ground for half-price.

'But it's a bear,' people said. 'Why not half-price?'

But the complainant, who happened to be on the Supporters Committee Executive, said it didn't matter – half-price was for juniors and old-age pensioners. The bear was neither, he said, so it should pay full-price. It was said that the real reason the Supporters Committee member took exception to the bear was because the programme seller was already getting into the ground for nothing and a free entry for him *and* a half-price for the bear was just too much for the old skinflint on the Supporters Committee to accept.

The programme seller who brought the bear to the ground argued that in bear years the creature was surely old enough to qualify for half-price. The club said this was fair enough providing nobody objected, but the man from the Supporters Committee Executive wrote another letter of complaint, saying that the bear's age would have to be proved. Of course in the end the directors had to decide one way or the other. In the absence of any document confirming the bear's age, they decreed that he would need to pay full-price – which was why the man took the bear off in disgust to Accrington Stanley where the club let *both* of them in for free in return for the prematch entertainment they provided.

'A *decent* club – Accrington Stanley,' Noah would say to the kids. 'Not like Blackburn Rovers or any of those other big-shot Premier Division teams who get too uppity and Fancy Dan for the poor folk who cough up their own hard-earned wages to support them. Accrington Stanley was a good club for the little people: for underdogs; for ex-pros who had to become programme sellers, and for bears.'

The kids liked the bear story. They had Noah tell it to them often.

'He shoulda let the bear settle it,' the kids would say. 'He shoulda let the bear bite that guy's fuckin' head off.'

Whenever anybody appeared who Tipper Gill thought

hadn't heard the story about the bear, he would get Noah to tell it in his matter-of-fact way. And Tipper Gill was always astonished and incredulous that people continued to believe what Noah was telling them, because he knew what Noah knew – which was that these were stories that Noah made up in his head.

Over the years, Noah had grown used to the clink of the bell downstairs, and the push of the heavy church door in the evenings, when he was in the Mustard Seed building alone – the slow tread on the stairs as if whoever was coming to see him was weighed down by what they needed to say. Noah would be clearing the day's junk from one of the battered armchairs when the visitor reached the door.

'I was just putting the kettle on for myself,' Noah would say. 'Fancy a cup?'

Usually, the people who drifted in were from Lowell's bottom end; more often than not it would be someone from the St Silas estate. There was a kind of order to Lowell, it seemed to Noah, akin to gravity. Maybe it was just that lives, left unattended, did slip from higher up to further down. The tenants at the top end of the estate kept neater gardens, or kitchens, or lives, and sometimes moved out altogether to one of the bigger towns along the valley – Haslingden or Rawtenstall – or got enough money together to organize a mortgage for the new Barratt estate on the land behind the Asda store, or a house in Lowell's small streets of private terraces. The tenants further down the estate, in the cul-de-sacs and maisonettes, seldom did. It was such a long way up, it sometimes seemed to Noah, and gravity or some such force, he always felt, was set against the Gills and Catlins and Quigleys in this way.

People came to see Noah if someone they knew was in trouble, or if they had been burgled – if they'd wanted to *talk* about it to the police and the police hadn't had the time or, in Neville Pascoe's case, the inclination. Women would come when their husbands had blown the week's money or been unfaithful, or when they themselves had spent up on the scratchcards. Hardest of all was when women came in with fears for their children, fears which their husbands could not grasp – when they came to talk about the possibility of things going awry with a new generation. Sometimes someone would tell Noah that, all in all, going on seemed harder than not going on, and Noah would listen to that, too, without telling them it was wrong to think like that, without telling them what they ought to think. It was mostly the women who came; it was mostly the women who tried to imagine how things could be different.

If it was quiet in the evenings, Noah used the time to write. He had written more since the trustees had taken the decision to sell the Mustard Seed Centre, since the sign went up outside and he had been set the task of finding satisfactory endings of his own. Noah kept imagining the figure in the immaculate dress suit with the white jacket – kept writing sentences, wondering why the man had come and what might follow.

The girl stood in the doorway. She had a small body and a plain face, the kind of face that children drew. Hidden away in her man's parka, she seemed even more slight than Noah remembered from that afternoon. The parka, with the hood up, seemed to swallow her. Her child was holding her hand. He was looking round the room. Downstairs, Noah could hear Linde dragging chairs across the hall ready to buff the floor as she did each week. He could hear the temper in the way she was doing it. It was not

Noah who insisted on stripping and buffing the floor every week but Linde herself. The ritual was her labour and her penance.

'I came to ask something,' Melanie Quigley said.

''Sokay,' Noah said. 'I was just putting the kettle on for a brew. You want one?'

'I came to say I changed my mind. If that's okay. About the nursery.'

'That's good.'

'You'll ask if they'll take him?'

Noah nodded.

'Just a couple of mornings.'

'Just a couple of mornings.'

'I wouldn't have to pay?'

Noah shook his head.

'And they won't take him off me?'

'You're a good mother to him?'

She watched Noah, and bit her lip.

'I'll tell them you're a good mother who wants a bit of day care two mornings a week.'

The boy was pulling to get away from the girl.

'No, Ryan,' she said. She was looking at Noah's face. 'You're him that used to have a go at Ronnie Roots, aren't you?'

Ronnie Roots, without ever getting his hands dirty, supplied most of the drugs that circulated on the St Silas estate. Noah used to stand in the empty road, shouting at Ronnie Roots's house, accusing him at the top of his voice of supplying the kids with freebies, and demanding that Ronnie Roots come out to face him, but he never did. It had gone on for a while. It had been a long time ago.

'I used to watch you,' the girl said, 'from the window. Everyone did. Weren't you frightened of him?'

Noah hadn't been frightened. He had known he'd had licence to do it. He had known he could get away with it. It had made no difference anyway. There was no one who would give evidence against Ronnie Roots.

The child was still pulling to be free of his mother.

'It's okay,' Noah said, 'he couldn't create any more havoc in here than Tipper Gill's kids or the food co-op lot.'

Reluctantly, she let go. The boy wandered into the middle of the room. He stood, looking round, then across at Noah. He shifted his weight from one foot to the other.

'Five?' Noah said.

'He's four in the autumn,' the girl said.

'He's big for nearly four.'

'He eats and eats.'

'I'm Noah,' Noah said to the boy.

'He don't talk much to people he don't know,' the girl said.

Noah opened a drawer in his desk and took out a rubber ball, the size of a squash ball but softer. He held out his palms, with the ball in his left hand, leaving a distance between himself and the boy. Then he made two fists. He crossed his hands, uncrossed them, blew on them, and held them out in front of the boy. The boy looked at him, then touched Noah's left hand. Noah opened his fist. It was empty. He opened the other fist to reveal the ball. Noah did the same trick four or five times. The girl had moved to sit on the edge of one of the old armchairs acquired by Tipper Gill years ago. Each time Noah did the trick, the boy guessed wrong. He showed no emotion, but he carried on guessing.

The bell rang downstairs. The front door banged and the echo rode through the building. The girl looked round.

'It's just the door,' Noah said. 'It's probably Linde.'

'It'll be my brother,' the girl said. 'He's waiting for me.'

'That's good,' Noah said.

'Gotta go, Ryan.'

The child tapped Noah's fist. Noah had forgotten about the trick. He opened his fist. It was empty.

'Ryan!'

The child kept his back to the girl. She took a step towards him. Noah held his hand up to ask her to wait a minute. He opened another drawer, and pulled out three smaller, leather-stitched balls. They were multi-coloured – red and blue and yellow – and the three of them fitted on to the palm of Noah's hand. The boy watched as Noah began juggling. The boy scowled in concentration. Noah kept the balls up in the air for several seconds, then caught all three in quick succession and held them out for the boy. The boy took them.

'You can't keep them, Ryan,' the girl said. 'They're just to look at. Now come on.'

'It's all right,' Noah said. 'Woolworths, ninety-nine pence. I'll get some more. He can practise.'

The boy moved back to his mother and took her hand, clutching the three balls to his chest with his free hand. They could hear Linde Wzinska's voice downstairs.

'You'll let me know?' the girl said to Noah. 'About the holiday?'

'I'll come down. I'll leave a note if you're not in.'

'I'll be in.'

There was Linde's voice again, scolding.

The girl steered the child through the door. The boy stopped in the hall and turned round.

'You have a ship?' he said to Noah.

'For the animals?' Noah said. 'Two by two?'

The boy nodded.

'You think I should have one?'

The boy nodded again, still not smiling.

'I'll think about it then,' Noah said.

Noah walked them down the stairs. Someone was leaning against the wall just inside the hall, smoking. Noah guessed it was the girl's brother. There was a likeness. He looked perhaps a year younger than Melanie. Linde Wzinska, ten yards away, was glaring at him.

'Where the fuck you been?' the brother said. 'You said you'd only be a minute.'

'I'm here,' she said.

'I've been waiting.'

'I ask him not to smoke,' Linde said to Noah. 'He thinks it's funny to drop his ash on thuh floor after I spend all thuh evening polishing it up.'

The boy drew on the cigarette. Again he knocked the ash on to the floor that Linde had stripped and partially buffed. There was a sprinkling of ash in the area around his feet.

'Don't think you're not too old for me to sort you out,' Linde said. 'I bring up two daughters on my own round these parts and I have plenty of messing with the likes of you.'

'Let's go,' the girl said.

The girl's brother turned to Noah. 'You sorted her out with this holiday then or what?'

'Was it too much to ask that you didn't flick your ash on the floor?' Noah said.

'Fuck off,' the girl's brother said.

It was after nine when Neville Pascoe and his partner came round to the Mustard Seed. Noah was polite but, having once seen the way Neville Pascoe, believing no one else to be watching, had arrested Tipper Gill, Noah was content these days to keep a civil distance between them. Tipper Gill had been released without charge four hours after the arrest and Noah had asked Tipper whether he had thought of making a complaint. Tipper had regarded the matter as unexceptional.

'I could complain, I suppose,' he'd told Noah, 'but they'd still have the uniforms on afterwards and I wouldn't.' He had grinned, but it was a bleaker kind of grin than the one he usually wore.

Noah told the two officers that Olwen Sudders hadn't been raped last night. She *had* been attacked by a man wearing a balaclava over his face, but she had beaten him off. Perhaps it had been a lucky blow she had struck, Noah said, or the way she had fought back in utter silence that had finally unnerved her attacker. The blood which Linde Wzinska had seen was from him, not her. She had clawed at his face or his neck – she wasn't sure which. The younger officer took notes as Noah spoke. Olwen Sudders hadn't been sure whether it had been her husband. Her guess was that it probably hadn't been him. Her husband, she said, knew how to hurt, and this seemed a more fumbled attempt. Being deaf, she hadn't heard her attacker coming up behind her. Perhaps the surprise, Noah said, helped her to fight back; there had been no time to freeze, to think about what was happening. She had just reacted.

'Fuck him,' Olwen Sudders had signed to Noah after she'd told him about the man who had attacked her, signing out each letter of the expletive with her quick, neat hands. 'Fuck *him*.'

When Noah returned to the hospital after locking up the Mustard Seed for the night Olwen Sudders was sitting in the chair by the bed. They had moved her on to the observation ward during the day. She signed, 'Hello.' She asked about her husband. Noah told her the police had gone to talk to him. He asked why she wouldn't talk to the police when they had come to see her earlier in the day. She shrugged. She tapped the arm of the bedside chair, asking him to stay a while. Noah sat down on the bed. In the next bed, a woman slept with her mouth wide open. Across the bay, another patient lay curled up in her dressing gown. A fourth woman was knitting while her husband read the newspaper he had brought her.

Noah Brindle and Olwen Sudders spoke with their hands. She asked him about the Mustard Seed going up for sale. She wondered what Noah would do afterwards. He said he didn't know, he hadn't really thought about it. They talked about how they first met. They laughed about Noah's cut lip and the swelling where she had caught him with her fist earlier that morning. She touched it with her finger, sheepish.

Olwen Sudders had first turned up at the Mustard Seed Centre because she had heard there was someone there who could sign.

'I won't write these things down,' she had signed to Noah, 'I won't, I *won't*,' stabbing the air with her fingers and fists to say it.

This was after she had stopped living with her husband, after the injunction against him coming near her, when she was learning to make a go of it alone. No one had seen much of Olwen Sudders while her marriage had run its course. Her husband had liked her to stay at home. Now and then he had whacked her to keep her in line. Then she had had to stay indoors until the bruising went down. In the end, he had started going strange. He put his hand through a wall – he said he was under pressure. He started saying he was the Angel Gabriel. He agreed to leave their flat in the maisonettes, but after he moved out he started spying on her. He demanded that she go to see him once a week for sex in the bedsit he'd rented in Bacup. He would make her kneel in prayer in front of him before the sex, but at least he left her alone the rest of the week. He started asking to wear her underwear. Finally, she went to see a solicitor, wrote out what had happened, and had the injunction taken out against him. The injunction said he wasn't allowed to go within four hundred yards of her or of the St Silas neighbourhood.

She found work with a private nursing agency providing care to housebound clients, and was sent as an auxiliary to look after a quadriplegic man. He'd been in some sort of car accident. He couldn't move from the base of his spine down, and he had learned to sign in the rehab unit before he'd learned to talk properly again.

Olwen Sudders did the night shift – ten till six. It suited her to be away from the flat in case her husband showed up in the night. After the second week, the man signed that he didn't like to ask but would she consider giving him relief. She asked what he meant. He meant sexual relief. He said he was sorry that he had to ask. He said he couldn't have proper sex any more. She signed that she was here only to take care of him – not for *that*.

The next night, at about ten o'clock, a woman turned up at the house. She had a small boy with her – her son. The boy was asleep. Olwen Sudders recognized the woman as one of the other auxiliaries. The quadriplegic man insisted that Olwen Sudders let them in. He said he had paid good money. The woman put the boy down on a chair and wheeled the man through into the bedroom. Olwen Sudders went into the kitchen to wash up. Later on, the child came through into the kitchen, whimpering. He had woken up not knowing where he was. Olwen Sudders nursed him and let him fall asleep on her lap, stroking his hair. A few days later she went to the Mustard Seed Centre for the first time, having heard that the man in charge there could sign.

'Why me?' was what she had wanted to say to Noah. 'Why *me*?'

The food co-operative was running that day. Olwen Sudders had asked him about it. When he told her, she was non-committal, but a few weeks after that she joined the food co-operative as a customer, and later began helping out as a volunteer. Then she had joined the writing group that Noah ran. The first piece she wrote for the group was a description of how, when she had gone to the agency to complain about the quadriplegic man, she had been sacked for refusing to go back to care for him.

She was sleeping now. Noah watched her. He saw a forty-year-old woman who could not speak and could not hear, curled in the sheets of the hospital bed, one eye half open, the way cats sleep or children nap. It was dark outside. A nurse came over to ask if he wanted anything.

He drove back in the dark, following the lights of the valley and the crouched black hills. People pictured their lives as stories, Noah Brindle knew. They saw a thread that pulled the random fragments of their lives together into a simple narrative, even though that thread might be invisible to anyone other than themselves. Olwen Sudders, and Linde Wzinska, and the other women who used the centre, and would soon learn to cope with its absence, all had lives drawn taut and given shape by these same invisible threads of narrative. Noah guessed that Elly Pascoe must have set out her story for the counsellor she paid with her evening wages from Asda. And Noah's own story was this: that he had come here to man his small boat in the always rising tide, that he was meant to have saved people from the floods, to have hauled them clear and waited for the storm to pass. He was meant to have imagined better endings than he had been able. The child in the centre had seen this much earlier in the evening; the child had known who every Noah was *meant* to be. But this Noah had let things slide, had coasted, had saved no one from the rising floods.

We fall short, Noah thought as he drove. We all fall short and this is how our stories end. And even as he saw the thread of his own life beginning to unravel, and even as he tried to think how the story of his life might turn out, he was imagining how the story of the man in the white dinner jacket would unfold.

On the ridge of the bypass which swept along the high stretch of the town, Noah stopped the car on the slip road and felt for the notebook and pencil he carried with him these days. Around him, houses gave way to the blanket of moorland before the lights of the next town took over and lit candles in the night for travellers hoping to find their way. The hourly bulletin on the radio said an aeroplane had come down in China – it was thought there were no survivors of the crash. The newsreader gave the evening's football results. The news finished. Music played again.

In the collision with Goose, he had dropped the piece of paper, Noah wrote in the notebook.

Noah drove home. There were two messages for him on his

answerphone. They were both from Elly Pascoe, asking him to call and giving him the number. When he rang, no one answered. He tried again later. He left a message to say he'd called.

He wrote for half the night. In the morning he found he had fallen asleep at his desk and dreamed of Mr George, and of the bear.

6

The Travelling Fair

And then he realized that, in the collision with Goose, he had dropped the piece of paper on which Dounleavey had written the address of the lodging house. Mr George approached an old newspaper vendor selling final editions of the *Lancashire Evening Telegraph* outside the railway station.

'I'm looking for somewhere to stay for the night,' Mr George told him, his voice a little too forced.

'Connaught, sir,' the old man said briskly, not quite catching Mr George's eye.

Goose knew where the Connaught was – everybody in the town knew – but he wouldn't go in. He led Mr George up the hill by the park to the high iron gates but would go no further.

'They have dogs,' he said. 'Dunkiss showed them me.'

They did. As Mr George approached the Connaught he could see the dogs, two of them, lying at the end of their chains.

It wasn't a boarding house; it was a hotel. It was the one good hotel in the town. It was the only place, Mr George suddenly realized, the old newspaper vendor had thought suitable for the almost-Dounleavey figure.

It seemed too grand and ornate for the town. Seeing it, Mr

George felt his courage waver and considered creeping back down into the town again to find some anonymous, damp lodging house for the night. But the thought of running into the pale-faced Goose who had guided him there made him go on, and he reasoned to himself that there must be a small boxroom in the eaves he might be able to afford for a single night. He could find himself more reasonably priced lodgings in the morning.

The lobby of the Connaught was high and tiled, and seemed to absorb any noise reaching it from the outside world. There were big plants in stone pots; there was a wide, red-carpeted staircase. The lobby clerk at the desk stiffened as the swing doors opened, then relaxed when he saw the dress suit, the white dinner jacket and the neat cummerbund.

'Good evening, sir.'

'Good evening,' Mr George said.

'You are with Alderman Cumpstey's party being provided for by the Town Hall, I imagine?'

Mr George explained that he wasn't with anybody, he just wanted one room for the night. Alderman Cumpstey, he would discover, was the incumbent Mayor; it was his inauguration which was being celebrated at the Town Hall.

The lobby clerk looked briefly down at the bookings register.

'Only the top-floor suite is available,' he said with a sigh, as if worried he might be losing the fine young man as a customer. 'Everything else is taken for the night.'

'If that's all there is . . .' Mr George began.

'There would normally,' the lobby clerk began hesitantly, 'be an advance deposit required for the top floor. We wouldn't usually offer the top-floor suite without a prior booking.' But he clearly would offer the suite to anyone who was almost Dounleavey – providing they had the money.

Mr George reached into the inside breast pocket of the white jacket, ready to ask how much the room would cost. He had never stayed in a hotel, and imagined in his innocence that a suite might be some kind of smaller single room. The only thing he could feel in the pocket was the calling card Dounleavey had given him on the train. He put the card down on the desk in front of him to free his hand and continued, with a growing sense of unease, to feel in each of the pockets, searching in vain for his money.

Then he realized. Dounleavey had it. The eleven shillings he had arrived with was in his own suit – the one Dounleavey was now wearing.

The lobby clerk picked up the calling card. He held it up, as if posing a question.

'Er, Dounleavey . . .' Mr George said vaguely. 'He said . . .'

The man pinged the service bell in front of him on the reception desk. There was a moment's delay, then a bellboy appeared in the lobby from a side door.

'Dunkiss, take Mr . . . ?'

'Just George.'

'Take Mr George to the top suite. He will be staying at the Connaught tonight as a guest of the hotel.'

'You have any luggage, sir?' the bellboy added.

'No . . . no.'

'Mr George has no luggage, Dunkiss. Show him around. Get him whatever he needs. You will need to sort things out up there – linen, coals and so on.'

Dunkiss – serious, round, his full-moon face as shiny as his boots and the buttons on his waistcoat – acknowledged Mr

George. He was short and barrel-chested, constructed like one of those inflatable toys weighted in the base to allow them to bounce back upright whenever they are knocked down.

Unsure how to proceed with the introduction, Mr George offered his hand. Dunkiss looked puzzled for a moment, then pleased, as he reached across and the two men shook hands.

'Follow me, sir,' Dunkiss said, and led the young man in the dress suit towards the wide staircase and up the first of several sets of stairs. By the time they reached his suite on the top floor, Mr George was puffing like the steam train that had brought him to the town.

'Just put your head between your knees,' Dunkiss said, 'and everything'll soon come back.'

After a couple of minutes the world stopped spinning and Mr George began to take in the room. It seemed to be at least the size of the hotel lobby they had left several floors below. There were two large settees set at right angles, and an array of good furniture; a floor-length curtain ran almost the full width of the room. There was a marbled fireplace where Dunkiss, having put on a pair of cotton gloves, was busy arranging coals from a copper scuttle. Mr George could see no bed or wash-basin and realized that these must be in other rooms, through the various doors that led off this main sitting room.

'What's behind the curtain?' Mr George asked Dunkiss, who was still busy with the coals.

'The pulley cord is over there,' said Dunkiss, pointing.

Mr George found the cord and pulled the curtain open. Behind it, beyond the long window, was an evening view of the town, with the still-clear outline of the moors in the distance, blank and grey and hemming in the small community. It was like a backdrop to a fairytale, with the huddle of men, women and children at its heart drawn by the coloured lights of the fair that shone brilliantly in the dark.

'Is that why the hotel is full – because of the fair?'

Dunkiss grinned. 'No one down there's got two farthings to rub together. Not them on the fair, and especially not them wandering round it. They couldn't pay for a night at the Connaught if they all chipped in together.'

'So who's here?'

'Guests of Alderman Cumpstey. Paid for by the Town Council. Them that the Alderman's invited to the Mayor's Ball.'

'Does the Council pay to put people up here every year?'

'They usually just invite the other Mayors from the district. This time, they've invited the shippers and the bankers and them that used to take the town's cloth and export it for sale. They've invited everyone who *used* to do business with the town before the Depression, to wine them and dine them – put them up at the Connaught with room service and everything in the hope that they'll get a favour or two back. That's capitalism, isn't it? You scratch my back and I'll scratch yours. And bugger the rest. It's being paid for with money from the Council's Ways and Means Committee. It's called hospitality in the Council minutes. They think that if all these people actually see the town – what fine men run the mills, and how dependent the town is on the trade – then these people, persuaded by their better natures, will go back to trading with the mills. Supply and demand. Economics.'

'Will it work?'

'Oh, I don't know about economics. I'm a *people* man myself. Dignity of the masses. None of that balance of trade stuff for me.'

'Is that why Dounleavey was invited to the Mayor's Ball?' Mr George asked.

'Oh, he's always invited, but the Mayor hoped he'd come this year especially. They hoped Dounleavey would be the town's spokesman – persuade the guests to revive the town's cotton industry. They invited Dounleavey to *represent* the town in dealing with these men.'

'Is that why Dounleavey's calling card had the effect it had downstairs? Because of the Mayor's Ball?'

'Dounleavey owns the Connaught,' Dunkiss said. 'He owns eight of the town's mills, too; and his estate runs from the edge of town into the Ribble Valley. But Dounleavey won't come. Beggin' your pardon if you're a friend of his, but he won't come, no matter how much the Mayor keeps hoping he will.'

Dunkiss had by now finished with the hearth. 'You want a fire lighting in here now?' he asked.

Mr George told him he was fine as he was. Dunkiss stood up, changed his gloves, and moved into the bedroom to put new linen on the bed. Mr George went to stand at the bedroom door, watching Dunkiss tucking in the corners and turning down the sheets with a surprisingly boyish eagerness.

'You don't *seem* like a bellboy,' Mr George said.

Dunkiss grinned, and went back to turning down the sheets. 'You see through my cunning disguise, eh? I am, in fact, not a bellboy. Not, at least, by calling and profession.'

'What are you, Dunkiss? Er, do I call you Dunkiss, or do you have a first name?'

'Oh, I have a first name, but everyone just calls me Dunkiss. It's part of my performing name – The Great Dunkiss. That's me. Saturdays round the market square, Bank Holidays in the park.'

'What does The Great Dunkiss do?' Mr George asked.

'Performances,' Dunkiss told him with dignity. 'Feats of athleticism.'

His most impressive feat, he told Mr George, was to have leaped across the width of the Leeds–Liverpool Canal. He had done that skimming the surface with his trailing leg. Another of his performances was to run over a tram's length of boxes of eggs without breaking a single one. He had escaped from barrels and chests in which – in the manner of Harry Houdini – he had been chained. And the previous Easter Day he had taken a challenge to run for six hours non-stop round the perimeter of the town square, racing all challengers at a sprint on any single lap of the course. People bet each time someone took him on, and he passed on the money he made to St Brendan's Orphanage in Haslingden. But it wasn't his *job*; it was his hobby. He was a weaver, like pretty much everyone down in the town square. He had operated eight looms in Cumpstey's Mill, until he was made overseer.

'So how come you're working here as a bellboy?'

'I was made redundant on account of the bad times. One of the first to go.'

'Isn't it unusual for the foreman to be laid off first?'

'S'ppose it is, but my situation was different to that of others. I was let go on account of my opinions.'

'Your opinions?'

'Yes, sir. I am a communist.'

'You are?'

'Got my membership card. Believing in the people, and the inevitable crumbling away of the old system. I think in the mill they was prepared to put up with me while things was going okay, mostly because the weavers liked me and worked hard for me. But when the Cumpsteys said there'd have to be a cut in wages if the mill was to be kept going, I objected. Said I'd lead the people out. Managers knew they'd follow me. So old Alderman Cumpstey was crafty. He announced there'd have to be just a few redundancies – the price of keeping the wages up – and one of them was me. And how could I be seen to object to that, sir? So here I am, since none of the other mills will take me on now, knowing my opinions – my principles – working as bellboy at the Connaught.'

'Are you a good bellboy?'

'I see no reason not to try my best. I don't know what the books say about it, but I reckon there's dignity in ordinary jobs. That's where the real heroes are. Besides, I find that I can get in my blows against the system in quieter ways. Like making sure the dogs are always overfed with scraps from the kitchen, so they'll not be taking a bite at anyone who happens to come trespassing in the grounds for a bit of lead off the garage roof to flog for sixpence on Chorley market. Besides, if you're good to people – pass the time of day with them – people're more likely to listen to your views and take your side . . .'

'Come the revolution?' Mr George added speculatively, and then, seeing Dunkiss staring at him, quickly wondered whether he should have done.

'Exactly,' Dunkiss said, suddenly gratified, his round face beaming. 'Come the revolution. When all men 'ull be brothers and everyone 'ull get a decent share of things.'

'You haven't read any communist literature, Dunkiss?'

'Not so's you'd mention. None of the clever words seem made for me. I get lost in 'em. Besides, when have I got time for that with six kids and a wife and working here all hours? My principles comes from closer to home – from personal experience, you might say. From when I was a boy. That's when you could say I came to my senses about things.'

Dunkiss had finished making the bed and was now moving through another door, into the bathroom, to set out the soaps and towels.

'Can I say something?' he said as he worked.

'Yes, Dunkiss.'

'Well it's just it seems to me, all in all, that just as I'm no bell-boy in reality, you don't seem to be a man who'd spend his time hobnobbing with the likes of Dounleavey.'

And so Mr George told him about coming to find work in the town, about Dounleavey and the change of suits, about Goose and how the boy had led him to the Connaught, how he had come to find himself with no money and how he couldn't in all conscience stay at the Connaught since he was not what the lobby clerk had taken him for.

'Stay!' Dunkiss urged him.

'I can't.'

'Think of it as a small blow for the *people*. Stay here as long as you can. Stay a week while you look for work, till you can afford lodgings. Who's to know?'

'No, no. You see I have to find a place for my father to stay with me.'

'Your father's with you?' Dunkiss asked.

Mr George shook his head and explained that he would be sending for his father as soon as he'd found the right place for them to stay, and a job to support them both.

'What kind of place?' Dunkiss asked.

'Some rented place where I can look after my father without it causing a disturbance to people. My father has bad dreams. He screams. It upsets people where we are now. And he has tinnitus – noises in his head that make him shout things out and bang about.'

'Has your da always been like this?' Dunkiss asked him.

Mr George shook his head. 'Not always. He was in prison during the war, and it's since then he's had the dreams, and the tinnitus.'

'He was in prison? In the war? A prisoner of war, you mean?'

'No,' Mr George said. 'He was in prison here in this country. He was a conscientious objector.'

'They give him a hard time when he was in?'

Mr George nodded. 'Things come back to him a lot at night. It bothers him.'

'I hope you're proud of your old man,' Dunkiss said. 'I hope you're real proud.'

The thought seemed to quieten them both for a while. It made Dunkiss – a moon-faced prophet in a kind of wilderness – melancholy.

They went downstairs where Dunkiss left Mr George in the sitting room overlooking the gardens. He had Sassy, the chambermaid, bring the young man some bread and cheese and a mug of tea ('It's on the house – another blow for the *people*') while he resumed the task of clearing up after the reception held earlier in the day.

'What do you do with all the food that gets left?' Mr George asked.

'I'm supposed to throw it away,' Dunkiss said. 'I sneak some of it back home when I can – for the children. But you can't get much past that old shark on the desk. He says it would encourage vagrants if it was known we gave it away. So what I can't get by him I feed to the hotel dogs.'

It was then that Dunkiss was called out by the chamber-maid. He was gone for several minutes. While he was gone, Mr George finished tidying the sitting room for him. When Dunkiss returned, he announced that there was news from the town – the fair people were packing up and leaving. What sort of town, he wondered, would force a travelling fair to pack up and leave before it had even set up?

They could see as they walked down the hill, even from a distance, that the rides and the tents *were* being dismantled, and that part of the fair had already left. The weavers, standing together on the edge of the scene, were watching, helpless to intervene. Goose was amongst them.

Some of the fairmen were barking orders. They seemed in a hurry now to leave. The animals were unsettled. The dogs at the end of their heavy leads were barking at those going by them; those roaming free were darting between legs and wheels; the bear, as tall as a man, stood on its hind legs at the end of the chain which tethered it to a post, scenting the change of pace; the clutch of very small animals whipped back and forth across their cages. The generators were being cut; the strings of coloured lights were coming down.

Dunkiss knew some of the travellers and went to speak to them. He had a showman's fascination with the fair. He was good enough to have joined a travelling fair, but by the time he was seventeen he'd had a wife, and then six children one after another, and he'd had his workers in the mill, and his principles, so the travelling funfairs had to go on without him.

It was one of the fairmen who explained what had happened. The elders of the fair had gone to the Town Hall as usual when they arrived in the town earlier in the day. They'd been put in a room and told to wait. They had waited and waited. The assistant borough treasurer, who usually dealt with them, was looking after the guests who'd been invited by Alderman Cumpstey and his colleagues to the Mayor's Ball. The clerk who was finally sent to see the fair people said that, because of the continued effects of the Depression, and because the Ways and Means Committee had exhausted its budget, its reserves having been spent on this year's Mayor's Ball, the Council could not allow the fair to stay for free in the town. The fair people would be charged a rent per stall to stay for the week. That was the message, the fairman told Dunkiss. That was why the fair was leaving.

'We won't stay in a place that wants to charge us money to entertain the people,' the man said. 'We won't stay in a place where the men in charge don't even come and tell us the news themselves.'

'But it's not the weavers' fault,' Dunkiss said.

'I know it's not, Dunkiss,' the fairman said. 'I know it's not. But we'll not be back in this town again.' And he carried on loading his caravan because soon he too would be gone.

They watched the last of the caravans pack up and go, and Mr George saw how much the fair's departure meant to Dunkiss, as if in being able to pack up their belongings and leave they had some magic which had always eluded him.

'You can leave, move on from one place to another whenever you like, but we are stuck in this place,' the weavers sometimes told the fairmen.

'So leave,' the fairmen would say, puzzled.

But the weavers would look at them as if they were mad, as if leaving demanded a gypsy magic they lacked, as if the weavers could no more contemplate leaving the town than they could imagine leaping from the summit of Pendle Hill, or swimming out from the jetty at Fleetwood Harbour and voyaging across the Irish Sea.

When Dunkiss was sixteen, as strong and as fit as he would ever be, he'd announced that he was going to walk to China. Word had spread, and on the market day in question people gathered in the town square to see him off.

'How long will it take you, Dunkiss?' people asked.

'Depends on the weather, I suppose,' Dunkiss had said.

He took a rucksack, and his savings from the mill, and he got as far as Hebden Bridge before he turned back.

So the fair went away, and the new Mayor's guests, the exporters, wholesalers and shipping executives, advised him simply: 'Cut your costs and cut your labour, there's a depression biting, don't you understand. We all have to make sacrifices to get through this thing.'

And Dounleavey had not come.

And only when the last of the caravans had pulled out of the square and long gone would the people who were left realize that the old dancing bear was still there, left behind, tethered to the post, sitting alone and disconsolate on the cobbles of the town square.

Dunkiss said they had to take the bear back with them. Left tethered outside the Town Hall overnight, the animal would have been at the mercy of stray dogs, or of drunken revellers coming out of the Mayor's Ball and teasing the bear for sport.

It was clearly past its prime. It seemed to gaze into the middle distance, as though it expected nothing of consequence to happen any more. It was a vague, uncommunicative creature. That was probably why the fairmen had left it behind. To them, it was just another mouth to feed, and it probably wasn't bringing in the money like it once had. Even Mr George – who'd never seen a fairground dancing bear before – had noticed that the bear's earlier performance had been half-hearted. Leaving it behind in the town to cause a little havoc and consternation had probably seemed like some useful small act of revenge on the Town Council.

The last group of people to leave the square was headed by Mr George in Dounleavey's dress suit, with Goose alongside him, and Dunkiss (in his hotel waistcoat and shiny boots) leading the bear on the leash.

Tatlow Street ran up, then down, in a straight line for half a mile. A high wall at the far end marked the yard of a mill, behind which ran the town's river. Dunkiss lived in a house tucked halfway along the narrow, terraced, cobbled street. He seemed to know everyone on the street, and those on their doorsteps acknowledged him as the group returning from the town square went by. People gathered round the bear and Mr George, to whom Dunkiss had handed the leash while he hurried inside his house.

'Does he bite?' one man asked.

Mr George didn't know whether he bit or not. He had never seen a bear before, never mind led one down a street on a leash, but there was something in the bear's vacant expression, in its sense of resignation, that encouraged the young man in the white jacket to casually stroke the animal's muzzle as he stood there waiting for Dunkiss to return, and to rub behind its ear. In response, the bear sat down heavily, its hind legs spread like a dog's. The people from Tatlow Street watched, respectfully, at a careful distance. Only Goose was brave enough to join in rubbing the bear's muzzle.

The bear seemed to accept the attention in an uncommitted sort of way.

'Is he yours?' a woman asked.

'He is now,' Goose said happily on Mr George's behalf. 'We got him off the fair.'

Dunkiss reappeared, having changed out of his hotel uniform into overalls, and carrying a gas lamp.

'I've been thinking,' Dunkiss said. 'I'll put the bear in Tatlow's Mill for the night. It'll be safe enough tied up somewhere in there. There's plenty of straw. That'll give me until the morning to work out what to do with it.'

Tatlow's Mill at the end of the street had been one of the first mills in the town, built before the Leeds–Liverpool Canal had been constructed in the 1860s. It was derelict now, but in its working life Tatlow's had been one of a series of mills built along the banks of the town's natural river and powered not by electricity, like all the later, bigger, mills, but by waterwheels constructed on inlaid weirs.

The mill hadn't produced any cloth since the First World War. It had been used for a time as a warehouse, but was vacant now, as the owner, owing a large sum of money to the Council for business rates, had been declared bankrupt.

They secured the bear out in the loading yard, then Dunkiss, holding aloft the lamp, led Mr George into the building. Inside, it was dark and damp.

'We'll find somewhere for the bear at the top,' Dunkiss said. 'If we leave the bailing doors open up there, then the bear won't have to be in pitch darkness all night. I don't want it taking fright and running amok.'

Dunkiss led the way up each flight of stairs. Mr George, following, pushed open the doors leading off each landing, curious to see what was left in the place. The door to the former carding room was stuck. Mr George gave it a shove and the door swung open. The room, sixty feet long, was filled with statues – carved wooden statues of saints and angels, as if a church had decided to close its doors and move its entire catalogue of religious statues and artefacts into that one room. Standing in the gloom, with Dunkiss's lamp half a flight of stairs ahead of him, it seemed to Mr George that he could actually smell the sweetness of newly worked wood and sawdust that he knew so well as a joiner, as if these artefacts were freshly carved. I am tired, he thought. I am simply remembering home. He closed the doors and hurried to catch up with Dunkiss on the next flight of stairs.

When they reached the top floor, they found it cluttered with debris. Supplies had once been winched up by a pulley system which still jutted out from the bailing doors over the loading yard. There were packing boxes, spools and shuttles strewn about the place, and straw everywhere. Dunkiss unbolted the bailing doors and pushed them open.

'If we secure him up here,' Dunkiss said, 'there'll be a bit of moonlight for him, and some fresh air coming in. He might be more settled, as well, being able to see some sky. I guess he slept outside when he was travelling with the fair. He should be all right like that.'

'I'll stay with him,' Mr George said.

Dunkiss looked round. 'You can't stay.'

'Why not? Somebody should stay. He'll be better off with some company, and it can't be anybody else – they're all too wary of the bear. You don't want him trying to escape or to go chasing after the fair.'

'But you're booked in at the Connaught,' Dunkiss said. 'You should stay there. I'll take care of the bear.'

'You've got a wife and six children and a house down the street. I'll stay with the bear. I'll be more at home here than in the Connaught. I'd only get lost in all those rooms.'

Dunkiss shrugged his acceptance. 'Well, all right, but only if you're sure. I'll bring you some tea across in the morning.'

They trooped back down the stairs to collect the bear from the loading yard.

Goose was waiting for them. 'Are you hungry, Goose?' Mr George thought to ask.

The boy nodded.

Mr George slipped open the button on his dinner jacket. He seemed to feel for his wallet, then leaned towards Goose and from the boy's ear produced a big hunk of cheese and an orange. The boy grinned and took them.

'Anyone else hungry?' he asked.

One by one the weavers still gathered around the bear came forward, hungry or curious or simply wanting to be part of the story. Each one of them in turn discovered that, somehow, the man in the white dinner jacket – the man who was almost Dounleavey – seemed able to produce from about their own persons bread and fruit and chocolates and biscuits, and it was only when everybody had been fed that Dunkiss realized that Mr George, with a magician's cunning, had somehow hidden about him all the leftover food from the buffet reception at the Connaught.

When the people from the street had gone, and a basket of remains had been collected and fed to the bear, the two men led the animal up the stairs to the top of the old mill.

'I wanted to ask you something, Dunkiss,' Mr George said as the two of them secured the bear for the night.

'Anything you like, sir.'

'I was wondering how it was that you came by your *principles*?'

Mr George had not met a communist before. He had only ever pictured them in his mind as exotic foreigners, as dangerous plotters, as angry men with beards, as spies, but here was Dunkiss, moon-faced, smiling, generous, anxious to secure the welfare of one old bear and worried about leaving a well-dressed stranger in an old mill for the night.

So Dunkiss explained that he had become a communist because of his support for Accrington Stanley. As a small boy, he had gone to watch the pre-war Accrington Stanley team every week, standing in the same spot in the Scratting Shed stand. It was a special kind of support, Dunkiss said, because most of the Stanley players lived in the same neighbourhood as Dunkiss in Accrington. Stanley wouldn't enter the Football League and become fully professional until 1921 and nearly all the players were local lads but gods nonetheless to Dunkiss. And they were all, to a man, wiped out on the Somme. The entire team joined up as part of the Accrington Pals at the outbreak of the war in 1914, when war had seemed a fine thing, even to the seven-year-old Dunkiss.

Afterwards, he saw it for what it really was: an enterprise that rich people ran – kings and politicians and those making profits from the bullets and the guns – in which ordinary people were used as fodder. The entire Accrington Stanley team slaughtered on the Somme – for nothing.

'Not for better wages, or jobs,' Dunkiss said. 'Not for better lives. They just got used. That's why I became a communist.'

*

'They're good people out there in Tatlow Street and all the other streets,' Dunkiss said. 'They just need something to do. They need some self-respect while we weather the storm, so no one gets the bright idea of having another war to keep the lads busy. They're good men but their children can't even go to Sunday school because they can't afford Sunday bests to wear and the priest won't let 'em into church wearing clogs and school shirts. They need reminding that they're as good as anybody else.'

'What does your wife think about you being a communist, Dunkiss?' Mr George asked.

'You know wives. They'd rather you were a good husband than a good communist.'

'Are you a good husband, Dunkiss?'

'Oh, I don't know. I don't understand women. Never have. It's not that she isn't a good person – she's just a puzzle. Being a good communist seems easier, somehow, than being a good husband.'

Everyone, even Dunkiss, had gone. The last of the spring snow was falling into the steady run of the river at the back of the mill. Mr George could see it falling silently past the bailing doors. The bear slept on the straw Mr George had arranged for it on the floor. Halfway through the night he had unfastened the bear's muzzle and taken it off. The animal had opened its eyes and looked at him, scratching itself, and then settled back to sleep.

'That was when I knew how the *real* story of my life would unfold,' Mr George liked to say to the orphans. 'With Dunkiss and the weavers there in Tatlow Street.'

And they would lie in their narrow beds in the long

dormitory, imagining Tatlow's dilapidated mill, and snow falling outside on the water, and Mr George, and the dinner jacket with the brilliant, crushed flower in the buttonhole, and the old bear asleep on the straw, and the scent of newly worked wood reminding Mr George of how far he had come, and of the work that in the morning would begin.

7

Pebbles

In the days that followed Josh Pascoe's arrest and his release, Noah Brindle would find himself looking out for the boy as he moved around Lowell. He would imagine Josh erupting in sudden furies against his mother, then subsiding into monkish gloom, while Elly moved between impatience and concern. Disturbed by the unfamiliar pulling tides around him, Noah would look at his watch at odd moments of the day or night and wonder what Elly Pascoe and her boy were doing at that moment. He would wish himself back in her warm lounge, drinking Elly Pascoe's tea from Elly Pascoe's mug, though some doubting inner voice kept saying that Elly and Josh should be left alone to sort things out between the two of them. But there would be no sign of the boy around Lowell; no glimpse of him amongst the casual evening huddles of youths in the yard outside the Mustard Seed, or riding his bike, or walking past the shops in that familiar bent-shouldered way; and Noah would wonder hourly whether Elly Pascoe still had the boy secured, and whether her son was tunnelling his escape beneath the town, or whether they had made their peace. Was this what Elly Pascoe felt for Josh? This weight? This gnawing curiosity? This desire to be a part of someone's life – the loss of *not* being? This fear that stemmed from spilling helplessly into another life, from not controlling what was loved or held important? Was this the accusation she had sometimes levelled heartily at Noah Brindle across the meaty smells and condensation of the Sandwich Box – that he rode above these things?

Elly Pascoe had taken the call from the police station at about quarter to ten.

They knew it was Neville Pascoe's son when they took him in, but Neville had gone off duty and they couldn't reach him. So they rang his ex-wife. They'd kept it quiet for Neville's sake, they told her. It would only be a caution, they said, even though the boy had technically assaulted one of the arresting officers, and resisted arrest. Just get him out of here, they said. He's been bouncing off the walls, they said. She could tell what they were thinking, scattered round the duty room in the station, pretending not to be watching while Elly Pascoe collected her son from the cells. To their minds, it showed how the boy needed his father. This was the proof. Here was the boy finally going off the rails, they were thinking, without the steadying influence of a man in the home. She could imagine all the sympathy there'd been for Neville at the station when Elly had thrown him out of the house three years ago. No matter that he'd been the one caught sleeping with the girl from the off-licence, when he'd told Elly he was putting in overtime. Things needn't have come to this if Neville's ex hadn't overreacted, they were thinking. Neville had just been having an Away Day; he hadn't deserved what he'd got. There but for the grace of God, they were surely thinking.

'They slipped him something. I think they called it a bomber,' Elly told Noah.

'Who did?'

'Josh won't say. I think it was that friend of his from school.
Damien. He was with him the other night when the police got
there.'

'Where'd *Damien* get it from?'

Elly shrugged. 'Apparently this Damien says it wasn't him
who gave it to Josh, and Josh won't grass on him or on anyone
else who's involved.'

'Where's Josh now?'

'I let him out for some fresh air. I told him half an hour for
a walk and not a minute longer.'

'You can't ground him for ever.'

'You just watch me.'

'You'll have him digging tunnels under the road to get out.
In fact there's probably an escape committee already.'

'It's not funny, Brindle. And just wait till that Damien shows
his face round here next.' She paused for thought. 'You want to
know what really hurts? It's knowing how Josh went off week
after week, telling me he was going to the youth theatre when
he was doing no such thing. He hasn't been there for months.
I know – I checked. God only knows what he *was* doing all that
time. He lied to me, Brindle. Every time he said "Bye" he was
lying to me. God, when I think back. He used to be such a *good*
kid.'

'He is a good kid. He just made a mistake.'

'And what happens if he makes another? If he keeps on making them? I feel like I don't even know him any more.'

In the kitchen, the boiling kettle had clicked off. Reluctantly,
it seemed to Noah, she climbed out of the sofa she'd been
sitting in with her legs tucked under her, and wandered through
to make the tea. Noah stood up, feeling as if he filled the place.

He looked around the room, feeling somehow breathless at the thought of being alone and surrounded by Elly Pascoe's things, at the centre – momentarily – of the small and (to him) remarkable life that was hers. It was the first time he'd ever been upstairs, in the flat above the shop. It was much smaller than his own place which seemed a kind of temporary refuge. His was somewhere to return to sleep, an ill-thought-out investment. There was nothing of *him* in it. Not like this. Elly's things seemed to fit together in a way he couldn't put his finger on. It was a light, low-ceilinged lounge with large impressionistic framed pictures on the walls. Books lay in twos and threes, as if she moved easily from one to another. There were three or four wall lamps which lit the place cleverly, making it seem bigger than it was, comfortable, peaceful.

From the window, he could see the outline of the Mustard Seed draped in darkness. When Noah left the centre to walk across, there had been three or four kids in the yard, leaning in a huddle against the shelter of the wall. The yard was one of the places where the kids in Lowell hung out at night. It was in the middle of the town, it was sheltered, and it was far enough away from the road to be sufficiently furtive. A morning trawl of the yard usually turned up a batch of cigarette stubs, lager cans, an occasional used condom. Last year there was a spate of small syringes being left, but these seemed to have stopped appearing for the moment. The front door banged, and Noah looked round. Footsteps followed on the back stairs and Josh came through the hallway, pushed open the door.

'Oh,' he said, seeing Noah standing at the window. He hesitated, hands in pockets, not sure whether to carry on through to his bedroom to avoid his mother, which seemed to have been his initial plan. He stood there looking, in turn, down at his shoes and across at Noah, not knowing what to do. He seemed cowed by the events of the last few days. According to Elly, he didn't remember much about the night itself. She had told Noah that Josh had been completely out of control for a couple of hours after they arrested him. It took three police-men to restrain him at one point. Several times, she had used the phrase the policeman used at the station – he'd been 'bouncing off the walls'. They'd concluded that it was the com-bination of the tablet he'd been given and the alcohol he'd drunk.

'How's things?' Noah said.

It was the first time Noah had seen Josh since the night of his arrest.

'Mum's pretty mad, I guess.'

Josh seemed relieved that Noah was leading the conver-sation, even if it was the dreaded topic of his arrest.

'She's worried about you.'

'I'm not a kid.'

'I know. But bad things don't just happen to kids. I mean, your dad's lot haven't caught that prowler yet.'

'That's just a weirdo. Damien says it's him on the estate who keeps the animals. He says everyone knows.'

In the kitchen, Elly could hear their voices. 'Josh?' she asked.

'What?' His tone with her was flat, dull, non-committal.

'You all right?'

The boy didn't answer this time, guessing that she'd simply wanted confirmation that it was him returning.

'How's your dad taken all this?' Noah asked.

'What do you mean, *all*?'

Noah shrugged.

Not being challenged, Josh conceded ground and answered,

'He's told Mum that he doesn't want me round there till I've sorted myself out. Whatever that means.'

'Do you think *he's* worried about you?'

'He's just embarrassed 'cause his mates at the station saw me like that, that's all. It's not like he *wants* me round at the house.'

'Why not?'

Josh screwed his face up.

''Course he wants you round. He's your dad.'

'It's all Tracey now.'

'Who's Tracey?'

'The woman he met from the singles club he joined after Mum and me left. Tracey this and Tracey that. And Lauren. If you visit them, you have to sit and watch *101 Dalmatians* twenty times and not speak while it's on, or else play Snakes and Ladders, and if you try to win you get told off 'cause Lauren cries.'

'What's your dad say?'

'He's the one that tells me off. And Tracey's always slagging Mum off. I've heard her. He can't wait to get shut of me when I go round. When I do go, he brings me back on Saturdays now 'cause he says he's working a shift or else doing the car or something on Sundays, and when I say I could stop and help he just gets stroppy and says wasn't I listening or something. It's because he just wants to be with Tracey and Lauren.'

'You don't *know* that's the reason.'

'Yes I do. I've biked past their house on Sundays and there's no one in and the woman next door says they've all gone out for the day.'

'Have you told your mum how you feel?'

Josh, shifting his weight from one foot to the other, pulled another face.

'Maybe you should tell her.'

'She wouldn't listen. Not now.'

'You want me to say something to her?'

'No.' He was definite. As definite as he could be, fog-bound and drifting. He stood there a moment longer, as tall as Noah's shoulder but stooping, as if he'd gained the height too quickly and been left searching for some misplaced centre of gravity, then he edged back. By the time his mother came through with the tea Josh had drifted away. Elly glanced round at the door, curious for a second, as if something had been mislaid. Then she looked across at Noah, shrugged in that 'Let it be!' kind of a way that Noah Brindle relished; smiled. It was as though her son had not left the room consciously, but instead, through some failure of concentration, some act of omission on his part – or theirs – had faded into absence.

No one had actually seen a prowler. No one had *seen* anything suspicious. For several months now, women had periodically reported a sense of being followed if they were out alone at night. It could almost have been put down to nervousness, a fear of shadows, if it wasn't for the messages.

The messages were posted through women's letter boxes in the St Silas district. Usually they were found the morning after some woman had experienced that sense of having been followed. The messages were spelled out using letters cut from newspaper headlines. People suspected Ripley from the estate. The messages asked for sex.

'Just sex?' Noah had asked Linde Wzinska, who had received one of the letters and thought she knew where it had come from.

'Wid bells on,' Linde had said. 'I tell him. I cut his balls off if he try that wid me,' she told Noah. 'He should be so damn lucky. He just say, "No, no, Linde, it weren't me that do it, I wouldn't do that kind of thing." But I see them magazines that the man reads. I know you see to him, Noah, but you don't know thuh man like I do – truly. I seen him watching my girls when they was growing up, getting changed in their bedrooms. I seen them curtains of his trembling.'

Linde Wzinska lived next door to Nathan Ripley on the St Silas estate. She'd had trouble with him for years. Ripley kept animals in varying combinations and in contravention of the rules of tenancy – dogs, ferrets, mice, chickens, a donkey, even a pig at one stage, in an overgrown and shit-laden garden – and Linde had fought a constant battle to get him evicted, but without success. A fair number of Linde's contributions to Noah's writing group in the Mustard Seed had detailed her battles with the Council bureaucracy over Nathan Ripley's tenancy. Noah consoled himself that, if nothing else, she had found a way to let off steam that didn't involve booby traps or Herman the Alsatian.

'It's just a game to them people in the Town Hall in thuh nice suits with thuh fancy offices,' she complained to Noah. 'Thuh tenancy officer they send out – God, he looks like he's just out of school! And I'm not his *sweetheart*. Why's he calling me his sweetheart? I tell him not to and he just grins at me like I'm just bouncing off him – like it's a game and he's always going to win.'

Linde, Noah knew, was short for something: Emilinde or Grunlinde – something like that. She could have been forty or she could have been sixty-five. She dyed her hair; it glinted purple under the big lights in the hall of the Mustard Seed. She was heavy and she slopped about in sandals because of the arthritis in her toes. She had brought up two daughters on the St Silas estate who were grown up and gone now; they sent cards at Christmas saying they wished they could have got back, but Linde's need to mother went on.

'You should listen to music,' Linde would tell Noah endlessly. 'Not always so much of thuh news about bad things. There isn't enough of the bad things? You think after listening all night to chickens and braying donkeys I want to hear *more* bad things on thuh news?' Her voice had a fizzing foreign edge that salted the flat, Lancastrian vowels she had lapsed into over the years since she'd first come to England.

'I like the news,' Noah would argue. He had a radio in his office.

'Don't you listen to music?'

'I used to listen to jazz music,' Noah said.

'Why not any more?'

'It makes me sad,' Noah said. 'So I listen to the news instead.'

'But why do you like to beat your brains out with all that pain?'

'It's not all bad news,' he would say.

'It's not good for the soul,' she would say, 'all that . . . oh, shpah!' And she would make a gesture with her fingers that Noah didn't recognize. 'You want me to find you some music on that radio of yours?'

And Noah would shrug.

Linde Wzinska worried about Noah Brindle. Sometimes she nagged him. She told him that she prayed for him. She carried a rosary in her handbag. She did the First Fridays every year ('in case the others have worn off'). She knew that Noah didn't believe in souls, or grace, or heaven.

'Listen to the news,' Noah would say to her. 'Do you *see* a pattern to things? Do you see a purpose being worked out?'

'Psh! And this once being a holy place,' Linde would say, looking up at the ravaged and flaking statues of the saints in their high alcoves in the hall.

In addition to working for Noah, Linde Wzinska also worked for a local firm which employed seamstresses to make orthopaedic supports. The firm sold them to health service trusts. The full-timers took home a hundred and twenty pounds a week and nothing if they were off sick. Linde couldn't sew because of her arthritis but she got two pounds an hour for doing the quality check and the packing. Twice a week she did two hours' cleaning in the chemist's shop next door to the Sandwich Box. She shuffled casually between each job. It's too late to hurry now, she thought. Sometimes she was late but she didn't care. Even when her employers reprimanded her, she didn't care. She spoke her mind. She would glare at them.

'You should be so glad I'm here at all,' she would tell them, 'with what you pay me. It's not *Christian*, what you pay me.'

Linde had lost jobs in the past because she had answered back, but there were always other jobs at the rate Linde had to accept in order to avoid being 'reliant', which, she was certain, was the worst thing anyone could be. She was scornful of those on the St Silas estate who collected 'money for nothing'. It was one of the reasons she was so scornful of her next-door neighbour, Nathan Ripley. Ripley only ever left his house and garden to collect his benefit and to shop with it. The other reason she loathed him was all the animals. He'd had goats for a couple of years and they chewed their way through anything. Linde would find them eating the flowers from her tubs or the rubbish from her overturned bin while Herman went berserk in the kitchen or jackhammered against his chain in the yard.

Sometimes, when she grew fed up with the Council, Linde called the police to have Ripley arrested, but he was still there.

Noah didn't mind if Linde was late for work. When she got there she was an organized and thorough cleaner. She had come to England in the sixties. Before that, she had worked in the offices of a freight shipping company in Poland, her birthplace.

'In charge of twelve girls in a respectable office in Cracow,' she would say, 'and now I clean floors. What do you think of that?'

As she was the only one who had worked in an office, Linde did the orders for the St Silas food co-operative. She calculated each member's weekly bill, based on whatever the wholesaler was charging that week, and then organized Tipper Gill to make the deliveries in the battered ex-Norweb Transit for those who couldn't manage to collect their orders.

Noah frequently saw Linde down on the estate. She was easily spotted because of her crab-like shuffle. She walked everywhere. 'Thuh exercise is good for me,' she would tell Noah if he tried to offer her a lift.

Whenever she shuffled along outside in her sandals, Linde rattled. At first, Noah had suspected that it was her arthritic toes which rattled, but it wasn't. She carried pebbles in her coat pockets. They were reminders. The pebbles that she carried in the left-hand pocket of her coat were there as a reminder of a particular problem she had to overcome, she had told Noah.

'And those on the right?' he had asked.

'Dreams,' Linde had said. 'Hopes for things. My father said to do it.'

One pebble on the left for each obstacle; one pebble on the

right for each small unrealized dream. Putting her hands in her coat pockets reminded her of them. Noah knew that her father had died in the Second World War when Linde could only have been a very young girl. He imagined that this was maybe the only memory she had of her father.

'How long do the pebbles stay in your pockets?' Noah had asked her.

'They come, they go,' she said.

Ever since Noah had learned about the pebbles Linde carried round with her, he found himself imagining all the women on the estate doing this – all of them with pebbles in the pockets of their coats. He imagined that this was what slowed them down as they walked around the estate or as they came up the stairs in the Mustard Seed. He imagined it was all those pebbles. He imagined that they were all reminders of the small dreams they were carrying, and of the obstacles standing in their way. He told Linde this.

'Tsh,' she said – meaning *foolishness*.

And so Linde had found a radio station for Noah Brindle to listen to instead of the news, and had weaned him away from the fortunes of brittle foreign democracies and the strength of the pound. The station played all the songs in the music charts which had a melody and which were sung well, and avoided anything that simply sounded like noise.

Over time, Noah had grown to like the radio station Linde had found for him. Sometimes his anxiety about the world compelled him to go in search of news of foreign governments along the dial, but after a while he found himself returning to the music. Old dogs and new tricks, Noah had sometimes thought, and smiled. The only problem with the radio station was that, in order to stay both tuneful and up-to-date, it seemed to have a very restricted playlist. Most of the songs seemed to come round again and again if Noah had the station on for more than an hour. Most of the songs (in Noah's mind) were sung by women. Or at least these were the ones that he remembered on his way home, or while he was making his supper, or lying in bed at night. These were the ones that stayed with him.

One voice had stayed with Noah for days when he had heard it for the first time.

'Is Annie Lennox,' Linde had told him when he asked her. 'Is fine woman. Is *strong* woman. See. It's better than all thuh bad news.'

'Isn't it ironic . . .' another voice had sung. 'It's like rain on your wedding day/ It's a free ride when you're already paid/ It's the good advice that you just didn't take.'

The same songs would be played over and over again. Noah learned to recognize the ones he liked in the first few bars and he would reach for the little radio and turn the volume up. The ones he turned up the sound for were usually those plaintive, female voices that ran in his head at night.

It had taken him months, after Linde Wzinska had found him the station, to realize that this was more than just chance, that he was drawn to these particular voices. They were posing the same questions over and over. They stayed with Noah because they reminded him of the women on the estate, with pebbles in their pockets weighing them down.

Linde Wzinska knew that Noah Brindle was always writing things down. She knew that he had once written a tiny book of poems. (It seemed tiny to Linde, who mostly read shopping catalogues.) It had been published by a small, co-operative publisher. It didn't pay much, if anything at all. He still had to come to work; he still had to deal with the real world – with the trustees who were almost bankrupt now, with the St Silas estate, with men who ate frogs and women who carried pebbles in their pockets. But still, she knew, he was always writing. She was amused and indifferent, because she knew so little about him, and because she was determined not to be caught asking. Noah realized this. Perhaps, for Linde, curiosity was a sin. He had said so to her. Linde, for her part, hoped that the Holy Spirit understood why he said these things.

One time, Linde had made a list of what she knew for sure about Noah Brindle – her boss – apart from his work in Lowell, and the fact that he was a good man who had lost his sense of there being a pattern and a purpose to things. She knew that Noah sometimes wrote things down, things he'd made up in his head; she knew the ridiculous story Noah Brindle told of how he got his name; and she knew that he'd had a wife a long time ago who had been killed in a car crash. And that was all she knew.

Linde Wzinska had only discovered he'd had a wife because her daughter had worked for the *Lancashire Evening Telegraph*. She had found the article about Noah Brindle's wife while she was going through the microfiche, researching something else. Linde wondered if that was why Noah Brindle no longer listened to the jazz music he'd once liked – why he only listened to the news.

Linde Wzinska found herself thinking a lot about Noah Brindle after she discovered that his wife was dead. Linde had even dreamed about Noah. It had been during the disturbances on the St Silas estate, when some of the youths had caused trouble for three nights on the run and when Linde, fingering her rosary like Braille, had watched a car burning down the street from her window. She had dreamed about a storm that threw down rain until the estate was washed away from the anchor of the earth and went riding on the flood over the streaming moors that had become an ocean. Frantic men bailed water from the houses or tried to steer to shore, but there was no shore there. And Noah? She saw him in the distance, hovering like a gyroscope above the squall of the estate, righting himself no matter which way he was buffeted or which way the streets and houses tilted. She dreamed the dream again a few weeks later, but Noah was not there any longer, though whether he had drowned or had been washed away on the tide she never knew.

Linde was right about Noah always writing. Even without a pen in his hand he was always struggling to make words work together in his head, coming to terms with the world he could not grasp in any other way. Each time Noah sat down with another blank white sheet of paper he felt a momentary panic about the story he was writing, like an attack of vertigo experienced in a car driven fast over a high bridge. He wondered about the kind of miracles the man in the white jacket would perform. He saw people waiting, patiently, in the loading yard of the old mill, and Noah waited too.

'I guess you're just a boring man,' Linde liked to say to him some days, as though she had just hit upon the joke. 'No story to tell of yourself, so you have to make some others up.'

'I'm an orphan,' Noah said to her, teasing. 'Orphans have no stories.'

'Shpah!'

'You had no orphans in Poland?'

'Sure we had orphans,' Linde would say. 'They were all *boring*!' And she would collapse with laughter, and all the pebbles in her pockets would rattle.

8

Tatlow's Mill

The bear was still asleep when Dunkiss appeared at the mill the next morning. The animal lay curled up on the straw, its cheeks puffing and blowing with the percussion of its irritable breaths. Mr George was sitting by the bailing doors. He had taken off Dounleavey's jacket and rolled the sleeves of Dounleavey's dress shirt up to his elbows. A quiff of hair was swept back from his open face. He had been awake for a while, listening to the water lolloping through the weir below where the waterwheel had once generated enough power to drive Tatlow's forty looms. Dunkiss was carrying a mug of hot tea. The young man smiled at him. Dunkiss nodded.

'Sleep all right? How's the bear been?'

'He was restless,' Mr George said. 'He seemed to dream a lot. I untied his muzzle during the night and he was more set-tled after that.'

Dunkiss nodded. 'That's good. I guess the animal must have taken to you.' Dunkiss passed him the mug. 'Here, this should warm you.'

The young man took the tea. 'I wanted to ask you some-thing.'

'What?'

'Last night, I kept imagining the smell of fresh sawdust in the mill. You said the mill was derelict, but this morning I thought I smelled it again. So I went back down to the second floor, to the big room down there.'

'The carding room?'

'Yes. I went to look at the wooden statues I saw on the way up last night, and I saw fresh sawdust.'

Dunkiss nodded. 'Darius Whittle. He's a boy who lodges on Tatlow Street. Funny fish – keeps himself to himself. He hangs around the mill sometimes. The statues are his. He carves them.'

'Why?'

Dunkiss shrugged. 'I don't know. He just does. He doesn't talk about them. Poor Darius doesn't talk about much. I don't suppose it does any harm him coming here, though. No one else has used the mill for a long time.'

The bear exhaled lazily, fluttering its cheeks.

'Is it late, Dunkiss?'

'Just after seven. I thought I'd leave you to lie in a bit. Thought you might need it. There's some people from the street knocking around in the yard. They're waiting to have a look at the bear – and the man in the white dinner jacket who brought it. I suppose news travels fast. I said to them they ought to wait out there. I said, "Mr George will barely be up yet, he'll have been minding that bear all night."'

Mr George crossed to the other side of the room and saw the people in the loading yard below. They were peaceable, shabby, a little vacant. They were unemployed weavers, Dunkiss said, back from queueing for work. If an overseer needed extra labour, he would take in a small number of casuals for a day's work at half wages, and so each morning by six o'clock a line of jobless men would have formed outside the gates of each of the big mills still producing cloth, in the hope of a day's employment. The weavers in the loading yard were some of those who had returned empty-handed to Tatlow Street. One or two were smoking, others were talking, waiting patiently. Small children ran around their legs, and all of them were there to see the man who was almost Dounleavey and the bear he had brought with him.

'What will they do now, Dunkiss – for the rest of the day?'

'Some of them will queue up again at twelve to see if an overseer will take them on for half a day. Some will go to the pub if they've the money, or go to the public library if they don't, and snooze with a newspaper next to a radiator to get out from under their wives' feet. Mostly, they'll just wait around till tomorrow. They're just waiting and hoping that things will get better. They don't know what they've done wrong for the mills to have stopped running. They're weavers. It's all they know. The only consolation is that they're all in the same boat.'

'They should have something to do,' Mr George said. 'Something more than just waiting around for hours for the chance of some work, or for some glimpse of a tired bear.'

''Course they should. I've been saying that myself ever since things started to get bad. But no one's bothered about weavers who don't weave. It's like they're not even *people* any more. That's the system, though, isn't it? If you're not *useful*, you're no one.'

The two of them fell quiet, watching the men who were no longer useful. Even the mill they were in was no longer useful. No one wanted it any more, unless you counted Darius Whittle sneaking in and out to carve his statues. Tatlow himself was long gone. The Council were trying to sell it off, but who had any use for a dilapidated old mill in the middle of a depression apart from poor Darius Whittle?

The bear shuffled and rose unsteadily to its feet. Dunkiss and Mr George watched as the animal looked around the room, squinting, struggling to work out where it was, then sat down heavily on its backside and began to scratch earnestly, scuffing up the bedding around it in a small flurry of dust and straw.

'What are we going to do about the bear?' asked Mr George. 'There's nowhere that will take him. Not even another fair, I shouldn't think. A farm wouldn't want him. He's not *useful* for anything any more. He's just a burden.'

'I suppose there's the knacker's yard,' Dunkiss said in the end.

The bear stopped scratching and looked at them. They fell silent. Then the animal turned round and flopped down in the straw next to the bailing doors, humphing through its snout. It lay with its back to the two men, looking out of rheumy eyes at the river, as if it had understood what they had been saying and was resigned to its likely fate.

'He deserves better than that.'

'Everyone deserves better than that. Even bears. But where would we put him?'

'There's this place,' Mr George said, looking around. 'This would be the only place round here big enough to keep a bear. We could keep him here – for the time being, at least. Until we thought of something better.'

'Someone would need to take care of him here,' Dunkiss said.

'Someone who understood about bears,' Mr George agreed.

'Or who understood this one,' Dunkiss added.

'Someone would need to exercise him, and feed him.'

'And they'd need to maintain the mill so the bear was secure and well looked after.'

'Someone would have to be here a lot,' Mr George agreed.

'They'd have to find another use for the mill. Something as well as just keeping the bear here; something for the weavers, perhaps.'

'And whoever it was would have to make this place their home.'

Which was how they came to keep the bear.

Asleep, it continued to dream as vigorously as it had on that first night in Tatlow's dilapidated mill. Awake, the animal padded around the mill on all fours, or walked rolling-shouldered behind Mr George, like some shambling dog. It was a vague and dissolute creature they had adopted. It seemed uninterested in learning new tricks, or even in extending any affection, hard as Dunkiss tried in those early days.

On the rare occasions the animal showed any signs of life, it was wary of something. Then, it would rise nervously on to its hind legs, sniffing at the air as if sizing up the threat. The bear had been trained to perform for long hours at a time and it seemed uneasy that so little was now demanded of it. It seemed to be expecting the worst. Whenever there was a sudden noise – Darius Whittle dragging blocks of wood around in the carding room below, or a gust of wind blowing a door shut – the bear would flinch, as if this were a prelude to a blow being struck. Mr George guessed that the bear had been hit frequently by the fairmen; perhaps that was how they'd trained it as a cub. They discovered a series of swellings and blisters underneath the fur on its neck, shoulders and the back of its head, where a short stick or a club had evidently been used. Maybe, they thought, this was why it was nervous of moving quickly, why it stood upright and sniffed the air anxiously whenever something worried it, why it usually feigned indifference about whatever was going on around it. The bear, it seemed, had rejected the world just as surely as the world had rejected it.

When they entered the Mayor's office in the Town Hall, the bear was upright and muzzled. The long, dark municipal corridors had set the bear on edge but they hadn't wanted to risk leaving it alone in the mill.

Dunkiss, who had come straight from an overnight shift at the Connaught, his hair licked down into some semblance of order, stood in front of the Mayor's desk, still dressed in his tight bellboy's uniform. On the other side of the bear stood a taller, blue-eyed young man in a white dinner jacket now shorn of its buttonhole but still immaculate. The three of them stood before the Mayor like refugees from a travelling circus.

'You want to *buy* Tatlow's Mill?' Alderman Cumpstey asked incredulously.

'We want to *use* the mill,' Mr George told him. 'We don't have the money to buy it. We want the Council to rent it out to us.'

The bear settled down on the floor at Dunkiss's feet while Mr George set out his proposal to pay a rent to the Council for the use of the mill. As a time-served joiner, his plan was that he should organize the renovation of the mill for the benefit of the local unemployed weavers.

'And you, Dunkiss?' the Mayor asked. 'What about you? I've had trouble with you before. Who's to say I wouldn't get it again if I let you loose in Tatlow's old mill? Who's to say you wouldn't go using the place to stir up trouble?'

'I'd just be helping Mr George. You have my word on that.

99

I'm all for the people, Mr Cumpstey, as you well know, but you can still have my word. You had it when you laid me off from your mill – I wouldn't cause any bother, providing no one else lost their job. I'd just be helping out Mr George. He's a good man. You'll do well by him if you let us use Tatlow's place. Besides, I'd have thought you'd have welcomed a friend of Dounleavey's making use of the place.'

The Mayor glanced up at Dunkiss. 'Dounleavey?' He looked across at Mr George. 'You know Dounleavey?' he asked.

'I travelled into town with Dounleavey,' Mr George admitted.

Dunkiss jumped in. 'Mr George is staying at the Connaught,' he said.

'The Connaught, eh?'

'The top-floor suite, Mr Cumpstey. I took him up myself. He's booked into the hotel as a guest of Dounleavey's.'

'Is this true?' the Mayor asked.

The young man in Dounleavey's white dinner jacket shrugged, reluctantly confirming this to be the case.

'And you would take personal responsibility for Tatlow's Mill and what went on there?'

Mr George agreed with the Mayor that he would do so.

Alderman Cumpstey pushed his chair back to give himself room to stand, and to pronounce on the deal. As the heavy oak legs of the chair scraped on the polished wood floor, the bear rose instinctively on to its hind legs, growling at the possible threat signalled by the noise. The Mayor froze. He thought about sitting back down but each slight movement he made was met with a further nervous growl from the bear which was facing him, eye to eye. Cautiously, having run out of other options, the Mayor reached over and took Mr George's hand.

Then, turning to face the bear, fearful of the animal's reaction, but unable to do anything else, the Mayor held out his hand. The bear paused, then (as the fairmen had taught it to do as part of its act) it reached for the Mayor's hand with its two forepaws and the bear and the politician shook hands. The bear's hot, sour breath spilt through its muzzle on to the Mayor, standing rigid with fear, waiting for the bear to relax its grip.

'I'm sure the Council would be prepared to waive the rent, and to grant leasehold of the property, providing our terms were adhered to,' the Mayor said, still held in the bear's grip. 'For a colleague of Dounleavey's.'

He edged away from the bear, then sat down in his chair, relieved to have put a little distance between the animal and himself. The bear dropped back on to all fours, happy that the threat had passed, and settled.

'I will arrange for a contract to be drawn up,' the Mayor said. 'I will be in touch in due course. Now, if that is all, gentlemen, will you please take that bear out of here.'

Within the week, Dunkiss arrived at Tatlow Street with an envelope delivered to the Connaught Hotel and marked for the attention of Mr George. Inside was a contract giving him full legal ownership of Tatlow's Mill and permitting business there for reasons of welfare, education and social recreation. There was also confirmation that the Council would make an application to the Diocesan Board of Social Responsibility on Mr George's behalf, for a stipend to oversee the running of the place. A handwritten note from Alderman Cumpstey asked for his personal good wishes to be extended to Dounleavey. The Mayor clearly saw his actions as a way of keeping alive the Council's hopes of persuading Dounleavey to save their cotton town – his mill included – from the worst economic slump in a hundred years. The day after Mr George opened the envelope, a large painted sign was erected over the entrance to Tatlow's Mill by several of the weavers under Dunkiss's command. The inscription, in bold lettering, read COMMUNITY HOUSE.

By the time the refurbishment of the old mill was completed it was said that half the people in the neighbourhood had been involved in helping out. Mr George had ensured there were jobs for everyone who wanted to be involved. Everyone felt their contribution, however small, had been necessary. Everyone felt that they had shared in the transformation of the place.

Ever since Tatlow's Mill had ceased producing dhooti cloth, very little had been done to maintain it. The roof leaked; many of the frames had rotted; some of its windows were broken; some of its floorboards were missing. Dunkiss and Mr George, with the voluntary workforce of Tatlow Street in tow, began working their way through the building, repairing, replacing, restoring – Dunkiss carrying timbers and joists it took three other men together to move, and hurling rotted floorboards from the bailing doors like sticks.

What they couldn't afford to buy for Community House, Dunkiss scrounged from dealers and second-hand shops, or somehow managed to get donated. He had a small handcart which was normally used to carry the accessories required for his performances as The Great Dunkiss, and every Friday, accompanied by Mr George and a Pied Piper-line of children, he dragged it round the town, collecting odds and ends – rugs, sheets, pots, books – that people were intent on throwing out. Someone in a big house even gave them an old piano, and Dunkiss tied it to the back of the already full cart and dragged the cart *and* the piano *and* Goose, who was riding on it, all the way back to Tatlow's Mill. The booty they gathered on these trips was either put to use in the old mill or else sold to the nearest rag-and-bone man, who happened to be Goose's dada. The money they made was put towards the Community House fund, administered by Mr George and kept by Dunkiss in a biscuit tin under his bed for use in emergencies.

Gradually, the leaks in the roof were repaired. The wood was replaced where wet rot had seeped up into the joists and beams. The ground floor, which had once been the weaving shed lined with looms, was cleared; the floorboards were mended, room dividers constructed, linoleum and rag-rugs laid down, and the space transformed into a recreation room. The winding room next door became a canteen. On the first floor they turned the old mill's accounting office into a classroom where Mr George was keen to put the weavers' enforced idleness to good use by teaching those who were illiterate to read. The second-floor carding room was to become a workshop in which woodwork and shoe repairs and upholstery could be taught. On the very top floor, the storage loft was stripped and cleaned. A space was cleared for the bear and bedded with straw, and a living area was created for Mr George, with a small galley in which to cook, a sitting room, two bedroom alcoves, and a pot-bellied stove, rescued by Dunkiss from an abandoned freight barge at the wharf and dragged home just like the piano had been.

For Mr George, at least, the final piece in the jigsaw was the armchair. After much searching, Dunkiss had finally found what Mr George wanted and brought it back to the mill one evening. Mr George had said the chair had to be high enough to afford a view of the weir through the bailing doors, and comfortable enough for a man to sleep in.

'They were going to throw it out,' Dunkiss said, 'just because there was a whisky stain they couldn't get out of one of the padded arms. It's perfect for what you want.'

The chair was set with care between the bailing doors and the pot-bellied stove. And when the work was almost complete and the converted mill was opened for business and people knew it no longer as Tatlow's Mill but as Community House, and when the storage loft was finally readied and made habitable, Mr George wrote the letter sending for his father.

The only real problem during the whole affair had been Darius Whittle's continuing presence in the building. Throughout the renovations, he had been adamant that he wouldn't move out.

Driven by some hidden music only he could hear, Darius Whittle relentlessly carved figures from whatever blocks of salvageable wood he could find. Over the course of four years he had all but stripped bare Tatlow's cargo barge in his endless search for wood in order to add to the army of saints – blind, hollow-eyed, hands pressed together or opened out, serene, unworldly figures – which seemed to fill the carding room. As to *why* he continued to make them, no one was sure.

Darius Whittle lodged in an upstairs room in old Mrs Greal's house two doors along from Dunkiss. He had been brought up by the monks at St Brendan's Orphanage out on the moors above Haslingden. St Brendan's was a bleak place, run with spartan discipline by the monks as they sought to instil a particular kind of unsentimental resilience in their charges. The orphanage had found Darius a job preparing fish for a stall on the town's fish market. He was punctual and diligent, uncomplaining about the ice burns, painstaking over the gutting and washing of the fish, and sullenly uncommunicative. After a year he was moved on from the back room to serve at the counter, and eventually he was put in charge of the daily orders and the financial accounts.

Darius spent virtually nothing of his wages apart from the money he paid as rent to his landlady. He walked to work rather than take a tram, he spoke to no one, and he smelled of fish, no matter how hard he washed. The women on Tatlow Street liked to tease him. 'Cat got your tongue today, lad?' they would shout down the street to him. But young Darius Whittle – fish stink and all – would hurry by, nursing a grievance against the world the way a woman might nurse a fractious child.

As Community House took shape, Mr George had asked Darius if he would consider letting the weavers share the carding room with him. When they had adapted it into a better workshop, he explained, Darius could make use of it as much as he wanted in the evenings when he came back from the fish market. Maybe, he suggested, Darius could help him teach? But Darius was unmoved – he would not share his space with anyone.

'You've got to get him out of there,' Dunkiss said. 'The workshop's the only thing left to sort out now before we're ready to open.'

'Darius needs to leave of his own volition.'

'But you've got the lease. You're *allowed* to force him out. I'll *carry* him out.'

But Mr George would not force Darius Whittle out of the carding room, and a stand-off ensued.

It was partly Mr George and partly the curiosity of the bear that in the end persuaded Darius Whittle to move out.

Each time Mr George spoke to Darius, the bear would hover close by, clearing its throat in a vague growl. The animal had taken an instant dislike to Darius, who insisted on shooing it away whenever it wandered near him. Darius repeatedly asked Mr George whether the bear oughtn't to be on a leash, or at least have its muzzle fitted, jabbing a finger disdainfully at the animal to emphasize his point. Mr George would explain that the bear was easier to handle *off* the leash; the animal was calmer and more settled, he said, without a muzzle.

'Of course I accept that you were here first,' Mr George said in the end, seeing Darius's weak spot, 'but if you choose to stay in permanent occupation of the carding room I don't really see how I can keep the bear away from you once Community House opens. He'll have to pass through here whenever he wants to urinate. Or whenever he's searching for food downstairs when he's *hungry*.' Mr George's emphasis on the last word seemed to give Darius something to think about.

It took more than two hours for the weavers to carry Darius Whittle's statues, work-in-progress and tools out of the mill and into their new home – the long, low, draughty bargehouse, with its unrepaired roof, on the other side of the loading yard. He had been offered any of the other, smaller unclaimed rooms in the mill but he had refused.

He was seldom seen, after that. Dunkiss maintained that this was because Darius was afraid of the bear, who certainly didn't like him. Sometimes, if the mood took it, the animal would give out a desultory growl if it caught a glimpse of Darius crossing the yard. Darius couldn't understand why Mr George had kept the bear, and said as much. He couldn't see the *point*. He thought it was frivolous. But then, as Dunkiss pointed out, Darius Whittle thought most things that were fun – football, funfairs, Dunkiss's feats of strength and Mr George's conjuring tricks – were frivolous.

It was fitting that the celebrations to mark the opening of Mr George's Community House should close with Mr George performing magic tricks for the children.

It was the kind of performance Mr George would come to be noted for over the years. With the skills of a natural conjurer, he would delight in staging ever more elaborate performances, as his belief that he could change the world strengthened and seemed to be reflected in the increasingly ambitious set pieces of magic he staged for those in his care.

But the performance to mark the opening of Community House was a straightforward affair. It took place in what had once been the weaving shed, on a makeshift stage of wooden packing boxes. As the new electricity supply had not yet been connected to the building, the light in the shed came from candles held by the spectators, adding to the sense of intimacy. It was a spontaneous show improvised as entertainment for the children, but it appealed just as much to the adults of Tatlow Street.

The weavers had no money to spare for music-hall entertainment, and after its dispute with the Council the travelling funfair no longer stopped in the town. And while the cinema was cheap enough up in the gods, it wasn't real; it was celluloid, it was make-believe. But to see Mr George, in the white dinner jacket he had worn on the night he arrived in the town, standing in front of them, making reels and drop-pins appear and disappear, and to see him pulling bobbins from children's ears and from under the hats of women, and making shuttles jump unseen from one bucket to another, seemed astonishing, almost miraculous.

The one regret that people had about the evening was that Mr George's father, who had finally arrived in the town, wasn't able to be a part of the gathering. Lawrence Littlejohn wasn't used to travelling. He was weary after his journey down from Annan. He had looked vague and confused, and had retired early. It had been a particular disappointment to Dunkiss, who had been eagerly awaiting the arrival of the former conscientious objector about whom he had heard so much. It was Dunkiss who had insisted that Mr George's father should stay in his house that first night to avoid the noisy celebrations at the old mill. And so, at the time when Mr George was bringing the evening to a close by speaking to the weavers about his hopes for the future, his father was already asleep in a narrow bed in Dunkiss's house, dosed heavily with laudanum and a tumbler of whisky.

Of course at that point, no one was sure what to call the new arrival. It wasn't until the following day that Goose began asking what he should call the old man. Dunkiss came up with the idea that 'Uncle' would be easier than 'Mister' since 'Mister' would be confused with 'Mister' George, and 'Lawrence' would be too much of a mouthful for the children of Tatlow Street who had taken to the bear. And perhaps 'Rolly' (the nearest the little ones could get to the name was 'Rollance') had a simpler, cleaner ring to it. Two days after his arrival Mr George's father let it be known through his son that *Uncle Rolly* seemed a good enough name to start a different kind of life.

*

It was a difficult transition. Uncle Rolly was unused to having so many people around him all the time. He wasn't really old, of course. He couldn't yet have reached fifty. He was a man plagued by noises in his head ever since his incarceration in Lancaster Prison during the Great War. He was old because of his past, and because he had been in retreat from the world for such a long time.

The day after his arrival, Uncle Rolly moved into the quarters he would share with his son in the former storage loft. He sat drinking mugs of sweet tea, and seemed content with his armchair, the view from the bailing doors, and the steady lulling noise of the water rushing through the weir below. He was less keen about the bear. He was uneasy with the idea that he should share his living space with an animal, let alone a former fairground bear lying in the straw in the corner. For its part, the bear, of course, was still awaiting its imminent fate at the knacker's yard. Each day it lay watching the new arrival with suspicion, as if *he* might be sizing the animal up – as if Uncle Rolly, poised and watchful, might be the slaughterman come to perform the deed at some sudden moment when he could catch the bear unawares.

'The bear does nothing,' Mr George's father complained, 'except lie there listlessly watching me all day. It's like being back in prison. It's like being spied on by some warder.'

It worried Dunkiss to think that the bear, in Uncle Rolly's imagination, could seem to be a prison guard keeping watch over him. But when he offered to look after the bear until Uncle Rolly had settled in, Mr George maintained they should leave the bear be. Leave them both to stew together, he advised – they'd be good for each other in the end.

*

Mr George found Dounleavey's place by accident. It was set back from the road on the edge of town, and Mr George had only realized it was Dounleavey's place because he had caught a glimpse of a white Rolls-Royce swishing into the drive from the main road, and had noticed the same crest engraved on the stone gateposts – the bear and the unicorn flanking the crown – as he had seen embossed on Dounleavey's headed notepaper. No one else could have an identical crest *and* a white Rolls-Royce, as Mr George knew Dounleavey did. It had to be Dounleavey's place.

The tram, having reached the end of its route, had headed back towards the town. In its wake was a sudden silence – like a sluice of cold air, Mr George always said. He had walked on for half a mile past the terminus. The town gave way, after a sequence of lavish but discreetly sited houses built by the wealthiest millowners, to fields with hedges that rode down into the tucks and folds of a broad valley and, after that, to rising hills and the clean, high edges of the moorland. Dounleavey's was the last, the most discreet, almost certainly the grandest house, secreted behind a frame of beech trees and the curve of the drive.

It seemed an odd kind of chance which had led him there. He had boarded the tram at random in the town as he'd done fifty times before in the months since his arrival, but this time his random route had led him to catch sight of Dounleavey's white Rolls-Royce turning off the road and up the private drive past the familiar insignia on the gateposts. Apart from the arrival of the Rolls-Royce, there was no obvious sign that Dounleavey was at home as Mr George walked up the driveway. He heard the doorbell ring distantly somewhere inside the house which seemed empty of life. Mr George rang the bell once more, and this time he thought he heard a noise – an inner door being pushed to quietly. After a few moments, the heavy front door opened. A butler, serious and unruffled, appeared under the stone porch.

'Trade?' the butler asked.

'No, no,' Mr George said, 'not trade.'

Behind the butler, Mr George could see the wood-panelled hall. There was a suit of armour at the bottom of the wide staircase. The butler waited for further explanation.

'I was wondering if Mr Dounleavey was in?' Mr George said. He had the excuse of the message from Alderman Cumpstey which he had promised, in a kind of way, to deliver to Dounleavey if he got the chance. There was also the excuse of asking for the return of his suitcase and the clothes Dounleavey had used to make his discreet exit from the railway station. But, more than anything, he wanted to tell Dounleavey about his work at Tatlow's Mill. He wanted to tell him about the hardships he had witnessed, and the difficult lives of the weavers of Tatlow Street. In a strange way he felt the compulsion – having found his own purpose – to offer Dounleavey a lifeline. He wanted to give Dounleavey the chance to become involved in some small way in the work of Community House, as patron perhaps, and to reawaken his faith both in men and in the world Dounleavey had grown so weary of.

'Mr Dounleavey does not receive visitors,' the butler said, 'though in any case he is away at present.'

'When will he be back?'

'Might I ask if you are known to Mr Dounleavey?' the butler said.

'We met on a train. A while ago, when I first arrived in the

111

town. I did him a small favour. I lent him my suitcase. He still has it. It was nothing really – and he did something for me. I wanted to thank him.'

'Can I take a name, sir? Perhaps I could pass on your request to Mr Dounleavey when he is next staying at the house.'

'Er, George.'

'Mr George?'

'Yes, yes. Mr George. That's how he'll remember me.'

'And is there a message, sir?'

Mr George thought for a moment, then asked for a piece of paper and a pencil. Sitting on the steps, he scribbled some details of his work at Community House and the things he hoped to achieve in the future.

Perhaps Dounleavey was there in the house, out of sight, still keeping all approaches from the town resolutely at bay. Or perhaps he was not. It was said by some that Dounleavey lived half the year on the Continent. It was said that he had married a countess. It was said he had drunk his liver to ruin. It was said that he had lost half his fortune one night at the casinos of Nice and won it back the next. But no one was sure. No one in the town was even sure what Dounleavey looked like. Whatever the truth of it, although Mr George would look out keenly for any kind of communication from Dounleavey from then on, nothing came. He imagined at first that Dounleavey might simply still be away, perhaps abroad, and that he hadn't yet got the message. But a week passed, then a month, then three. Only after six months did Mr George finally allow himself to think that Dounleavey would not be responding to his note, and that his role in Mr George's life had ended just as it began, with their single chance encounter on the train.

'I guess we're on our own now,' Dunkiss would say when Mr George would mention Dounleavey.

'You and me – and the weavers,' Mr George would agree, 'and poor Darius.'

'And the bear,' Dunkiss would say. 'Don't forget about the bear.'

9

Remembered Love

Noah had known the riots were coming on the St Silas estate. Ronnie Roots had sent a message to warn him. Ronnie Roots had the message delivered to Noah through Tipper Gill. It had been clever, that. Wide-eyed Tipper Gill had no sense of who *not* to trust in the world and so he had run the errand for Ronnie Roots to tell Noah that trouble was brewing.

They hadn't been real riots, judged by big-city standards. They were not even thought of as riots. People in Lowell thought of them as troubles – as disturbances. This was Lancashire; this was just a former cotton town. On the first night, a reporter from a national newspaper – a youth with a donkey jacket and a mobile phone – was on the estate giving the local kids fivers to go and find another car to trash. No one was sure how he'd been tipped off; people suspected Ronnie Roots, of course. Down the road, Neville Pascoe's colleagues in the police community unit were handing out Mars bars to the kids if they promised to go home. The kids did circuits of the estate all night, collecting fivers and Mars bars until the fivers ran out and until the smaller Catlin children were sick on the grass after all the Mars bars they'd eaten, lacking their football coach Tipper Gill's iron constitution.

It was the attraction of the Granada TV van which swelled the numbers, kept things going for three nights altogether, and encouraged youngsters down from Haslingden and the outlying villages. A couple of nights there were stand-offs with the police – screams on the estate from the gangs of roaming kids whooping like Indian braves, stones pistoned through the air towards the small police line, sirens wailing, Noah frantic. People wondered how things had come to this. For half an hour it seemed like the end of the world had come, although, in truth, it was just twenty youths whose parents were indoors watching telly, and a can of petrol syphoned from a rusty Mini Metro. A couple of vacant properties on the estate were left charred; there was some looting; and the family who had been setting themselves up as rivals to Ronnie Roots were firebombed out of their house. Some of the people who ran errands for this rival family were assaulted in the general mêlée – one had a punctured lung and was on life-support for a week afterwards until he pulled through.

In the middle of all this mayhem, two of the Catlin boys wandered up to the Mustard Seed and started a fire in the back porch which got out of hand and threatened the whole building. Noah, choking in the smoke, rescued stupid things in case the fire spread – the big food co-op scales, the writing group's work folders, Tipper's trophies. Afterwards, he slept for seventeen hours and woke astonished to discover the smell of his childhood orphanage's turpentine and bleached-wood floors in his nostrils. Battling a fierce headache, he drank mugs of sweet tea and drove back to check the damage to the centre before going down on to the estate to see how bad things were in the aftermath of the disturbance.

It scared the Council, whose remit covered three towns in the valley and a fair acreage of moorland rising towards the Yorkshire border. So they commissioned a team of consultants to research the problems on the St Silas estate, because the estate was now a problem.

They discovered there was someone employed by a local charity in Lowell who worked, in part, on the St Silas estate, and found they had a file on him. For a long time, this man had been petitioning alongside the local tenants group for the refurbishment of the estate. They found invoices submitted by the centre he ran in a former church; the invoices were for basketball posts, which no one could account for. They brought Noah Brindle in.

'What are these people like?' they asked him. They hadn't seen Noah Brindle before. They were from Chief Exec's and from Corporate Policy and the like – the ones who had commissioned the consultants' survey to find out what needed to be done. Noah was old enough to have been their father. He envied how closely they'd been able to shave. Their chins reflected light as if they'd polished them. Noah felt too big and badly put together around them.

'How long have you worked out there with these people?' the man from Chief Exec's asked him.

'A long time,' Noah said.

'You see, we want to know, from you, what's happening out there,' Corporate Policy said. 'You could be our eyes and ears.' They had seen pictures of the cars on fire.

Noah imagined telling them that these people ate frogs through their gummy mouths.

'It's pretty much like the Town Hall, I guess,' Noah said.

'How so?' Chief Exec's asked him, puzzled.

'Some are shits,' Noah said, 'and some are saints. And most are in the middle making the best of what they've got.'

'What do you know about Ronnie Roots?'

Noah looked at them. 'What do you want to know?'

'The Housing Department believe a man called Ronnie Roots might have had a part to play in the disturbances.'

'What do the Housing Department say?'

'They say they're only able to keep records if there's an official complaint – from another tenant.'

'Let me guess,' Noah said. 'There are no complaints against Ronnie Roots.'

'The Council's policy is that anonymous complaints aren't formal.'

Noah nodded.

'Do *you* think this man was involved,' Corporate Policy asked.

'I guess he probably was,' Noah said. 'It's hard to say with Ronnie Roots.'

'You don't see much of him yourself?'

Noah shook his head. 'People say he doesn't leave the house much. Some reckon he never comes out in daylight. Others say not at all.'

There was a pause. Noah was not anxious to fill it. Chief Exec's worked on a question to help them out.

'If there was one thing you could do today, that would help the situation on the St Silas estate – just one proposal that we could take away and act on that would change things for the better – what would it be?'

'Anything?' Noah said.

'Anything. That would help things. In your opinion. That we could do to make a positive impact.'

Noah thought. 'I would get the Housing Department to fix Mrs Wzinska's window frames. It would be good if she could put wallpaper up again.'

They thanked Noah for coming in.

Noah Brindle knew that Ronnie Roots *did* come out, although Noah had only ever seen the man twice. Both times had been in the middle of the night, so maybe people were right in that – maybe Ronnie Roots never came out in daylight. His most recent sighting Noah remembered well because it had been snowing that night, and because it was so late, and because Noah, alone in the Mustard Seed, had been crying.

The first time, walking home after a visit, Noah had just seen him from a distance, but he knew the huge, forlorn figure, struggling along on his own, heaving one leg out at a time in a parody of a walk, must be Ronnie Roots. He was about the same height as Noah, but much heavier, though it was hard for Noah to tell exactly how much heavier because of the vagueness of the outline the man made in the dark – he was wearing what seemed to be a cloak. Noah mistook it at first for a monk's habit. It turned out to be a hooded dressing gown made of some thick towelling material. Noah had watched him walk to the end of Tipper Gill's football pitch, shuffle round, and go back the way he had come. Even four hundred yards away, Noah could hear the figure rasping impatiently for breath.

On the night Noah saw him for the second time, it had only just stopped snowing but the fall of snow had settled and Noah wanted to get out for a while to clear his head. The air felt sharp on Noah's face, pressing on his forehead, and clean in his lungs. It made his eyes water. Earlier on, Noah had heard the shouts and screams of the small children sliding on the skid lines in the Mustard Seed's yard. The bigger kids, he knew, would have been using the more reckless slopes beyond Tipper Gill's football pitch. Noah had walked down there. From the bottom of the slope beyond the bushes, where the river ran, he heard that same rasping breathing he'd heard once before. Noah climbed down the slope and found the man lying naked on his back on the riverbank. From the slide marks, Noah guessed that the man had somehow lost his footing, slipped down the bank and fallen in the river. He didn't seem to be injured – just exhausted amongst the collection of household refuse forested in the bushes between the towpath and the river. The man couldn't breathe – he was gasping like a fish – and he seemed to have lost his dressing gown in the struggle to get out of the water. The other remarkable thing about the man was that he was covered in fierce sores and pockmarks; they were all over his skin – on his arms and legs and the blubber of his torso, and on his face. It was this, Noah realized – the psoriasis – that compelled him to wear the towelling robe. It was, Noah guessed, all he ever wore. On the evidence of the scratch marks the man had made all over his body, anything more close-fitting would have driven him mad.

'Can you stand up?' Noah asked. But the man just lay there on the ground, gasping, naked, covered in sores, looking up at Noah. He was slowly turning blue.

In the end, Noah had managed to get the man to write down his address on a piece of paper. The man wrote down only one word: Roots. Noah knew where the house was. It was the house with the Landrover outside, with the hardwood door and double glazing, and the hanging baskets.

Noah found a makeshift sled abandoned earlier by the kids. He harnessed himself to the sled's rope, then he dragged Ronnie Roots along the bank to where the gradient levelled out, and then all the way to Ronnie Roots's house.

A week later there was a message left in the Mustard Seed asking Noah to go and see Ronnie Roots, but Noah didn't go. A few days later, an envelope arrived for him. Inside was a little over two thousand pounds in crushed notes. Noah guessed it hadn't even been counted. He had sent it back. Occasionally, after that, scribbled notes arrived for Noah, information which the sender clearly thought might be helpful to a man in Noah's position – to a man trying to sail his small vessel against the prevailing wind.

The team of consultants sent in by the Town Hall started off using one of the vacant flats in the maisonettes overlooking Tipper Gill's football pitch, but after a week declared it unsuitable and settled for a series of daylight raids from out of town. They wore trousers with braces and chunky jumpers and huge leather boots with seams on the outside and dangling leather brand tags clipped to the eye holes.

Noah knew that all the kids on the estate admired the boots. The survey team had moved their base out after some of the kids had asked the survey leader if they could try his boots on. The man drove a Mazda 626.

'Is that the one with the ABS and the traffic guidance system?' Lewis Roots asked him, pushing his eight-year-old head inside the car when the survey leader lowered the window to ask for directions. 'Fuckin' tin box, Jody says. You could get a decent BMW – the Three Series – for what you paid for that.'

Another boy shoved his head through the window. 'Bag of crap, BMWs,' Jody Catlin said, peering into the car on tip-toe. 'Lexus, that's what you want, mate.'

The survey leader had his car rifled twice. One of the kids tried to sell him back his own leather attaché case after it had gone missing the week before. Near the bottom of the estate one day, the survey leader got lost in his Mazda. Each road looked the same and seemed to bring him back to where he'd started. The petrol gauge was on red. He kept the window up, feeling increasingly tight in the chest, his face salted with anxiety. He drove round and round, looking for a way off the estate. It was growing dark when he ran out of petrol. The car coughed, and stopped. He waited, and tried to think of a plan. Finally, he got out and started walking, looking around. Within a few minutes, he was surrounded by a group of kids who seemed to have drifted in from nowhere.

'You got them boots, mister?'

'I'll let you have them if you help me,' the survey leader said.

'Honest?'

'Show me how I get off this place?' he asked.

'What about the boots?'

'Just show me.'

The boy who had spoken looked around, then pointed.

The survey leader turned, and began walking.

'You shouldn't have done that, Jody,' Lewis Roots said.

Jody Catlin shrugged.

They watched in silence as the survey leader walked in the direction Jody Catlin had indicated – across the gulley where it flattened out, past the maisonettes, and beyond the bushes that flanked the river. The field beyond ran up to the reservoir at the top. After that, it was the West Pennine Moors. The man walked slowly; relentlessly. He would not look back at them. He just kept going, as if he had no choice, as if he had to keep walking or something would crack open.

'Where did he get to?' people wondered whenever the kids mentioned it. Noah smiled when they told him. He said he didn't know where the man might have gone.

Todmorden, they liked to think. Todmorden was fourteen miles away. It was so far away that they had different weather there because of the hills, and they spoke funny.

There were seven women sitting around the room. They were waiting for Noah Brindle. Noah had told Linde Wzinska that he had an appointment, and that after that he was going to see Olwen Sudders. He had told her they should start without him.

The women sat waiting in Noah's office, hoping to hear Noah and Olwen coming up the stairs, but there were no footsteps, no sign of them. Olwen Sudders had not been to the writing group since the night of the attack.

It had been Morag Gill's idea to move the writing group upstairs into Noah's office. Linde hadn't approved. In her view, all activities should take place in the hall or one of the smaller meeting rooms. Noah's office was his private place. But Noah himself hadn't minded; he thought it helped to persuade the women that the sharing of what they had written, or what they felt, about a book was not meant as a test. It wasn't a way of catching them out. They were not in a classroom. This was a place of safety, a kind of sanctuary from the lives they left at the door downstairs when they arrived, and that they would each slip on like overcoats when they left.

The women were still shy of sharing their feelings, of the intimacy of performance. At the start of each week's session they would gossip, talk, laugh. When someone was ready, they would go first with the piece of writing they had worked on during the week or talk about something they had read. If no one wanted to read, or if they had finished early and were reluctant to leave, they would ask Noah to read one of his poems. Noah would take down the book from a shelf, find a thumbed page, and read whatever came to his mind. Noah tried not to read often to the women. It was an occasional thing, resorted to only if he was sure it would help the meeting along or assist in winding things up for the evening. When he read, the women sat still, quieted by what Noah Brindle had done with simple words. What little they knew of Noah seemed to be buried in these private poems.

'How do you think of those things?' Morag Gill had said to him once in the group. 'How did you *see* it like that? I can't *see* things like that.' And Noah had shrugged helplessly, not knowing what the sad magic was, knowing only that sometimes, for reasons beyond him, he seemed able to catch particular moments in words – words that, once uttered, would melt like ice, releasing their captured meaning inside the head of someone reading them years later and miles away.

Noah hadn't shown anyone the completed chapters of his book. The lives of Mr George and Dunkiss stayed in his head, weaving patterns of love and resilience in him. The first question he asked of almost everything he came across now was, 'How would this person or that incident add to the world I am creating in my head?' It seemed to Noah that his long body was continually crouched in concentration, taking in the smallest gestures of people around him. Noah Brindle missed nothing, though no one ever quite caught him staring at them, as he fought to take up the threads of the story which was growing inside him.

*

123

When Olwen Sudders had first started coming to the writing group in the Mustard Seed, the other women found it difficult. They hadn't known how to deal with her. They were unsure who she was behind the armour of silence wrapped around her. She made them nervous, speaking so fluently with her hands. She seemed, despite her exclusion from the world of sound, oddly complete and defiant.

It was Morag Gill who generally read Olwen Sudders's writing to the others for her. Olwen Sudders wrote about how it felt to have no voice, to be excluded by sound from the wider world, and to live under the cloak of words like *deaf* and *dumb*. It made the other women in the group – more used to compiling lists, to the recitation of events – uncomfortable. It was unsettling and unsatisfying for them. They pitied her physical limitations, but they were not entirely sorry on those weeks when she did not attend. And when Morag Gill read what Olwen had written – diligently, uncomprehendingly – it distanced Olwen Sudders still further, to have *her* words run through the echo chamber of a separate, unconnected voice. It made the words seem frivolous and spiteful and not her own, even though, as Noah knew, she was the most talented writer of all the women who came.

It was Olwen Sudders who changed the situation in the group. It was she who moved them on in a way Noah had not been able to. One week she signed to Noah that she had written a story. It was a kind of fairy story, she explained. It was about eight women. Each of the women in the story had been a princess, but each of them had had a spell cast on her by a goblin. The first princess had her eyes blanked out, the second had her ears filled with soft wax so that no sound could get through, the third had her voice taken away, the fourth her arms rendered useless, the fifth her legs impotent, the sixth was unable to sleep, the seventh was given a dreadful forgetfulness and the eighth the curse of giving birth to a sequence of stillborn children. Olwen Sudders gave the eight princesses names identical to those of the women in the writing group. She also insisted that, on this occasion, Noah should read the story out loud since he was the only outsider and everyone else in the group was involved in what she had written.

In the story, the eight women decided that the one thing each of them desired was to be free of their particular curse. So they journeyed to the end of the world to find the only wizard powerful enough to break their spells. Olwen's story took the women across deserts and through forests, and to dangerous kingdoms which they survived only by helping each other to overcome the obstacles they faced.

Eventually, they reached the wizard's castle. They were admitted, and the wizard agreed to lift the particular spell cast on each of them. He did so by asking each woman to take off her ring and put it on to a table. The wizard told them that for as long as they stayed in the castle grounds they would be free of the spells, but that if they wanted to leave they would have to take back one of the rings and the particular spell associated with it as a passport into the outside world.

The women stayed in the castle with the wizard for a year, happy to have their spells lifted, but in the end they all agreed that they would like to go home. They decided that the fairest way of allocating the burdens of the eight spells was to draw lots and in this way let each woman choose the burden she would take back with her into the world. As her name was drawn, each woman in turn moved forward to the table and selected a ring to wear and a spell to be cast under, and only when all eight rings had been chosen did they see that each of them had chosen the same ring and the same spell they had arrived with – not because their own burden was any less cruel but because in each case it was preferable to the unfamiliarity and strangeness of the others.

All of the other women in the writing group had, until that time, forfeited surprise in what they wrote and occupied their own well-worn territories on the page. Morag wrote doggedly about happy childhood memories. Theresa wrote about the curse of looking after her mother who couldn't remember who she was any more. Linde always wrote about the day she'd just had – her jobs, her battles with Nathan Ripley in the house next door. But the story Olwen Sudders told, and which Noah Brindle read in his slow, sonorous, poet's voice, seemed to free them of their doubts about her and the shackles they'd imposed upon their own imaginations. After that, they were more at ease with Olwen Sudders and more forgiving of what she wrote, and more adventurous in their own writing.

On nights when Olwen Sudders didn't turn up, they began to see that the group was unsatisfactory without her, despite her alien inability to talk. So it was that the women were content to wait for a while before starting the group, in the hope that Noah might have persuaded Olwen Sudders to come. They wondered, secretly, whether eventually Olwen would write about the assault. Maybe she would get Morag or Noah to read it to the group. Maybe she was writing even now, they thought. Maybe she was searching for words that would embrace the act, the aftertaste, the residue. Perhaps she was sitting in her flat right now writing, 'Fuck him, fuck *him*.'

'Have they arrested Ripley?' someone asked.

'They took him in to ask some questions this morning.'

'About Olwen?'

'Yes,' Morag Gill said. 'And other stuff.'

'What other stuff?'

'The letters. The threats to *do* things.'

'There was a tip-off to the police,' Morag Gill said. Dorothy, by her side, watched the see-saw movement of Morag's lips as she spoke. 'It was anonymous,' Morag said.

'They should cut thuh man's balls off,' Linde said. 'I think it's disgusting.'

'They're only asking him questions,' Morag said. 'I don't think they've arrested him yet.'

'Men!' Linde said. 'How come they always have thuh brains in thuh pants?'

'You're lucky if they're *there*,' Theresa said. 'Mines wasn't.'

Linde laughed and banged the desk. 'Janice Catlin, you know what she told me?' Linde said. 'She says she was talking to her eldest one while he's lying in his bed in the middle of the day, and she's trying to get him up, and she says, to cheer him up, "What would you have if you could wish for just one thing to make your life better, son? What would your one thing be?" And do you know what he tells her? "A bigger dick." Dat's his one thing. A bigger dick. And he says that to his mother. God, I'm glad I have daughters.'

Noah Brindle had listened to the women in the centre talking about how the prowler could be Nathan Ripley. They all had their own ideas about what should be done to whoever had been following women about the town at night and leaving messages cut from newspapers. Most of the women – except perhaps for Morag Gill – seemed willing to advocate 'a taste of his own medicine' for whoever was responsible. As for Morag, she found it hard enough to get beyond trying to imagine what the *purpose* of such a compulsion was. Why would someone trail a woman at night? And would he take all that trouble to try to catch her just for sex? Only that? Was *that* the prize on which everything could be staked? She had asked Noah. Noah had said yes, he guessed that it sometimes was.

Morag had first asked Noah this question about Nathan Ripley several weeks ago, when she had come to the Mustard Seed to tell him about the letter the tenants group had been sent by the Town Hall. The letter had asked if Morag, as chairman of the tenants group, would become a member of the Regeneration Board which the Town Hall were setting up to co-ordinate a scheme to regenerate the towns along the Rossendale Valley. There was just over seven million pounds in the fund. Some of the money might be spent on Lowell at the end of the valley. Some of it, as a result of the consultants' survey, might be spent on the St Silas estate. As the Regeneration Board had to be a 'partnership' between the public, private and voluntary sectors, Morag would be a community representative. She and Noah guessed that the riots, and the survey which had followed, were the reasons Morag, as chairman of the tenants group, had been invited. It had made Morag dizzy to think of it, panicky, so she had taken the letter to show Noah.

Morag Gill, Noah remembered, had once confessed to him that all through her adult life she had found herself playing a secret game called 'When Jesus Comes for Me'. In the game, she imagined what she would do when Jesus finally came to her, when she had paid sufficient dues to help her choose the life she wanted, not the one she had. And Noah realized that Morag Gill, clutching the letter from the Council, had at last come to believe that she had now paid her dues. They talked about her hopes for the estate, and about the prowler, and about Morag's sense that Nathan Ripley's life was ruined but that her own would now soon be mended.

Noah felt closer to Morag Gill than to anyone else on the St Silas estate. Unlike Linde Wzinska with her melancholy lack of expectations, unlike Nathan Ripley with his hopelessly straying goats, or Melanie Quigley raising her son in the flat emptied of all her possessions, or Ronnie Roots, or even Tipper – all apparently unanchored by experience – Morag Gill seemed to have a past which bequeathed to her beliefs about the world and which left her sounding echoes to find the depth and meaning of things. She seemed to be the only one he knew whose days weren't simply about reacting to the flotsam coming downstream by clawing either right or left – it made no difference which – or simply going under on impact and leaving it to fate whether she'd come up again. Or maybe it was just that the pieces of Morag's life (because Noah knew the key) made sense. They added up. They told a tale, he knew, and had an end in mind, and the end was Jesus coming.

Noah saw her most mornings when she came to the centre. Morag took a walk with Dorothy each day after breakfast and after the chores they did together while Tipper still slept. On their walk, arm in arm, they talked, and Dorothy remembered words and used them, hard and shiny and one at a time – like stones bowled at things. They walked through the estate and up to the Mustard Seed so that Morag could check whether any tasks needed to be done for the food co-operative or the tenants group. Sometimes she would just talk with Noah, or drink tea while Noah made phone calls or did the books or his paperwork, and Dorothy sat – quite still – taking in the movement.

'She likes things happening round her,' Morag Gill had said

to Noah. 'Don't you, love?' And Dorothy would be watching: heavy, placid, hands pressed into her lap, grandmotherly, determined, deliberate. People sometimes mistook the two women together for sisters, but they were not.

'I've been reading a new book,' Morag Gill said to the women gathered in Noah's office. The others looked round, wary that Olwen was not there, and that Noah had still not returned; wondering whether or not they should wait, but happy at least that someone else was offering to go first. This thing they did was still a form of confession; they still felt a sense of walking out on to a high wire. Morag unearthed a book from her shopping bag. It was a copy of *The Grapes of Wrath*, and she held it up for the others to see.

'It was a film,' Morag said. 'I saw it years ago. Henry Fonda. I didn't know it was a book. Not then. I've not written anything about it yet,' she said, 'but I wanted to say I'm glad I got round to reading it. I told Noah I'd seen the book in the Oxfam shop – fifty pence – and he said I should get it and have a go at reading it. I hadn't really thought a book that was just about farmers travelling in a truck to California would be much cop, especially having seen the film. The film's always better, isn't it? You can see the thing there in front of you; you haven't got to imagine it. At least I thought that before I started reading this.'

Morag picked up the book and held it in front of her, looking at it, feeling the weight of it.

'He was an American who wrote it,' she said. 'He's dead now. He'd been with them – the farmers, the ones who all lost their farms because of the dustbowl. They all made this trek from Oklahoma towards California. California was their dream and they packed up their belongings in their trucks and just drove there 'cause they had nothing else to do. It really happened. It's a true story. You'd think in a book it'd be boring. Like history. Like a story in history or something. But it's . . .' She fought for a word. 'Listen,' she said. She flicked to a page she had marked. 'Listen to this.' And she read.

'"In the wet hay of leaking barns babies were born to women who panted with pneumonia. And old people curled up in corners and died that way, so that the coroners could not straighten them. At night the frantic men walked boldly to hen roosts and carried off the squawking chickens. If they were shot at, they did not run, but splashed sullenly away; and if they were hit, they sank tiredly in the mud."'

Around the room, the other women listened, but Morag was no longer conscious of them. She was reading for herself.

'"The women watched the men, watched to see whether the break had come at last. The women stood silently and watched. And where a number of men gathered together, the fear went from their faces, and anger took its place. And the women sighed with relief, for they knew it was all right – the break had not come; and the break would never come as long as fear could turn to wrath."'

Morag continued to look at the book – at the page – even though she had finished reading. She didn't close the book. No one in the room said anything. They were all in their own private worlds. Finally, Morag Gill closed the book and put it down in front of her. The others waited for her to speak.

'It's not really about history or farming at all,' Morag Gill said. 'Well, it is and it isn't. Does this make sense?' She looked for Noah for help, then realized that he wasn't there.

'It's about . . . it's about . . . well it's about people who are just ordinary. Trying to survive. Trying to make it through. They just want to get to California, to the orchards, to work there because there's nothing left of their farms, and it's not their fault that there's nothing left of them. The book's about trying to get by in the olden days, and about these men – they're just farmers – trying to stick together, trying to fight for each other. And this one family the writer made up to show what it was like. The Joads – that's the name he gives to the family. It's about trying to stay human and not just fall away into something else. I don't know – I don't know how to say it. California's their dream. They have nothing left, and that's their dream. In a way,' Morag said, 'the book's about what Jesus preached. It's about having the courage to try and stand up for what Jesus said and not just sitting back and wishing for it. It's about putting things that Jesus said in the bible into action so those who aren't strong enough to take care of themselves get taken care of, don't get forgotten and trodden under. So it's not a free for all. Like the Sermon on the Mount. Like Jesus said in the Sermon on the Mount.'

She stopped.

Her voice had grown stronger as she continued to talk. Now, the silence among the women in the room seemed sudden and remarkable.

The others weren't used to her speaking like this. They wondered how it was she had been able to. They guessed it was because she had something to hope for now; they guessed it was something to do with the Council asking her to sit on the Regeneration Board.

At first, Morag Gill had said to Noah that she would refuse the invitation. She said if she went she'd make a fool of herself. The idea of sitting round a table in the Town Hall down in the valley with all those men in suits who knew more than she did scared her. She dreaded the possibility of saying something stupid or going blank. But in the end she had accepted.

Linde said, 'What happens to the men in thuh book? Thuh farmers? What happens to thuh story? Do they get there? To California? You should tell us.'

'You have to read it,' Morag Gill said. 'You have to read it yourself. Then you'll see what happens in the end.'

Only Linde was still at the centre when Noah got back. She was straightening up, moving furniture back with vigour, sweeping even narrow corners and inlets, wanting (Noah felt) to apologize for the group having taken place without him – but, instead of using words, she had spring-cleaned the place because words only came out of her as scoldings.

'How is thuh deaf woman? Olwen?' She reached for the broom she had been using, as if she needed it to anchor her.

'I didn't get there,' Noah said. 'My appointment ran late.'

'What appointment can anyone have at this time?'

'My ear infection,' Noah said. 'The doctor wanted to see me after my course of antibiotics was done.'

'Doctors! What do they know.'

'Not as much as you, I bet.'

'Don't you be so cheeky, Noah Brindle. You're getting headaches with this thing? This ear infection.'

Noah shrugged, meaning maybe yes.

'That's stress. Headaches are stress. It's because thuh centre is closing down. I have thuh headaches quite a lot myself. It's thuh stress. I always have paracetamol in my bag. You want me to get some?'

Noah reached into his jacket pocket and took out a small

plastic bottle which rattled with pills as he shook it to show her. 'So, are you going to tell me how it went tonight? I suppose everyone thinks the group can run without me from now on?'

'Tsh!' Linde said, stamping with the broom.

'What's tsh?'

'Some people seem to want to read some funny stuff in that group lately. What's wrong with a nice simple story so you know where you are? What's wrong with knowing thuh ending?'

Linde said that the other women had felt safer walking home tonight while Nathan Ripley was being held by the police. She was triumphant that the police had arrested him for the attempted rape of Olwen Sudders. Listening to her, Noah couldn't help but wonder what things were going round in Nathan Ripley's head in his police cell. What was the catalyst which, if the police were right, had brought him into fateful collision with Olwen Sudders? What was he thinking now, as Olwen Sudders herself sat alone in her flat in the maisonettes, writing out, 'Fuck *him*, fuck *him*.' Was Nathan Ripley hanging on to some kind of hope, some memory of goodness in his life as the waters began to rise around him?

Noah himself knew the importance of a memory or a hope to cling on to. Noah remembered love.

Morag Gill knew it too. Morag – with her man's face and her farmer's shoulders – had told Noah that, when she opened the letter from the Town Hall inviting her on to the Regeneration Board, her heart had boom-boom-boomed for the whole day, and that when she had finally arrived for the first meeting and had walked down the chandeliered corridor on the top floor of the Town Hall she had felt herself breathless. It was as though her life was starting over again, just as she remembered it doing when she was fourteen and Our Lady had appeared to her and had said that one day Jesus would come and He would save her.

10

Educating the Bear

The Diocesan Office sent someone round to Community House every three months to monitor the spending of the modest stipend. Fr Fearon was a junior member of the Diocesan staff. He was a desk man – short and thickset with a cultivated sense of holiness. He clasped his hands together a lot and spoke of 'we sinners' even though the weavers could tell that he didn't include himself in that category. He was bothered by Darius Whittle's fish-scented louring night-time presence in the bargehouse, and by the menagerie of curious saints Darius had surrounded himself with; he disapproved of the presence of the bear – his reports called it 'unhygienic'; he objected to the language of some of the weavers, usually when they were chasing a football round in the loading yard. He had hoped, he said, for a more *redemptive* atmosphere overall. He had hoped for more tutoring in scripture, for more spirituality, and thought that Mr George should make daily worship compulsory for those attending Community House.

'If the men choose to pray, they can pray. If they want to read the newspapers each morning, that's up to them,' Mr George would say. 'Christianity is what's done, not what's said.'

The cleric's reports were submitted on his return to his

superiors, who would pass their memorandum on to the full Diocesan Board. Mr George never really knew what happened to the forms. He guessed that, despite the cleric's concerns, Fr Fearon was satisfied enough to recommend continuation of the stipend, since the next quarterly payment always arrived in due course from the Diocesan treasurer. It was this money that enabled Mr George to offer Sassy – who, it transpired, was Dunkiss's younger sister – a full-time position helping him at Community House.

Dunkiss himself continued to work at the Connaught. After each shift, he would run back across town to Tatlow Street, still dressed to the waist in his Connaught bellboy's uniform, a pair of baggy white football shorts falling below his knees, and a pair of crusty, oversized workboots.

With Dunkiss's work, his running, and his weight training, his performances as The Great Dunkiss had become less frequent, and were now reserved for special occasions or as part of Mr George's own weekend entertainment for the band of ragged children who played in and around Community House.

Saturday afternoons, however, when Accrington Stanley were at home in the League, were sacrosanct, and Dunkiss continued to arrange the rest of his life around that fact, donning his colours each match day and walking the four miles to his former home town, Accrington – with Goose now accompanying him – to pay homage to *his* team.

Stanley were not a glamorous team. They were a small-town side dwarfed by their local rivals. But Blackburn Rovers and Burnley held no appeal for Dunkiss.

'Stanley are *the people's* team,' Dunkiss always insisted.

Three years after his arrival in the town Mr George was

finally persuaded by Dunkiss and Goose to go to see Accrington Stanley play for the first time. Mr George had never been to a football match before.

'You *should* come,' Dunkiss had told him. 'I think the team's going to be on a roll again come the spring.'

It seemed that few others shared Dunkiss's optimism. Not many more than two thousand hardy souls turned up in the sleeting rain alongside Goose and Dunkiss and a shivering Mr George to watch Stanley play York City early in 1936.

'A goal in the first ten minutes should warm us up, eh!' Dunkiss said hopefully. He knew as well as anyone, though, that this would be a small miracle.

Within a minute of the game starting, kicking up the slope and against the wind, Stanley had taken the lead. Dunkiss, confirmed as a prophet, was speechless. Beside him, leaning against the terrace barrier, Mr George stood grinning and slapping him on the back. Within ten minutes, Stanley had scored a second and the red shirts were running riot. By the time the final whistle blew, the roof was being cheered off Peel Park by the supporters applauding a 7–2 win.

'You can't stop coming now,' Goose said happily. 'Not after that. The team need you here.'

In the months which followed his first visit to Peel Park Mr George became increasingly concerned that Goose seemed to spend more and more time at Community House and hardly any at home. Goose seldom seemed to have been washed and even less often fed. His dada, the rag-and-bone man from Navigation Street, brought the boy up alone. He had a horse and cart. He couldn't afford a sign and had chalked on the back of the cart: MULLIGAN RAGS AND BONES EVERYTHIN TAKIN.

Goose would explain, if ever he was asked, that his dada worked late on the cart, and that he did an extra round on Saturdays in the outlying villages. His dada's last visit on Saturday afternoons, Goose said, was at one of the pubs in Belthorne village where the landlord gave him his tea and a pint of bitter for his troubles before his journey back to town. Now that Goose was older his dada didn't get back to the house, Goose maintained, till eight o'clock on a Saturday. And on a Sunday, Goose said, his dada locked the house to go to see an aunt in Burnley who was very old and didn't like children and needed jobs doing round the house all day. As a consequence, Mr George allowed Goose to have the run of the mill at week-ends, feeding him, letting him go to the football with Dunkiss, enlisting his help with the bear, and only chased the boy home in the evenings at eight o'clock when Goose's father would have arrived back home (according to the boy) to take care of him.

It was for children like Goose that Mr George had by now begun to run a Sunday school in Community House. The children who came were, by and large, those who were not allowed into the parish Sunday school which was overseen by the Diocesan Office. Mr George spoke frequently about the matter to Fr Fearon when the junior cleric called on his quarterly visits, but to no avail. Fr Fearon, with laboured patience, always repeated that certain standards were necessary; only children of regular church-goers, properly dressed, could be allowed to attend the parish Sunday school.

'But these children are the ones who need a Sunday school *most*,' Mr George argued.

Fr Fearon would purse his lips. 'Then maybe you could use your undoubted influence amongst these people to persuade them to do their Christian duty by giving worship in church, and bringing their offspring with them.'

Within a month of Mr George's school starting up, there were sixty children queueing outside the old mill on Sunday mornings. Fr Fearon wasn't happy. He was concerned, he said, about the *number* of games being played, and the *extent* of the football, and the sheer *din* that the children generated throughout the day – God's day, the day of rest, of prayer. His reports said so, though the Diocesan Office seemed curiously unwilling to respond to Fr Fearon's objections.

By the time the draw for the third round of the FA Cup had been made the following year – pairing Accrington Stanley with Blackburn Rovers – Mr George had become as avid a fan of the Reds as Goose and Dunkiss. As the day of the big match grew closer, however, Goose grew noticeably quiet. Dunkiss wondered if it was nerves at the prospect of the cup tie against their mighty local rivals.

It looked at first like more dirt on the boy's unwashed face. It was Mr George who finally realized that it was a bruise, bluegrey and the size of his father's fist. Further investigation revealed that Goose had a broken molar in his upper jaw which had become more and more painful as the week had worn on.

Mr George paid for Goose to see a local dentist who pulled out the remaining shard of tooth. The next day, when some of the swelling had begun to subside in the boy's face, Mr George and Dunkiss cleaned Goose up in the bath tub. Under the film of dirt his skinny rabbit body was layered with bruises and scab marks.

Goose's dada was sprawled out on the settee in the front room when Mr George entered his house. The curtains were pulled

shut against the light; a half-empty bottle was on the floor
beside him. The dark room stank of cats and urine. Goose's
dada was fully dressed. He was snoring. He smelled of drink.
Mr George let the door slam shut behind him. Goose's dada
woke with a start in the forced darkness.

'Clear off out, you swine,' he muttered. He rubbed his eyes,
then reached for the bottle by his side. Mr George, standing
over him, gently knocked the bottle over with his foot. The
contents began to spill out on to the floor which was already
filthy with a gauze of cat hairs, Capstan Full Strength ash and
the domestic debris of months past.

'What the . . . ?'

The man swivelled unsteadily to sit up, throwing a fist
vaguely in Mr George's direction as he did so. He looked up,
and realized that it wasn't his son in the room.

'Who are you?' he mumbled. His head seemed to hurt.
'Here, I know you. You're that bloke runs the old mill. I hope
you ain't come to complain about the boy, 'cause I'm sick of
him.'

'I've come with a message,' Mr George said.

'Just leave him to me,' the man said. 'I'll knock some sense
into him when he gets back, the little bugger.'

'I've come to say that I know what you did to Goose last week.'

'What?'

'I know what you do to him. I've had him examined and
attended to, which is more than can be said of you.'

'Tsh! You know what a doctor charges these days? Huh?
This business ain't so good that I can chuck money around on
stupid kids that get in the way of things.'

'I've come to say,' Mr George said, 'that if I hear you've laid
another finger on that child, you'll have me to answer to

directly. One more blow and I'll be back. And I'll take the boy off your hands myself for good. Do I make myself clear?'

The man was groping for the bottle on the floor beside him; he could hear its contents still leaking slowly away. Mr George stepped across and kicked the bottle out of his reach. It smacked into the skirting board.

'Do I make myself *clear*?'

The man gathered himself to stand, then thought better of it, unsure whether he was capable of rising if he made the effort. 'Oh yeah, guv,' he said, trying instead for sarcasm. 'Real clear.' He fell back into the settee.

On his way out, Mr George heard a scuffling noise coming from the kitchen. He went through the dim middle parlour and opened the door. The horse was standing in the kitchen, gazing out into the backyard. There was a pile of steaming horse shit on the stone flags of the kitchen. The sink was full of hay.

That weekend, Stanley surprised everybody by holding mighty Blackburn Rovers to a draw and earning an unexpected cup replay. All weekend, children played out the match again and again in the loading yard and rehearsed the goals they hoped for in the return match at Peel Park.

It wasn't until Sunday evening that the note arrived at Community House. There were dirty fingerprints on the envelope, which was addressed to 'The Gaffer, Tatlow's Mill'. It had been delivered by hand. Dunkiss had found it and brought it to Mr George.

'Who's it from?' Dunkiss asked as Mr George read it.

'It's from Goose's dada.'

'What's he want?'

'Twenty pounds.'

'For what?'

'For Goose.'

'He wants to *sell* his son?'

'He'll let the boy pass into my custody if I provide him with a consideration. Twenty pounds is the consideration he'll agree to. If not, he'll stop the boy coming round to Community House again. He says if Goose is found here, he'll set the police on to me for kidnap. He says he's consulted a lawyer about his rights as a father.'

'What'll you do? We don't have twenty pounds. Nothing like. There's less than six shillings in the biscuit tin.'

'We'll send him a reply, Dunkiss. I'll do the note tonight and you can take it round to Navigation Street tomorrow. I'm going out in the morning. I have some business to attend to.'

He wouldn't say what the errands were.

Dunkiss delivered Mr George's reply after breakfast the next day. The note said that human beings were not cattle to be bought or sold. It also said that Goose (or anyone else for that matter) was welcome to continue using Community House for as long as he wanted to.

Mr George didn't arrive back at Community House until the middle of the afternoon. Dunkiss met him at the gates.

'They took him. Goose's dada and a policeman. They came and took him back to Navigation Street. The policeman said it's a father's right by law to have his son. Goose's dada says he's leaving town tomorrow and he's going to take Goose with him.'

There had only been Uncle Rolly and Sassy and some of the weavers in the mill at the time. No one had known what to do. They had had to restrain the bear – it had kept growling at Goose's dada and the policeman and Goose had been crying as they had dragged him back to Navigation Street.

*

They found Goose's dada shovelling slag from the backyard into roughweave sacks. He looked up at the two men as though he had been expecting them. No one spoke. To Dunkiss's surprise, Mr George took a brown envelope from his pocket. He handed it over. Goose's dada took it and looked briefly inside at the contents. Then he nodded, and with a flick of his head indicated that the two men should go into the house. Mr George and Dunkiss found Goose sitting alone on a mattress on the floor of his room.

'Pack anything you want to bring,' Mr George said. 'You'll not have to come back here again.'

'Where'm I going?' Goose said. 'Not to St Brendan's?'

'No, not to St Brendan's.'

Dunkiss realized there had been money in the envelope that hadn't come from the Community House fund. Neither Mr George, nor Uncle Rolly, he was certain, had anything like twenty pounds of their own. Dunkiss knew, of course, that the money had to have come from somewhere.

'You had nothing to sell that was *worth* twenty pounds.'

But Mr George would not say, either then or later, how he had come by the money which had bought Goose from his dada and freed the boy to be adopted by him.

It was always said that Goose's adoption – his becoming Mr George's first *kind-of* orphan – was what made the night of the cup replay so special.

'Everything happens for a reason,' Mr George declared. 'You just need to have faith that you will be allowed to see what that reason is.'

All the ingredients were there: the magical cold snap in the air, the whiff of strong Bovril in the Scratting Shed stand, even the bear – brought to a football match for the first and last time because Mr George had felt that everyone should have the chance to be part of the story of the night. Even Uncle Rolly came. Only Darius Whittle stayed away, but it seemed that everyone else in Tatlow Street set out for the match that night.

The party from Community House was so late getting into the ground (eleven thousand people were somehow shoe-horned into the tiny terraces of Peel Park) that they missed Blackburn Rovers taking the lead after four minutes. But the Stanley equalizer did come, just as everyone felt sure it would. In the dying seconds of the match Blackburn seemed to have bundled a winning goal into the Stanley net in a flurry of fists and knees, but the bear rose and stood and bellowed in a protest that sounded across the football field and over the stands like a ship's foghorn. The Rovers fans crammed into the Len's Cooked Meat End on the far side of the stadium felt the hairs on the backs of their necks rise, and the referee – after a moment's pause – blew for a foul and disallowed the goal.

In extra time the pitch grew muddier and heavier. 'Like the Somme,' Dunkiss would say afterwards. And as if in memory of the Stanley men of 1916 the Reds forced home first one goal and then another against the tiring Rovers, and someone tossed a grinning Goose skywards after that third goal and a dozen pairs of strong arms caught him safely, and the shouts of the crowd at the final whistle – like the reverberating sounds from a fired cannon – were said to have been heard by a farmer on Pendle Hill eleven miles away.

As war in Europe drew closer, the highlight of the Community House year had become the procession of weavers, carrying lanterns and led by Mr George, which wound its way up to the

Children's Fever Hospital on the final Sunday in Advent. Sacks of gifts, made throughout the year in the workshop as men served their joinery apprenticeships under Mr George, were towed up there on Dunkiss's cart, which was pulled by the harnessed bear as if it were some Christmas sleigh. The bear, as far as anyone could tell, seemed to enjoy the chore.

It was Uncle Rolly who had discovered, quite by chance, that the bear was short-sighted. It seemed likely that it was the culminating effect of the beatings the animal had suffered while it was with the travelling fair. This discovery proved to be the final hurdle in the rehabilitation of the bear. With an old pair of Uncle Rolly's spectacles strapped on to its pear-shaped head, the bear suddenly found that it could see the world clearly again. A whole new life seemed to beckon for the animal. Its rejuvenation even encouraged Uncle Rolly back into the world a little. Uncle Rolly was still wary of *people*, but with the bear's example before him Uncle Rolly gained enough confidence alongside it to carry out the kind of tasks he had shied away from for years – shopping, walking, visiting the library. It was the bear, Mr George would always maintain, who seemed to invest Uncle Rolly with the courage to face the world again. The two of them usually went together to the growing list of engagements the bear was now invited to, the most important being the weavers' annual Christmas parade up to the Children's Fever Hospital.

The year that war began and the Football League was suspended, with Accrington Stanley riding high at the top, Dunkiss dressed the bear in a red blanket, and fashioned it some antlers from beech wood.

The children cheered as the procession made its entrance into the hospital grounds. The bear, harnessed to the cart, seemed happy to take the hullabaloo in its stride as it was stroked and patted by those children well enough to come out into the fresh air and for whom Mr George performed a selection of his magic tricks. The bear was said to have stood on its hind legs in the courtyard, clutching one of the lantern poles, as the weavers held sheet music and performed 'Once in Royal David's City' and 'Silent Night' for the staff and patients. Snow had begun to fall, and the whole ensemble was illuminated by the lantern held by the bespectacled bear. It was said that the bear even seemed to join in with the singing – a growled accompaniment – as the children too ill to leave the wards pressed their noses to the glass to watch.

Dublin was one of the children watching the spectacle from the ward that night, but he was always sceptical about the claims made about it. Dublin had been a sickly baby, stricken with a bout of polio when he was just a few months old, and then afterwards with the tuberculosis which would so limit his life and cause him to be abandoned at the hospital. He was, of course, too young to have had any clear memory of that Christmas, although he would insist, when asked, that he *could* remember being lifted to the window by one of the nurses to see the weavers arrive. Dublin always maintained that he could recollect no bear being with them. Even if there *had* been a bear, he would say, it would surely not have stood clutching a lantern in its great paws as the snow fell, or sung carols with the weavers. But he did concede that if it *had* been a former fairground bear it *might* have been able to tow a cart up to the hospital in the way Mr George always said it had.

By now Mr George seemed to be capable of anything he chose. And as his fame spread, so did his influence. It was rumoured that Alderman Cumpstey and his fellow councillors sometimes called on Mr George to ask for his advice on how to deal with the continuing hardships faced by the weavers as the Depression in the town (as everywhere else) wore interminably on. It was even said that, in the general panic and uncertainty following Alderman Cumpstey's death (he died in his sleep on the day that Hitler annexed Czechoslovakia), Mr George was offered, but refused, a seat in a safe ward and the Mayorship of the town.

It was Goose who had first asked if Mr George was Jesus. It was a child's kind of question – literal and uncomplicated. But such had been Mr George's effect on the town that Goose's childish question hadn't seemed *so* extraordinary. People could understand why it was that a child like Goose – albeit a slow child, a cloddish child – could have thought such a thing.

By now, Mr George had adopted not only Goose but the polio-stricken Dublin, whom he had come across at the Children's Fever Hospital that Advent night and saved from the inevitable rigours of life at St Brendan's. As Mr George's charges, the two boys lived in Community House. Dublin, being very young, slept with Sassy, for whom Mr George had created a private room and a nursery on the unused floor beneath the storage loft. Goose, however, was allowed to sleep in a room next to Mr George's in the converted loft. It had been designed for Uncle Rolly, but he preferred to sleep in his armchair. Goose had his own set of chores around the old mill. He swept out the workshop every evening, tidied up after the bear, and attended to Uncle Rolly – with an idiot grin permanently fixed on his face. His exuberance did sometimes have to be restrained, however, and Goose was cautioned several times about hurtling into Mr George's room at all hours of the day and night. Finally, Mr

George had to ban Goose from entering the room uninvited, but by then Goose had already caught sight of the marks on Mr George's body.

'What marks?' Dunkiss asked when Goose whispered to him the day after he'd seen them.

'Like Jesus had. Like saints get. Like Fr Fearon says saints get so they can share Jesus's suffering.'

'You mean stigmata?'

'Yes, that's them. Stigmata. On his feet. And the marks made when the soldiers whipped Jesus after Pontius Pilate had sentenced him to death.'

That was when Goose first asked if Mr George really was Jesus.

Dunkiss had already received his call-up papers when he gave his final performance as The Great Dunkiss at Community House. Many of the weavers had already been called up, or had signed up of their own volition. The others had all the work they wanted at the suddenly booming munitions plants. Only poor Darius Whittle seemed left out of this general motion of events, having been rejected by the armed services on account of his flat feet and an asthmatic chest.

Dunkiss's pacifism had been one of the earliest casualties of the war. He had been increasingly horrified by the picture emerging from Europe of the bully in Berlin stamping his way through country after country – horrified by what Hitler was doing to ordinary people. It was Uncle Rolly who let Dunkiss see that this war might be different from the last one, that maybe it was for a better purpose, that perhaps its sacrifices might not be so pointless. Uncle Rolly, it was said, gave Dunkiss the permission he needed to go to war at the age of thirty-three.

Dunkiss was officially too old to be drafted for combat. Mr George, however, knew an officer in the armed services who was persuaded to intercede on Dunkiss's behalf. After much endeavour and, because of his age, a series of medical examinations and physicals in which he broke three army endurance records, Dunkiss was eventually taken into the Royal Signals as a wireless operator. So it was as a farewell to Dunkiss as much as anything that his last performance was staged in the loading yard of Tatlow's Mill in the spring of 1940.

It was also the last hurrah for Community House. A crowd of several hundred people, many of them soon to go to war or back on leave, crammed into the yard. Even Darius Whittle was there, and was loudly cheered when Mr George, strolling round the yard as Master of Ceremonies, shook hands with him and then proceeded to pull three sprats from his ear and a small trout from his shirt pocket.

Eventually, the signal went up that Dunkiss was ready and Mr George introduced – 'for one final time before his overseas engagement' – The Great Dunkiss. They cheered and stamped their former gaffer in Cumpstey's Mill as Dunkiss strode on to the stage like a champion boxer in his bright red robe.

The illusion involved the disappearance of The Great Dunkiss from an apparently solid, locked box, within which he had been strapped and tied. Dunkiss, stripped down to his showman's pantaloons and running boots, climbed on to the top of a specially constructed table with drop-leaf sides. Mr George fastened Dunkiss's legs together with a narrow leather strap which he wrapped around his feet and secured to a metal hasp screwed into the table. All of this was carefully examined by an observer from the audience. Next, Dunkiss's outstretched arms were fastened to the table top by leather thongs which bound his wrists to two more metal hasps. Finally, Dunkiss was blindfolded.

The frame on to which Dunkiss was tied was levered forwards by Mr George, using the old mill's winch, until Dunkiss was tilted upright and facing the audience who could now see him firmly secured. Mr George then proceeded to 'fold' the sides of the table around him using the hinges he and Dunkiss had manufactured in the carpentry room – first the sides, and then the two front panels which served as doors. When he had finished Dunkiss was completely obscured from view 'inside' Mr George's Magic Box. The two doors were then padlocked together by the observer on the stage and a large white sheet was dropped over the closed box. After the few seconds it took to fix the winch into position, the box was gently raised off the ground. When the sheet was finally pulled away by Mr George, and the box was unpadlocked and opened, the box was empty. Dunkiss had disappeared.

The box was then lowered to the ground; the sheet was dropped over it again. At this point, Mr George tried out the magic phrase he had been rehearsing. There was a short theatrical pause until The Great Dunkiss, now magically unshackled, pulled the sheet away from inside the box and made his re-entrance. The weavers applauded and cheered. Dunkiss, beaming, bowed low. He and Mr George shook hands and the two of them acknowledged the raucous applause all round the loading yard. It was in the general mêlée that followed that poor Darius Whittle was famously heaved into the river behind the mill by a bunch of weavers eager for one last event to cheer the day, and Mr George and the bear had to wade in and rescue him.

The trick, of course, was in the straps which had secured

Dunkiss. They were made of a fine-quality but well-worked buckskin leather. The straps were perfectly sound when inspected by any member of the audience but, however firmly they were tied, they were sufficiently pliant to 'give' very slightly if enough torque was applied. Dunkiss was strong enough to be able to work his way out of his bonds in only a few seconds. In fact, the only real challenge was to ensure that he made his escape *before* the box was hoisted off the ground so that he could unfasten the trapdoor in the stage and make his escape. Once the box was lowered back down to the ground Dunkiss slipped back from underneath the stage and 're-appeared' in time to take the final round of applause beside the man in the white dinner jacket.

The next day, the two men packed Mr George's Magic Box into two trunks and stored them away in the old mill to await the end of the war, and Dunkiss's return.

By this time Mr George was beleaguered with half a dozen adopted orphans who would otherwise have been threatened with life at St Brendan's – or worse. The brothers of St Brendan's were embarking on a programme of shipping their orphans overseas to a fellow colony of Brendanites in Australia, and with the weavers leaving for the war or usefully employed in the war effort, Mr George finally saw his chance to convert Tatlow's Mill into a *real* orphanage of his own. Sassy had already been telling him for a while that he couldn't go on adopting children in an ad hoc way while he was also running Community House; the situation was starting to get out of hand. The obvious thing to do was to turn Tatlow's Mill into what it was, in reality, halfway to becoming already – an orphanage.

*

Perhaps Mr George still had moments of doubt about the life he had committed himself to. He was still a young man, and the project of turning Community House into an orphanage took all of his time – all of his *life*. He still needed to ride the trams alone to give himself the chance to think and reflect in private, especially when, as sometimes happened, he received letters which were marked PERSONAL AND CONFIDENTIAL. But these bouts of reclusive reflection always passed. He was committed to his task, and unsparing of himself. In that sense, he was a driven man. Sassy was still by his side, of course, and happy to follow him. So was Uncle Rolly. As for the bear, it had dealt with so much change already that it seemed to weather the transition from Community House to orphanage without much distress. Uncle Rolly continued to keep his distance from the children, but the bear seemed finally at ease in its own bear skin. Mr George would always say to people that the bear had by now come to learn the one lesson that was most guaranteed to allow a little contentment into a difficult life – that habitual mistreatment at the hands of one human being was not an accurate means of assessing the motives of all men.

11

Baking Cakes

When Morag Gill went to the Town Hall for the first meeting of the Regeneration Board, the commissionaire downstairs directed her to the second door on the left after the Council Chamber, but Morag counted the second set of shut doors leading into the Chamber as 'one' and so she turned left a room too soon.

In the room a dozen people in suits were sitting round a committee table. Some of them looked up as she came in, curious, then they went back to their own private conversations. There were a few vacant places at the table, each set with agendas and reports, waiting for those who had not yet arrived or who could not come. It had been raining; Morag's coat was wet and she was conscious as she sat down in the chair nearest to the door that she was making a puddle. Her hair was stuck to her forehead after the walk from the bus station. Around her in the big high room, all the men knew each other. There were whispers and smiles. Morag, of course, know no one. She had never been upstairs in the Town Hall before, having only ever visited the Collecting Halls to pay the rent or the counter in the big Victorian lobby to make a complaint on behalf of the tenants group. She kept her head down and fiddled with her spectacles, which were steaming up with condensation now she was out of the wet and in the heated committee room. She rummaged in her shopping bag for the letter inviting her, as the representative of the St Silas tenants group, to sit on the Regeneration Board. She found it, damp and crumpled into tissue. She smoothed it out and put it down on top of the other papers in front of her and waited for someone to say something to her but no one did. Someone laughed out loud, and the sound rose like a musical note. A man at the front asked if there were any apologies. He welcomed people to the meeting. Morag didn't understand some of the things that he was talking about in introducing the agenda – finance allocations, slippage, aggregation. She waited for him to start talking about the St Silas estate, about the improvements they were hoping to make, about rescuing lives, about *salvation*. She imagined what she herself would say, what questions they might ask her about her ambitions for the future of the estate. She wondered how Dorothy was doing back home with Tipper. And then she saw that everyone was introducing themselves, one at a time, round the table. Morag's heart thumped. She fiddled with her letter. It was getting closer to her turn. She looked at the agenda. Her breathing was short. She began reading the agenda very slowly. It was at that point that she understood what she had done, and the panic, like a flush of adrenalin, rose in her face and made her giddy. The sudden realization, like a punch, threatened to capsize her even though she knew she was sitting quite still. 'Take all this away from me, Jesus,' she prayed. 'Let me be back in the living room with Dorothy knitting.' She thought of Tipper in his red football shirt, snoring in the chair, with the telly on, and each minute familiar and well polished like sand-stone worn down to the grain. She thought about running out into the street, but she could not move. The man on her right spoke. The room swam around her. It was her turn to speak.

'Mrs Gill,' she said, too loudly. 'St Silas estate.'

That was all she said. She could hear her own voice drifting away from her over the table, like a child's balloon, rising into the air, irretrievable. The pause went on and on as everyone in the room seemed to be watching Morag's gaudy balloon float upwards. Morag kept her head down. She stared hard at the words on the page. She wanted someone to rescue her and lead her out of the room, but no one did. Some time later there was a call for a vote about something. Someone asked for 'all in favour'. The men round the table raised their hands. At first, Morag did nothing, but more and more of the men were raising their hands and slowly Morag raised hers. They had been watching her slyly – waiting to see what she would do. It had become, she would say to Noah Brindle later, a kind of sport. She could *see* the sport it was for them but there was nothing she could think to do to stop it. She couldn't think what else she could do but raise her hand too. After a moment she drew it down. She thought she heard someone stifle a laugh. She just stayed there, turning the pages of the reports attached to the agenda that meant nothing to her. The meeting went on around her at the table. When it was over, the men left in groups of two and three, carrying their sheafs of paper and the reports from the meeting. She could hear laughter at the end of the long corridor.

Morag sat there, waiting for them all to leave. After a while, the lights in the room went out. She got up and left, walked across town and caught the bus back to Lowell. She wrote a letter to the person whose name was on her invitation to the Regeneration Board, saying she had been ill and hadn't been able to get to the Town Hall for the meeting. She told Noah Brindle what had really happened. To everyone else, she said that she had missed the meeting because Dorothy hadn't been well.

Morag Gill had a man's face, and hair that stayed stubbornly flat to her scalp no matter what she did to it. When she was a girl, it helped that she was Catholic and could content herself that Jesus had been crucified on a cross, with nails punched through His feet and the palms of His hands, while Morag only had the clumsiness of her big face and her farmer's shoulders to contend with.

When she was twelve, Morag had hollowed out a shrine in the escarpment of the tip behind the house, placing in it a porcelain replica of the Blessed Virgin Mary which she'd won as a school reading prize, a tin jug of holy water from the church, and bunches of daisies. She carried the hope that one day the Blessed Virgin Mary would appear to her, just as she had done to the children of Fatima and Lourdes.

Every Lent, Morag gave up sweets and chocolate; loving chocolate, she couldn't conceive of anything more urgent to give up for the good of her soul. Her parents were devout, confused, superstitious. Not knowing for sure what wasn't wicked, to play safe they imagined that everything *could* be and shied away from every possible experience that had not been mapped out for them by the Church or the lives of their own parents.

When Morag bled from her first period, she couldn't face telling either of them. She prayed at the shrine she had made to Our Lady. Not sure what was happening, she imagined that this was the outward sign of some previously unsuspected inner impurity. She hoped that it would bleed away and leave her cleansed. She hoped Our Lady would come to her. She bled and bled and marvelled at how much evil was in chocolate, and maintained a devotion for hours at a time until one day it seemed to Morag that she might actually have had a vision, or something very close. Our Lady had said that Morag should sleep on the floor for a week and learn the Hail Mary backwards and that, if Morag did these things, Jesus Himself would one day come for her and save her. In the meantime, the bleeding would be curbed if she felt sorry for her sins.

At seventeen, she'd never kissed a boy and Tipper Gill with one good eye seemed so much fun and hardly a devil and he kissed her on the mouth like he didn't *care* what she'd say. There was no one she could tell about the things going round and round inside her, always connected with Tipper's face and Tipper's one good eye and one dull one, insisting and insisting and promising something so foreign she didn't have the imagination to understand it. How it came to sex was hard to say.

Dorothy was the result. It was a clean and simple truth – like poetry, like baking a cake. So simple that it had no need of words and so she never *said* it, though she *knew* it. The simplest truths always had a little poetry about them: that those not baptized were left stranded in limbo until enough prayers had been accrued on earth to set the souls of such creatures (black babies, Protestants) free to float up to heaven – trapped bubbles rising to the water's surface; that the Communion host was Jesus's flesh; that eating meat on a Friday – the day Our Lord's flesh had been violated – was a mortal sin. Dorothy was her punishment for the lascivious act she had committed with Tipper Gill. Dorothy was the weight that she would bear as a result. She never doubted it for a moment. She knew, beyond all need to say it, that doing the one thing had given rise to the other. Like baking cakes.

She never said it.

Not to her parents. Not to the doctors. Not to Tipper Gill who married her five months pregnant, grinning hugely still. Her mother hadn't attended the ceremony at the register office and forbade Morag's father from going too, though her father went, after which no word passed between Morag's two parents for half the summer, till one day Morag's mother had dropped the teapot she'd been given as a wedding present, saw it shatter and screamed.

Morag had idolized her father, a man who had paid for piano lessons for her and had preferred her company to his wife's and called her his *princess*. He had cried when Morag, in white, had taken her First Communion. She had polished his shoes for him every evening. Shoes were the real indication of a man's pride in himself, he told her. He had a music box which had been his mother's. He let Morag wind it up each night and while it played he made up stories in which the two of them flew away over the hills and the sea on a magic carpet. There was a picture over the mantelpiece of a Tyrolean village. The villagers were all gathered in the square for some kind of festival – the men wearing lederhosen and beaming smiles, the women in petticoat skirts and white linen blouses, with flowers plaited in their hair. Morag's father said they'd go there one day, the two of them. Always it was just the two of them, and Morag never thought to question it. The music box was painted with figures similar to those in the Tyrolean picture, even though it had 'A Gift from Cleveleys' stamped on the bottom. Each time it played, the music box was a kind of promise that one day they'd go – the two of them. But then there'd been Tipper, and after that her father had died before they'd had the chance to go.

While he was alive, Morag thought of her father as gentle, as wise, but in the years after his death, when Morag's mother grew older and more bitter about being left alone, remembering her husband sourly, her small heart shrivelled to the size of an apricot, Morag began to think that perhaps her father had only been cautious, or afraid – of what, she didn't know.

Her father hadn't been much taken by Tipper Gill, but he said nothing once it was clear they'd have to marry. He had gone to the wedding alone. Pale and solemn, her father had stood – shoes polished – amongst Tipper Gill's rag-bag family of cousins and dilapidated uncles. It was 1962. They played rock and roll at the reception at the working men's club. Tipper got drunk and threw up over the snooker table.

The baby had been diagnosed after a year, though the signs had been there earlier, unfurling like the petals of a bud.

Morag remembered the moment they told her. The stopped clock, then the tiredness, the need to sleep, the shuffle of doctors, the way things ebbed from her: decisions, certainties, the consolation of real love.

'She'll love me in her own way,' Morag had said to a man in a white coat. He was a doctor, or maybe a porter. Someone called to her. In a room with high walls of frosted glass was another man she hadn't seen before. It was hard to follow what he said. His voice was soft and vague and his words tumbled confidently at her. She guessed he often had to give difficult news. She thought of all those other lives going on even as he was speaking; all those bits of bad news, all that tiredness. The doctor was talking about her, saying she was just unlucky, it had been a chance in a million. But Morag knew that he didn't really understand how the world was constructed. He was a doctor, not a priest. He couldn't see the real connections between things; that all actions had consequences, that one thing always followed on from another. He said there were places the baby could be sent, where it would be looked after. He said it would be no picnic if she kept it herself. He meant because she was so young, because – in ways that he could measure – she knew nothing. It wasn't just a matter of intelligence, or even of looking odd. The child wouldn't be able to display affection as normal children could. He gave it a name – the condition. Morag looked at the floor. And what would she do when the child was grown up? When it was an adult, but not an adult, always dependent on her, never leaving her for a separate life of its own? But Morag knew that Dorothy was the weight that she would bear all her life and she wouldn't have the baby sent away.

When Dorothy was six they moved to the newly built St Silas estate from the street where they had rented a two-up two-down. They moved because the terraces were going to be knocked down in the town's clearance programme and because, since Tipper had no job, the rent on the new flat would be paid by the Council until he got one, and because the newly built estate on the fields at the bottom end of Lowell – shining new, pale-bricked, threaded with rainwashed empty streets and passages, with rising clump-grass fields behind – reminded her of the picture of the Tyrolean village which had hung over her father's mantelpiece.

*

'We have to learn to dance,' Morag said.

They had been one of the first families to move on to the estate. Morag waited for others to arrive. She kept thinking of the Tyrolean village above the mantelpiece in her parents' house, and the people dancing together in the street during the summer festival. But Tipper would have none of it.

'Why do you want to dance?' Tipper asked. 'There isn't anywhere to go dancing round here.'

'It's just something we have to do,' Morag said. 'I can't explain. It's just necessary.'

'And who's going to look after *her* while we're dancing?' Tipper said.

And so Morag Gill had enrolled herself in a dancing class, which she paid for by doing alterations to wedding dresses. She did the work in the evenings while Tipper was out in the dark field in the shadow of the maisonettes, the field he intended to mark out eventually, when it had been levelled, into a football pitch. On Saturday mornings, while Tipper still slept, Morag walked up into town with Dorothy and learned to dance in the room above the Co-op. The rest of the class were young couples who were engaged or going steady and full of possibilities. Alongside them, Morag danced with the six-year-old Dorothy's head pressed to her stomach as she learned each set of steps over and over until the wedding season ended and Morag's dancing money ran out.

When Morag first saw people dancing on the streets of the St Silas housing estate, Dorothy was a teenager and Noah Brindle had begun his work at the Mustard Seed. Morag remembered telling him.

'Am I going mad?' she asked Noah. 'Perhaps I am.' And she

told him there and then – the first time she had ever said it out loud to anyone – that, once, the Blessed Virgin Mary had appeared to her.

The first time she saw the dancing was shortly after Barry Catlin had made a pass at her. Tipper had just been given bail for looking after some boxes for Ronnie Roots which turned out to be on the police list.

Barry Catlin was the man who helped Tipper to run the junior football teams on the estate. He had stiff, wirewool hair and dentures that forced his cheeks into a grin; he dressed in second-hand suits that didn't always have full sets of buttons, and ties that didn't match anything else he wore. His voice was loud, hard to shape into whispers or confidences. Until he had been made redundant he had worked at the ordnance factory in Lowell. He worked part-time as a security guard at the Asda retail park. Barry Catlin especially liked the uniform which was embellished with braid and a cap. He kept the cap on the chair by his bedside at night. He practised saluting in his bathroom mirror.

Barry Catlin organized the fixtures for Tipper Gill's teams. He wrote them out in painstaking longhand, his tongue sticking out from his mouth as he wrote. He had once attended two days of a coaching course in Haslingden on which Noah had found him a place and from which he had withdrawn prematurely for reasons that were never clear, but Barry Catlin referred to it often in devising strategies for the boys to put into practice on the pitch. As with the fixtures, he wrote these plans out in detail with arrows and figures spread across the paper like neat hieroglyphics. The kids ignored the formations, preferring just to chase after the ball as and when they fancied.

While Tipper refereed, Barry Catlin would watch from the touchline, tripping over words, semaphoring frantically for the boys to move into space or to drop back, and the kids on the pitch laughed to each other in their private game of pretending never to see him or hear his spluttering instructions.

Sentences had always been assault courses to Barry Catlin. He liked words. He liked latching on to them. Once he caught one, he'd use it over and over for months in every conversation he could cram it into, chewing it down to the knuckle until it was spent, after which he'd go in search of another. *Indolence* was one. *Perception. Incidental. Desultory.*

One season, he'd spent more and more time round at Tipper Gill's house. 'Can't move for folk at our house,' he'd say, explaining it. 'Got to have some thinking room.' He would bring a few cans.

Barry Catlin's wife Janice didn't leave the house much. 'She has a condition,' Barry would explain. Janice took pills. Barry wasn't sure what they were, except that they seemed to keep her own particular ship steady.

Barry Catlin was attentive to Morag in a way that Tipper, ever since Dorothy's birth, had not been. He would open doors for Morag, make her tea, listen to things she said. One night he and Tipper Gill got drunk. Tipper went to bed and Barry Catlin made a hesitant and stumbling pass at Morag on the settee. A few days later, Morag saw people dancing in the street for the first time.

Morag and Dorothy had been crossing the estate when, without warning, the people began dancing to the music of her father's music box which she could somehow hear quite clearly in her head. A boy who had been kicking a football against a wall took the hand of a girl passing by. Youths began a simple waltz with a line of old women queueing at the bus stop across from the junior school. A taxi driver – his battered Datsun Cherry parked nearby – was dancing with a woman passenger wearing a brown coat and tam-o'-shanter and clutching a shopping bag. And then other people came out of their houses, in dress coats and vests, bleary-eyed, cigarette-butted, blue-chinned, curlered, curious, and seeming to hear the music of Morag's music box, and danced the same steps Morag had learned herself until the tune finally wound down. When it came to an end, everyone returned, unhurried, to their houses or to the solitary occupations they had been drawn from. It wasn't alarming. It was beautiful. And Morag cried when it was over.

'Did you see that, Dorothy?' Morag Gill said each time it happened after that. 'Did you see everyone dancing, my lovely?'

'Dancing,' Dorothy would say.

'Yes, my lovely, yes.'

When concerns about a prowler had first begun to spread in Lowell, the person who came to Morag's mind wasn't Nathan Ripley – the suspect – but Barry Catlin. It wasn't because Morag believed it was Barry (she felt sure it wasn't him) but because of that night when Barry had got drunk and made a pass at her and because of what followed. She couldn't conceive of who might actually be doing the prowling. The link in her mind between Barry Catlin and the prowler was sex. Talk of the prowler always brought to mind the time Barry Catlin had professed his sudden, desperate love for her – after all the uneventful years they'd spent in close proximity on the estate. 'I'd make you a better husband than Tipper,' Barry Catlin had told her that night. 'You're pure and good. I'd worship you. I'm nothing and you're pure and good.' And he had wept as he'd said it, unable to look at her even though he was drunk and slurring the words which his need of her was ripping from him one by one.

Barry Catlin waited a year before he could bring himself to call at Tipper and Morag's house again. Riddled with shame, he had written to Morag, apologizing in schoolboy words for what had happened. He'd written a formal letter of resignation from all involvement with the football teams and offered to step down from all positions of responsibility (Tipper had made him club chairman, there being just the two of them to choose from). Morag had persuaded him to stay on with the football. She wrote a note saying there was no need for him to give up something he enjoyed doing so much just because of one silly mistake, and so he continued to help Tipper with the football teams but was careful not to get caught alone with Morag too often. Whenever he did come across her, he would smile foolishly – panic fluttering in his heart – and talk about Janice's condition, or about the way the back four for the St Silas under-elevens were playing too flat and kept getting caught on the break when balls were knocked over the top.

'It's obvious,' Linde Wzinska said. 'Thuh prowling started about a year ago, yes? And that's when my youngest, she moved out to go living with that boy.' Her mouth shrank in disapproval of the boy in question. 'So that's it. Ripley, he's spent all these years watching my girls from across the way, hiding behind thuh damned curtain to get a look at their titties. Then when the last of them goes off a year ago he has to go wandering on to the estate to do thuh thing he does – watching thuh women. I don't suppose he wanted to stand there watching a big lump like me.' She laughed, at what she had said and at the thought that she was a big lump.

Noah had to admit it was a neat theory, but even after the police had arrested and questioned Nathan Ripley he couldn't believe that Nathan was the prowler, was the man who followed women, who posted sexually explicit messages through their letter boxes, who had begun assaulting them. Knowing what Fred Wyke had told him, Noah felt sure that Nathan Ripley couldn't be the prowler.

Fred Wyke had been Nathan Ripley's social worker since his client had first arrived in Lowell.

'I've had enough,' he told Noah. 'Mary's been on at me for years to finish. She thinks I'm too devoted to the job. It's not that, Noah – I've just been frightened. I'm frightened of what'll happen if I stop. I think something awful will happen if I stop.'

They were intending to close the office in the town and transfer the Lowell team up the valley. The memo said they were centralizing into more cost-effective generic teams. They were also losing one in four jobs in the process.

'No bugger else gives a shit,' Fred Wyke said to Noah as he gave him a potted history of Nathan Ripley's life. 'That's why I'm telling you.'

Noah contributed to the whip-round the Social Services team organized for Fred Wyke, the proceeds of which bought him the set of Wainwright Guides he wanted. Fred and his wife were moving to Kendal, near her sister's, and every so often after that Noah got a postcard with some Lakeland mountain or other on it, and a report from Fred of a daylong expedition on to the fells. He seemed happy. He would sometimes remember to ask about Nathan Ripley. As time went by, he tended to ask less. Fewer postcards came. Noah took it as a sign that he'd managed the break.

Nathan Ripley was not visited as often by the authorities. He was passed around, added to the caseloads of people who didn't much care for him and who were too stretched anyway. Noah came to be Nathan Ripley's main contact with the world. Noah called round most weeks when he was on the estate. He taught Nathan how to play patience and one Christmas he bought a solitaire board for him, but he could never get close enough to feel he *knew* him. Nathan seemed to lack some instinctive rhythm; he was too conscious of himself, unnerved by the idea of *being* someone that others might choose to weigh or measure. The sense of Nathan as incomplete didn't repulse Noah but drew him on. There was a kind of recognition in it, as if here in Nathan was Noah's own inarticulate and damaged underside flipped up and exposed to the harsh light of inspection.

Noah brought library books round for Nathan to read; Nathan liked children's books, books with the right number of illustrations, with mice that talked and hedgehogs who wore waistcoats, and especially with bears. Noah would sit on the midget chairs of the children's room in the public library, knees jammed under his chin, sifting through the boxes of books to try to find the ones that would give pleasure to Nathan, and this business of choosing became a kind of intimacy between the two men where no other was possible. There was an innocence about Nathan – a lack of natural guile – that Noah came to like, even to admire, crippled as it was by the things Nathan didn't talk about, and constrained by the louring fatalism that hung over him. Wondering, once, how he might describe Nathan Ripley to a stranger if he had to, Noah thought: he is waiting, as a child might do, for the sky to fall in on him.

Nathan Ripley cut his own hair. His brown suit was the one he had been given at Newlands; the price tag was still inside, Fred Wyke had told Noah. His shaving was uneven and he tended to make small nicks that bled and hardened into scabs he seemed oblivious to. No one on the estate was surprised when he was arrested for the assault on Olwen Sudders. People could tell there was something funny about him. His expression – the only one he had in public – seemed to be one of continuous surprise. If people spoke to him, he froze, and seemed only partly to hear them. Linde Wzinska and her dog, especially, unnerved him, though he'd liked playing with her children when they were little until Linde had stopped them coming over to see the animals.

Nathan Ripley had enjoyed living at Newlands. He would have been happy to stay on there, but the rules said people had to leave after a year, or two at most. That was the idea; it prepared the residents to live on their own again. Newlands was a big house, with twenty residents at any one time, and four staff who lived in a flat on the top floor. Nathan Ripley didn't know where Newlands was. He guessed it wasn't far from Lowell because that was where they'd moved him to, but 'not far' might have been five miles or it might have been a hundred.

At Newlands, he had enjoyed the routines. There was a comfort to routine that kept at bay the panic that Nathan was prone to. They always started workgroup at nine o'clock, followed by feedback; they took turns in making lunch; they had activities after lunch, followed by feedback again; they took turns to make dinner; then they had counselling, and once a week there was the big House Meeting.

A couple of times, in his counselling hour, Nathan had cried when he'd told Alice, his counsellor, about the things his dad had made him do, and had done to him, until he was fourteen. He liked Alice; she smelled good; he liked the things she wore. He liked watching her when she wasn't looking. No one hit him in there as they'd done at the place he'd been sent to after all the trouble. The staff at Newlands didn't wear uniforms or chains of keys; the doors weren't locked like in the other place. He didn't know how long he'd been in the other place, though he remembered them teaching him to shave in there. He remembered three men holding him down in the wash-house.

The policemen who came for Nathan kept asking him about a woman called Olwen Sudders. They asked him how he'd got the scratches on his neck – whether it was Olwen Sudders who had given them to him. Nathan admitted to them that sometimes he did follow people, and watched them if he liked them, but that was all he did. He said he couldn't remember if he'd followed Olwen Sudders. He couldn't remember what she looked like. When they showed him a picture, he still couldn't remember. Nor could he remember where he was on the dates they kept repeating. The policeman in the car on the way to the police station said it was funny how he couldn't remember much about anything. The police station was like the other place he'd been to before Newlands. There were men with keys. The door was kept locked. He didn't like it there, without the routines that day by day kept him safe. People – grown-ups – were scary, Nathan Ripley knew. His routines were what kept people at bay. He could be comfortable sometimes around children, and with animals (excepting Linde Wzinska's dog).

Animals weren't scary. He gave names to all the ones he kept. He called one of the rabbits Alice, although the rabbit didn't ever cry. He wondered if *his* Alice was old yet. He wondered if *he* was old. He was glad that no one hit him in the locked room at the police station.

The rumours around Lowell were that Nathan Ripley had admitted to trailing Olwen Sudders, then later on to attacking her. People breathed a sigh of relief that the prowler had finally been caught. For Morag Gill, it was a sign of a new beginning, and she said so to Dorothy.

It was Noah who had persuaded Morag Gill to go back to the Town Hall. She went to the next meeting in Noah's car with Dorothy sitting in the back, holding her knitting on her lap. Noah and Dorothy waited in the car park while the meeting ran. Noah read through the chapter he had recently finished writing while Dorothy knitted. Knit, purl, knit, purl. Her expression did not change as she worked along the line from stitch to stitch. *A Spitfire did a roll in the skies above Tatlow Street on the day the war in Europe was won*, Noah had written. The bear, he knew, would be gone. The children would now only imagine the bear, and the lives of the weavers before the war, and the way that Mr George had arrived in the town.

After that, Morag started taking Dorothy with her to the meetings. They travelled from Lowell by bus. It became a regular journey, and although Morag had not yet spoken at any of the meetings, the commissionaire at the Town Hall knew her and Dorothy to nod to, and she knew which committee-room door to go in. At one of the meetings they passed round copies of the prospectus which the Regeneration Board had commissioned. It outlined the remit of the Board and the

objectives it hoped to accomplish in its three-year life insti-
gating schemes up and down the Rossendale Valley. There
was a colour photograph taking up most of the front cover, of
the summer roofs of the houses on an estate, with picturesque
hills like a backcloth behind them. It reminded Morag of the
painting which had hung over her father's mantelpiece when
she was a child, and it struck her how much closer she was
now to being happy than she could remember being since
she had been a child and loved her father and dreamed of
Jesus.

One of the bids for funding to the Regeneration Board was
for the St Silas estate in Lowell. The proposal was to sell off the
dilapidated maisonettes at the bottom of the estate to a
Housing Association. The remaining houses would be damp-
proofed and refurbished, and have new sills and doors. The
Council would landscape the estate and fence off all the gardens, and develop a crime prevention strategy. If the
Regeneration Board approved the scheme, almost a million
pounds would be available. They were going to build a new
community centre, and an all-weather football pitch. The land
down by the maisonettes, including Tipper Gill's pitch, was
going to be sold to the Housing Association. There were pages
of figures towards the back of the brochure with costings, performance targets and outputs for the scheme. It seemed so
simple to Morag, who was curious that the shape of seemingly
permanent land, and of lives, could be altered so fundamentally
by money and a simple act of will, when all along the prospect
of change had seemed, to her, so fantastical.

The only problem left now, it seemed to Morag Gill, was
Nathan Ripley – because the St Silas estate had a prowler and
because Ripley (questioned about the assault on Olwen Sudders

and held for the magistrate's hearing) had been released from the police station and was free to stalk again.

He had returned unannounced. No one had seen him come back – it must have been sometime late in the evening. It was Linde Wzinska who was the first one to notice that Nathan Ripley was back in his flat.

'Thuh police must be stupid or what is it?' she said to Noah.

'They haven't charged him,' Noah said. 'They mustn't have any evidence that it was Nathan who did it.'

'He admitted he did thuh thing,' she said, indignant.

'How do you know?'

'*Everyone* knows,' she said. 'You're thuh only one, Noah Brindle, who doesn't. All it is, you know – they don't care about us. They just say sure, send the rapist back to live in that place. We're just rubbish to them, that's all. And you're going – what do *you* care?'

The solicitor appointed to represent Nathan Ripley had obtained his release. The confession, made to Neville Pascoe and his colleague and repeated some time later in front of the duty solicitor, was eventually ruled out for lack of corroborative evidence. Nathan Ripley could give no convincing account of where the attack had happened, or descriptions of the notes made from newspaper headlines, and there was nothing in his flat to link him with the crime. The scratches on his neck, it was decided, had come from one of his ferrets. His confession was deemed to be a meaningless result of his panic.

It was a reporter on the *Citizen* who first referred to a campaign to get him moved off the estate. Morag Gill, egged on by the others, had called the paper, a weekly free-sheet that ran half a dozen news stories sandwiched in between the ads and the weekend TV pull-out. The junior reporter had taken details over the phone, then put the three-paragraph story in front of the editor.

'Is it a campaign?' the editor asked. 'Campaigns are always good.'

The reporter rang Morag Gill back. 'Is it like a campaign against this man that you're running?'

So far it had just been a complaint by the tenants group to the Housing Department in the Town Hall, who had said they couldn't move Nathan Ripley off the estate on the basis of inconclusive police interviews. The trainee reporter took a photograph of some of the tenants – Morag and Dorothy, Linde Wzinska, and Barry Catlin – across the road from Ripley's flat. The photograph showed that Ripley's curtains were closed even though it was the middle of the day. It lent an air of seedy menace to the place which pleased the reporter whose name – rare for the *Citizen* and rarer still for its junior – ran on the byline.

The editor asked if there was any more to come. The trainee reporter found it surprisingly easy to find out more, despite getting nowhere with the man who had been Ripley's social worker in Lowell, and whom he'd visited after tracking him down to Cumbria. He spent two days digging for information back in Lowell and then worked with the editor to organize the information into the following week's front-page story.

The article said that Ripley had spent nineteen years in a secure mental hospital. It said that he'd had a conviction in 1968 for sex offences against two children. It printed facsimiles of articles in the *Daily Express* about the case. It referred to Ripley's alleged confession to the attack on Olwen Sudders. It said he had admitted to the police that he sometimes followed people. It said the St Silas estate was a community living in fear.

The police themselves refused to comment. Social Services said only that they could confirm that Nathan Ripley had been known to them for some years. In an editorial, the *Citizen* asked whether normal families should be exposed to the dangers of having a man like this living in their midst.

'What do our readers think?' the *Citizen* asked. 'Send your opinions in to the address below.'

'One thing that beats a campaign,' the editor told the junior reporter, 'is a write-in.' He asked if there was any chance of getting the women to mount a vigil outside the bastard's house.

Nathan had liked the brass bed they gave him at Newlands; it was old and it dipped in the middle and cradled him, and creaked reassuringly each time he moved in the night, when he was awake and the other three men in the room were asleep. He liked the still winter mornings in the garden before any of the others were up, when he stood on the edge of the tree-sheltered lawn, watching warm breaths unfurl from his mouth like smoke and rise into the air. He liked the tinned pears they sometimes had. He liked the spoons they used that were heavy and coppery with age. He liked the big community room with the fireplace and the frayed carpet, and the piano by the garden window. He liked the wooden banister rail that twisted its way up the four storeys of the house and the way it smelled of polish and was patterned with gouges that, Alice told him, had been made by a bear which had been kept there during the war. He liked the way Alice would smile in a special kind of way after telling him about the bear. He had told Noah about Alice, and the bear.

When he came to leave Newlands, he took one of the spoons

with him. He slipped into the kitchen and put it in the pocket of his jacket while everyone was gathering in the community room to say goodbye to him. Alice was quiet for once and Nathan watched her, straightbacked, fingering the spoon in his pocket. They presented him with a clock whose glass he would afterwards have the compulsion to touch every evening. He had been at Newlands almost three years, longer than anyone else had ever been. They made a joke that they wouldn't let anyone else sit in the chair he'd always used at House Meetings because, they said, they would always think of it as Nathan's chair.

Since the police had let him come home, Nathan had stayed indoors most of the time. If he went out of the flat, people on the estate pointed at him. Some of the shop people in Lowell wouldn't serve him any more. Once or twice, men obstructed his way and made him stop in his tracks and said why didn't he just fuck off back to fucking queerland or wherever the fuck he came from. He kept the curtains of the flat closed all the time now because otherwise boys peered through the window and banged on the glass to try to surprise him and make him jump. Some of the flat's windows had been broken. They had been repaired after it had happened because Noah had reported the damage, but they had been broken again subsequently. Things had been written in spray paint on the front of the flat, on his door, and on the bin store in the communal yard. Noah came round to check on him every day now, but the trouble always came after Noah had left. The goat had disappeared and he'd had to bring the rabbit hutch inside the flat because people kept letting the rabbits out; two had been taken, and only Alice was left.

*

Linde Wzinska said to Noah, 'I think you should take a look.'

'Why me? Call the police if there's something wrong.'

'I'm not calling thuh police for that man. But I think some-one should come round and have a look. It smells so bad in there.'

Silverfish scuttled for cover when Noah first went in and put the light on. He cut the body down. The thin white fingers of each hand were clenched. Something slipped out of Nathan's jacket pocket as Noah levered the body on to the floor. It was a spoon. He closed the eyelids, and stroked the tousled hair that – combined with those permanently startled eyes – had given Nathan the look of a wild Stan Laurel.

'Where's the sense, Nathan?' he said. It occurred to Noah that he was comforting a man – already dead – who had once put his finger inside a five-year-old girl's vagina and then after-wards helped to dress her and made tea for them both with sandwiches and cakes on doilies. Noah sat with him on the kitchen floor for a long time. He realized he was still repeating the same sentence, and that the clock over the mantelpiece had stopped.

Before he made the necessary phone calls, Noah went round the flat, tidying up. He traced the awful smell to the faeces that the intruders had left in the hallway the day before when Noah hadn't called in. He scooped the shit into a dustpan, wiping the smeared lino with a cloth. He opened all the windows to get rid of some of the smell. He supposed they'd done it on the way out – whoever *they* were – after they'd written on the living-room wall. Noah went through Nathan's drawers. He found nothing surprising except that Nathan had kept the notes people had pushed under the door. They were in the sideboard cupboard, folded neatly. The animals were dead, though they were all back in their cages, arranged in still life. Noah guessed that Nathan must have done it when he'd found them, putting down fresh straw and food as well.

The only things Noah removed were the notes that Nathan had pinned up over the mantelpiece. There were two lists. One of them detailed Nathan's daytime activities. It said: 'Workgroup, Lunch, Activity Group (animals), Dinner, Free Time.' The other was a kind of weekly menu sheet. Lunch was soup and soldiers. Pudding at dinnertime was always tinned pears. Under each day it said: 'Washing Up – Nathan.' Noah folded the two notes and put them in his pocket.

12

The Faith of Angels

War meant orphans, and a steady stream of them arrived in Tatlow Street – victims of bombing raids on the big northern cities. Some of them were passed into Mr George's supervision for just a few days or weeks, until their symptoms of shell-shock or despair diminished. For others, for those too difficult to place, for those with no one or nothing left, the orphanage would become their home. The most remarkable of these war orphans was found in the rubble of a house two days after it had been destroyed in one of the Luftwaffe's early wartime assaults on the Manchester conurbation. She was huddled against the body of her mother; her grandparents' bodies and her sister's were also discovered in the shell of the house. The footprints in the dust suggested that the child had found them first. She had passed through a holding station for displaced children, and two orphanages, with a number written on the ID tag to her wrist. She had refused to communicate in any way. She wouldn't allow anyone to touch her. At one point she had bitten an orderly's hand and drawn blood. By the time she was placed in the second orphanage it wasn't clear who she was or where she had come from. When Mr George found her she was four and had been classified as mentally sub-normal. She was being kept in a locked ward in a special unit. No one knew her name or had given her one.

Mr George was tipped off about the girl by someone out of town who had heard about his work with difficult children. When he went to see her she glared up at him from under a fringe cut institution-short to combat the lice, arms hugging her legs to her chest as she crouched on the floor. He sat on the edge of the bed and raised his hat to her, but didn't try to approach her. He asked her whether she remembered her family, whether she'd *had* a family. He asked whether she wanted to come and live in an orphanage with other children. She didn't answer or try to impress him – this man who was offering to take her out of her locked ward to a place with other children, with animals, with no locks. She was not frightened, he would maintain afterwards. She simply didn't *care*. She had seen hell; it was heaven she didn't believe in.

Mr George said nothing for a few moments. Then he pulled out some photographs taken with his Box Brownie. The photographs were of Walter, the newest infant orphan, of Sassy and Goose feeding the goat they had acquired, and Dublin in his callipers, playing football with Goose in Tatlow's yard. He laid them down on the floor beside her, one by one, without a word. She didn't touch them – they might have been a trap – but she looked at them. When he finished, he stood up and told her that he was leaving now. He said he knew that she could understand him. He said he knew that she was smarter than she pretended to the staff. He said the staff would leave the doors unlocked for five minutes. If she wanted to come with him she could do but he wouldn't force her. She had to *choose* to come with him to the orphanage.

He drove away convinced that he would never see her again.

It was only some time after he had set off in the juddering second-hand Alvis that he realized she was in the car with him. She was lying down on the back seat, lulled by the Alvis's engine. He had no idea how she'd managed to get into the car without him seeing her. She had no shoes on. She was holding the photographs.

Three or four times a year the authorities sent a man from the armed services to Tatlow's Mill. It was always the same man. He was an RAF officer who was also a doctor, Mr George explained to the children. That was his job – to look after the pilots and the bomber crews who were injured or who got sick. Pilots, like orphans, he said, sometimes got sick and needed doctors. To the silent girl he had rescued from her locked ward and to the other orphans in his care, it must have seemed the most natural thing in the world that the services should choose to send someone to inform Mr George about the course of the war, and that the Chiefs of Staff should ask him what they should do next.

'The officer *couldn't* know things like that about the war,' Dublin, aged six, would say, not daring to voice his young doubts directly to Mr George, but complaining instead to Goose. 'Someone who's only a captain wouldn't get to know about all the tactics of the Prime Minister.'

'But Mr Churchill says the orphans have to be told about the war,' Goose would retort, voicing what all the other children believed. 'That's why Mr Churchill sends the man. Maybe he's Mr Churchill's doctor too.'

The RAF officer, smart in his blue officer's uniform, was younger than Mr George, as thin as a boy but with a sense of command about him. He would spend most of the day with Mr

George, telling him the news of Dunkiss's war (according to Goose's version) and confiding the difficulties the Allies still faced in winning the war. Then he would ask Mr George for his advice just as, before the war, the Council had come to Tatlow's Mill to ask for his advice. Afterwards, Mr George would walk with him back to the railway station in the town and see him on to the London train, back to where Mr Churchill, who had despatched him, was running the war.

These visits seemed to trouble Mr George. It must have been hard, the children reasoned, for him to be burdened like that with the secrets of the war, and to have to think of different ways to win battles and rescue spies caught behind enemy lines. These secret things he was left to ponder after the captain's visits seemed to weigh on him; they made him sad; they always left him riding the trams alone for a few days afterwards. And then, quite suddenly, in the summer the war ended, these visits ceased and the officer was seen no more.

A Spitfire did a roll in the skies above Tatlow Street on the day the war in Europe was won.

Sassy and Goose were returning from the neighbourhood picture house with the children – fourteen of them, walking in twos and holding hands. It was Dublin who spotted the plane overhead. Dublin was always scanning the skies above Tatlow Street for aeroplanes. He had fallen in love with them while watching the weekly Pathe newsreel from his warm seat down in the dark of the picture-house stalls. That was how they had followed the progress of the war – Dublin as a small boy, and Goose passing through his adolescence, and the other orphans and unplaced evacuees learning the names of the tanks and the insignia of the ranks on the uniforms, cheering at the cartoons, watching the news in a pitch of excitement as if this were another scripted and reassuring feature to revel in.

Dublin loved the aeroplanes. His obsession continued after the war but it began, like so many things, in Tatlow Street. The aeroplanes were everything that Dublin himself was not. Sometimes the newsreel would show a distant dogfight captured on film between a Spitfire and a Messerschmitt, or a line of fighters taking off from an RAF base and climbing into the sky, and Dublin's small hands would grip the arms of the seat or the metal struts of his callipers in excitement as he followed their acrobatics on the screen, imagining himself to be as dexterous and free and unshackled from the earth as they were.

It was easy for the orphans, crouched in the stalls, to believe that what they saw each week on the newsreel was happening at that very moment. It was as if they themselves were playing parts in the North African campaign, or the D-Day invasion, or in the final drive across Germany in the spring of 1945.

'He's there. It's Dunkiss! *Dunkiss!*' Goose would shriek, jumping up and down on his seat as the newsreel showed a group of men in uniform in North Africa, eating from billycans and smiling foolishly for the camera, or boarding an aircraft in France, or racing across a field in Umbria. There amongst them, Goose was frequently convinced, was Dunkiss. There seemed to be little doubt for Goose or the other children (who had either never met him or were unable to remember what he looked like) that Dunkiss was steadily, surely, everywhere on the Pathe newsreel, leading the troops and the children with them to victory. And each week they hurried home to tell Mr George about Dunkiss, and about the state of *their* war.

'We've won in Italy!' they would yell, rushing back through the loading yard. Or, 'We've landed in France with the Yanks,

Mr George!' Oblivious to the fact that Mr George *knew* that the Allies had won in Italy, and that they had landed on the Normandy beaches with the Americans, because he listened to the news each day on the big wireless, and because he knew the officer from the air force.

Mr George was in the loading yard in the May sunshine when Goose led the charge back into the mill, shouting out that they had won the war because Germany had just surrendered at the pictures. He listened to the news and dealt with the general clamour of the orphans' return from the picture house; then Dublin and Sassy, hand in hand and bringing up the rear, came through the open gates and Dublin was pointing up to the sky, and there was the Spitfire approaching fast overhead. They looked up from the loading yard to see, and it was then that the Spitfire did its roll – over and round and throbbing with power right above them by now. The plane whooshed above Tatlow Street and Dublin, eyes wild, mimicked the sound, 'Whoo-oosh', and everyone knew the Spitfire had done the roll because the war was over.

Perhaps it was the Spitfire flying over Tatlow Street which finally convinced Mr George of the need to speak to them all that night. He had known all along that eventually he would have to share with Sassy and the children the secret he'd kept from them throughout the war. 'Before the war,' he had often rehearsed in his room in the rafters of the old mill, 'we had to find some money to bring Goose here to live with us.' He would pause, and notice that his heart was beating faster. 'It wasn't a lot of money,' he would press on, 'but it was much more than we had – Dunkiss and I and Uncle Rolly – at the time.' And by that point his face would have clouded over and he wouldn't be sure any longer how to go on, and once more he would postpone the idea of telling anyone about the imminent loss of Tatlow's Mill.

The only way of raising the money for Goose – to pay Goose's dada off – had been to offer something in return. And the only thing he'd had was Tatlow's Mill. And so he had sold the mill, then rented it back from the new owner on a five-year lease. It hadn't seemed such a risky thing at the time. After all, the place hadn't even been an orphanage when he'd agreed to the deal. It had been a project for out-of-work weavers. It had been Community House. Five years had seemed enough time to complete his work. Even when he had come to establish the orphanage, he hadn't been unduly worried. When the war broke out, he had gone back to the new owner to ask to be released from the agreement because of the orphans he now had in his care. The man would agree only to extend the lease as far as the end of the war but no further. At the end of the war the lender wanted his building. He had a legal document. He had plans. As for the orphans, he said, they weren't his problem. And now the Spitfire had done a roll over Tatlow Street because the war – in Europe at least – was over, and Mr George was finally being forced to explain that he hadn't been able to get the lease extended any more.

And so, on the night the war was won, he began, 'You will not all remember that, once, we had to find some money so that Goose could come and live here.'

He told them that he might have to arrange to have the children transferred to St Brendan's. Unless there was some kind of miracle, he said, he would go to see the warden of St Brendan's at the end of the month. It would only be temporary – until Dunkiss came back and the two men between them were able to organize another home for the orphanage. The children

185

looked across at Goose as he spoke. They were doing a kind of ragged arithmetic involving the sale of Tatlow's Mill and the purchase of Goose's freedom.

Lying in their bunks that night, they all understood that there was no chance of a reprieve for Tatlow's Mill, because Mr George had told them the name of the man to whom he had sold the mill as premises for a wholesale fish business. All the children recognized his name. Even those who had not been a part of Tatlow's Mill before the war had heard of Darius Whittle. They had all pictured poor Darius – with a shiver – gutting and heading his glassy-eyed fish, or surrounded by his eyeless wooden saints in the old Tatlow Street bargehouse, or hiding his wages each week in a box in his upstairs room in Mrs Greal's house. And yet none of them, drifting to sleep in their bunks that night in the mill, were troubled. They were sure that they would *not* be sent to St Brendan's, or for transportation, or to Canada; they believed that Mr George would surely find a way to keep them with him; they knew, with the faith of angels, that they would all be safe.

It was a week later that Mr George went missing.

Afterwards, the story was that he'd been away conducting more negotiations with the Diocesan Board, still trying to raise the money that would enable him to keep the children with him. The truth was that he had gone up on to the moors to think and to be alone. On the second night there had been a storm. At least two of the sheep grazing on the fellside had been washed down the scree by the force of the waterslides. Mr George had been out on the tops, shouting to God, soaked by the rain, begging for a miracle, demanding that God *say* what He wanted of him now that he had been led into this seeming cul-de-sac. He had been brought back to the mill in the back of a farmer's truck the next day and carried to his room. He was delirious for several days with a fever.

And the miracle?

Just timing. Miracles are surely nothing but timing – like Mr George's feats of conjuring; like the way Mr George had made Dunkiss disappear from the Magic Box.

The letter from the Dounleavey estate said that Dounleavey had died in South America. It said that Dounleavey had followed the fortunes of Mr George's work. It said that Dounleavey (whether through contacts, or favours, or money, the letter didn't say) had been the influence behind the decisions made by the Diocesan Board in support of Mr George's projects on Tatlow Street.

Mr George read on, astonished at how much Dounleavey had known about his work. He had often wondered what had become of the man he had met on the train – the man who had lost faith in the world. Dounleavey had gone abroad when war began to seem inevitable in Europe. It had been a personal decision. He had died alone in a hotel room in Buenos Aires. One of the hotel maids had found him. Mr Dounleavey had enjoyed a good life, the letter stated. His wishes in death were not to be taken as a sign of regret or of some imagined need for redemption. He simply had a mind – the letter said – to conclude some unfinished business.

'Is this heaven?' Goose had asked.

The place had not been lived in for six years. The gardens had run wild behind the high hedges. The courtyard was green with moss. The stable doors had rotted and hung from their hinges, and two of the stable roofs had collapsed. In the bell tower, the untethered clapper smacked randomly against the lip of the bell, chasing the sound round the stableyard. Inside the house, a pipe had cracked in the thaw after one of the winter freezes and the leaking water had rotted two of the downstairs carpets. The smell of cats was strong, the banister rail had been clawed, and the suit of armour had been toppled and lay in pieces. The curtains were drawn. The wardrobes had clothes still hanging in them and the beds were still made up with linen sheets, as if Dounleavey, in taking flight, had abandoned more than the house.

But upstairs the ceilings were high and the windows were wide and let sunlight flood in the length of the long rooms when Mr George pulled back the heavy red velvet curtains, and there was nothing he could see that he and Dunkiss wouldn't be able to take care of when Dunkiss returned from the war.

Mr George had led them all up to the Big House after the street party in Tatlow Street to celebrate the end of the war. He had even put on the mothballed white dinner jacket for the occasion. In the absence of the bear, which had itself become a casualty of the war, Goose had been put in charge of the new goat for the journey. Tiring on the march up the hill and out of town, Goose had clambered into the first of the four carts carrying their belongings from Tatlow Street and pulled the bleating Gomorrah up after him. Vacant tenure was what Darius Whittle had asked for; vacant tenure Mr George had given him. Goose and the goat had climbed down from the cart as they neared the Big House. The view down into the woods, over the miles and miles of quiet patchwork fields and out to the ship's bulk of Pendle Hill, must have seemed like the pastures of heaven to Goose.

And so he had asked if it was heaven.

'It's the Ribble Valley,' Mr George said.

They all agreed that night that the bear would have loved the procession from Tatlow's Mill of which they had all been a part; it would have relished leading the crocodile of children and belongings out of town to the Big House. The bear had come to revel in that kind of public show, and it was a sadness that the animal had not been there to enjoy the day.

It was inevitable that the bear would never adapt to being muzzled again, or to being put on a chain in a fenced compound in the corner of the loading yard. But the local wartime authorities – made jumpy by the avalanche of instructions being circulated by the government about foreign nationals, public health and wartime livestock supplies – had insisted on the bear being confined and had come round regularly to check. Having been threatened with having the animal confiscated if he did not comply, Mr George had done his best to ameliorate the situation. The cage had been spacious; the chain was long and light; Sassy fed the bear on all the scraps and Mr George and Uncle Rolly came over to talk to the animal each time they passed through the loading yard. But it wasn't enough; it could never be enough. The bear had made a run for it on the one night when Mr George had forgotten to replace the muzzle after dosing the animal with its medicine for the chest ailment it was by then prone to. It had chewed its way through the chain and begun working on the mesh of the cage with its old, blunt teeth. Sometime during the night, without a sound, it was away – perhaps, Uncle Rolly thought, to find a better place to die; perhaps, Mr George liked to think, to go in search of a new fair which might treat it with a little dignity.

As they were growing up in Dounleavey's place, the orphans liked to imagine that the lamp which Mr George would light each night at the top of the bell tower was there for the bear.

Goose liked to say that it was there in case *any* stray bear came by the valley. As time passed, Goose (the only orphan who could clearly remember the bear) would keep watch; he would never catch sight of the creature but he liked to think that the light gave hope to any stray and wandering bear who needed it.

Of course, the orphans needed a school to go to, and there was no school within walking distance of the Big House. Tram fares into the town every day for twenty-four children would have bankrupted the orphanage within a month. Any children in the neighbouring houses (and there never seemed to be any) were undoubtedly sent away as boarders to private schools. After much debating, it seemed that, if the orphans couldn't get to school, the only answer was for a school to come to the orphans.

So it was that Uncle Rolly's ancient teaching certificate was dusted down and despatched to register the orphanage's school with the Education Authority, though it was Mr George who, in reality, did the teaching, taking responsibility for this as he did for every aspect of his orphans' lives.

Mr George called the silent child sitting attentively at the front of his class Rachel. She liked to listen to music on the big wireless in the study. She let herself be hugged, and eventually she allowed herself to cry. And she learned to use a kind of signing of her own invention and began to communicate with people, but she didn't speak and Mr George saw that her voice had gone for ever.

In this way Rachel grew up in the Big House, writing her thoughts down. The other children would find her notes magically scattered round the house – in drawers she knew they would look inside, between the covers of books, nailed to the branches of trees they liked to climb. They were Rachel's versions of whispers. In this way she would pass on snatches of poems on scraps of paper. Rachel liked poems. She liked the sounds they made in her head, which was the only place she was not silent. She liked the economy of poems. She liked the way they concentrated ideas into as few words as possible. It was the way she herself would have liked to speak had she been able. Rachel liked the poetry of people she knew were still living. Death had claimed enough victims in her life. She liked the thought of them still breathing, eating supper, seeing trees, and she had Uncle Rolly find poems for her by such writers.

> I peel and portion
> A tangerine and spit the pips and feel
> The drunkenness of things being various.

She copied the poem on to the back of a cake wrapper as she and Dublin sat in the long kitchen one November afternoon. She made Dublin read it out loud. They were with Sassy who was baking, and were watching orange leaves, wide as hand-prints and dried to paper, hanging from the sycamore outside the window. They both smiled. They were happy to agree with Louis MacNeice, whoever he was, wherever he was sitting down to tea or, like them, looking out at trees.

On Rachel's eighth birthday Mr George presented her with the research he had done on her family. He had unearthed two photographs – one of Rachel's mother, one of the family (including the infant Rachel herself) – and had talked to neighbours who remembered the family and recalled that Rachel's father had been in the merchant navy. His ship had been sunk by a German U-boat in 1941. Mr George had written everything down for her in a hardbacked notebook and had stuck the two photographs inside as well.

She decided to take back her own surname but chose to keep *Rachel*.

'Rachel's who I am,' she wrote down when Dublin asked her why she didn't take her real name back. 'The other name died when the bomb fell.'

After that, the orphans would sometimes find other notes that Rachel had left in particular places around the grounds. They were addressed to her mother and her sister. They wouldn't say much – just hello, just bits of news, or sometimes lines from poems which rang bells for her in her silent head. Dublin found one in the bell tower one day and asked Mr George what he should do about it. Mr George said just to leave it where he'd stumbled across it. He said it was just Rachel whispering to her family.

The bell tower at the far end of the courtyard was Dublin's particular bolt hole when he wanted to be away from people – when the incessant hum of life in the Big House became too much for him. It was Dublin who, along with Mr George, rang the bell each morning for the orphanage. It wasn't a rule, but everyone understood that this was how things were. The two of them could be seen crossing the courtyard in the mornings, cast in the dim light of the lamp in the bell tower. Dublin and Mr George would first go into the chapel – a converted stable – and Mr George would pray for a few moments. Sometimes Dublin would stand at the door and wait for him, scanning the gunmetal sky for signs of lights from passing aeroplanes; sometimes he would sit beside Mr George in the wooden pew halfway down the chapel, his callipered legs placed out in front of him. He would look at the rough wooden altar or watch Mr George – dismissive of the whole business of praying (the astonishing leap of faith which this act entailed was beyond Dublin), but happy enough to be out in the morning air, clanging the bell for the children.

Before the ringing of the bell, they had to extinguish the gas lamp at the top of the bell tower. The lamp, lit the previous evening, could only be reached by climbing the metal fireladder which ran inside the bell tower, and then clambering out on to the balcony. It was a feat which Dublin, clad in his callipers, could never have managed. Instead he would watch each morning as Mr George ascended alone and doused the lamp. After that the two of them together would pull on the rope which hung down the length of the bell tower, hauling it down then letting it rise in rhythm, ringing in each new day for the orphans in Mr George's care.

They had rung the bell in the bell tower for Dunkiss. The moon-faced Dublin in his callipers and the tall, stooping, silent Mr George pulled on the rope for Dunkiss. Across the quiet Lancashire valley people heard the bell's weeping peals. The Great Dunkiss was dead.

Dunkiss's children came up to the Big House for the service, with his wife. She had scowled but didn't object outright to Mr George's proposal that Dunkiss be buried in the bottom field down in the valley so that he could be close to the orphanage.

'He was such a *large* character,' Mr George said to her, 'that he seemed to belong to everybody.'

'I wanted him for myself,' she said, knowing she had long ago lost Dunkiss to the world. She seemed less sad than angry at Dunkiss for dying. She had married him, pregnant, at six-teen. He had been her world, but his horizons were too wide for her to comprehend. She had been baffled by his wish to go to war and suspected that war, like the business of Community House, was an excuse for him to leave her. She was also affronted by the instruction Dunkiss had left, in the eventuality that he didn't come back from the war, for the inscription he wanted on his headstone. She didn't cry at the service. Dunkiss was already lost to her long before his death.

Mr George didn't tell Dunkiss's wife how he had died. What was the point? he had reasoned to himself. What good would it do? He even kept it from Sassy and Uncle Rolly, neither of whom, he felt, should be asked to bear the weight of *knowing*. Their shoulders were not as strong as his; he thought of them, in some ways, as children who needed to be pro-tected. As for himself, he felt responsible for the death of Dunkiss. He thought of it as a judgement on *him*. People said afterwards that the effect of Dunkiss's death was to make him redouble his efforts with his orphans. He felt he had to suc-ceed – with the work of the orphanage, with the salvation of *every* child – for the sake of Dunkiss's memory and for the price that Dunkiss had paid.

It was the man who had visited Tatlow's Mill during the war – the RAF doctor – who, on his one and only visit to the Big House in the autumn of 1945, had revealed to Mr George how Dunkiss had perished. Dunkiss, Mr George was told by the officer, had constructed a radio receiver in the prisoner-of-war camp, made out of parts scrounged from the compound. What they didn't have they got by bribing one particular guard who spoke pidgin English. Dunkiss, a Signals man, had been asked to try to cobble the receiver together. It was good for morale to hear English voices on the radio and to know about the gains the Allies were making.

The guards found the receiver under the floorboards during a search. They guessed Dunkiss, the only Signals man in the hut, must have been involved. They realized from the parts which had been used that one of the camp guards must be implicated, and suspected one of the Koreans. They wanted his name, and the name of the English officer who had given the order for the receiver to be constructed. Dunkiss would say only that the radio had been his idea, and that he had made it alone.

They put him in a bamboo cage on the edge of the compound. The cage was too low for him to stand and too narrow for him to lie. It was positioned out in the open where there was no shade. When the Japanese put him in the cage, he had already lost three stone as a result of the work, the diet, and the dysentery in the camp. On a few occasions, the others from the hut managed to smuggle water and scraps across to him during the night. The authorities in the camp left him in the cage for twenty-four days. After they let Dunkiss out of the cage, he never walked again.

He died in the infirmary three weeks later, principally (they guessed) of kidney failure caused by the blow of a rifle butt in the stomach. In the week before he died, he was sucking powdered milk from the finger of the chaplain and his eyes were drawn back deep into his skull. The captain said he had weighed barely four stone when he died.

It was odd to think of Dunkiss, who when he left for the war had never been further than Hebden Bridge, dying so far away. It was hard to think of a man who had jumped the width of the Leeds–Liverpool Canal, who had pulled a barge faster than a horse between two canal bridges, who had hauled a piano halfway across town to Tatlow's old mill, being too weak to get out of his cot to reach the latrine, being unable to clean the excrement from his hollow buttocks and the sticks that were his legs.

Sassy kept Dunkiss's boots. Sometimes she brought them down and polished them. Goose had stood beside her at the funeral when she wept helplessly and, stricken, had leaned over her, too anxious to touch her lest she should break into a hundred pieces.

Her brother's death cut the final line that connected Sassy to the outside world. After Dunkiss's death the whole world beyond Dounleavey's old place receded from her like a tide, until there was nothing in her life except Mr George, and the ritual of daily duties that bound her ever more firmly to the Big House. She had been eighteen when she had left Dounleavey's Connaught Hotel and gone to work for Mr George. She had been little more than a girl (with a rough and ready father and a remarkable brother whose very public prowess and persona had always overshadowed her own less delineated life) when she came to work at Tatlow's Mill. She had spent almost all her working life in the employ of Mr George. When Dounleavey's own particular miracle had offered a new start out of town, she had agreed, without a word of protest, to become a kind of live-in housekeeper at the Big House while she and Mr George waited together for Dunkiss to return.

And that was the key, of course. Mr George was the key. How could she, at eighteen, *not* have fallen in love with Mr George? How could she *not* have promised herself that she would follow him to the end of the earth if he asked her to? Her life became her service to him. She shared Mr George's load. She allowed him to confide in her, to lean on her. She watched him shape his small republic. She sewed and cleaned and dressed grazes and dried away tears. But it was his vision. He led and she unquestioningly followed, waiting for the day when, finally, he would realize (as he surely would) that he was also in love with her and would ask her to marry him.

To be fair, it was hard for anyone to be privy to any of Sassy's thoughts or dreams. Her clothes were nondescript – knowing Mr George paid little attention to appearances, she had no great interest in what she looked like for anybody else. She had few possessions of her own. Those who had seen inside her room could testify to its spartan appearance. Like Sassy herself, it had a kind of transient, waiting quality. There was a scattering of books, her crocheting things and a couple of modest framed paintings she had brought with her. There was a small wooden chest as well for her clothes and winter boots. And, on the chest, as the years ran on and she waited for her own private revelation with George Littlejohn, she kept Dunkiss's boots. Sometimes, in the evenings, she polished those boots in her spinster's room, holding them like a lucky talisman.

They never saw the RAF captain again after 1945. Delivering the news of Dunkiss's death to Mr George appeared to be his final act in the life of the orphanage. The captain, of course, had been the one who had pulled strings to get Dunkiss into the Signals when Dunkiss, at thirty-three, had been struggling to find a way to enlist, and the inhabitants of the Big House supposed that he felt a measure of responsibility for what had transpired.

On the final Saturday of the first post-war Football League

season, Accrington Stanley scored eight goals in an 8–4 win which might almost have been designed as a final salute to Dunkiss. Mr George was not there to see it. He was in the town arranging a headstone for the grave. The inscription on the stone read:

Ernest Dunkiss
(1907–1945)
The Great Dunkiss
Founder of the Dounleavey Orphanage

It was Mr George's idea that they should hold a Founder's Day celebration each year in Dunkiss's honour. The final letter that the orphanage received from the mysterious RAF officer came a month after the funeral service. The letter confirmed that arrangements had been made for a former colleague of his to perform an aerobatic display over the valley on that first Founder's Day.

13

Candles

Noah had the radio on as he drove up the motorway. He had woken with the decision firmly in his head to drive up to Cumbria. He wanted to tell Fred Wyke about Nathan in person. He hoped Fred might want to come with him to the funeral. The only other possible mourner had been a cousin of Nathan's in Macclesfield to whom Noah had sent a note but it seemed unlikely, after thirty years of silence, that the woman would elect to come to Nathan's funeral.

Noah didn't do much motorway driving. He realized partway up that his knuckles were white wrapped around the wheel. When he came off the motorway at the South Lakes turn-off to follow the Kendal signs, he felt relief that there was less traffic. He felt more able to relax. For the first time in half an hour he was conscious of the music playing on the radio.

'What if God was one of us?' the girl on Linde Wzinska's radio station was singing. 'Just a slob like all of us/ Just a stranger on the bus/ Tryin' to make His way home?'

The voice had a bleak, break-your-heart quality. It was Noah's favourite song of the moment. He didn't know why. Noah didn't know the name of the girl who sang it. He imagined her having long hair, big eyes, a curious, warm face.

He imagined her travelling to a small bar in New York with a big guitar case. It would be snowing outside. She would be late, distracted. She would nod quickly to the bartender who would shrug and go off to pour her a black coffee and find her a Danish while she set up, because he somehow knew she would not have eaten. She would try not to catch the owner's eye. She would sing to the two dozen people in the dark bar from the small stage set in the corner. After a couple of songs, the tightness in her throat would begin to go and she would start to relax into the music. Afterwards, off duty, the young bartender would stay behind and wait for her.

The ancient fells that Fred Wyke had developed a passion for long before he'd quit Lowell were in view now. Maybe there was a lesson in this for Noah. It was almost three months since he had been told by the Dounleavey Trust that his present contract to run the Mustard Seed would be his last, and he still had no plans, no idea of what kind of life there might be for him when the centre became a cash and carry or a carpet warehouse. He had already found the turn-off he was looking for on the drop into Kendal. He knew he must be close now. Seeing the lines of the fells, it occurred to him that Fred Wyke himself might be up there. If the house was empty, he supposed he could leave a note giving Fred the details of Nathan's funeral.

'Back up to heaven all alone,' the girl in the New York bar sang. 'Nobody calling on the phone.'

Noah turned into the cul-de-sac.

They were bungalows with longish drives. Fred Wyke's turned out to be the one at the far end. He saw Fred sitting at the window. He seemed to be watching the hills. Noah wondered whether he ought to have rung ahead to say he was coming. He got out of the car and walked up the drive. Fred Wyke, turning in the window seat, saw Noah, took a moment to think, then waved. Noah held up a hand. Fred Wyke disappeared from the window. Noah waited at the front door. Then Noah saw Fred's silhouette appear through the frosted glass.

'I can't find the key,' Fred said. 'You'll have to go round the back.'

'Fred, it's Noah. Noah Brindle.'

'Noah? You'll have to go round the back, Noah.'

'Okay. It's good to see you again, Fred.'

Noah walked round the side of the bungalow. There was a back door but when Noah tried it, it was locked. He walked on round to the back garden. He tapped on the back window, peering into the kitchen. It looked well kept. Fred Wyke had disappeared.

'Fred? Back door's locked too. Fred?'

A woman came up the back path through the garden, carrying a carrier bag in each hand.

'What do you want?' she asked. She didn't seem happy to see Noah.

'I came to see Fred,' Noah said.

'What about?'

Noah guessed this must be Mary. He'd never met her. He wondered if he'd stumbled into a marital row of some kind. He wondered if this was why Fred Wyke's wife was *walking* back with the shopping. 'There's a funeral in a couple of days,' Noah said. 'Of an old client of Fred's in Lowell. I came to tell him Nathan had died. I thought he might want to come to the funeral.'

'We know Nathan died. Someone came round – a reporter.'

'What did he want?'

'He wanted Fred to tell him what Nathan had been locked up for. Are you a reporter?'

Noah shook his head.

'So who are you?'

'Noah Brindle. Fred knows me. He was going to let me in the back way, but he seems to have gone missing for the moment.'

'He knows not to let anybody in when I'm not here.'

'Why would he not let anybody in?'

'Noah Brindle?' she said, ignoring his question.

'Yes.'

'You're the one he used to send postcards to.'

'That's right. He hasn't sent any for a long while. I guess it's not been the weather for walking.'

'Well, Noah Brindle –' she put the shopping down and began searching her coat pockets for the key – 'you'd better come in.'

She guided him into the kitchen, and told him about Fred.

'You hear about it,' she said. 'But nothing prepares you for it when it's someone you know. When it's someone who's been your life.'

'Is it hard to cope?'

'Fred might have told you, I was a nurse. I've seen it all before in other people. Dealt with it. The problem now is I'm not spared from knowing exactly what's going to happen. I know how Alzheimer's develops. I know it's . . . irredeemable.'

'How long's he had it?'

'How long? The last twelve months, he's been on a gradual slide. Before that, it was a bit more hit and miss. You know, he'd have good days and not so good days. But I knew there was something not quite right even back in Lowell when he was still working. Just little things. I kept hinting it was time for him to get out but he was a bugger for work, not that they appreciated it. And then you look at what it's cost him in the end. It doesn't seem fair after the things he spent his life doing.'

'What's he like with you?'

'He knows me, but on the bad days even that's a bit dodgy. He gets me confused with his mother sometimes. That's why I have to lock him in the house when I go out. A couple of times he's gone off on his own and got lost and neighbours have had to bring him back.'

Fred Wyke, dressed, but in slippers, came into the kitchen. 'Some tea for Noah, love?'

She smiled at him. ''Course. Don't worry, I'll make it – you go into the lounge with Noah.'

They remembered their childhoods. Noah told tales about the orphanage. Fred told him about the time he was chased out of an orchard with two other boys, apples spilling from under their jumpers – how they'd heard a shotgun blast out, how they'd just carried on running. They laughed. Noah went to see how the tea was doing. In the kitchen, Mary Wyke had been standing listening. She was smiling.

'Thank you, Noah Brindle,' she said.

He shrugged. It seemed such a little thing next to the mountain she climbed every day. Noah produced a small phial of tablets.

'Could I have a glass of water?'

She poured him one, watching him shake out two tablets. 'What are they for?'

'Ear infection.'

He swigged back the tablets.

'Carry the tray in for me?' she asked.

He carried the tea tray through and put it on the table in the lounge. She followed him in and passed him the phial he'd left in the kitchen. When he left, later in the afternoon, she walked him down to his car.

'Are you married, Noah Brindle?'

'I was.'

She nodded. Noah got in the car.

'Don't tell anybody,' she said. 'What he's like, I mean.' She made him promise. 'I know you'll keep it,' she said. 'You're good at secrets, Noah Brindle.'

'How do you mean?' he asked. The engine, in neutral, was ticking gently.

'I'm a nurse,' she said. She smiled. 'If those pills are for an ear infection, you've got the oddest ears I've come across in thirty years.'

She told Noah what she remembered a doctor telling her. It seemed, to her, the most human, the most useful, piece of advice she had been offered during that desperate period of her life. Each morning, the doctor had said, she should write down the three things that were most important to her. She should keep the piece of paper in her pocket, he had said. She'd asked him what for. He'd said she should think of it as a map – think of it as giving directions. Noah reversed slowly in the road. As he drove away, he saw that she was waving. He could see Fred at the lounge window. They were both waving.

No one else from the tenants group would go to the funeral – Linde Wzinska said she knew the man was probably in hell so what was the point – so Morag and Dorothy went alone.

It was the first time Morag had been inside a church since Dorothy had been born. The God she knew couldn't be chanted at from a pew any longer. She couldn't, after Dorothy's arrival, be a part of all those hopeful communal prayers recited like recipes. The idea of being saved was no longer a hypothetical Sunday nicety – it was something she lived for daily, looked for in the small signs of her life. She had not even had Dorothy baptized as an infant. Sometimes she wondered what difference this might make. Would it matter to Dorothy? Would it be important later in her life? After she died? Morag didn't know. How did people know?

The two women struggled up the steep steps of the cemetery chapel and into the porch, side by side, step by step. It was a comfortable rhythm to walk beside each other after all these years – not forced, nothing conscious any more. It was as if they were one person and not two. The kids on the estate sometimes sang 'Jake the Peg' at them if Morag and Dorothy were out on the street.

It had outraged her at first. It had reduced her to tears that people could thrive on other people's oddities. In the end she had made a kind of peace with it. It was, she decided, a kind of Calvary. And the best thing to do with the kids was usually to ignore them. They'd learn themselves, soon enough, that life didn't care who it was cruel to. That was surely the point of the tests that God, like some curious and dispassionate scientist organizing experiments and measuring the results, set for people.

Edging into the church, the two of them shuffling into the back pew and sitting down, Morag suddenly saw the funny side of it – two women, three legs, stride by stride for a full life. She saw it the way the kids must have seen it, and she had to put her hand to her mouth to stop herself from snorting out loud. Dorothy put her hand to her mouth too, sharing the secret.

They had caught the bus up to the cemetery. Morag had not asked Noah for a lift. She was frightened of what he might say, or do, in the aftermath of Nathan Ripley's death. She hadn't seen him since, and she expected blame.

They had moved the special meetings about Nathan Ripley out of the Mustard Seed to avoid Noah. She had concluded that Noah's silence was condemning. He is lost to me now, she had told herself, not knowing exactly what the phrase might mean, even though it had passed through her mind several times. She was aware that you could know someone for many years and still not be sure – absolutely sure – how they would react, whether they would be angry or resentful. She remembered the only time her father had ever been angry. She was sixteen when it had happened. Soon she would meet Tipper Gill with his one good eye and one that strayed. It was New Year's Eve. Her father had been drinking sherry – he was a Christmas-only drinker. He'd said he had a plan. He fancied running his own small business. He'd seen a little tobacconist and sweet shop in the town. He'd said he wanted them to consider it. His proposal came out of the blue, although it was evident he'd given a lot of thought to it. What do we know about that sort of thing? Morag's mother said. That's not for us, she'd said. She'd laughed at him. He'd gone upstairs, and come down later to retrieve the sherry bottle. Eventually they heard bangs, and something broke or shattered as it hit a wall. In the morning, Morag's father, with a cut above one eye, didn't remember anything about it, and the tobacconist's shop was never mentioned again. Morag's parents both wished her Happy New Year. They called each other Mother and Father as they always did in front of her. The memory came back to Morag years later when she was told that her father had killed himself. She had thought of it often since then. It was the thing she thought of now, sitting in the back pew of the cemetery chapel, afraid of what Noah

Brindle might say when he saw her there. She had come to Nathan Ripley's burial not for Ripley but for Noah.

She had sometimes wondered what would have happened if she had gone upstairs that New Year's Eve to see her father in his room with his bottle of sherry, and tried to soften the blow of her mother's scorn. If she had shown him that she wasn't siding with her mother. Or if she had spoken to him about it in the days or weeks that followed – would it have changed something if she had been brave enough to try? But she hadn't been brave enough; she had yielded to her mother just as she had yielded to the other members of the tenants group about the campaign against Nathan Ripley.

She had always believed that her father had blamed her for taking sides, and that it had never been quite the same between the two of them, father and daughter, after that. It was this, and not Tipper's arrival on the scene, that was to blame for spoiling things between them.

With Tipper, too, there was a similar failure to gain absolution, this time for producing Dorothy. Tipper looked at what other people might see – in his family, in *him* – and held Morag responsible. His answer had always been to ignore it, and to seek sanctuary in the football in which he immersed himself. Tipper was not so much repulsed by Dorothy as perplexed. He was out of his depth, and not just with Dorothy. Morag's nurturing of Dorothy brought out an aspect of his wife that Tipper hadn't guessed at and which took Morag beyond his own small orbit, making it impossible to make amends.

Standing at the front of the chapel, Noah Brindle and the priest were the only other people in the church. Dorothy looked around. Dorothy liked the stillness of the chapel; Morag could tell because she had let go of her mother's hand. It occurred to Morag that she should perhaps pray, or make a confession of some kind, but knowing how to seemed beyond her.

Morag listened to the service, such as it was. The priest spoke a little about Nathan Ripley. There wasn't anything in what he said that she didn't already know. Noah had told her about Nathan's past. He had come round to her house when the campaign to have Nathan Ripley moved off the estate was beginning to unfold. Noah had tried to persuade her that Nathan Ripley couldn't have assaulted Olwen Sudders. But in order to persuade her, he'd had to tell her something worse – that a long time ago Nathan had done terrible things to children (and been punished for them). But he was too frightened of adults, Noah had said, too separate from the adult world, to dare (or even want) to assault one. Noah had trusted her, and now he believed she had betrayed him and told the *Citizen* about Nathan's past, even though it wasn't Morag who had leaked the story.

He'd said, 'He did a terrible thing. I don't deny that, but it was thirty years ago. Doesn't he get the chance to change?'

Morag had replied, 'It's all right for you – you can sit in judgement on these things. You don't have to live here. You drive home at night. You're leaving for good soon.'

'The kids are lobbing stones through his windows because they think it's all right to. It's wrong. You're wrong.'

It was wrong but necessary, she'd wanted to say. Instead, she'd said, 'You know what, Noah, I don't care. I just wish he'd go. I'm sorry his windows are bust but I just wish he'd get the message and go so we can all get on with our proper lives.'

He'd said, 'Is that why you've been keeping clear of the centre – because you know it's wrong?'

'You haven't got any right to lecture me, Noah Brindle,' she'd said. 'Anyway, things are getting better without your help. The Regeneration Board are going to give us the money to sort the estate out. We don't need your help any more.'

She realized now that what she'd wanted to say to Noah was that stopping the campaign to oust Nathan Ripley was beyond her. It simply wasn't possible, not even for Noah's sake. But she couldn't say it. However illusory, the idea that it was *her* campaign, that such a thing was in her domain, was in the end too glorious and fragile a thing to surrender.

When Noah had gone, she had realized there was more she'd wanted to say: that even though they had fallen out over this she still respected him, that there was a time when she'd even thought of him as Jesus – come to save her. Over the years, she had, of course, come to see that he was not – not because of any omission or particular wickedness on his part (though his attachment to Accrington Stanley struck her personally as bizarre) but because of his humanity, because she caught him crying once, because he couldn't change things, because his face was full of small and wondrous imperfections, because she did not feel spiritual but earthbound and fleshy around him. She'd wanted to say that the price she would pay for *not* stopping the campaign was the knowledge that Noah Brindle would think less of her, and that this was almost unbearable. What she'd wanted to say most of all, of course, was that she loved him. With the priest humming the final words of the service, before the unmourned coffin of Nathan Ripley slid forward for cremation, she realized that this was her confession.

*

Afterwards, she took Dorothy to the front of the chapel to look at the candles. A dozen of them had been lit and were propped upright in rows in the metal rack to one side of the pulpit. Dorothy had been watching the flames. She reached into the tray beneath the rack and picked out three candles. She examined them. They were the thickness of her own stubby fingers. She held them up to Noah and smiled at him, because smiling was what she did for Noah. Noah, in his overcoat, looking bleakly cold in the draughty chapel, smiled back. He reached for the candles Dorothy was holding in her hand, then he lit one, using one of the candles already burning in the rack. He passed one of the two remaining candles back to Dorothy and the other to Morag. Then he held his candle over Dorothy's until Dorothy's candle was lit. He let her watch it, let her hold it tight, then he guided her hand towards the rack and helped her to place the candle in one of the vacant holders. Morag watched. There was no one else in the chapel; the priest had gone. Morag was surprised how peaceful it was. Noah held his candle out for Morag. She raised her candle and kindled a flame from it.

The three of them watched the candles burning steadily. It was very quiet. Morag could hear her heart beating, not fast but firm, as if it would beat for ever, having come this far. She could feel Noah's presence, and Dorothy's. She kept watching the candle as she listened to her heart beating.

14

The Tiger Moth

It became Mr George's fate to take in difficult children. The truth was that, as the relationship between Mr George and the Diocesan Office became more strained, the Big House increasingly became a kind of dustbin facility, left to cope with the children whom the other orphanages, like St Brendan's, wouldn't take or couldn't handle and whom Fr Fearon couldn't place anywhere else – the absconders, the chronic bedwetters, the firestarters, those too wilful or disturbed to speak or those inexplicably retarded or unco-operative. Somehow they all ended up with Mr George. And as the years slipped by, the Diocesan Office would find that, however much it disapproved of Mr George's outspoken views or his methods, it had come to rely on him – because he would never turn any child away; because he believed that anything was possible.

Mr George reached a stage where he truly did believe he could work with any child, no matter what problems they brought. After all, Mr George's own father had howled in terror as he slept every night for forty years. After that, the terrors of the small children brought to the Big House seemed normal. The news of his approach, and of his success with apparently irredeemable children, began to spread. Orphans were placed with him from farther afield. Mr George found himself being described as a pioneer. Occasionally he was asked to give talks about his work. Someone suggested in an article that Mr George's orphanage was the first recognizable therapeutic community in England for disturbed children. People wondered what his secret was. They wondered how it was that Mr George could succeed with children where better-staffed and more fully equipped institutions and better-qualified professionals had failed. The Diocesan Office, however, were suspicious of Mr George's growing reputation. They disliked the notion that he was some kind of pioneer. They saw him as a maverick running an unorthodox institution. They put up with him because of his apparent ability to deal with difficult-to-place and seemingly irredeemable orphans.

By the late 1950s, the Big House had thirty-four orphans. Working alone, it was easier for Mr George to teach thirty-four children of different ages in one classroom rather than split them up. Solomon and Gifford sat at one table. Walter (in his astonishing hand-me-down yellow-fleck fisherman's sweater) and Gordon (who no longer ran away, to Scotland or anywhere else) sat at another. Jacob (a chronic bedwetter) and Flo (a big-boned girl with red hair, who had set fire to two previous orphanages) were on another table with Megan. Megan was epileptic and had been transferred to the Big House from St Brendan's, where the brothers had reduced her to a virtual zombie by dosing her on bigger and bigger quantities of pheno-barbitone in order to curb the fits which terrified them. And so it went all the way round the classroom in which they gathered every day.

There were no outsiders. If Megan had epilepsy and

sometimes fitted because her phenobarbitone level had been reduced by Mr George to allow her to function normally in class and with her peers, it made her different but not an outsider. If Rachel, returning nightly from her studies at the local teacher-training college, didn't talk and only wrote notes, if redheaded Flo threw tantrums and sometimes harmed herself, if the handyman Goose stood grinning at the moon or talking out loud to himself in the grounds, if Jacob wet the bed so much that people sometimes wondered whether the pipes had burst, the same principle applied. Mr George's boast was that, providing he had the room, any child who wanted to could come to the Big House. The only rule was, once there, *they* accepted everyone else in the house in the same way. No one was turned down because of who they were, or what they had done, or because Fr Fearon's Diocesan Office described them as incorrigible in the assessment reports which invariably preceded a child's arrival at the Big House.

The flurry caused by the news that Walter had seen real naked breasts was well remembered in the Big House. Walter was sixteen at the time and discovered a previously engineered hole in the wall of the second-floor linen cupboard which looked into the girls' bathroom – a legacy of some previous post-war orphan passing through the orphanage in its early days.

Sexuality takes everyone by surprise. Before it envelops us it is so unimaginable that when it happens it seems to arrive from nowhere. One week the road ahead is clear and wide; the next it is crowded with uncomfortable cravings and beckoning images of bare flesh. Walter's own interest in the business, however, seemed more financial than erotic, and as the proprietor of the viewing hole he made a killing charging sixpence a time for a peek at the dark secrets of the second-floor linen cupboard (particularly when Walter's customers knew that Flo's ample breasts were on display).

The topic wasn't so different in the girls' dormitory, except that the girls tended to think about the charms of *older* boys – the farmers' boys down in the valley, and the grammar-school youths who earned money at weekends caddying at the neighbouring golf club.

Flo was the most blatant – the most provocative – in showing her interest in boys, even though she wasn't the oldest, even though (perhaps because) she was far from the prettiest. She liked to pretend that she was older than everyone else. She liked to say that she didn't want anything to do with the other orphans – that she would rather mix with normal people from real families. It was just Flo's way, Mr George said. She was really still a child like the rest of his charges. She was really just as nervous about herself and what the world thought of her as every other orphan in the Big House. That was why she'd been moved around so much from place to place; that was why she'd set fire to two of her previous orphanages, why they had thrown her out, why Mr George had needed to come to her rescue (though you could never tell she had been rescued from the disdain she sometimes liked to show for the Big House). But at the time of Walter's discovery of the hole in the linen cupboard Flo seemed to have finished her own growing up.

Mr George was used to it. Every year seemed to be a time of sexual awakening for one or other of his charges. If it was Flo's turn in 1960, he knew it would be the turn of others the year after.

When the inspectors came round each year, one of the questions they would routinely ask Mr George was how the orphanage dealt with 'bodily issues'. Each year, he told them the same thing – that he dealt with all such matters in a Christian manner, and informed by Christian values. He didn't exactly know what *they* understood by this, but it seemed to be sufficient to satisfy them. *He* just meant that he relied on telling the truth. In explaining sex to his orphans, Mr George dealt plainly with the whole subject. He saw no point in doing otherwise, having so many children growing up under one roof, who would trade furtive secrets and discoveries whether they had a sexual education or not. He didn't want his orphans having sex out of curiosity. He knew about girls getting pregnant out of ignorance from his days in Tatlow Street. After the war he had been disturbed by the suicide of a St Brendan's girl who had drowned herself in the canal after menstruating for the first time and not knowing what was happening to her. It seemed common sense to ensure that *his* orphans knew the facts of life early enough to avoid these things. No secrets. Mr George dealt with burgeoning sexuality in the same way that he dealt with Megan's epilepsy, with Goose's slowness, with Uncle Rolly's night-time madness: out in the open. Of course it didn't stop boys hiding in the linen cupboard at sixpence a time, but it helped in other ways.

The inspection in 1960 was led by an official called Fish. Mr Fish carried a shiny brown briefcase everywhere he went. He was some kind of curate who had not been with the Diocesan Office long, and he was very thorough. He wore a bow tie and his nose ran continually so that he sniffed at regular intervals. His colleague was a mouse of a woman whom he introduced as Miss Wallop and then proceeded to ignore. She spent the whole day following mutely in his wake, not saying a word, even through lunch which they ate together in silence.

They went through the books, discovering (as always) that the stipend and the money provided by the Town Hall for the children it had referred barely paid the bills, let alone covered the upkeep of the Big House. It was only the income from the annual Founder's Day event and the sales of vegetables grown on the allotment that kept the building at least partly maintained and which paid a kind of wage to Sassy and an allowance to Goose as handyman. But at least, they concluded, the Big House could somehow juggle its debts for another year.

When Mr Fish and Miss Wallop were done with the accounts, they reviewed the plans for the forthcoming Founder's Day celebrations, checking, amongst other things, that the Tiger Moth pilot's licence was in order so that no insurance liability could fall on the Diocesan Office. After that, the inspectors met with a group of the younger children for the purposes of the inspection report – to test them on their algebra and spelling and their religious knowledge. Elsewhere in the house, Mr George continued to teach the remaining older portion of the class, assisted by Rachel, who had finished college for the summer break.

Mr Fish's habit with the small children was to pick on the least attentive child in the room. He picked on Solomon, a boy who had a habit of wandering in and out of class at will.

'What can you tell me about Jesus?' Mr Fish asked. Solomon had been staring out of the window.

Solomon thought. 'Jesus cared for the children,' he said, 'and healed the sick, like Mr George.'

'Yes, child, Mr George runs the orphanage but he doesn't heal the sick like Jesus did.'

'He healed Gifford.'

Gifford, in the yellow fisherman's sweater now bequeathed to him by a growing Walter, nodded in confirmation. Gifford, who had arrived the previous year, was a small nervous boy and a chronic asthmatic.

Sassy, who was supervising the smallest children, shifted uncomfortably. 'It was just an asthma attack,' she said warily. 'He just calmed Gifford a little until the boy could breathe.'

'The doctor said Gifford was *dying*,' Solomon insisted. 'He said Gifford was going to suffocate to death.'

'The doctor said there was nothing else he could do,' one of the girls confirmed.

'So Mr George healed him.'

Gifford himself put his hand up. 'And when Mr George came here he only had a few shillings in his pocket and nothing else, and Jesus gave him the orphanage to run.'

'He had his white dinner jacket on when he first came,' Solomon said. 'The one he wears on Founder's Day when he does his magic tricks.'

'And he came on a steam train,' Gifford added. 'Mr George can do *anything*.'

'Yes, yes. That's enough.' Mr Fish brought his handkerchief out and blew hard.

The tour of the facilities was next. Mr Fish and the taciturn Miss Wallop were led by Sassy round the grounds of the Big House, and then through the various rooms of the orphanage as they sought imperfections which could be noted in the report. Mr Fish complained about there being a goat in the chapel; he didn't like the noise of the antiquated heating system; he noted various leaks, and a damp patch on one of the walls. Miss Wallop pointed out the dirty towels left lying on the floor after two of the boys had failed to deposit them in the wash basket that morning.

It was in the girls' dormitory that Miss Wallop found the scribbled note on the floor near the waste basket. She picked it up and began to read. Her face slowly tightened. She held out the note for Mr Fish. He read it twice, as though hoping he might have misread it the first time. But he was not mistaken.

They entered the classroom where Mr George was tutoring the older children. Everyone stood up, but they could sense that something was wrong. Mr Fish was unwilling to sit down. Miss Wallop lingered by the door. She was looking at the children sideways on, pretending *not* to look. Mr George had stopped teaching. Mr Fish brought the piece of paper from his pocket.

'I have just found this in the girls' dormitory.' He looked deeply unhappy. He brandished the note at Mr George whilst declining to go so far as to let it go.

Mr George read the note, nonplussed.

'I want to know who the culprit is,' Mr Fish said. 'I want to hear what the child responsible for *this* has to say.'

Mr George shrugged. 'That isn't possible.'

'And why not?'

'Because it's Rachel's note, and Rachel cannot speak.'

It was true. Everyone could tell that it was one of Rachel's notes. Rachel stepped forward.

'I would like to know the meaning of this,' Mr Fish said. Rachel signed animatedly to Mr George. Mr Fish didn't worry her; she was not easily worried by a perspiring, bow-tied inspector.

'Rachel wonders if you want her to explain why she wrote the note,' Mr George said.

218

'Those words do not bear repetition in any setting,' Mr Fish said. But he was too late. Rachel had already signed the contents of the note in asking Mr George her question. 'Women can masturbate too, Flo,' her note said, 'that's what your clitoris is *for*!' And since everyone in the class could sign to some extent they all knew what Rachel's note had said.

'We were talking in the dormitory,' Rachel continued to sign. 'Flo said it wasn't fair that boys got something to play with between their legs as they got older, and girls had to wait till they were with a man to get to play with it too and have some fun. I told her she shouldn't be rude. I said there'd be plenty of time for sex when she was older and she'd found someone to love, but she carried on saying it.'

So Rachel had scribbled the note to Flo. It wasn't Flo's fault that she didn't know till then. She pretended she was so grown up that people sometimes forgot that she wasn't.

'Who put this nonsense in your head, girl?' Mr Fish demanded.

Rachel glanced at Mr George. He nodded his permission. So she wrote out a note, wanting to explain directly to Mr Fish, who couldn't sign. 'Mr George explained to us about masturbation.'

Mr Fish looked at Mr George as if this might be a joke. Then Rachel passed Mr Fish a second note she had been scribbling. 'It was after we learned about contraception – prophylactic rubbers and things,' the second note said. Mr Fish read it, horrified.

'Don't you find this kind of behaviour unacceptable?' he demanded.

'I don't see how it's unacceptable,' Mr George said. 'It's just a part of growing up. I don't encourage body hair or acne but they seem to appear just the same as all my children grow up.'

'So do I take it that you encourage this . . . gutter talk?' He held aloft Rachel's notes.

'I suppose I encourage the older children to be open about sex and what they feel. Changing into grown-ups is frightening enough without having to hide what it's like.'

Mr Fish's nose was running again and he was searching for his handkerchief. 'But surely you are denying these children the value of a Christian upbringing if you permit them to conduct themselves in so lewd a manner and go unpunished – if you allow a younger girl to be so blatantly corrupted by an older one in this fashion? Where will it end?'

'You're surely not saying I should tell them that it's *the stork* that brings babies? Or that I *don't know* what is happening to their bodies when they come and ask me why they are changing? How can that be the Christian truth when we both know it isn't? I teach the orphans that Jesus died on the cross for them. That they must honour God. That He devised conception as a way of procreating and that sex is a gift from God to be enjoyed, preferably within marriage. I tell them masturbation, especially for boys, but also for girls, is just a way of addressing the urges that will one day lead to sex. You'd rather I told them *nothing* about the business of growing up?'

Mr Fish was scribbling furiously in his notebook.

'You'd rather,' Mr George added, 'young girls from my orphanage threw themselves in the canal because they didn't understand they were simply menstruating for the first time?'

'I really think I will have to take this back to the Diocesan

Office for consideration,' Mr Fish said, still writing. 'And I should add that I am not at all happy that such a conversation is taking place within earshot of my fiancée.'

The children looked across at Miss Wallop in amazement. They had assumed that the two adults had barely been introduced. Miss Wallop, standing over by the door, continued to say nothing.

'I'm afraid that I feel compelled to call a halt to the inspection,' Mr Fish said. He had finished writing. He was collecting up his papers and notes, depositing them hurriedly into his shiny brown briefcase. 'Fr Fearon will doubtless have something to say.'

And with that, he hurried from the room, followed three paces behind by the vacuous Miss Wallop.

The orphans knew that Mr Fish was upset. They weren't sure, though, exactly why. They thought everybody knew that boys masturbated as they grew up. They thought everybody knew that girls could too if they chose. It surprised them that someone could think there was something wrong in that; that it might in some unfathomable way make them bad Christians. They didn't worry about it for long, though. They had more pressing things on their mind that particular week in the summer of 1960. They had Founder's Day approaching. They had Dublin's last flight in the Tiger Moth to prepare for.

Founder's Day was the one time of year when Mr George's self-sufficient world looked outwards. It was an occasion to which the whole town was invited and at which Mr George's orphanage could show off its best face.

Founder's Day was summer dresses and shirtsleeves, and the rustle of tablecloths on trestle tables. It was the smell of

Sassy's cakes, baked in relays from early in the morning – the smell wafting across the courtyard and lingering on the warm breeze. It was raffles and white-elephant stalls, children's games and tombolas. It was music from the rickety tannoy, and old friends from Tatlow Street milling around the house and gardens. It was also an occasion for another one of Mr George's performances. Since they had moved to the Big House, these had become grander and more elaborate each year, taking place on the outdoor staging he had constructed specially for the purpose. He had made a motor car disappear; he had made a woman float across the stage; he had turned Gomorrah the goat into an elephant. His favourite, however, was the Magic Box trick he had first performed with Dunkiss in Tatlow's Mill and which he had reprised several times since the war.

But above all, ranking even above the performance of Mr George's annual illusion, Founder's Day was about the Tiger Moth which Tom Travis brought each year to perform a display of aerobatics – barrel rolls and stall turns and loops – and to provide five-minute rides over the valley for five shillings.

When the war ended, Tom Travis had exchanged his RAF Hurricane for a Bristol Wayfarer which he had flown for a freight company, and then for a Fox Moth when he had joined up with a couple of brothers who held the franchise for joyrides over Southport Sands. For his first few years at Founder's Day, Tom had borrowed one of the four-seater Fox Moths he flew over Southport Sands. By 1951, however, he had enough money saved to set up on his own in the freight-transport business and he arrived in the bottom field that year with an ex-RAF Tiger Moth – painted canary yellow, with room for only a single passenger sitting in front of the pilot. Dublin, whose war had been spent idolizing RAF aeroplanes in the distant skies and at the picture house every week, fell instantly and completely in love with it. As a result, Mr George arranged for Tom Travis to give Dublin a special flight of his own over the valley, and this – Dublin's annual struggle to wedge his callipered legs into the front cockpit, and his flight in Tom Travis's yellow Tiger Moth – became another tradition of Founder's Day.

Dublin was the only occupant of the Big House to distrust Mr George's contention that *anything* could be accomplished. Dublin wasn't convinced that the world could be conquered. It had beaten Dublin himself by setting the clock ticking irre-deemably against his own life while he was still a child, and it would probably beat Mr George in the end with some unan-ticipated roll of the dice. He said as much. Dublin was never frightened of saying what he thought. His sentence of death had freed him to say anything; it allowed his natural cynicism a free reign. Only in the weeks leading up to Founder's Day did Dublin allow himself to yield to boyish enthusiasm. Only at that one time of year, anticipating the distant insect hum of the yellow biplane as it came down the valley and prepared to land in the bottom field, did Dublin allow himself to give way to an imagined future – to dreams.

The arrival of the Tiger Moth was the highlight of Dublin's year. As he grew into adolescence he came to know almost every-thing there was to know about Tom Travis's aeroplane. He knew that when Tom took paying passengers up for flights he would glide down from his thousand-feet limit and sideslip in to land as quickly as possible to avoid wasting engine time. He knew that most Tiger Moths spun to the right if the engine speed dropped to forty miles an hour; he also knew that Tom Travis's plane could be ruddered into a left-hand spin for its aerobatic routines because the wartime anti-spinning strakes had been removed. And he knew that what was best about the Tiger Moth – better even than the barrel rolling or looping the loop – was that when Tom eased back the throttle in the cathedral of air over the valley, Dublin, in the passenger seat ahead of him, could hear, above the idling engine, the music of the wind in the wires.

The other thing that Dublin knew all about was his sickness. He knew that the doctors believed he wouldn't live beyond the age of twenty-five. He was reconciled to it. His only regret was that at some point in his shortened life he would grow too sick to be allowed to fly any more.

'Maybe in your case,' Mr George sometimes said to him, 'you'll get to thirty, even thirty-five. It's been known for people with your condition to get to thirty-five.'

'Who wants to get to *thirty-five*?' Dublin would snap.

Mr George would think. 'So maybe you'll only get to twenty-five,' he'd say. 'Shouldn't you aim to make it the best twenty-five you can? You're clever enough to do all kinds of things. Achieve things that people will remember you for.'

'What *for*?' Dublin would protest. 'I have polio and my lungs are shot. Soon I won't even get to go up in the Tiger Moth. And I'm going to be dead by twenty-five. Who'll remember me then?'

He was a ferocious sceptic. He waged war against anything woolly minded or well meaning that smacked of condescension or of hypocrisy. The biggest of these, of course, for Dublin, was religion. 'All the stuff that Goose likes so much,' Dublin would say dismissively. 'Angels and arks. Stories! Just stories.' He was amazed that people believed them and took comfort from them. 'Why do people kid themselves?' he would say. 'There's nothing afterwards. We live, we die. There's no plan to it. There's no plan to anything.'

Mr George, with a degree of relish, called Dublin 'my doubting Thomas'. He regarded Dublin as another challenge. He believed he would win through in the end, amazed but tolerant that Dublin couldn't yet see the workings of God's grace.

It was an evening early in 1960 – the year in which Flo for one felt that she had finished her growing up, in which Mr Fish turned up for his ill-fated inspection. Mr George was giving a talk to the Manchester Federation of Oddfellows about his work, when the Big House received a phone call to say that Dublin had collapsed in the town and had been admitted to hospital. Mr George returned from Manchester at around midnight, received the news from the doughty Sassy, who, as ever, had waited up for him, and turned the car around to go to the hospital.

They kept Dublin on the ward for a week, and after that Mr George sent him to convalesce by the sea for a month. The day Dublin returned to the Big House, Mr George pushed him up the drive in a wheelchair. He carried walking sticks across his lap. Mr George had warned the children the night before that Dublin was gradually losing his ability to walk, and that he'd had to postpone college until a time when he had regained his strength.

What finally got Dublin walking again, albeit in short bursts, was the prospect of flying in the Tiger Moth again that summer. Tom Travis had always insisted, however, that he could only take Dublin up in the passenger cockpit as long as Dublin could walk to and from the plane unaided. It was a condition of the insurance policy: the single passenger in the front cockpit had to be able-bodied enough to comply with the safety regulations. It was clear now that, barring a miracle, 1960 would be Dublin's last flight.

*

The yellow biplane flew down the valley from Clitheroe. Later in the morning the paying visitors from the town would begin to arrive, but for now preparations were halted as everyone watched Dublin's last flight.

'It wouldn't have been fair on him,' Tom Travis had told Mr George, 'letting him think that he *might* be able to go up again next year. He's too sick this year – with the sticks and everything – but I'll risk it and let it go this once. But as far as next year goes, I owe it to him to be honest so he gets used to the idea that he can't go up again.'

The hum became the rip of the engine, and Rachel, Walter, Goose and the rest of the orphans, along with Mr George and Sassy, watched the pilot glide down and sideslip in to land just like they'd seen him do so many times before. They listened for the singing of the wind in the wires as he came low. They saw him drop and touch the ground – skipping, bobbing, bumbling, slowing to a crawl, taxiing fussily so that the plane's nose, when it was parked, pointed into the wind – then settle within a hundred yards of the spectators. Tom Travis still had the throttle open, waiting until the airscrew had stopped rotating. The engine noise was still very loud. Everyone could see that, in the front passenger seat, Dublin was laughing.

And that was that.

That evening they talked in the kitchen when the last of the visitors had gone home. Dublin was absently polishing his glasses, closing his eyes as he imagined being up in the air again. He was still smiling, just as he had been when he had been helped from the cockpit that morning, recounting every detail of his last flight. He struck Rachel and the others as being more alive than he'd been for a long time, and they took it as a promising sign that after his flight Dublin had managed to walk at least part of the way back up the hill to the Big House and for once had seemed unexhausted by the effort.

The day after Founder's Day was the only day in the year when Mr George didn't get up early to douse the light on top of the bell tower and to ring the bell alongside Dublin. The day after Founder's Day, Mr George always left Dublin to ring the bell alone. As a rule it took him until long after midnight to finish clearing the grounds after the event. For one day, he reasoned, Dublin could ring the bell on his own, and they could let the gas light burn until after breakfast.

Rachel lay awake in her bunk, realizing that she hadn't heard the bell. She guessed that Dublin, like Mr George, had decided to take that one morning off. And she thought she would get up and ring the bell herself for that one morning. She had watched Dublin perform the same chore often enough, so she was confident she could manage it. She was only surprised that, on the day after his last Tiger Moth flight, Dublin should have decided not to ring the bell, that he should have preferred to stay in bed.

She was wrong.

He had been up very early. Perhaps he had not been to bed at all, it occurred to her later. His body was lying at the foot of the bell tower. The fall had killed him. The doctor said he had been there for a couple of hours. Rachel remembered calculating that he must have jumped at first light.

The following week a letter came for Mr George from the Diocesan Office. He thought it might be offering condolences for Dublin's death. It wasn't. It was from Fr Fearon and it was about Rachel. It was about the note that the inspector, Mr Fish, had found in the girls' dormitory.

The letter from Fr Fearon referred to the need to re-establish Christian values in the orphanage in relation to matters of decency. It asked Mr George for suggestions on how this might best be achieved in the light of 'the incident'. The letter also wanted Mr George to specify the action he intended to take against the girl who had written the obscene note.

Mr George didn't speak at the service for Dublin. It was as if he couldn't find the words to make sense of Dublin's suicide, as if he couldn't, for once, explain the *point* of what had happened – the sudden and brutal intrusion of that premeditated act into the version of events he himself had envisaged. In the following months, however, he began to accept more and more invitations to speak on matters of public morality. As if anxious to provoke the Diocesan Office even more, he began to send them copies of his speeches. He began to argue publicly for more openness in sexual education. He began to criticize more forcefully the brothers at St Brendan's for the suffocating regime they ran and the levels of punishment they inflicted. He castigated the authorities for their slum-clearance programmes and the shoddy high-rise flats that the Council were throwing up in their place on the edge of town. He talked publicly for the first time about an offer of money that the golf-club committee and some of its acolytes on the Council had made him on the condition that he despatch his troupe of orphans to St Brendan's and allow the golf club to convert the Big House and its grounds into a new clubhouse and eighteenth hole. It was an allegation that the councillors he implicated denied – implying skilfully that the offer of a Council grant to help develop the work of the orphanage in other parts of the town must have been misconstrued by the gauche and unworldly Mr George. As for the letter sent to Mr George by Fr Fearon, he burned it.

15

The Bigger Picture

Barry Catlin suddenly had the impression that Janice was standing behind him. Hunched at Noah's desk in the Mustard Seed, surrounded by the customary litter of records and IOUs from the boys for their unpaid subs, Barry was sure that his wife was there in the doorway. Without looking round, he could sense Janice's shape and he was suddenly grateful that he had finished his string of phone calls for the evening and that she hadn't overheard.

Barry Catlin didn't like using the telephone. He barked down it. He clicked his dentures in the awkward silences, and pushed anxiously at his wirewool hair with his free hand. He regarded the telephone as treacherous.

'It's Barry Catlin chairman of St Silas's are you all right fine thanks yes. What?'

He held his breath while talking as if he was diving underwater. He rose to breathe, dazed, at the end of sentences.

It was hard for people to tell how old he was. The broken veins on his face gave him the shiny, rouged cheeks of a drinker, even though he drank moderately and usually at the insistence of Tipper, and the cigarettes that had turned the tips of his nicotine-stained fingers to leather had reduced his voice to gravel.

Barry did the admin for Tipper Gill's football teams. Tipper himself couldn't be doing with that side of things. Tipper left all that to Barry. He had to arrange fixtures and kick-off times for each of the teams the two of them ran. He had to report details back to the league secretary, whom everyone else knew as Jack but whom Barry Catlin always addressed as 'Mr Secretary', even though he and Barry had worked together at the ordnance factory. He had to make sure that the lads knew when to turn up for matches. He had to book the referees and pay them their fees if St Silas were the home team. He had to sort out registrations and fines and collect weekly subs from all Tipper's lads who never had the right money, or enough money, and who regarded it as a game to avoid paying Barry whenever they could.

'I paid double last week,' they'd say, 'you said you'd make a note,' and he could never tell which of the kids were lying and which were not.

Barry Catlin would never make his rounds of phone calls from home. He always came to the Mustard Seed Centre where he could make them in the privacy of Noah's office. Noah knew to leave Barry to plough through his paperwork and his phone calls alone. If the younger kids – the under-elevens or under-thirteens – were in the centre, they found excuses to hang around the office, listening to him gasping through his business on the phone. They liked hearing him clattering into the sentences of the person at the other end of the line, missing cues, drying up, shouting 'What?' or 'Are you still there?' They did booming impressions of him that echoed round the rafters of the main hall until Tipper caught them and walloped them.

'Jesus!' Tipper would yell at them. 'He's doing all this for you lot!' But it didn't stop them.

*

At school, Barry Catlin had always struggled with the work. He was slow to grasp things. Over-cautious and hesitant, he was usually last to finish. He had been famously excluded from woodwork after falling behind and then, in his hurry to catch up, sawing the tip of his thumb off and being taken, ashen and shamefaced, to hospital. Miss Doughty made him work on needlework with the girls after that, and he was teased all through school for it. It wasn't as if he could compensate in the playground. He had no ball sense. Even though he loved football the nature of the game – its balance and aggression – mocked him in return and he took refuge in the Charlie Buchan football annuals he collected. Miss Doughty liked to make her pupils stand up at their desks to recite homework; Barry, frantic, would lose his way, reddening, biting his lip, closing his eyes and wishing the ordeal away until Miss Doughty lost patience with him again.

He had left school at fourteen. His handwriting even now was childish and inelegant; mental arithmetic was still a mystery beyond his reach. As a consequence, running the club's affairs didn't come easily to him. It wasn't as if he didn't have other responsibilities to occupy his mind. He had his part-time job at the retail park, patrolling the perimeter of Asda and Shoe Express and Burger King in his uniform; he had half a dozen children of his own that he could scarcely control; he had the dog called Denis Law that he walked several times a day. Then there was Janice.

Not long ago Barry had received a call up at the centre to say that the dog had got out of the house and was on the loose (Janice was always leaving the door open), and that Janice herself was having another one of her turns. Janice sometimes went missing for a few hours. She usually turned up somewhere on the estate. Once, some people came home to find her sitting on their settee in the dark. This time, the caller said, she was sitting on the pavement down near the maisonette blocks. Barry rounded up the dog and put some food down for it (Janice hadn't fed it), then he went to coax Janice back home.

'Come on, love,' he said. 'It's getting dark, you should come in.' He was looking up at the windows of the flats all around him. He guessed that people were watching. It was like being in Miss Doughty's class all over again, standing up in front of everyone and not knowing the words.

Janice gave him a look that he knew well.

'I suppose you went for the dog first,' she said.

Noah had offered more than once to give Barry a hand with the running of the club's affairs, but Barry always refused these offers of help. He chose to wade through the work alone. He would spend hours in Noah's office in silent and mounting frustration, surrounded by pieces of paper. The mornings after his sessions at the Mustard Seed everything in the office smelled of the cigarettes Barry had smoked all evening, and Noah's waste bins were crammed with the spoiled notes and calculations Barry had thrown away.

Noah grew curious about the clutch of files Barry Catlin kept in the Mustard Seed's office. In the end he decided to read through them. He told himself he was just checking to see how much work might need doing to straighten out the club's finances. He expected chaos.

The files were immaculate. Every money transaction was scrupulously receipted. Addresses and contacts for the other teams in the league – in fact for every team the St Silas boys had ever played – were listed alphabetically. The same had been done for the referees. Barry had noted every boy's weekly subs going back years on a Z-sheet that folded out the length of Noah's desk. There was a record of everyone who'd ever turned up for one of Tipper's training sessions. The fixtures for the teams were catalogued in the same way. Friendlies were written out in blue, cup matches were in green. Results and teamsheets had been transcribed minutely into margin spaces in Barry Catlin's painstaking, schoolboy-best handwriting. There was even a description of the weather conditions in which each match had been played. Noah read through the complete set of Barry's files. He wondered how many drafts it had taken for Barry to get things to look like this; how many binfuls of scrap paper; how many long and anxious draws on Woodbines.

Occasionally, Noah took down the football-club files again and followed the thread of the transcribed tables and lists and calculations as Barry Catlin continued to update them. And it struck Noah that here was the reason Barry wouldn't accept any help in managing the club's affairs. The sum of Tipper Gill's and Barry Catlin's world was recorded perfectly here. It was a puzzle with myriad parts that Barry Catlin himself was continually solving. By contrast, his life with Janice and the kids had no such sense of order about it. It could not be solved. Over Janice's frame of mind (as over the behaviour of his rampant children) he had no such influence or control.

Sometimes, Barry would take one or other of the files home with him for the evening to show Janice.

'Under-fifteens are six points better off than this time last year, love,' he'd say, pointing to the comparative tables. 'And that's with four of the lads still having another year till they're top age.'

It meant nothing to Janice, who would nod and hand the file back to Barry.

'I'm going for a bath,' she'd say.

The bath was Janice's refuge. Baths meant that Barry had failed to lift her spirits. Baths meant that retreat had been sounded for another day.

Sometimes Barry would imagine that, instead of staying at home with her television and her pills, Janice had followed him to the Mustard Seed Centre. He would picture her being moved to wonder at the alchemy of his secret work there. Sometimes he would imagine himself laying bare the sum of their own shared life and, in this way, resolving those things which had eluded the two of them.

But when he finally looked up it wasn't Janice standing there in the doorway. It was Elly Pascoe. He remembered – looking across the room at Elly Pascoe but thinking of Janice – how love, or something close enough, had been promised in the days when he and Janice were courting; how the future had not seemed complicated.

'Is Brindle around?' Elly asked. But Barry Catlin only looked at her, as if he had been expecting someone else.

She knew Barry. He was often at Noah's centre. She knew he helped Tipper Gill with the kids' football on the estate. He was an odd man – polite, intense, vaguely ramshackle in his improbable second-hand suits. He smelled a little. It was more than his distinctive aura of cigarettes. There was something faintly tragic about him, Elly Pascoe thought, but it was the tragedy of a clown and it made people laugh.

Like everyone else, Elly Pascoe knew that Barry Catlin had once made a pass at Morag Gill. It was hard to imagine

awkward Barry Catlin in that way – filled with passion and tenderness. It was one thing everyone knew about Barry Catlin:
that he had made a (failed) pass at his best friend's wife. Even
the sound of it seemed funny to people – that he had done
such a thing, out of the blue; that he had failed; that the two
men were still best friends and ran the kids' football on the St
Silas estate. It was like a weight that Barry was forced to carry
round with him. He was like a medieval man sentenced to have
a line of pots and pans tied to his waist and to trail them behind
him wherever he went in his village. The more earnest he tried
to be – the more serious he was about the business of helping to
run Tipper's football teams – the more ridiculous he seemed,
with the rattle of pots and pans dragging in his wake.

Elly Pascoe tried again.

'I was looking for Brindle?'

Barry Catlin emerged from his daydream. He seemed flustered; he wiped his nose with his hand; his voice, when it came,
was too loud.

'He's out with Tipper, love. You need him for something?'

Elly Pascoe instinctively stepped back half a pace as he
shouted the words across Noah's office, then nodded.

Barry was lighting up another cigarette. The air was shiny
with the residue of his smoke. Noah didn't encourage smoking
in his office so Barry brought his own ashtray and vainly tried
to waft all the smoke out of the open window before he left.
There was no way he could get through his office evenings
without smoking. He waved the match vigorously up and down
in an effort to put it out.

'I was trying to sort this Whalley Juniors match out,' he said.
His voice was still loud. It was always loud – somehow slightly
off key. It was something else that made him a comical figure.

'They keep cancelling messing us around they shouldn't be allowed to do it. The league secretary –' he pronounced it secker-terry – 'he ought to stand up to them but he never does so by rights we should have had the points last season when they cancelled.'

He was holding the cigarette in the very tips of his fingers. He drew hard on it, as if for oxygen.

'Is Brindle due back soon?'

Barry pondered, then pushed up one of the big sleeves of his Al Capone suit and looked at his watch. 'Not yet, love, no. He'll be back when he thinks I'm done. You want to sit down and wait? You want a coffee or anything? Noah lets me brew up whenever I want.'

'I don't know where Josh is,' Elly Pascoe said. 'He's disappeared.'

Elly hadn't meant to tell him about Josh. She had only come over to the centre to tell *Noah* that Josh was missing. It was, she supposed, a kind of apology, because even in her distress at Josh having been missing since this morning, she still saw Barry Catlin as a clown and she felt guilty about it. Confessing to him about Josh's disappearance was an attempt to restore a sense of dignity to this man who had done her no damage and meant no harm.

Instead, it made Barry seem even more foolish. It stopped him in his tracks. He didn't know what to say in response. Like a swimmer suddenly aware that he was out of his depth, he froze. He drew on the cigarette again. The silence between them became difficult, and Elly Pascoe regretted making the confession.

'Kids,' she said weakly.

'They're beggars are kids,' Barry Catlin said. He bit his lip as he'd done in Miss Doughty's class forty years ago. In the end, realizing that she was happy simply to wait for Noah, he said, 'Can I do something?'

'Maybe you could go and get Brindle for me,' Elly suggested.

'Yes, I could, I could,' he said, as if he had just hit on the idea himself.

He stood up at Noah's desk, brushing flakes of ash from between the stripes of his lapels. He stubbed the cigarette out in his ashtray and began coaxing Denis Law out from under the desk. He seemed relieved that he had something to do. An errand. A good, simple deed. A Samaritan's task that a serious, grown man might undertake. Barry fastened the lead to the small dog's collar and very lightly stroked its muzzle as if to reassure the animal. And in that moment Elly Pascoe saw the tenderness which had led this man to declare his feelings to Morag Gill.

But when he put his coat on and led the dog out of the centre, the picture of Barry Catlin which Elly Pascoe had in her head was one in which a line of pots and pans were tied to his waist, trailing behind him as he hurried down to the estate on his errand, and in which people hearing his approach smirked to each other and said, 'Aha, that sounds like the clown Barry Catlin coming this way!'

Even playing on the shortened pitch, and letting the kids do most of the running, Noah was out of breath.

The bulldozers had carved their way through the earth as far as the centre circle of Tipper Gill's pitch. The centre circle was the boundary of the land which the Council had sold to the developers.

It was for the matching funding, Morag Gill had told the

members of her tenants group. Each major scheme had to attract funding to match the amount offered by the Regeneration Board. That was why Morag had persuaded the other members of her tenants group to approve the sale of the maisonettes and the land adjacent to them, and why she had wanted to persuade the tenants left in the dilapidated maisonette blocks to move to other properties on the estate.

Morag had explained to the maisonette tenants that they were being offered five hundred pounds each to move out. She went round the maisonettes one by one with Dorothy, explaining the deal that was on offer. Of those who would open the door, some needed convincing. One or two were grateful.

Another part of the Regeneration Board's plan to improve the St Silas estate was the new all-weather football pitch for Tipper Gill's teams to use. But Tipper had become uneasy when Morag had told him that his existing pitch would have to be sacrificed. They had argued, which was rare. They usually coped with disagreements by engineering distance from each other. But Tipper didn't like the idea that he'd lose his own pitch, and part-way through the season at that. Neither did he like the fact that the promised new pitch – the one with the floodlights – wouldn't begin construction for several months yet.

'But we'll have to play the rest of this season's matches away from home,' he said.

Morag wouldn't be swayed. She saw the sale of the maisonette blocks as a chance to get rid of some of the more troublesome tenants who were bound to use their money to leave the estate before they were collared for back rent. She foresaw new people coming to live in the private properties – nice people who would be keen to join the tenants group.

'We don't really *need* floodlights,' Tipper had protested finally, 'or a changing hut. What if they don't build the new pitch? Can't we just keep *our* pitch? Why can't we just call a halt to it?'

'Because we need the land the pitch is on to persuade the developers to get involved. Without the land there's no deal. Anyway, the Regeneration Board promised you can have the new pitch.'

She grew angry with Tipper. She felt he was behaving like a child. She told him he couldn't see the bigger picture. That was the phrase Morag had learned from Councillor Porrit, who chaired the Regeneration Board and who encouraged everyone to see the bigger picture.

Councillor Porrit was a short untidy man with a ginger beard and a withered right arm which he hadn't had full use of since a childhood bout of polio. Some of the other members of the Regeneration Board didn't like him. They saw him as being too abrupt, too plain-spoken. He had a way with sarcasm that came from his days as a full-time union convenor at the ordnance factory. He had cut his union teeth at a time when management were always promising that the latest batch of lay-offs weren't part of some grand asset-stripping plan to close the factory down in stages. People said Councillor Porrit had a chip on his shoulder, but Morag liked him in comparison to the smooth Council officers and business people on the Board, with their good suits and bonhomie.

Councillor Porrit always made a point of talking to Morag in the informal lull before the Regeneration Board meetings began. He told her he'd been born on an estate like St Silas's. He said he knew what it was like trying to improve things from the grass roots. He confided to her that he had grown a beard because it had always been hard for him to shave with only one good arm. Morag shared with Councillor Porrit some of her dreams for the St Silas estate. He nodded solemnly, saying the world needed dreamers. He wondered if she'd ever thought of taking up local politics herself, perhaps standing as a councillor.

For her part, Morag felt an affinity with Councillor Roy Porrit. She saw how he had triumphed over the withered arm which restricted him physically, and she likened this to her own predicament of having Dorothy as a kind of appendage to her life. She watched how Councillor Porrit controlled the meetings of the Regeneration Board, keeping the trustees and their various agendas in order, steering them all towards his own vision of the bigger picture. She began to compare Tipper unfavourably with Roy Porrit. She determined, for Councillor Porrit's sake, to try to see the bigger picture in everything, and she used her vote to side with him whenever he needed help in steering parts of his bigger picture through.

'What do you think?' Morag had finally said to Tipper. 'That Councillor Porrit's doing this just to cheat *you* out of a stupid football pitch?'

The newly deserted blocks of maisonette flats were surrounded by wire-mesh fencing. The compound for the Portakabins and the heavy plant machinery occupied half of what had formerly been Tipper Gill's pitch, and the fencing ran just shy of the halfway line.

Tipper used what was left of the pitch for five-a-side. The security lights from the builders' compound helped to illuminate the remaining portion of the pitch and allowed them to play on longer in the evening. But sometimes the ball flew over the fencing into the compound and someone had to retrieve it by crawling through the hole the lads had cut away in one of the fencing panels. Each time this happened it gave Noah the chance for another breather and to flex his stiffening knee, but when they restarted he was still out of breath. When, finally, Tipper yelled, 'Next goal wins for tonight' across the pitch, Noah offered a silent prayer of thanks.

Tipper – his one good eye staring fixedly at the ball – won possession deep in his own half and started moving forwards, head down. He beat one opponent, then, faced with Noah, decided to outrun him round the outside. Noah, to Tipper's surprise (Noah had given up running two games ago), began to track him back stride for stride, forcing him wide of the goal. Tipper ran wider; Noah went with him. At the last moment Tipper shot, off balance, from an acute angle. Noah dived in to tackle. Tipper's lack of distance judgement let him down and the ball sliced off his foot and ballooned over the fence. Tipper and Noah fell into a heap together, panting. Still lying on his back, Tipper blew for full-time.

'Someone get the fucking ball,' he yelled.

But by the time he and Noah had got to their feet, all the kids were already walking away and Tipper had to find the ball himself. He got stuck coming back through the tiny hole in the fencing and ripped the nylon of his tracksuit top. He stood cussing, trying to unhook himself from the wire. When he got back to the pitch he saw Noah leaning against the goalpost, vomiting, and Barry Catlin walking towards them across the pitch.

'I just did too much,' Noah said, 'that's all. I just feel queasy.'

'You're a pillock for doing it at your age,' Elly Pascoe said, smiling. 'What about your knee?'

'I'll put some ice on it later. It'll be all right.'

242

'You want a cup of tea or some water or something?'

'No, I'll be all right.'

He didn't feel all right. He realized he should have dropped out of the five-a-sides earlier. He was fifty-one, for God's sake. He was on medication. He thought he was going to vomit again. But he couldn't say so to Elly Pascoe who, although she was trying not to show it, was working hard not to panic yet over Josh's disappearance.

Elly had told him Josh had been missing since this morning. She'd rung the school when he hadn't come home but he hadn't been there all day. The school had mentioned Josh's other recent unauthorized absences. Then she had rung any friends of Josh's she could think of ('God knows there are few enough of them nowadays,' she said), but none of them had seen him today or had any inkling where he might be. From what they'd said, it sounded like he hadn't had much to do with any of them lately. One or two of them had said Josh had been acting funny. He'd left no message anywhere, and now it was dark, and just before she'd come down to the centre she'd discovered a sleeping bag and bits of his clothing missing from the flat.

She wasn't frantic yet, but she was moving in small but significant stages towards it. Noah's own bad guts seemed trivial by comparison. Elly had been desperate enough to ring Neville, her ex, to see if Josh might have gone round there during the day. Elly and Neville had argued on the phone. He'd sounded unconcerned. She'd demanded to know what Neville was going to do about their son running away from home. He'd said Josh couldn't be reported missing for twenty-four hours. She'd said didn't he care what happened to Josh? He'd said that was rich coming from her when she'd been the one who had ended the marriage and left Josh with no father. She'd called him pathetic and slammed the phone down.

She told Noah all she did these days was argue. She had been arguing with Josh for weeks. They didn't talk any more, she said. It was just 'Good morning' and then into round one.

'What about?' Noah asked. He felt gaseous, and had started sweating again. He wondered about asking for that glass of water.

'We argue about anything. The favourite one at the moment seems to be Damien Tunney. It's Josh's mock exams in a month and he's always going out instead of revising. It's Damien Tunney's influence, I know. He's into all sorts. Josh told me he does drugs – that was when we were talking. I forget what sort. Sparklers or something. He gets them from that Quigley boy – the brother of that girl you organized the childcare for.'

'Melanie?'

'Yes, her. Her brother works for Ronnie Roots. Someone told me in the shop. When he's not in prison. He gives these sparklers and things to the kids for free to get them into it. Damien Tunney's always hanging round with him. I know – I've seen them myself. So what's he want with Josh? Why can't he just leave my son alone? Josh won't take it seriously when I try to talk to him. He just tells me to *chill*. He just says he's not a child. He says he can handle things. I say, "What things?" He says, "Nothing." Then we start again. That Damien Tunney, I'll kill him if he's anything to do with this. God, if it's drugs, Brindle, I'll die.'

Noah lifted his head. He was going to say, 'No you won't. Josh is too good a lad. He'll turn up.' But he didn't. He felt the swell of his stomach turn like a tide inside him, smelled the air sickly with Barry Catlin's Woodbines. The ground swayed under his planted feet and Noah threw up again right there in his office in front of Elly Pascoe. It was a compulsive, jerking rhythm, clawing the last of his stomach's contents from him. When it was over he felt cold in his bones, aching in the cave of his chest, and miraculously washed back up on dry land.

Elly Pascoe put a hand on his shoulder. He sat there, shivering. Afterwards they both smiled about it. And only when they opened the door of the office did they realize that Barry Catlin had followed Noah back up to the centre. He was smoking in the corridor, waiting with Denis Law to see that everything was all right. He offered to clean up Noah's office. Elly Pascoe said no, she would do it, but Barry could go and get a glass of water from the kitchen downstairs.

Barry fetched a glass of water and stood over Noah.

'Better yet?' he barked after each sip.

When Barry had finally gone home, Noah went outside into the yard. He breathed the cold air and sipped his water while Elly Pascoe finished inside. He felt better. His ship, for now, had stopped rolling. He shook his two evening tablets from the phial in his coat pocket.

They were not for earache. They were for the illness which had been diagnosed last year when Noah had finally gone to see the doctor about his earache. The blood test had picked it up.

It was being treated with courses of tablets; two weeks, then a gap of a week, then two weeks of tablets again. The doctor who had first looked at the test results said that Noah's white-cell count should have been ten. He said it was two hundred and twenty. Noah had asked if it had a name – this thing he had. The doctor said yes, it had a name.

The tablets brought the count down. Sometimes the count

went up, but the tablets brought it down each time. They had so far. Noah had asked about side effects.

'Your hair won't fall out, if that's what you mean,' the doctor said. Noah might get tired now and then. And his libido might suffer. Noah laughed.

'Is that a joke?' the doctor asked.

'Could be.' Noah thought. 'Will I die?'

'We all die,' the doctor said. 'Do you mean are you dying?'

'Yes,' Noah said.

'I've had someone coming to see me for thirteen years who has the same condition you have. There are no hard and fast rules with leukaemia. We'll make you an appointment to have a check-up with the specialist every four months. Do you have someone to tell? Someone you want me to talk to about the condition? Family?'

'I'm an orphan,' Noah said.

No hard and fast rules. That was what his doctor had said. And it was true. You could place your faith in the bigger picture, but it didn't always work out that way – unless you were a Ronnie Roots or a Councillor Porrit and you could shape the world to your design and bugger the people who got in the way, and the consequences.

When Noah had helped to set up the tenants group, it had seemed to be a first small step in a bigger picture. But the Council was deaf to their appeals. Morag and the other women seemed ridiculous, until one of them had the idea of setting up a food co-operative. It was such a simple idea, and, miraculously, it seemed possible that it might work, especially when Noah's innumerable telephone calls resulted in someone being appointed from the district Health Promotion Unit to help the women set up and run the project. The co-ordinator was involved for a number of years, until funding cuts led to the withdrawal of the post and the need for Morag and the others to take responsibility for managing things themselves. It seemed a kind of turning point – St Silas people making a go of things on their own. There was even the promise of a grant from the Council to turn the project into a full-blown community business, with management training for those who were now running it. But only weeks after the women had taken sole charge of the project their entire wholesale purchase of fruit and veg – enough for the one hundred and fifty tenants who were customers of the co-op by now – was stolen. Since there was no sign of a break-in, it was assumed that one of the women had forgotten to lock up the night before. When people arrived at the centre for their grocery order the next day, they had to be turned away empty-handed. The culprits were never found, and the co-op nearly folded.

The article in the *Citizen* reporting the launch of the venture some years before had been two paragraphs. The news of the theft was splashed across the front page. It made the whole thing sound like a shambles. YES WE HAVE NO BANANAS, the headline smirked. The possibility of a Council grant evaporated. People drifted away.

Noah recalled the incident because the feelings of frustration and helplessness he'd had then were returning tonight with the news of Josh's disappearance, seeing Elly Pascoe angry and desperate, and Noah unable to do anything other than listen. While Neville Pascoe and his colleagues were getting ready to scour the moors and to alert their colleagues in the cities, Noah could do nothing but listen to Elly's fears.

Elly Pascoe, fearless till now in Noah's eyes and tempered

within her small and wondrous form by all she had been through, feared the worst. Perhaps that was only natural with your own child, Noah thought. It wasn't something he was qualified to speak about. The expression on her face when she'd been telling him about it said that she had done her utmost – on her own for the most part – and still, in the end, she had failed her son by not protecting him, or protecting him too much.

This was the first time Noah had seen Elly Pascoe frightened, and he was struck by how desperate he was to help her – and by how helpless he was to ease her pain. He had a ridiculous urge to ride out into the hills to search for news of Josh that would bring her solace. To bang on every door he could get to, asking about her son. To drag the driver out of every passing car and demand news of him. *What do you mean, you haven't seen anything? Think, you idiot – think. You must have seen something. A boy hitching with a sleeping bag. Josh! You couldn't miss him.* What else could he do? He could ring bells. He could broadcast an appeal. He could run through the streets and fields of the town for Elly, shouting for the boy, all night, every night, pleading for a sight of Josh's flop of blond hair, his long limbs, his still-unfinished face that was clearly Elly's but not Elly's, until he grew tired, weak, until he sank, inevitably, defeated, into some final muddy field out on the moors.

16

The Truth and the Light

Flo appeared at the door of Mr George's office late one evening. Mr George thought she was ill, or sickening for something. Flo didn't often go looking for Mr George – his ability to see through her when she was trying it on made Flo edgy; his refusal to jump up and down with fury when she did something designed to rile him made *her* mad.

Mr George was doing the accounts – he called it robbing Peter to pay Paul.

'Hello, Flo,' he said.

Flo was shifting her weight from one leg to the other.

'Something the matter? Can I help?' He put his pen down. It was late and Flo should have been in bed but something about the way she looked made him hold back from saying so.

Flo thought. 'Would you make me leave if I did something bad?' she said.

'I thought you *wanted* to leave,' Mr George teased her.

Flo was always telling people that she wanted to leave, but there was nowhere else in the county that would take her after she'd set fire to two orphanages.

'I'm being serious,' Flo said.

'All right. No, I wouldn't make you leave.'

'No, I mean if it was something *really* bad.'

'I still wouldn't make you leave. You want to tell me what's wrong?'

That was when she burst into tears.

It had been several hours since the three boys from the golf club had had sex with her. She'd been too upset to say anything when she had come back. She had thought they were nice boys, she said – grammar-school boys who caddied at the golf club and who, to her amusement, referred to Mr George's orphanage as the Zoo. She'd liked one of them in particular. She'd let him put his hand inside her jumper the week before. He'd been trying to persuade her to have sex with him. And that afternoon they'd been in one of the greenkeeper's sheds on the golf course. Flo had agreed in the end because he'd been a nice boy and because he went to the grammar school, but she'd said he had to wear a rubber and that the other two boys had to go outside. The boy produced a condom and the other two went out. But when he'd finished, the boy tried to persuade her to have sex with the other two as well. Flo had said no. He persisted. Flo refused. They argued. Then the other boys came back into the greenkeeper's shed and had sex with her anyway. She had struggled but they had just laughed at her and said to keep still and she'd enjoy it. Neither of them had used a condom. They had left Flo in the shed afterwards. They told her she was a good shag. They said at least they knew now that the girls who lived at the Zoo were good for *something*.

She cried again. Mr George tried to get her to say who the boys were but she wouldn't.

The real trouble began six weeks later, after it became clear that she had missed her second period.

*

Mr George was still weighing things up when the Diocesan Office, hearing the news of Flo's pregnancy, despatched Mr Fish to the Big House.

'What is the girl's health at present?' Mr Fish asked.

Mr George said that Flo wasn't eating much, that she cried a lot, that she was confused and unhappy.

'The girl's interests are surely best served by sending her to the Bentgate Hostel.'

Mr George shook his head. 'That isn't the way we work with children here. You should know that. If Flo is old enough to have a baby, she's old enough to be part of the discussion about what should happen to her, and what should be done about her pregnancy.'

'Fr Fearon would prefer that the girl was sent there.'

'I don't think Flo is ready for a move just yet,' Mr George said.

'Ready or not,' Mr Fish said, 'in our opinion she needs to go.'

'But she's still very distraught,' Mr George said. 'You know about the circumstances of the conception – that those boys forced themselves on her.'

'That is *her* version. It isn't one we are necessarily convinced of. As I understand it, the girl doesn't dispute the fact that she had intercourse voluntarily, at least with *one* boy. It seems more likely that she invented the incident concerning the other boys out of panic. In any case, all of this only confirms our suspicions that what she needs between now and the birth is the firm guidance and supervision that the Bentgate Hostel can provide.'

'Flo is considering the possibility of a termination,' Mr George said.

'Absolutely not. That is not an option the Diocesan Office can agree to you even discussing with the girl.'

'Why are you so keen to burden the world with another orphan? Flo is fifteen. She can barely take care of herself, let alone a baby. She's an arsonist whose previous institutions couldn't cope with her. And she doesn't even want to have a child.'

'With proper guidance, those things can be attended to.'

'I don't see how being shipped off to a hostel miles from here is going to help anyone, least of all Flo.'

'I ought to warn you that Fr Fearon has sanctioned me to take the girl away with me today if I think that the decision is merited.'

'Merited how?'

'In the best interests of the mother, *and* the child.'

'Flo's in my orphanage, and you're not taking her anywhere,' Mr George said. 'She will stay at the Big House. You tell Fr Fearon that I'll take Flo to look at the Bentgate Hostel myself. If she decides that she might get the help up there that she needs to have the baby, then I'll deliver her to the door myself in a week's time when she's had a while to get used to the idea. In the meantime, she stays here with me.'

The Alvis panted its way up the long hill. The Bentgate Hostel was set back from the open moorland road. The institution was hidden behind a high wall. Flo sat in the passenger seat of the car. She hadn't said anything since she and Mr George had left the Big House.

Flo remained silent as they were taken round the building.

'Why are there bars on the windows?' Mr George asked.

The man leading them round looked at the bars as if he had not seen them before. 'Well it's not a hotel, is it?' he said.

The nun who ran the hostel told Mr George about the regime. 'There is a focus here on education,' she said. 'Many of the girls are sadly lacking in the moral character needed to bring up a child. The hostel sees *that* as a priority. We offer close supervision of the girls at all times, and the staff conduct periodic searches in order to make sure there are no compromising objects in the girls' possession.'

'Such as?' Mr George asked.

'Coathangers, knitting needles, that kind of thing – in case one of our charges is tempted to induce the foetus herself. Occasionally a girl, succumbing to temptation in a moment of madness, will go to ingenious lengths to attempt to terminate her pregnancy before time.'

She ran through the rest of the rules – mealtimes, schooling, nursing care, the rules for escorted travel beyond the walls.

Mr George turned to Flo. 'Is there anything you want to ask, Flo?'

'Why can't we just go outside when we want to?' Flo asked.

The nun looked at her, then turned to Mr George. 'We generally find,' she said to him, 'that allowing a girl out whilst she is carrying can be a disruptive influence.'

'It's a *prison*,' Flo said.

They drove back in silence.

He was doing his late-night rounds that evening when he came across Flo in the scullery leading off Sassy's kitchen. Flo was sitting on the stone floor, rocking back and forth. At each forward roll her head was hitting the brick of the scullery wall. He sat down next to her. Flo carried on rocking. She only stopped hitting her head on the wall when he restrained her and put his arm round her.

'What do you want, Flo?' he whispered.

'There's a way,' she said. 'There's a way you can get rid of it. There are people who'll do it.'

'Are you sure?'

'I want rid,' she said. 'Please.'

He could barely hear her.

A woman answered when he rang.

'Surgery,' she said.

Mr George asked to speak to Dr Carmichael.

'Which one?'

'Are there two?'

'John and Roland. The two brothers run the practice as partners.'

'John,' Mr George said.

'He's seeing a patient at the moment,' the woman replied.

'Can I make an appointment at the surgery?'

'Are you on the doctor's list?'

'No, I'm not. Would you tell him it's George. Littlejohn. It'll be all right, I promise you. Tell him . . . tell him I'm bringing someone with me to see him.'

It was at the next Family Meeting in the Big House that the announcement was made that Flo had been to see a doctor out of town. (Mr George had driven her in the Alvis to Ripon in North Yorkshire.) The doctor had examined Flo and talked to her and had agreed to Flo's request for a termination of her pregnancy.

Mr George explained to the orphans in the Family Meeting what a termination was, and why Flo was going to have one. Flo herself said nothing. She had bundled herself tightly into one of the armchairs and sat biting her nails throughout the meeting. Solomon wandered across the room to get a closer look at Flo.

'How come,' Solomon asked, doing the calculation in his head, 'if Flo is carrying a foetus – how come she's thinner than she was before? Shouldn't she be bigger?'

Mr George explained to Solomon that Flo was poorly. He said that he and Flo would be travelling back to the doctor's (he didn't say where it was) sometime during the next month and that this was when she would have the termination. He asked Flo if she wanted to say anything. She shook her head. Solomon carried on looking at her, but Flo stayed curled up. Over the next few days she seemed to spend most of her time curled up like that in corners of the house. She was waiting for what came next. Everyone was waiting for Fr Fearon's next move.

When the intervention came, it came not from the Diocesan Office but from the Town Council, whose assistance Fr Fearon had enlisted. It came from Alderman Darius Whittle. But by that time Mr George had already slipped Flo away into hiding. Nobody else knew where she was. Nobody else knew that, in order to make sure she was kept out of Darius Whittle's reach, Flo would not be coming back.

Darius had grown heavier in office. It hadn't shown as much in the occasional photograph Mr George had seen of him in the local press over the years. His face was not as narrow or as harried as it had been in Tatlow Street, haunted as it had been by the bear and the tauntings of the weavers. These days, Darius looked distinctly well fed. His suit was expensively cut and he no longer smelled of fish. His eyes, though, retained their old quick and curious sense of suspicion.

His story was a well-known one in the town – how he had entered Town Hall politics on the back of the success of his wholesale fish business in Tatlow's Mill, and had courted the daughter of a prominent town councillor with whom he had business dealings. It was Darius, Mr George knew, whose first act as a youthful Chairman of the Transport Committee had been to shut down the town's much lamented tram service as part of a struggle for power between competing Town Hall factions. Five years later Darius was in control of the key Finance and Planning Committee. The Town Hall was his. He was also a rich man.

It was hardly a secret that Darius Whittle had made much of his money on the back of his Council connections. His major coup had been signing the Council contracts to have clusters of high-rise flats built in the town by the firm part-owned by his own father-in-law and his wife. It was around that time that he had also bought his way on to the golf-club committee with the promise of finding a way to secure Dounleavey's old place for them to convert into their new clubhouse. It was Darius, people said, who had brokered the bribe offered to Mr George for the sale of the Big House and its grounds to the golf club, and who had then skilfully deflected the allegations when they limped out into the open.

They met in the garden of the Big House. Darius's chauffeur sat waiting in the municipal limousine parked in the drive. The two men sat on adjacent benches. Each waited a while for the other to speak first. Finally, Mr George broke the silence.

'You've done well for yourself I hear, Darius.'

There was a short pause. 'Since you fished me out of the river behind Tatlow Street?' Darius suggested, without a hint of irony in his voice. 'I've worked hard. I've done well. Better than that football team of yours.' Accrington Stanley, as ever, were languishing at the foot of the Fourth Division.

'May I ask you a question before we begin?'

Darius nodded.

'Are you here as Alderman Whittle, or as a member of the golf-club committee, or as a property developer, or perhaps as a member of the Child Welfare Board? Or perhaps this is just a social visit to chat about old times?'

'Think of me, for today, just as Darius,' he said. 'I always felt that we understood each other, you and I. Even in those distant Tatlow Street days. I always felt we wanted, more or less, the same thing.'

'The same thing?' Mr George said.

'Of course. You simply got there before me. I was just a later starter – just an orphan smelling stubbornly of fish. But I only ever wanted to be like you; to have influence over other people – authority.'

'If you can't see a difference between us after all this time, Darius, then you're dafter than I thought.'

Darius seemed to give the matter some thought. 'You remember,' he said, after a pause, 'when I was a boy – not much more than a boy – how I used to work with wood in Tatlow's Mill in the evenings?'

'You used to carve those figures from roof beams and barge posts,' Mr George said. 'They were astonishing. You had a real talent.'

Darius seemed to take no pleasure from Mr George's assessment of his craft. 'I wasn't sure,' he went on, 'why I was drawn to do such a thing at first – until I started watching you and I realized that what I wanted was to be like you. I wanted an army of people of my own to do my bidding, to respect me, just like that rag-bag army on Tatlow Street respected you. After you arrived – after you started your work on Tatlow Street – I started to realize that I wanted all those wooden saints I'd carved to be *my* men just as you had yours. I did it so that I could be someone like you.'

'But you're not like me, Darius. You would hate being like me. Look at the things you couldn't have in order to be me – no life of your own, no privacy, no family. You're not like me. You have a choice. You can be who you *want* to be.'

'That's the thing,' Darius said, shaking his head. 'It's not that simple. You can't. Once you set things in motion, you can't stop them. You shouldn't try. Do you think perhaps that's what fate is? Do you think I was fated to bring you down?' He shrugged, as if he was tired of trying to work it out. 'I didn't know,' he went on matter-of-factly, 'until last week, that you had no teaching certificate.'

'I always wondered when *that* would catch up with me,' Mr George said. He seemed unsurprised at Darius's discovery. 'My father was never up to teaching but there were so many relief teachers around at that time – schools muddling through with whatever help they could get – and there was no one to question who "Lawrence Littlejohn" was. People just assumed, when I started teaching the class, that Lawrence was my middle name – that it was my certificate.

'I could have trained, but there was never the time. There was always so much work to be done; so many orphans no one else wanted to deal with. Is that what this is about, Darius? You're going to try to get me to hand Flo over to you by holding the teaching certificate over my head? If I surrender Flo to you, you'll keep quiet about my not having a certificate? Let me carry on running this place and teaching my orphans here?'

'That was the original idea.'

'It wouldn't work, Darius. You must know that. You know I'd come after you if you did that. I'd make an issue of your business dealings, your perks on the side, your methods. That tactic you tried when your golf-club buddies wanted to get their hands on the Big House – you've probably tried the same kind of thing with others. I'd find those people. I'd listen to them. I'd use it.'

'Exactly,' Darius said flatly. 'You see, we are so much alike, you and I. And then I'd have to up the stakes by making a big issue of the rights of the unborn child, of the abortion you would have allowed the girl to have – and turn *that* into the crusade. I'd have to turn *you* into the monster, and then it would get so messy.'

'You'd do that?' Mr George said.

'Of course,' Darius shrugged, 'if there wasn't any other way. But I won't need to. I anticipated that. That's my job – to anticipate things before they happen. You're fighting on *my* territory now. You think I'd stop at a measly teaching certificate? As I said, you can't stop these things once they start.'

'But you *can* stop them, Darius. Leave the girl alone. Let her have the termination. She was raped for God's sake.'

Darius shook his head. 'Events have their own momentum. I told my people, "You have to understand the kind of person you're dealing with here. This man isn't like the rest of them." So they listened. They all listen these days. They are all my men these days. I carved them all. They owe me allegiance. That's why I have to keep winning. If I don't, their allegiance to me will be lost. That's what I mean about the momentum of events. I said, "You have to find something on him that means he can't possibly fight back, because he'll be dangerous now unless you do."'

'I know you had us followed to Ripon when I took Flo there,' Mr George interjected. 'And I know you had somebody sent to snoop around asking questions over there. I know you know about Ripon.'

'Not Ripon,' Darius said. 'Though it was Ripon that led me to it. If you hadn't gone to Ripon, we would never have come across the doctor. Small towns are terrible that way. You know that, of course. No matter how hard you try, you can't keep secrets for ever in a small town. There's always someone who's heard something they shouldn't. That's how we found out about the doctor. That's what persuaded me to dig further. Not Ripon. Annan.'

Mr George looked sharply at Darius.

'I know about Annan,' Darius said. 'I know what happened before you first came here, before you got on that train and met Dounleavey and set yourself up in Tatlow's Mill. I know *why* you came here. That's the advantage of having all those people who owe you allegiance. You send them off to look for things and they dig and dig like squirrels until you tell them to stop.'

He said it without a trace of victory in his voice. 'There *is* a difference between the two of us,' Darius said. 'In your position, I would never have taken the risk of going to Ripon. I would have sacrificed the girl before I did that. I would have sent her off to the hostel to have her bastard child and have it put in St Brendan's, out of the way, to safeguard the rest of what I had.'

'What do you want, Darius?'

'I know you won't pursue me now. I know you can't. Now at least we can concentrate on the girl.'

'All this, Darius, for one girl?'

'Funny,' Darius Whittle said, watching Mr George intensely

with those scrupulous eyes, 'I was going to ask you the same thing.'

It was Rachel who eventually went to see Mr George in his office later that evening. Rachel was due to move out of the Big House. She had been offered a job in a school for the deaf in London. It was her dream. The place was famous, even abroad. Rachel had beaten off over eighty other candidates for the post, and the fact that she was leaving soon suggested to the others that she would be the best person to talk to Mr George about Darius Whittle.

Mr George was sitting in his chair when she went in. She signed to him that she had been nominated by the others to find out what Darius had said. He seemed pleased to see her. He asked her to sit down and, for a while, he didn't speak. Finally he said he had a story to tell her. He said he thought it was about the right time anyway, and so, in Rachel's twentieth year, he told her how he had come to arrive in Lancashire with so little money, and a single cardboard suitcase, in search of a life to begin here.

'There was once a young man,' he said, 'who, growing up, fell in love. It came as a surprise to him that someone might fall back in love with him. He was used to being set apart because of things his father had done which had earned them both the dis-approbation of the small town in which they lived. He wasn't used to feeling as if he *belonged* anywhere, and love is nothing if not a sense of belonging. He had never expected love, in the same way that he'd never expected to belong.

'He nursed his father; he took up an apprenticeship as a carpenter and joiner; he prayed to God to help him understand the world a little better than he did, and he began to help out in the

Sunday school run by his local Church. The object of his love helped out at the same Sunday school; was gentle and kind; a little younger than him; made the earth stop spinning on its axis and hold its ancient evening breath when they were together; made him laugh; came from a well-respected family in the town; had ambitions to be a doctor; was twenty when the family found out.

'The Carmichaels were reluctant to have the other man arrested because they feared that John Carmichael would be implicated. They didn't want to jeopardize his future career as a doctor. His father was a doctor, and his uncle was a surgeon. They saw the carpenter as the villain who had led John Carmichael astray. They regarded it as a disease, something that could be cured providing they could keep the other man away from him. The carpenter thought of it only as love. He was astonished at the anger it unleashed – the vitriol; then frightened. It was impossible afterwards to explain how it felt – the sense that he was so different he could never again belong anywhere.

'An ultimatum was given to the carpenter to go and find work in another town. When the two men were caught talking together for one last time, the carpenter was given a ferocious beating. He was told that the next time it would be his father who would get it.'

'What did they do?' Rachel signed.

Mr George turned round and lifted his shirt up for Rachel to see, and she saw the marks on his back – the stigmata that Goose had seen before the war. She saw how the angry purple welts – several inches long – were raised up from the skin.

'They used their belts for the whipping, tying him down to do it. He was unconscious when they finished. It was in the

262

days before antibiotics, and the wounds turned septic. He was sick for a long time. When he had recovered enough, he packed a case and told his father he'd send for him when he had found a job and somewhere for them both to live. Every so often the marks flared up and became inflamed again and started itching. He would scratch them. Sometimes they bled; he had to rub ointment on them and sleep without a shirt.

'He was told that if he tried to contact John Carmichael again, they would have him put into prison. He told himself it wasn't this he was frightened of – it was what would happen to Uncle Rolly and what might happen to John Carmichael. So he left John Carmichael to make his own life. It was John who was posted to Warton airbase in Lancashire during the war and found Mr George. He would come round to Tatlow's Mill in his RAF uniform and they would talk. It was John Carmichael who helped Dunkiss find a way into the services at the age of thirty-three, and who signed up Tom Travis for his Founder's Day aerobatic displays. But when the war ended, so did their fleeting contact. It was too much to risk – for both of them. John Carmichael set up in his own medical practice, and Mr George refocused his energies on his work with the orphans in the Big House bequeathed to him by Dounleavey. He didn't see John Carmichael again until he had no choice but to see him for Flo's sake.

'I'm going to resign as director of the orphanage,' Mr George said to Rachel. 'It's the only way I can ensure that the Big House will continue to stay open. I can't risk fighting Darius. He was right about that. And I can't risk John being dragged into this. He could lose his practice, his livelihood. What chance has a homosexual doctor of keeping his practice if it comes out into the open? If I resign, Darius shouldn't be able to touch the Big House. I don't think he will. He'll just claim my resignation as the victory he wants.'

'You can't resign,' Rachel signed. 'You shouldn't resign. You haven't done anything wrong.'

'If I stay, I'll be painted as a moral danger to the children,' Mr George said. 'Fr Fearon and the rest of them will have a field day when they know the truth. A fag teaching boys how to masturbate – that's what they'll say.'

'But you *can't* go.'

'Why not?'

'Because. Because – what about your father, and Sassy? What about Sassy? What will *she* do?'

'What about Sassy?'

'You know what about her. She's in love with you.'

'Sassy? No, no. Sassy loves her children here.'

'Sassy loves you, you know perfectly well. She always has. That's why she's stayed all these years. You know that. Stay, for her sake – and if you have to go, let her go too. Talk to her. Tell her she's free to go. She has no other life except for the Big House, and you.'

'I'm going, Rachel. And alone. It's the one way I can ensure the work I started can be completed. Sassy ought to stay with the children until things are finished here.'

'But without you,' Rachel signed, 'there'll be no one to run the Big House. Not when I take up my post in London.'

Mr George took Rachel's hands in his. 'I've thought about that. There's only one solution, Rachel. *You* have to keep it going. I can't have outsiders coming in finishing my work. They wouldn't understand. Sassy will stay but she can't run the place. Uncle Rolly's too old.'

'But my job in London?' she signed. 'I'm meant to start next month. They're waiting for me. I want to go. Why not admit defeat and close the Big House if Darius has you so beaten.'

'Because that's not what's *meant* to happen. The Big House is the purpose of my life. Now it must be the purpose of yours, Rachel, or else we have both failed – everything we've worked for will have failed. There isn't a choice. You must turn down your job. There will be time for other things. It's the Big House that needs you most now. *You* will keep it going for me, Rachel, when I've gone – you and Sassy. You will finish things for me. Besides, someone has to stay and cheer Accrington Stanley through their latest crisis.' He smiled.

'But what if I was meant to work in London?' Rachel insisted.

Mr George shook his head slowly. 'I think this is the reason you were allowed to survive the air raid in the war. This is why I was allowed to rescue you – so that you could take over now and keep safe everything I've worked for. And I'll come back and visit – on Founder's Day.'

Rachel thought for a long time. 'I'll stay,' she signed finally. 'But you have to let Sassy go or else she'll just spend her life waiting for you to come back. Without you, there's nothing for her here. Tell her she *has* to go, or she never will.'

Several weeks later Rachel met him in the porch of the Big House after supper one night. It was dark. Rain was sweeping in from beyond the ship's bulk of Pendle Hill down the valley, and yet he seemed set on going out.

Two weeks had passed since Mr George had written to the Diocesan Office confirming his intention to stand down. All the children knew by then. Mr George had told them at the

Family Meeting that he was going to retire. He told them it was because of his health. He said it was his heart. He said his heart wasn't so good any more.

'Is it breaking?' Solomon had asked. Solomon was ten years old. He was chairing his first Family Meeting.

'Yes, Solomon,' Mr George had said. 'It is breaking. That's why I have to rest it.'

The gearbox of the Alvis had finally seized up after the long drive (twice) into Yorkshire and back, so Mr George walked the mile from the house in the rain. The car was parked in a lay-by on the main road. The windows were misted with condensation from the wetness of the evening and the car's heater. There was a man sitting in the back of the car and a driver in the front. The driver, uniformed and with a peaked cap, was staring out of the rain-smeared windscreen as if he was weary of waiting but dare not show it. Mr George opened the rear door of the Council Mercedes and came face to face with Darius Whittle.

He climbed in and dried himself as best he could with his handkerchief. He settled himself.

'I gather,' Darius said after a moment, 'you've written to the Diocesan Office telling them of your intention to resign.'

Mr George nodded.

'Has the girl had her termination yet?'

'Sometime last week,' Mr George said. 'I gather Flo is well. She's in good hands.'

Darius thought. There was a pause until he said, 'I have a proposition. I want you to consider having it all back.'

'Having what back?'

'You can have everything back. You can go on as before; the orphanage, the stipend, new orphans being sent to you. That's what you want, isn't it? To be able to keep changing the world your way. Just like I change it my way. You've demonstrated that you were prepared to go to the very brink, but you must see that to drag this thing out any further would only be a waste of your particular talents. And if the orphanage fell apart without you I'd have an institution full of unplaceable children.'

'It's too late now, Darius. It's over. You know too much and you will use it.'

'What's fixed can be unfixed. You shouldn't be so arrogant as to think you are the only man around here who can perform feats of magic.'

Darius – his offer made – leaned towards Mr George in the back seat of the Mercedes. He held out his hand, like a sailor offering to pull a drowning man from the sea, his eyes shining with exhilaration. But in the front seat the eyes of the driver were still glazed and unseeing (perhaps through fatigue, perhaps through the tedium of having seen this kind of thing acted out many times before), like the dull, unseeing eyes of the wooden saints Darius Whittle had once spent his nights carving in the second-floor carding room of a now demolished mill.

Goose was assigned to drive him down to the railway station in the patched-up Alvis on the day he left. As the car coughed into gear in the yard, no one knew for sure whether or when he would return. Hindsight, of course, is easy. In hindsight it was clear he would not come back. There were already unsubstantiated rumours circulating in the town that Mr George from the orphanage was a fag, that he was bent as a nine-bob note. People were already wondering whether he'd *done it* to the orphans. They were already starting to look at Mr George's orphans differently – scrutinizing them more, leaving looks hanging there for them to see. Letting it leak out like that seemed to be Darius Whittle's final act of revenge on Mr George – because he hadn't agreed to stay and run the orphanage on Darius's terms.

All the children believed he'd be back in time for Founder's Day. That was why no one cried as he made his way across the yard, carrying his case to the waiting car. All of them believed he would be coming back – when his heart was better. That's how he'd planned it. It was another lie. It was what the world did to people. It made men lie. It conspired to make them less than they were. And so he left, driven away to the station by Goose in the patched-up Alvis, with a cardboard suitcase and a little change in his pocket.

'Did he talk to you about what *you* will do?' Rachel signed to Sassy. 'About perhaps starting afresh somewhere?'

Sassy nodded. 'He told me he's coming back,' she said. 'I said I'd stay and help you. I said I'd wait for him.'

Other things came to fill the lives of those he left behind in the Big House – Gifford's passion for the space race; Megan's support for the Ban the Bomb campaign and for any other underdog's cause that she could liken to her own disenfranchising epilepsy; Uncle Rolly's night-time terrors which – as he grew into his eighties – returned to haunt him after dark and shot him nightly in the heart; the quirky jazz tunes Rachel had been introduced to during her teacher training and had fallen in love with; and, three months after Mr George's departure, the arrival of a young man called Noah – with a bag on his shoulder and a note in his jacket pocket from Rachel saying, 'I can't run this place *alone*, Noah – it's beyond me. Help me, please.'

Rachel had met him at the college where she had worked

towards her teaching certificate. They were the only two orphans in the year's intake. Noah was the only other student who could sign and could therefore speak out for Rachel if the cause arose. When he knew her well enough, he told her about the regime he had endured in the institution he had been brought up in. He struck her as being like a cork, submerged a thousand times but always rising stubbornly to the surface without fully understanding why. Rachel was the only one who did not see Noah's orphan's stutter as an insurmountable obstacle, standing in the way of his wish to teach. She was the one who saw past the stutter and admired the shy, intuitive, resolute soul obscured by it.

'Have faith,' she had written down, offering him her older-than-her-years smile, and somehow this had seemed sufficient to him. In turn, she communicated easily with Noah about her dream of working in a specialist school for the deaf – in a silent world unencumbered by speech. Noah was happy to watch her fast hands signing words; she seemed to him to be someone who might quietly climb from the rubble of any conflagration.

What they finally recognized in each other was the survivor whose heart had not soured. After that, everything was easy. When Noah responded to Rachel's invitation and arrived at the Big House to help her manage the place, he was already familiar with her tales of Mr George and the founding of his remarkable orphanage. He already knew of the bizarre menagerie of children it had nurtured, of Uncle Rolly's night-time screams, of Goose talking to trees, of Dounleavey's place, of Founder's Day, of the bell in the bell tower which Dublin had rung at the start of each day, and the lamp which had lit the way for lost and wandering bears. And finally Noah recognized it all – it was the world he had risen up towards each time his head had been forced under the water and he had fought his way back, choking, almost dying, to the surface.

At first, the little ones frequently asked when Mr George was coming back. At first, Sassy hurried to catch the morning post in case there was news from him. Still dreamy from fighting Uncle Rolly's dragons with him the night before, her heart would leap a little if the telephone rang, always secretly thinking it might be Mr George. But it never was. Slowly, Sassy's heart leaped a little less and she learned to seem more casual when the phone rang. In time, she stopped hurrying for the post and waited for one of the children to take it to the office which was Rachel's and Noah's now.

It was during this time that Rachel showed the remaining orphans how to whisper to Mr George; that she taught them how to write him notes and leave them in places that were special to them. 'That's what you do,' she signed, 'when you need to say things to people who aren't coming back, when you cannot simply shout but when you need that person to hear.'

When Founder's Day rolled round each August and Tom Travis brought his Tiger Moth, they would ask if *he* had heard anything of Mr George. He would shrug. He said he'd had a couple of postcards in the early days, but nothing since, not even when Uncle Rolly finally passed away. Ironically, after all the years of torment from his dreams, he had died peacefully in his sleep, free at last from the fear that the guards might once more be coming for him. It was Noah who stammered his way through the eulogy.

That year, Gifford had Apollo space missions on his mind; that year, Rachel had her first set of poems published by a small northern press and dedicated them to Uncle Rolly; and that year the ramshackle state of the Big House finally began to threaten their continued existence.

Six years of neglect after Dounleavey had abandoned it, and more than twenty years of orphans crashing about the place, had taken their toll. The stipend Mr George had received from the Diocesan Office to pay for the building's upkeep was now gone, and Mr George had left no clue as to how to compensate for its loss. To Rachel's growing despair they now found that they couldn't even afford to patch things up, let alone undertake the major work that was needed on the roof, the wiring and the dry rot. No matter how earnestly they saved or how hard they worked – and Rachel and Noah worked every day until they dropped – it was not enough. Like Accrington Stanley in their final fatal season when their gate receipts were falling and their costs were mounting, the Big House was living on borrowed time. Their only hope was to stay afloat just long enough to see the majority of the orphans through their stay.

The orphanage was quieter than it had been in Mr George's time, and not solely because of the loss of the abrasive Flo who, after her abortion, had finished her education with foster parents in Yorkshire. Uncle Rolly and his night-time dreams were also gone; Goose was getting older and quieter; and Sassy seemed less connected to the outside world than ever. Mr George had promised he would come back for her (Sassy still insisted on laying a place for him each mealtime at the long table in the kitchen) but he had not. As his promise faded, so Sassy became of less use to Rachel and Noah in helping to manage the orphanage, more insistent that things be done as they always had been in the old days, more prone to moods if they weren't, more confined to her spartan room as the effort of believing in Mr George's return slowly sapped her of the strength to live in the real world. There were also fewer orphans in the Big House since the Town Hall had ceased making referrals to the orphanage. Those who were still there formed part of Rachel's now silently animated classroom, signing back to Rachel with their hands – a teaching technique she had hit upon by accident as a way of ensuring that everyone in her difficult and demanding class got a turn to speak.

In the afternoons, Noah worked with individual orphans, painstakingly teasing out the shrapnel of their fears and torments like shards from old wounds. As he worked he'd hear Rachel's music floating round the house. Miles Davis and Duke Ellington drifted out into the hallway from the empty classroom where she was marking books, or working on a poem she was shaping. This was her voice. These tunes, and the poetry, were her way of communicating how she felt when scribbled notes would not suffice.

When the business of keeping the Big House going became too much, when Rachel resented it or felt its weight bending her, she played bleak Thelonius Monk laments. 'I am twenty-seven and I am old and worn out,' she once signed to Noah, slapping her palms down on the table in front of her in frustration. 'This was *my* life – he had no *right* to take it from me.' When she needed a sense of escape, or wanted to be lifted from the gloom, she played astonishing Louis Armstrong rags or Charlie Parker solos so loud they could be heard two storeys up in the boys' dormitory. The first time Noah kissed her – suddenly, breathtakingly, unexpectedly – Louis was playing a miraculous solo on 'Potato Head Blues'.

Rachel said the music was appropriate for the Big House. Louis Armstrong, she pointed out, was raised in a coloured-waifs' orphanage; Duke Ellington never lived in a home and spent his entire adult life in hotel rooms; Miles Davis was a heroin addict, so were all his band; Thelonius Monk went a little mad; Lester Young, conscripted, was court-martialled and imprisoned and in the end drank himself to death; Charlie Parker was committed to an asylum as a young man and when he died in his early thirties he was so raddled with drink and drugs the doctor completing the death certificate guessed his age to be sixty.

This was why Rachel called it the music of the dispossessed. Long after the Big House finally closed, whenever Noah heard jazz tunes being played, he'd close his eyes and see the Big House inside his head, and the last of Mr George's dispossessed, resilient orphans fighting their demons. Jazz was genius born of suffering, Rachel taught him, created by black men in a country that was not quite theirs. It reminded Noah of the way in which Rachel – thinking of his stutter and the reticence of his life until he had found his place alongside her – had once described *him*: as a man passing through a country that was not quite his. The Big House, Noah had felt moved to confess to her, was the first place in his life where he felt he belonged in any meaningful way, and she had leaned across and kissed his forehead gently after this confession. And so it was that strange, insistent tunes which people couldn't quite catch, but which haunted them in their intensity, painted the colours of silent Rachel's moods in Dounleavey's old place as she and Noah struggled to complete the work that the long gone Mr George had set her.

17

The Meaning of the Blues

Janice had become worse when Barry was made redundant, though exactly what it was that she suffered from and how she might get better remained a mystery to him.

Barry's redundancy came at a bad time. Janice had just given birth to their youngest and money was tight. She put on weight. She started objecting to Barry going out all the time, meddling with his stupid football. The other kids were playing up. The doctor told Barry she was just having a blue period. 'Just try to buck her up,' he said.

Barry came home one day with a medicinal tonic he'd bought from the chemist.

'What's this for?' she asked.

'It's for you,' Barry said. 'To make you feel better.'

'I don't want *this*,' she said. He remembered her pouring it down the sink in front of him.

'I could have taken it back,' he said. She threw the plastic bottle at him and went back into the living room.

She started walking out of the house at odd times, leaving the baby alone. Social Services took an interest for a while, but she would never have done anything to harm the baby. It was as though she had forgotten for a while that she *had* the child. She always came back.

She would walk up the high street – 24-Hour Taxis, Ear Piercing, Fiesta Spares – past the Mustard Seed Centre, to the nice shops, pushing the baby in the pram with the two youngest children walking beside her. There was a red dress in one of the shop windows. It was a size ten, and expensive, and it wouldn't have fitted Janice anyway who, after so many pregnancies, had filled out to a size sixteen, but she would stand outside the shop, looking at the dress in the window until one or other of the kids would start to whine.

She told Barry about the dress.

'We can't afford it,' Barry told her. They already owed one of Ronnie Roots's collectors money they'd borrowed for the kids' Christmas presents the year before. 'Besides, it wouldn't fit you.'

'It would give me something to *aim* for,' Janice said as if he were stupid not to see this.

Barry ruminated on the business of the dress.

In the end, he realized that he would have to commit a robbery. It was the only way he would be able to afford the dress. He couldn't just rob the shop, because people would see Janice wearing the stolen dress. Fiddling the football club's petty cash and doctoring the accounts was unthinkable, and he couldn't get himself another job to pay for the dress because there were only part-time jobs going and his benefits would be reduced accordingly. Nor did he want Tipper involved. Tipper would only take charge. It would become Tipper's plan and he didn't want that. It had to be a robbery. Something easy. Something he could manage on his own. Somewhere he had knowledge of the layout.

That was how he'd first hit on the idea of robbing the food co-operative. Janice had never felt up to getting involved in the project but Morag was. Barry spent a lot of time up at the centre; he knew how the co-operative worked; he knew the Mustard Seed wasn't alarmed; and he knew where Morag Gill kept her keys.

It was a simple idea. He would sell the produce himself. He would make enough money from selling one week's bulk-buy to get Janice her dress, and that way he would make things all right.

When he entered the centre using Morag's keys sometime after midnight, Barry found twenty-five pounds in the change box, to be used as the cash float the following morning, and three hundredweight of fresh fruit and veg ready to be bagged into orders by the volunteers.

The amount of produce took him by surprise. He hadn't expected there to be this much. It took him more than four hours to wheel barrowloads of the fresh produce out of the Mustard Seed, across the estate and into his backyard shed. What was left, he stored in the empty house next door.

After a couple of hours, and fourteen or fifteen journeys with the barrow, it became a kind of penance. His back hurt so much that he couldn't straighten up, and a line of pain ran up from his lower vertebrae into the base of his skull.

When he had finished he slept for twelve hours and woke up when it was dark again. Janice thought he was sickening for something. She said it was the drenching he'd got at the football over the weekend. She said it was his own fault. In the middle of the night, Barry moved all the fruit and veg into the attic so that none of the kids would stumble across it. The following day he began plotting who he could sell it to. But by that time, everyone on the estate was talking about the food co-op having been robbed and he realized he wouldn't be able to sell any of it to tenants on the estate.

Over the next few days he went round to every greengrocer in the district. Some refused outright.

'What do you think my normal suppliers are going to say, dickhead, when I tell them to take a hike for a fortnight and then go grovelling back to them?'

One or two greengrocers agreed to take some of the fruit Barry had stolen but changed their minds when they saw the deteriorating condition of the specimen batch Barry had brought along.

'It's just a bit bruised,' Barry protested.

'Of course it's bruised. Who's going to buy bruised?'

The produce began to go off and still Barry couldn't sell it. The fruit rotted first. The sacks of apples and crates of oranges began to sour. The bunches of bananas went black. The twenty pounds of mushrooms and the stacks of cucumbers shrivelled. The softer fruit – the mangos and imported grapes and South African pears and strawberries – began to darken and grow fur. Then the vegetables began to go off. Janice said she felt nauseous. She asked if they had a gas leak.

'It smells like turds,' the kids said gleefully.

'It could be mice,' Barry said.

In the end, he was forced to go up into the attic in the middle of the night again and scoop the putrid mess into dozens of carrier bags and, having got it downstairs, to wheelbarrow it out into the front garden. He had spent the previous day digging a hole three feet down and eight feet across in order to dispose of the evidence. He told Janice he was checking for a gas leak. He shovelled the three hundredweight of rotting fruit and veg into the hole and covered it over with topsoil. With the leftover soil he made a rockery by the fence and had to spend a tenner of the co-op's petty cash on trays of pansies and trailing ivy to decorate it.

Janice had no sympathy for his condition. 'I said all this running around for Tipper wouldn't do you any good,' she said.

He had an urge in the weeks that followed to tell someone about the robbery. But Tipper would have been miffed that Barry had kept him out of it, and he couldn't tell Noah because it was Noah's centre he'd stolen all the produce from. Morag Gill would have been the person he would have liked to confess to, but by that time Barry had already made the pass at her on Tipper's settee, and so a confession to Morag wasn't possible.

Instead he slept with Melanie Quigley, because Melanie sometimes slept with men for money. Barry paid her with the rest of the petty cash he'd taken from the centre. It wasn't so much for the sex that he did it. It just seemed like something he had to do – a kind of achievement after the failure of the robbery. It was like the pass he had made at Morag Gill. *That* hadn't simply been for the sex, either, although since the baby's birth his sex life with Janice had become virtually non-existent.

The idea of sleeping with Melanie came to him after he found the magazines. At the time, Barry was making an effort to keep busy as a way of keeping his guilt at bay: he made sure he was back home for the kids after school; he was sympathetic to Janice's various ailments; he tried to keep on top of the housekeeping, even in Shaun's bedroom. Shaun was his eldest son, and refused to do any kind of cleaning or tidying of his room.

That was when Barry found the magazines. It occurred to

him that it was odd he hadn't noticed them sooner, since there were so many that Shaun's mattress arched in the middle. There were some in the wardrobe in a couple of cardboard boxes, along with a collection of videos, and more in a suitcase on top of the wardrobe. A lot of the magazines were German and Dutch. Barry had never seen magazines like this for sale in the shops. He realized they'd come in the post when he found brown envelopes with foreign postmarks at the bottom of the suitcase. Shaun had a locked drawer in his bedside cabinet, but Barry didn't bother looking for the key to it; he guessed there were just more magazines inside.

He took a couple of the magazines out of Shaun's room; ones with ordinary sex in them, with only people – group sex. The first one had three girls and a man photographed outdoors on a barge. The other magazine had photographs set in a women's prison, featuring female guards and inmates having sex. Barry hid them in his shed, and when Janice had gone to bed he brought them in and looked through them and masturbated. But when he'd finished and wiped himself clean, and carried on flicking through the pages, he felt uneasy; he felt the pictures were mocking him. It was as if the people being photographed were taunting him because he couldn't manage real sex with a real woman any more, just as he couldn't manage a real robbery to pay for a red dress, or make his real wife happy, or keep a real job. He put the magazines aside and rooted out his Charlie Buchan football annuals. But the feeling stayed with him. That was when he decided he would buy real sex with a real woman.

He wasn't brave enough to approach a stranger – he had never been to a prostitute before – so he had to pick one he knew. Plenty of people knew about Melanie. It was Tipper who'd told him. She wasn't a pro, but she did it for money when she was short, when her brother was living with her and cadging off her, or when the child needed something.

Barry had heard somewhere that, afterwards, men were usually filled with self-loathing. Seeing a prostitute apparently had that kind of effect. But Barry felt elated. It wasn't the sex – it was daring to have done it. It was pulling it off. It was a small victory for him – for Barry Catlin.

Sex with Janice was largely a matter of routine. There were no frills; there never had been. Neither of them had had the courage to risk asking for anything new or different over the years. But the magazines Barry had been looking at persuaded him to ask Melanie for something other than the straightforward missionary position. When he'd paid her the fifteen pounds, he asked if she did anything else. At first she'd been worried about what he meant.

'My brother's coming back in half an hour,' she said.

Barry got flustered. He told her he wasn't a weirdo. He tried to tell her how the situation had come about – why he was paying for sex with her, about Janice, and Shaun, his eldest, though not about the robbery. He told her he had shaved and had a bath. She shrugged, then smiled – a small, tight smile. She understood. She found him funny. She put her finger to her lips to make him stop talking.

It was easier after that. She told him where to stand. Then she flicked her pumps away and took off her jeans and knickers. She could easily have been his daughter because of the age gap, but she wasn't. It didn't make it dirty, just different. He thought if she'd been more obviously *grown up* he might have been too cowed to sustain a hard-on or to go through with it. He thought she was lovely. She'd washed her hair that morning and he could smell the cleanness, and had grown hard already at the thought of the sex. She told him to take his pants off. She took a condom out and rolled it over his hard-on. Then she climbed matter-of-factly on to the bed and positioned herself in front of him on all fours with the white cheeks of her bum facing him and, looking round, she guided him into her.

He didn't feel the need again. Shortly afterwards he took the security job, even though his benefits were cut accordingly, and Janice asked him what the point was. He liked the job, and the uniform. Some of the girls on the checkouts reminded him of Melanie, but although he enjoyed slyly watching the slight swish of their breasts under their tabards as they walked by, and the way they flicked their hair back contemptuously, he didn't have any urge to have sex with them, even if he didn't have to pay.

Barry didn't tell Tipper that he'd had sex with a prostitute. Sometimes he was tempted, because his friendship with Tipper was like that. But what happened with Melanie was something he kept to himself. After that, it was easier to cope with his wife's sarcasm and all but the darkest of her moods. The thought he carried round inside him of Melanie – white legs, vague smile glancing back, small round bottom – put him out of Janice's reach.

He saw Melanie now and then on the estate in her parka, pushing her toddler to the nursery. Sometimes she would acknowledge him, sometimes not. He wished he could ask her how things were, but he knew that he couldn't. He had an urge to call round for an occasional cup of tea, to smell her washed hair, to put his head in her lap.

After he'd filled in the hole in the front garden Barry had regrassed it. But every now and then strange seedlings grew between the grass stalks and pushed their way through the clusters of rockery pansies. If he did nothing then within a few days these seedlings would begin to resemble the early stages of cauliflowers and potato stalks, fruit bushes and carrot tops. Even when he got Tipper to find him some paving stones and flagged over the garden, the shoots continued to grow through the cracks between the slabs, and he had to keep remembering to pour in a mixture of sesame-seed oil and vinegar – his grandma's cure for rheumatism – to keep them down. Secrets, like dreams, he was reminded, needed constant attention lest they somehow escaped and ran amok. To be incessantly reminded like that was a kind of madness, and whenever it happened he thought of Melanie, and sometimes of love.

Noah always saved the Wednesday jobs section until the evening. He would hide away in his office every week with a pint of tea steaming in his Accrington Stanley mug and a packet of biscuits. Usually it was no more than curiosity. Now and then he would ring up and ask for details. Only twice had he ever got as far as starting to fill in an application form before losing interest and putting it aside.

Noah's system with the Wednesday *Guardian* was this: he would circle jobs within a salary band running from five thousand pounds a year less than the Dounleavey Trust paid him (hardly any) to five thousand pounds more (numerous), and exclude those above that figure (about half the jobs in the paper). Then he went back to the beginning and deleted the ones where he obviously needed to be a woman, or from an ethnic minority. Then he put a line through jobs that were live-in, and jobs in parts of the country that didn't appeal to him – places with no football team he'd heard of, or no hills, or no discernible local accent. Finally he worked on deletions via job categories – Forestry Commission, Inland Revenue, town halls. From the little he knew of town halls – from Fred Wyke's tales of internecine wars in the committee rooms and of lowly foot soldiers like himself having to genuflect to fat-headed councillors – Noah couldn't imagine working in one.

He usually ended up with an average of half a dozen undeleted. He tried to imagine what it might be like to work in one of those places. Where would he live? Would the natives be friendly? Could he make a new start so far away at fifty-one? The descriptions of the required candidates rarely helped. Even the most straightforward jobs asked for qualifications he hadn't heard of (NVQs, BTECs), experience of strategic planning at a corporate level, and proof of on-going professional development.

There were three jobs in today's paper that Noah felt he could do and that were in places he liked the sound of: for Barnardos in Carlisle; on a community-development project in Exeter; with the Cyrenians in Canterbury. He wasn't qualified enough for any of them.

He looked at his watch. He thought about ringing Elly. The police were heavily involved in Josh's disappearance now that he'd been officially 'missing' for three days, and his details had been circulated to all the local forces. Noah had rung Elly twice today already. There was no news of Josh. He'd said he would call round after work. Elly should have been on the tills at Asda but she'd rung in sick. Noah decided to lock up early and go across to see her.

Last night she had talked about Josh – not about his being missing but about *him*. There had been a kind of reckoning up in the way she'd spoken. It was a reflective confession, born of the sudden physical distance between mother and son, and the fear of what this might signify. She had tried to remember what it was that sparked so many arguments and somehow couldn't. She remembered that she could never persuade Josh to lift the toilet seat before he had a pee; that he left the hot tap running and emptied the cistern; that he left damp towels stuffed down the side of his bed and dirty cups on top of his wardrobe. He'd had all term to organize his GCSE project file and still, as far as she knew, hadn't got past the list of contents and two sentences of the introduction. Josh wouldn't talk about it. He wouldn't talk about anything. He hung about in the town for hours – she guessed with Damien Tunney. As soon as he came home he made straight for his room, and if Elly asked where he'd been – he'd always say, 'Nowhere' – they'd be off again arguing with each other.

'It's like having a dog in the house that's not housebroken,' Elly had said. 'But when I try to talk to him about any of it, he just tells me to chill.'

Noah put his jacket on and went outside to check the building. There had been a few half-hearted attempts to break into the centre by some of the kids from the youth club. Their favourite trick was to insert a marble under the pole on an emergency exit door so that even though it looked secure it could still be opened from the outside, or to lodge a peg in one of the window frames to stop the window from locking. It was easier to check from the outside than to go through each room on the ground floor.

There were three youths by the gate in the yard. The face of one of them was partly lit by the streetlight. It took a moment for Noah to recognize Melanie's brother. He was shrugging, listening, coaxing, and then passed something to one of the younger boys. The boy put it in his pocket, looking round instinctively, and zipped up. It was the timing that bothered Noah. The transaction had not come at the start of the conversation as it would if it had been a simple errand. There had been some negotiation, and an agreement of terms. Melanie's brother said something; all three of them grinned. One of the boys was a Catlin (the middle one of Barry's brood of six); the other was Damien Tunney – Josh's friend from school. Both of them had been in the youth club earlier in the evening. Noah guessed that Melanie's brother had been hanging round waiting for them outside the centre. They caught sight of Noah. Damien and the Catlin boy slid out of the yard, leaving only the older youth, unconcerned.

People knew, in that vague public way in which such things were known in Lowell, that Melanie Quigley's brother worked for Ronnie Roots. Tipper Gill said that even the police knew, but they were only really interested in those operating further up the line. They weren't even *that* bothered about Ronnie Roots who was himself only a middleman, Tipper maintained. He just organized other people to move drugs around the estate – people like Melanie Quigley's brother.

Noah did a circuit of the centre, checking the windows, the emergency exits and the boarded-over door to the belfry. He came round past the front buttress with its For Sale sign jutting out in yellow and blue. He stood at the foot of the steps, watching the empty yard, and a voice close by said, 'What you looking for?'

Noah turned round. Melanie's brother had lit a cigarette, and was leaning back against the wall of the Mustard Seed. One leg was raised with his foot pressed against the stone behind him. He held a mobile phone to his ear with his free hand, waiting for someone to answer his call.

'I seen you watching us.'

'Did you?' Noah said.

'There was nothing to see. Was there?'

'You tell me,' Noah said. 'What's your name?'

'Why, what's yours?'

'Noah.'

'What, like the fucking bible?'

Noah was almost a foot taller, heavier, thicker set. The boy gave up on the call he was trying to make, turned off the phone, slipped it into his pocket, drew on his cigarette, and looked away.

'What were you doing?'

'I told you, nothing. Them two won't say nothing either.'

'You forget. I was watching you.'

'Why? You fancy me or something?'

'What did you give the boy you were with?'

'What boy?'

'In the yard.'

The youth shrugged.

'Damien. Josh Pascoe's friend. Josh has gone missing. You know anything about that?'

'Don't know no Josh.'

'But you know Damien. I watched you give him something.'

'Didn't give him anything.'

'In a packet.'

'Ask him.'

'He's not here. I'm asking you.'

'Who knows what you saw. Maybe you're just an old man who can't see straight in the dark.'

'I know what I saw.'

'I told you. I don't even know no Damien.'

'Did you sell him something? In a packet? Are you dealing in my yard?'

'I got nothing on me. You want to check?'

'Yes, I want to check.'

'No you don't, you just want to feel me up. You're a dirty old man.'

Noah stepped forwards, pinned the youth to the wall with one big hand, and turned out all the pockets of his leather coat, looking for money or for more packets. The youth didn't resist, just rode with it.

'You enjoying yourself then?'

The youth stayed floppy as a rag doll. There was nothing on him. Noah let go.

'What've you done with the money?'

'Fucking shirtlifter.' The youth was grinning now. 'I know about you. Ronnie told me about you. He said not to do this place over when I told him there was stuff in here.' He gestured behind him at the Mustard Seed. 'He wouldn't say why, though. You got something on Ronnie, then, or what?'

'Enough,' Noah said. He would normally have backed off. But he didn't want to walk away. 'You've got a mouth on you,' he said. 'It'll end up getting you into trouble.'

'Give Ronnie one as well did you?'

'You don't listen, do you?' Noah said. He felt himself tensing.

'You must be fucking desperate.'

'That's *enough*!' Noah shouted, his voice rising out into the darkness. He had reached across to take hold of the youth again. Blood punched through him.

'Fucking Tarzan, eh? Tarzan of the Jungle.'

Noah hit him. A single strike with the back of his hand. It

sent the boy falling back against the wall of the old church and down on to the ground.

Noah was breathing hard.

The boy, down on the floor, was smiling.

'Tosser,' he said. 'Think I'm scared? *Tosser.*'

He was laughing.

Noah put the radio on low in his office. His heart was beating hard. His hand hurt. He sat there in the dark for a while.

He had gone back inside, wanting to calm himself before he went across to see Elly Pascoe. He put the desk lamp on in the office, plugged in the kettle, and sat back down. The three job adverts he had cut out were still on his desk. They were on top of the notes for the closing chapters of his book – details of Mr George's fate, and the lives of the orphans he'd reared.

Noah could see now that a good writer had to write in a way that left the characters alive and breathing at the end. The reader had to believe that the characters would continue to live even when he'd finished the book – in contrast to a fairy tale or a romance. In a fairy tale the point of the writing was to conclude things, was to draw a firm line underneath and to close the story so that there could be no more. Happy ever after. The *point* of a fairy tale was that nothing significant could ever follow.

What surprised him was the need he'd felt to hurt the boy. He had wanted to hit Melanie's brother until the boy stopped leering and, for a split second, until he'd stopped breathing. But he had walked away.

The warming filament began to murmur. The kettle's noise began to rise. There was a bang as something fell. It startled Noah and he looked up. The noise didn't sound as if it was coming from outside the building. Noah remembered how Damien Tunney and the middle Catlin had disappeared from the yard, and he wondered whether the appearance of Melanie's brother was meant as a distraction to help the other two get into the building undetected.

He moved across the room and turned the kettle off. The noise subsided. He flicked off the desk lamp. The only light was from the porch outside. Noah stood in silence with the office door open. He could hear something being dragged across a floor somewhere in the building.

Noah took the big metal torch, went down into the main hall, and flicked the lights on. It was empty. He opened each of the side rooms in turn and swept them with light from the torch. Then he heard the noise again – it was coming from the belfry. Noah wondered if they had broken in the back way and somehow secured the door behind them. He climbed the concrete steps of the steeple, moving towards the belfry. Halfway up he turned the torch off. As he reached the top he realized he was carrying the torch as a cosh. He stood in the doorway of the belfry. There hadn't been any bells in there for years. It was used as a storeroom. It was dark and damp. Noah waited, swallowed, letting his eyes get used to the dark. He could smell woodsmoke, and the lingering incense of a candle. Then there was a movement in the far corner, and a scrape on the floor. Noah couldn't make out what it was. He turned the torch on. It was a moment before Noah saw that it was Josh.

'Did you sleep here last night?'

The boy nodded, hesitant.

'Were you cold?'

Josh shrugged. His legs were bundled against his chest; his

pallid moon face resting on his knees. He wouldn't come downstairs, not even to Noah's office. He'd started when Noah had taken a step across the room, in case it was some kind of trap or trick, so Noah had stayed where he was over by the doorway.

'I'm not going back,' he'd said. 'You can't make me go back.' His face was white. Noah saw how alike the two of them – mother and son – were.

'Are you cold now?'

'I'm all right.'

'Can I sit down?' Noah said.

'Are you going to tell her?'

'She's worried sick, Josh.'

'You haven't got to say.'

'For how long?'

'How long?'

'I mean, how long are you planning to hide out up here?'

Josh looked at him.

'Well,' Noah said, thinking things through out loud, 'I suppose I could bring you something to eat at night for a while – when people have left the centre, I mean.'

Josh nodded.

'I could get in a few extras on the centre's shopping day. Linde wouldn't notice.'

'You'd do that?'

'Well I can't let you starve to death up here now I've found you,' Noah said.

'They wouldn't blame you.'

'Yeah, but I could be held responsible for the death of a minor if they could prove I'd been up here. Fingerprints and stuff.'

'Yeah?'

'So I'll have to feed you.'

'Yeah, okay then.'

'There is one thing, Josh. I'd need to know if there were drugs on the premises. The centre could get shut down – you know?'

'You've been talking to my mum again.'

'She's worried about you. She thinks Damien Tunney is trouble. I saw him buying stuff tonight from that lad who works for Ronnie Roots. I know he's dealing for certain.'

'I know,' Josh said. 'I was watching from up here. I saw them. Damien's into whizz, trips, things like that. He's a pillock.'

'What about you?'

Josh shook his head.

'What about when you ended up in the cells?'

'That was one time. You have to try once.'

'Why don't you tell your mum that?'

'What's the point? She wouldn't believe me. She's always on my back. She thinks I'm still ten. That's why I go out all the time. It gets too much.'

'What do you do?'

'Dunno. Just walk, just think. That's why I left. I love her and stuff. She'd not have me back anyway after this shit. And no way I'm going to my dad's. I'd just bunk off again if anyone made me go there.'

'Maybe you could write to her then. Let her know you're okay. I could post a letter. Not from Lowell, though. I'd have to post it from a different town. Throw her off the scent.'

'Yeah,' Josh said. 'Like in that film on the telly the other week.'

'I'd have to get you some other bits.'

'Like what?'

'Well, you'll need soap and towels, and a shaving kit in a while. But there's a bigger problem.'

Josh looked puzzled.

Noah seemed to be thinking the problem through. 'You ever see *The Wooden Horse*?' he said finally.

'No.'

'The Allied prisoners in the German POW camp built this wooden vaulting horse. It was hollow, so that one of them could hide inside it when they carried it out into the compound every day. They placed it in the same spot each day – over the trap-door that led to the tunnel. You could do that. I could get the horse Tipper's kids use for fitness training in the yard.'

'What for?'

'Well, you'll be going to college before too long. Then eventually you'll have a family. So you'll need a way of getting in and out of the belfry undetected every day.'

Josh was grinning.

'You'd have to make a start soon, though. There's a foot of tarmac down on that yard. You'd need to get through that before you even reached the clay.'

'Pillock,' Josh said.

'That's weird,' Noah said. 'That's just what your mum says.'

Barry Catlin had been drawn back to Shaun's bedroom. Shaun usually stayed in his room, but tonight he was out. Barry didn't know where Shaun was. He hadn't asked. Even with the younger ones, Barry didn't ask where they were going any more. They came and they went. Sometimes he shouted at them. Sometimes, when Janice was a mess, he made the tea for them – hot dog and chips or pizza.

Barry had liked it when they were all little. He'd even liked cleaning up their shit and their sick – things that would sink Janice into despair. He'd liked playing I Spy, Lego, and football in the yard, and watching children's telly with them. He'd been more than Barry Catlin to them then, but now they seemed to know more about the world and how to navigate its currents than he did.

He hadn't known what drugs looked like until Tipper had shown him some the other night. Not smack, Tipper said – smack was different. What Tipper showed him looked like coloured transfers on small pieces of rice-paper and gelatin squares. Tipper said vaguely that you put them on your tongue. Smiley faces, stars, penguins. They were drugs? They seemed harmless. Like children's things. Tipper said that Jody had been swapping them for Mars bars after under-elevens training.

Jody Catlin had told Tipper that someone had given them to him. He hadn't said who. That was why Barry was in Shaun's room. He was curious about the locked drawer in the bedside cabinet. He'd wondered if that's where the picture squares had come from. Barry forced it with a screwdriver.

Inside, there was a Reebok shoebox, some Tipp-Ex, pens, Pritt Stick, pieces of an old watch, addresses, old football cards, cigarette packets, and two Rolo chocolates which he fed to Denis Law who had followed him into the room. Barry opened the shoebox and shook all the contents on to the bed. He was puzzled at first. There were squares of paper, but they weren't like the gelatin sheets with pictures on that Jody had been passing out at football training. These were small pieces of paper with letters and sometimes whole words on them. There were hundreds of them, cut from newspapers. Some of them were glued on to strips of paper to form words. SHAG, LICK, FUCK,

CUNT, CUM, ARSE, YOUR, ME, DICK, WET. On bigger pieces of paper, his son had arranged full sentences and stuck them in place. Messages. To women, it seemed.

There was a complete message: I WATCHED YOU COME HOME WENSDAY NIGHT. YOU HAD A WHITE TOP ON. KNOW WHAT, I WANT YOU TO TAKE YOUR WHITE TOP OF FOR ME AND RUB YOUR TITS IN — SO'S I CAN LICK IT OFF THEN LICK YOU OFF. I'LL DO IT SOON FOR YOU. JUST SEE. He hadn't sent the message yet because he was still waiting for one last word to glue into the space.

There were local women's names and addresses written down on a list in the lid of the box. One of them was the deaf woman – Olwen Sudders.

Noah was sitting on one of the packing boxes.

'Were you ever married?' Josh asked.

Noah paused, then nodded.

'What was she called?'

'Her name was Rachel.'

'What happened?'

'It was a long time ago.'

'It's okay if you don't want to say.'

They fell silent again. Noah watched the pale-faced boy for a while. 'You're a good listener,' Noah said.

'Mum used to say that. When she threw Dad out. We used to talk a lot then. We used to walk a lot, up on to the tops, and she'd talk.' Josh smiled at the thought of it. Elly's smile. Simple and wondrous.

'She died in a car crash – Rachel. It was before I came to Lowell. A long time ago.'

Josh nodded.

'Rachel was in the passenger seat. I was driving. A car hit us head on. He'd had about six pints. He was a barrister in a Manchester firm. He got twelve months suspended. Banned for a year. It was only afterwards that they told me she was two months pregnant.'

'Do you think about her?' Josh asked.

'Sometimes.'

'What's it like?'

'What's it like remembering her?' Noah thought. It seemed like a long time before he spoke.

'She used to like jazz,' he said. 'I've never been able to listen to it since she died. She used to have me listen to musicians she liked: Duke Ellington and Chet Baker and Miles Davis. I can't really remember the names of the tunes any more. She used to tell me about the musicians – who they were, why they played music the way they did.'

He paused again, reaching for words.

'It's like the way I remember Miles Davis played the trumpet on the records Rachel played for me,' Noah said. 'It leaves you a bit fragile, and bleak, but still hopeful. "The Meaning of the Blues" – that was one of them. That was a tune she liked. It doesn't take the pain away, but it helps to hear it played out like that.'

Noah smiled. 'I haven't heard Miles Davis play in twenty years,' he said finally. And then, 'I don't know what it's like, Josh – I really don't know.'

They could hear the wind outside blowing an empty can across the yard. Josh shivered.

'You cold?'

'Mmm.'

'You want a jumper?'

Josh nodded.

Noah slipped his coat off, then dragged his fisherman's sweater over his head.

Josh put it on.

'What are those marks?' Josh asked.

'Marks?'

'On your back.'

Josh had seen the welts on Noah's back. Three of them – thin red lines, slightly raised on his otherwise smooth skin.

'I've had them since I was a boy.'

'How'd you get them?'

'They were made with a belt – a long time ago. They're called keloid scars. Sometimes, especially in the winter, the tissue gets inflamed and turns purple, as if the scars were fresh.'

'Who did it?'

'One of the brothers who ran the orphanage.'

'What had you done?'

'I can't remember now. We got hit a lot. It wasn't unusual. I must have just caught one of them on a bad day when I got those.'

'Where was it?'

'It was over Haslingden way,' Noah said. 'It was called St Brendan's.'

18

The End of Accrington Stanley

Slow men in white with bubble heads paddled across the screen. Around the television in the Big House they crouched breathlessly, watching the ghostly ballet unfold.

Now and then Gifford – who along with Goose had kept an almost continuous vigil since the blast-off at Cape Canaveral five days before, and was by now dull and bog-eyed with fatigue – still felt the need to explain it all to the others. It came from being with Goose, who had been Gifford's principal disciple in following the space race in the Big House. Everything had to be explained to Goose (with his flapping legs and his now thinning hair) at least three times before he was happy.

'Armstrong will be opening the hatch before too long and stepping down,' Gifford announced, leaning forward on the settee. There was a small amphitheatre of people gathered round the television for this latest highlight of the voyage.

'Men walking on the moon,' Gifford had been saying all summer. 'It's *history*. We should make sure we're a part of it – we shouldn't miss a single minute.'

Unlike Dublin with his private Tiger Moth obsession in years past, Gifford wanted everyone to be as enthusiastic as he was – to be a part of his obsession – and, even at sixteen, was crestfallen when they weren't. The nervous intensity which triggered Gifford's still-frequent bouts of asthma was also the engine which drove his curiosity – in particular his fascination with jet aircraft and space rockets. The climax of this obsession was to see a man walking on the moon. And there in the Big House – six months before the decade's end and six months before the orphanage was finally to close – they were watching astronauts Armstrong and Aldrin floating inside the lunar module resting on the moon's surface.

They had seven orphans left with them in the summer of 1969. Rachel and Noah had known that this would be their last year when a large part of the roof had been blown away in a spring gale and it became apparent that Gordon's temporary repairs would suffice only for a few months. What they needed, he said, was a completely new roof before the onset of another winter – unless they were thinking of abandoning that part of the house permanently.

There was other work that needed to be done and Noah had asked Gordon (now a time-served joiner) to assess it for them. The whole house needed rewiring. In fact, Gordon and the electrician he brought in were so worried about the state of the wiring that they insisted on fitting a fire alarm. 'Just in case,' Gordon said. The indoor plumbing also needed attention after a sequence of spectacular bursts that reminded those old enough to remember of Jacob at his urinous best. Noah and Rachel couldn't afford any of the repairs. Rachel had already taken out a personal loan with the bank a couple of years before, to have the dry rot in the dormitories dealt with. Meeting the repayments on that loan was as much as Rachel and Noah between them could manage with the little money they had coming in.

They had agonized over the matter for some weeks after Gordon delivered his verdict on the extent of the necessary renovation. They would, they decided, celebrate one last Founder's Day, and after that they would prepare to offer the Big House to the golf club.

On the television, they were showing a rerun of the landing of the lunar module. It was getting on for midnight but all the orphans were still up. They had been given permission to stay up to watch the moon walk. Only Sassy was missing. She was in her kitchen, crocheting, having made it plain that she wasn't bothered about watching 'moon stuff' as she called it. 'The moon is up there every night,' Sassy had said to Noah earlier in the week, when everyone had been talking about it. 'Why spend all that money on finding out it's just a piece of rock?' Sassy had no curiosity about things any more. Sometimes it was easy to miss the fact that she was there with them at all.

Everyone else was gathered in the study with Rachel, huddled round the television screen, waiting for the big moment – for the moon stuff. No one wanted to go out into the garden with Noah for some fresh air. They said they'd call him if the module's hatch opened or if anything happened.

From the garden, Noah could see the moon. He'd brought Gifford's binoculars outside with him and, sitting on the bench by the lawn, he looked up into the night sky, imagining the astronauts in their tiny capsule somewhere up there in the stars.

Noah sat there for a long time. Only gradually did he become aware that he was not alone in the garden. There was an old man standing by the tree that marked the far border of the lawn. Noah guessed he must have somehow walked up the driveway without being heard. He carried a rucksack over one shoulder, as if he had walked a long distance. Noah's eyes adjusted so that he could see the man more clearly. His stubble, perhaps two days' worth, was silver. His face was leathery. His hands were sunk into the pockets of his padded jacket. He was standing very still, like a ghost. His eyes, set deep in his head, seemed tired. Noah didn't know how long he had been watched, or how long the ghost-like figure might have continued to stand there silently if he had not finally called out to him.

It was the way the ghost was looking at the Big House that first made Noah think it might be him.

'Are yu-you Mu-Mr George?' Noah called.

Noah had never met him. He had seen photographs of the man around the Big House, but it was difficult to recognize this shabby man as the same person. Besides, everyone in the Big House, even Sassy, had long been reconciled to the fact that Mr George was gone for good. And yet here was this ghost of a man in the black of night staring up at the house as if he recognized it – as if once, in a different life, it might have been his. It was this sense of familiarity and loss in the man which gave him away. That was how Noah knew.

The two men stood looking at each other. Noah couldn't speak for a moment. He felt the weight of the binoculars in his hand.

'They're ab-bout to walk on the mu-moon any minute,' he said foolishly, explaining why he was out there in the garden at such a late hour. 'The Yu-Yanks.'

Noah couldn't think of anything else to say.

Mr George didn't know about the moon stuff. He didn't

seem to know anything about the Apollo mission, which had been in all the newspapers and on the wireless and television for weeks. But he did know about the decision to sell the Big House. That was why he was there. He had come back for the final Founder's Day.

At first, Sassy had refused to believe that it was really him. Then, as if the fact of his return was too much, she fled back to the kitchen and sat sobbing until Mr George, prompted by Rachel, went to comfort her. It was Sassy who took responsibility for cleaning him up the next day. He looked less bedraggled after a bath and a shave, and they dug out some of Noah's clothes for him to wear, but he remained a distant figure.

He said very little in the first few days. He spent most of his time with Sassy in her kitchen, as if he was wary of being around children, or nervous in a larger group. As for Sassy, she was happy enough to have him to herself as much as she could.

'He *promised* me he'd come back,' she said to Rachel triumphantly. 'Now, he's home for good.' She was flushed with victory.

Everyone had assumed that Mr George had come back to save the orphanage, and yet he didn't seem at all concerned when Rachel tried to interest him in the damage to the roof, or the state of the orphanage's finances. Rachel wrote a note for Noah a few days after Mr George's return, when she'd tried once again to discuss the imminent closure of the Big House. 'There's no magic left in him,' the note said. And it was true that he was far happier sitting with Sassy, or mooching with Goose in the grounds, or gazing out of a window, listening to one of Rachel's quiet jazz tunes, than helping them plan what would happen when the Big House closed. He seemed – much as he used to say himself about Goose – to be 'in a world of his own'. He didn't like talking about what he had done in the years he had been away, or where he had been. It transpired that at one time he'd been driving freight lorries for a living. He also mentioned working on the ferry boats in the West of Scotland for a time. It seemed he hadn't stopped in any one place for long.

When he began to spend a little time with the children, they found that he would rather listen than talk. As a result, they competed to bring him up to date on events – how Accrington Stanley had gone bust and been expelled from the League the summer after Mr George left the Big House; how Megan and Jacob were at university together; how Walter was teaching undergraduates; how Tom Travis had a dozen aircraft now as part of his company at Blackpool Airport and still appeared in his Tiger Moth at Founder's Day each year and would do so one last time this summer.

It was Mr George's idea to mark the occasion with one of his performances, as he had done in the old days.

'Something to remember,' Mr George said. 'We have to do something special for the *last* Founder's Day.'

Mr George listened to the various suggestions as to what his final performance should be – suggestions which involved motor cars, elephants and lunar modules. Then he said quietly that he thought he already knew which trick he wanted to perform. He said he wanted to attempt the escapology routine which he and Dunkiss had first performed for the weavers at the beginning of the war. He thought this would be a fitting end, and he nominated Goose to be his stage assistant on the day.

The only one who objected to the plan was Sassy.

'He's too old now to be going about doing stunts like that,' she complained, fearful of anything that might jeopardize her imagined future happiness with him. But the chorus of approval from the children, and Rachel's relief that he was at least showing an interest in *something*, drowned out Sassy's note of caution.

Noah and Goose helped Mr George to sift through the accumulated junk of more than twenty years until finally they came across the props for the illusion. They were stored in one of the travelling chests which had been carried to the Big House on the great march from Tatlow Street, along with some of Dunkiss's possessions, the rusty key to Tatlow's bargehouse and the bear's leather muzzle.

As the big day approached, he seemed to lose a little of his vagueness. But Rachel and Noah still couldn't get him to look *beyond* the preparations for his performance.

'It'll be all right,' Noah said to Rachel. 'After Founder's Day he'll help us work out what to do.'

She nodded, unconvinced.

The day before the event Mr George decided to hold a rehearsal.

'We should have something more theatrical than just a wooden box,' he announced when he had twisted his arms out of the leather straps and slipped away, on cue, through the trapdoor in the stage floor. 'We should have a curtain or something to drape over the box to make the trick look more dramatic. A purple one, or red. Red would be good.' He was concerned that people were harder to impress than in the old days. People took things for granted these days; they demanded to be entertained. Sassy would have nothing to do with it, but Rachel came to the rescue, suggesting the use of one of the old red curtains from the now abandoned and partially roofless boys' dormitory.

'Hu-happy now?' Noah said to him when Rachel had demonstrated how the floor-to-ceiling curtain was long enough to completely cover the wooden box.

For the first time since his return, he smiled.

Tom Travis arrived by car the night before, leading a small convoy of fairground attractions he had persuaded to come to mark the last Founder's Day. The residents of the Big House stood watching them meander up the valley like a procession of multi-coloured dinosaurs mounted on the backs of small lorries. The two humps of the unbolted, travelling Ferris wheel led the procession. Behind it, a dodgem ring, a carousel, a children's train ride, a hamburger and candy-floss stall, a huge pipe organ, a generator for the pipe organ and for the string of lights Tom had brought for the top lawn, and a helter-skelter crawled in single file up the drive, through the yard, past the bell tower, and round the back into the grounds.

The next morning as Founder's Day got under way people paid their shilling to Gifford at the gate. All the regulars who had turned up every year to support the Big House were there. There were also, that last year, a lot of unfamiliar faces – people from the town who were curious about the Zoo, about the *queer house*; people who had heard that Mr George had returned and were curious to see this man who could perform feats of magic and who had got away with teaching orphans how to wank.

The day, as it wore on, grew noisier and gruffer than in previous years. There were the traditional carnival tunes from the carousel and the children's train, but there was also the pipe organ pumping music, and the deeper, constant rumble of the generator, and the young people's transistor radios bleating pop music. Mingling with all these noises were the smells of Sassy's cakes, onions frying on the griddle of the hamburger stall and hot oil from the engine of the Tiger Moth.

Mr George had turned out for the day in the old white dinner jacket which had once been Dounleavey's. It was more grey than white these days, going threadbare in places. As he had lost weight in his years away it was also noticeably too big for Mr George. But Sassy had cut his hair the night before, and she had cut a flower from the garden for the buttonhole, and brushed the jacket down after breakfast, so that he would *look the part* as she said. Everyone envisaged him performing his old familiar escapology routine with his old familiar style in Dounleavey's dinner jacket and hoped that perhaps, in this way, a little of his magic might return. So it came as a shock to discover that, unnoticed, he had changed costume for the performance of his magic trick.

He was meant to have waited for the tannoy announcement before he made his entrance from the Big House, so that the rides and the music could stop. But for some reason, perhaps through nerves or simple overeagerness to proceed, he came out early, even before Noah had managed to bring the red curtain from the house on to the outdoor stage.

It was the laughter which first alerted Noah to the fact that Mr George was already making his way towards the stage. Noah saw then that he had changed into the faded red knickerbocker shorts which Dunkiss had worn in the original performance. Mr George must have found them amongst Dunkiss's things in the trunk. He was also wearing Dunkiss's orienteering boots, which Sassy had kept in her room all those years. On Dunkiss the outfit had looked imposing but on Mr George it looked clownish and bizarre. That was why people were starting to laugh, and were pointing at the eccentric-looking figure walking slowly through the reluctantly parting crowd. The pantomime was completed by Mr George dragging the red velvet curtain over his shoulder. The curtain was so long that he hadn't been able to bundle it up under one arm and so its length trailed behind him as he walked. One of the youths who caddied at the golf club placed a foot on the trailing curtain as he passed. Mr George was jerked to a halt. He turned to look behind him. He saw the youth but said nothing – simply waited until the youth lifted his boot and allowed him to proceed between the sniggering ranks of spectators. Another man holding a beer in his hand stood on the trailing curtain. Mr George in his pantaloon shorts and boots looked back again. It was as though he understood the game by now. Goose appeared, pushing his way through the crowd. He gathered up the trailing red curtain and the two of them walked towards the stage.

A small boy stepped in front of Mr George.

'*That's* Mr George?' the child said, incredulous. 'He couldn't make an elephant disappear.' The boy sounded cheated, as if he had expected so much more. 'He couldn't do *any* magic. He's just an old man.'

'Show us your pecker, George,' a woman from the crowd suddenly shouted. 'I'll show you what you're supposed to do with it.' She screeched with laughter.

There were more hoots of derision as more people saw Mr George and then the unco-ordinated and childlike Goose mount the stage. Hearing the laughter, Goose grinned, bowing deeply to the crowd, who reacted with more incredulous laughter.

'Can you turn *him* into an elephant?' someone shouted at Mr George.

'He's already turned him into a *donkey*!'

Mr George leaned across and whispered something to Goose, who proceeded to fasten the straps round each of Mr George's wrists, and to bind his feet. He folded the hinged sides of the box around Mr George, enclosing him completely. Above them the Tiger Moth was soaring over the treetops on the latest of its flights. On the stage, Goose was carefully draping the heavy velvet curtain over the top of the fastened box. Then everyone watched him wait for Mr George to effect his escape – to signal to Goose (as Noah and the others knew) by tapping on the underside of the stage when the moment was right to remove the curtain and open up the box.

Noah didn't see anything after that because that was when the generator blew.

Like a lot of the fairground equipment the fairmen brought to the Big House in that final year, the generator was an old machine that had given long service. It was bound to fail at some point, but it was the timing of its failure that was so dramatic. The generator coughed twice, spluttered, and then belched an explosion. Its baritone hum was thrown into a more frantic, insistent pitch, as though the dynamo inside was being driven with increasing speed and an unsettling degree of recklessness, and smoke began to spill out of its rear end. At the same time, the pipe organ being powered by the generator went haywire and began, as if suddenly confused, to play several tunes at once and at a deafening volume. The string of lights which had been hung all around the top lawn flashed on and off, then, quite suddenly, began to shatter one by one like a sequence of pistol shots.

In the kitchen, Sassy saw smoke everywhere, and set off the fire alarm. The combination of the smoke, the clanging fire alarm, the maddened pipe organ, the squealing generator and the pistol fire of the bursting lights created chaos. People fled the grounds, blinded by the smoke, ducking each time a light burst as if they were under fire.

Eventually, after several minutes, someone found the right connection to disable the generator. By then the majority of the crowd had evacuated the grounds and were already heading home. Even after the generator had been silenced, light bulbs still continued to burst in the swirling white smoke, firing occasional shots overhead. Then the pipe organ began to wind down, slowing to a series of unearthly groans which descended lower and lower down the musical scale until – in one long, final, funereal yowl – it sighed and fell silent.

Ten minutes had elapsed since the generator had blown. The smoke from its exhausted motor thinned, and slowly Noah found that he could see again. None of the rides were running. The only noise that could be heard was the drone of the Tiger Moth out over the valley, oblivious to the evacuation and the explosions down below.

All this time, Goose had been waiting. He had been instructed to listen for Mr George's signal – the tap from underneath the stage. So, dutifully, Goose had obeyed. All through the pyrotechnics of the generator exploding and the lights blowing up and the fire alarm clanging and the crowd fleeing, Goose had stood there waiting for Mr George's signal. Finally, as silence fell, he took it upon himself to pull the red velvet curtain away from the wooden box. There hadn't been a signal. There had been no tap from underneath the stage. Goose dragged away the curtain and one by one unfastened the hasps holding the wooden box shut.

They said at the hospital later that it was evident he'd had heart trouble in the recent past. That was why he hadn't been able to escape from his bonds inside the box. Perhaps Goose had tied the leather straps a little too tight – it was hard to know and harder still to criticize him for it. Perhaps Mr George had cried out for help, realizing he was too weak to break free, feeling the strain on his heart as gunfire and smoke filled the air, but the din of the noise and the crowd's panic and the heavy velvet curtain would have muffled any such sounds or signs of struggle.

Goose pulled open the top of the box, and then levered down the sides. People saw Goose begin to cry. He looked down at Rachel and the others from the stage, not knowing what to do, then looked back at the figure inside the box, dressed in Dunkiss's pantaloons and boots. Mr George's arms were outstretched, fastened to the sides of the table by the leather straps. His legs were pinned together. His head had slumped forwards and to one side. He was dead. Below them, in the bottom field, the Tiger Moth was coming in to land.

19

Allegiance

The rumours seeped out slowly. Tipper, not knowing what else to do, watched in a kind of slow motion as Morag's dreams for the estate faltered – first hairline cracks appeared, and then a sizeable tremor reduced them swiftly to rubble.

Everyone except Morag had seen that it was only a matter of time. Councillor Porrit made the usual noises. He said he would fight the allegations. He claimed it was just a smoke-screen set up to protect the kind of tawdry politics he himself had targeted in his attacks on the leadership of the Town Hall.

The caucus in power at the Town Hall had identified auditing irregularities in the Regeneration Board's finances; then they produced evidence of a pattern of inducements offered by Councillor Porrit in an attempt to aid his own putative bid for the leadership of the Council. The inducements were financed by firms bidding for contracts to carry out construction and renovation work on behalf of the Regeneration Board. One politician pledging support for Councillor Porrit was revealed to have taken eleven trips abroad over the course of the last year – to Sweden, Hong Kong, America and Italy – as a 'consultant' for such firms. Councillor Porrit himself had attended a four-day European Regeneration Conference in Lausanne, along with two members of the Board and its finance manager. The costs of the conference, including first-class flights, were paid out of Regeneration Board funds. The bill came to eleven thousand pounds, including restaurant bills of one thousand four hundred pounds. The drinks bill over the four days totalled eight hundred and ten pounds. Another seven hundred and thirty pounds had been charged to phone calls and payments for videos and laundry. None of it was paid for out of a thirty pounds a day incidental-expense allowance each of them had claimed. Other evidence came to light, showing how Councillor Porrit had manipulated the other members of the Regeneration Board to ensure new projects were sited in the wards of those councillors whose backing he sought. In some cases the locations of projects funded by the Board had breached the guidelines.

The Regeneration Board was suspended. The finance manager took sick leave with stress. Each of the existing members of the Board, including Morag Gill from the St Silas tenants group in Lowell, was questioned. Morag defended Roy Porrit vigorously. She fell into every trap they set for her, and left the hearing in tears after forty minutes.

Councillor Porrit adopted the time-honoured war strategy of withdrawing to a more defensible position. He resigned from a series of posts, including that of Chairman of the Regeneration Board, and fought for his political life having returned to the status of humble ward councillor, still publicly proclaiming his innocence.

The night Councillor Porrit's resignation came to light, Tipper sat and watched Morag put her and Dorothy's coats on and go out to catch a bus to Councillor Porrit's house. The councillor had been drinking all day. He'd had the local press and radio round. He didn't recognize Morag when he answered the door.

'You're parasites, the lot of you!' he yelled in her face, clutching a glass. 'I can see that other bugger lurking by the bushes. Is that your accomplice?'

It was Dorothy.

All these things floated across the face of Tipper Gill's life as clouds float across the sky. He had never been able to see the bigger picture. These events were far away and out of reach, as if he might have dreamed them. How such things happened and what propelled them were equally mysterious to Tipper, who watched the consequences of them reflected in Morag's face.

It was Morag's single-mindedness that had drawn him to her. At nineteen, he had already done two separate stints in Borstal and was drifting out into the wider world with no sense of *where* he was going. Resolute Morag, who knew what she wanted and seemed determined to get there, was someone he could moor his flimsier vessel alongside. With this in mind he courted her.

Morag, with her farmer's shoulders, was two years younger than Tipper. They met at the Blue Dahlia Coffee Bar in Haslingden. She went with a single girlfriend. She wasn't one of the groups of girls who went there, clamouring like geese, stopping off for a drink on the way to the cinema or the Mecca Dance Hall. She wasn't *anxious* to be part of a crowd like most of the girls chatted up by Tipper. She wasn't as easily impressed by Tipper's chequered history – by the time he'd spent in Borstal and the single, exotically damaged eye on his cherub's face. She had an independence from those around her that intoxicated him and that he craved. It was Morag, not Tipper, who was the strong one.

Tipper had worked his way through a range of institutions. He was small for his age, often in trouble, easily led, but not vicious and always *wanting* to please. He was already a follower of Manchester United – of the Busby Babes of the mid-fifties. *He* could be a Busby Babe. People *called* him a baby – he stayed small and angel-faced until he started losing teeth to decay in his early twenties. He watched Big Duncan Edwards, a few years older and a kind of brother in Tipper's mind, emerge at the age of sixteen as the most spellbinding of the Babes. Someone told Tipper that Duncan Edwards would win a hundred caps for England – he'd be one of the greatest ever – and in his mind Tipper rehearsed playing neat one-twos with Big Duncan, in preparation for the time when the two of them would come of age together.

During his first term in Borstal he watched the casual violence around him – on the landings, in the kitchen, the common room or the shower block, out of sight or in full view of the wardens (it made no difference) – with a swelling sense of panic. Tipper himself had never hit anyone. What saved him from being picked on was his ability on the football field. At fifteen Tipper could dribble defenders, had two good feet, and could beat a full-back for speed. Other boys *noticed* him for that and so, despite his size, he avoided the gauntlet of seemingly random violence around him.

At night, lying behind the locked metal door, unable to sleep, he imagined Big Duncan Edwards watching over him from the foot of the bed. Big Duncan told him to hold tight, to keep out of trouble. Tipper hoped secretly that Duncan might get caught pinching a few quid from Bobby Charlton's jacket in the Old Trafford dressing room so he'd get sent to Borstal for a few months and they could be room-mates.

313

Instead, Tipper was befriended by his room-mate, an older
boy with a weasel face, who taught him dirty jokes, and how to
play cards, and persuaded Tipper to run errands for him and
pinch food from the kitchens where he worked. Tipper was
light-fingered and quick. Soon he was being directed to steal
from other boys. It was a sort of game, until the two of them
came up against George Bentley – a veteran of the system at
seventeen and whose watch Tipper stole in the shower block.
George Bentley's minions questioned Tipper, then let him go.
Two days later, Tipper's weasel-faced room-mate was dropped
twenty feet from the overhead landing on to the canteen tiles,
his head slamming against the side of a metal table just before
he hit the floor at a shocking angle.

'Remember what happened to him,' George Bentley told
Tipper, 'and there won't be no misunderstandings now you're
with me. You *are* with me?'

Tipper nodded.

The authorities didn't take action against anyone after the
incident as far as Tipper could make out. It was nothing
unusual. George Bentley had a reputation for ruthlessness –
he'd knifed an older man in a quarrel over a stolen car.

The chaplain was the only other person who took an interest in Tipper. He was a red-faced Irishman whom none of the
wardens took very seriously. The chaplain pointed out to
Tipper that George Bentley was bad news, a lost soul. But
Tipper kept remembering the weasel-faced boy falling from
the landing, the crack as his weasel face hit the table a fraction
of a second before his body hit the floor.

The chaplain got Tipper into the choir. It turned out he
had good pitch. He enjoyed the singing. The choir sang at the
local church on Sundays, and in between services Tipper

salted away candlesticks and offertory cash for George Bentley.

At one point Tipper was given a careers interview. 'What sort of job do you want to do?' he was asked.

'Play football,' he said. He was guileless. He stole the careers adviser's nameplate and a half packet of Richmonds from the desk.

'There must be *something* you want to do?' the man had said. Tipper knew what he wanted. He wanted to play football with Duncan Edwards. He wanted to be one of the Busby Babes winning the European Cup. He wanted *not* to be the weasel-faced boy.

It was the chaplain who arranged for him to work with the piano tuner who came to repair and tune the piano used to accompany the Borstal's choir. When Tipper got out, the piano tuner offered him a job as his bag-carrying apprentice. Tipper worked with him for four months – taking the odd piece of jewellery or silverware from spinsters' sideboards, pinging piano wires like a double bass with his tuning fork to sound rock and roll tunes – until a wire sounding C two octaves above middle C snapped while he was bent right over a piano. The wire just missed his left retina but seared the adjacent muscle tissue controlling his eyeball.

Afterwards, Tipper could no longer judge the flight of a football. It left him with a view of the world that lacked depth or perspective. He was on the sick for half a year, fearing he'd lose the eye completely. It left him with a stigma. Sometimes, especially when he was tired or under stress, his eyeball would oscillate rapidly, unable to fix on an object.

By the time Tipper came off the sick he had already established a routine of running errands for any of the George

Bentleys he could latch on to around Haslingden and Lowell, and he spent his free time in the Blue Dahlia Coffee Bar. Good singing pitch meant nothing to him. He'd only wanted to play football for Manchester United but one good eye and one that wandered put an end to that. The night Duncan Edwards – at the age of twenty-one – died of his injuries after the Munich air crash, Tipper smashed all the windows of the Blue Dahlia Coffee Bar in a rage of grief. He wasn't used to having feelings. He'd grown numb after the weasel-faced boy was dropped. In the days that followed the crash he kept seeing Duncan Edwards falling from the tilted, doorless aeroplane. Each time, he saw him thrown towards the earth, his head catching the table edge before his body slammed on to the Borstal tiles. Tipper, looking up each time, saw it was George Bentley pilot- ing the plane; he was laughing.

In the months that followed, whilst Matt Busby and United began the task of building a new team, Tipper dreamed of play- ing football with those of the Busby Babes who had died in the air crash. The team had only eight men and had to borrow a goalkeeper (Harry Gregg having survived the crash), but in Tipper's imagination they had to play against a full team and so Tipper found himself playing too. All the way through the dream he kept shouting for the ball, but each time Big Duncan Edwards or one of the others passed the ball to Tipper it came to him out of a depthless background that made it hard for him to judge, flat-footing him, playing tricks, and he lost pos- session to the other side.

Tipper had wanted to call the baby Duncan if it had been a boy. He didn't tell Morag. He wouldn't go into the room with the doctor when they were breaking the news.

'What's he know about my child?' Tipper said, smoking a cigarette pinched between two fingers and a thumb.

'We have to listen to them,' Morag said.

But Tipper shook his head. He left the ward and wandered round the hospital while Morag went in alone to see the doctor. She found Tipper a couple of hours later, sitting on a wall by the bus stop.

'Is it going to be all right?' Tipper said.

She nodded fiercely, meaning that they were going to let her keep Dorothy. She didn't know what Tipper meant.

When Dorothy became a toddler Tipper would watch Morag playing with her, making up endless games in which she acted and responded and in which Dorothy looked on.

'What are you doing *that* for?' he said. 'She doesn't understand.'

He didn't know whether he felt worse for Morag or for himself that he couldn't play those games with Dorothy. Instead, Tipper waited for Dorothy to do things so that he could react. Whenever he tried to show her something, she watched him quizzically. It was like sending out radar signals and waiting for echoes that never came.

Tipper would play football with the local kids for hours in the street. He liked them giving him lip so he could give it back, grinning. He liked just being able to be *Tipper*. He had imagined that being a father would give him licence to avoid being a grown-up all the time. When he played football with the kids, he played as one of them. If they broke a window, he ran with the rest of them. He was always anxious to win, seldom holding back in the tackle, providing a running commentary on each match in Kenneth Wolstenholme's voice.

The night before Manchester United finally won the

European Cup, he arrived home with a television in a holdall so that he could watch the match. Morag asked if the television had to go back.

'Oh, sometime,' Tipper said vaguely.

The evening after, Tipper and all the kids replayed the match out in the street, fourteen-a-side, then flopped down in the summer's evening heat, drinking bottles of Tizer Tipper had bought to celebrate. They talked about the match – about Best and Law and Charlton – until the kids were called in by their parents one by one and only Tipper was left. When he finally went in, Morag was bathing Dorothy in the sitting room.

'You missed tea,' Morag said.

Tipper looked curiously at the clock. He was carrying the ball, and the Tizer empties.

'It's cold now,' she said. 'I don't suppose you want it any more?'

He felt queasy from all the Tizer and the running around. 'I'll make something later.'

'We've nothing much in, and I've no money.'

Tipper fished in his pocket. He produced three pound notes and some change. He handed it all over to Morag. She didn't ask where the money had come from. It was never clear with Tipper how he came by money – he just seemed to produce it when they needed some.

'I'll take the broth that's left over from tea up to my mother's,' Morag said, 'and I'll get a few bits at the Co-op on the way back. I'll make you some egg and chips later. Are you all right with Dorothy for a bit?'

'How long will you be?'

'Not long,' Morag said impatiently. 'Just *play* with her.'

Dorothy wandered from room to room in her dressing gown. Tipper played with the toy xylophone Morag had bought for her sixth birthday. He was tapping out tunes he had heard on the new television. Each time he heard a musical phrase, he copied it back in the same key on the xylophone – the way he used to do on the piano for the chaplain at the Borstal. Dorothy came back into the room. She stood, watching him – small eyes, large moon face – then took the wooden mallet and started hitting the metal notes randomly. Tipper let her hit away, but the random notes jarred on him. After a while he told her to stop but she carried on, not looking at him. He took hold of her hand to make her stop the noise. She didn't react, but kept staring stolidly at the keys. So he moved his hand – holding hers – over the keys and tapped out one of the programme signature tunes. He copied the same tune three or four times, holding her warm hand in his. Then he let go. Dorothy tapped out the tune on her own.

'Do it again,' Tipper said.

'Do it again,' Dorothy repeated.

Dorothy did it over and over.

When Morag arrived back, Tipper showed her the trick. But when he tried to teach Dorothy a different tune – holding her hand the same way and tapping the keys – she kept repeating the first tune again and again until Tipper got mad and banged his hand on the table, making Morag jump, and when Dorothy and Morag had both gone to bed he took the xylophone out to the yard and put it in the bin.

Each night, Morag and Dorothy said prayers together. Sometimes Morag shamed Tipper into joining in, and the three of them kneeled together and prayed. Tipper would sometimes wonder what Morag prayed for. He guessed that Dorothy just kneeled and waited until it was time to get up. Tipper himself

319

prayed for Duncan Edwards. Sometimes he prayed that he could see with both eyes again so that the football didn't take him by surprise and play tricks on him. And sometimes he prayed for God to make Dorothy normal, but God never did, and the next day – as they always did if they went out together – Morag and Dorothy would lock arms as they walked and Tipper would walk a couple of strides behind them.

Tipper had not long been out of prison when they moved on to the St Silas estate. They were one of the first families to move there. Some properties were still being built, and most of the finished houses were still empty. Morag seemed to feel all this was a good thing – a clean slate, she said. She told Tipper things would be better on the new estate. She meant the burden of Dorothy; she meant jobs for Tipper. There were inside toilets in all the houses up there, she pointed out; there were electric fires; there were gardens. So the Council were bound to make sure that the place stayed nice. As if to mark the change, he remembered, she had told him she wanted to learn to dance.

Morag had always been anxious that things should be better than they were. Tipper hadn't minded them as they were. He'd liked being at the centre of things in the old street. Without people around him all the time, he wasn't sure who he was – and he had no wish to learn to dance.

On the new estate, those few people who were already there stayed hidden, and there were no kids for Tipper to play football with. On the new estate Tipper missed the open layout of the street, the bookie's, the pub, the routines and the schemes that made him feel part of the world.

After they moved, Tipper started dreaming of Duncan Edwards again. But now, in Tipper's dreams, Big Duncan wasn't playing football with Tipper – he was wandering round the rain-washed, empty alleys and cul-de-sacs of the new estate, forlorn, and Tipper had no idea what he was meant to do about it. He found it difficult to settle into any kind of rhythm. He drank more than he had done before. Morag badgered him to find a job. During the day he went back down to his old stomping grounds, telling Morag he was going down to the Employment Exchange or round the building sites. He had a couple of casual flings – with women he'd known years back at the Blue Dahlia Coffee Bar – involving sporadic, good-natured sex, but he knew he would always go back to Morag because Morag was the one he *needed*.

Down at the bottom of the estate, the maisonette blocks were still being built. The builders came and went every day and Tipper developed a habit of wandering down to watch them. At night, wary of seeing Duncan Edwards's bleak expression in his dream again, he prowled the building site and the huts for things to steal, and during the day he'd wake up late, often having fallen asleep in his armchair, eat, then go out and watch the builders working on the maisonettes, making friends with them, telling jokes and cadging cigarettes. Until one morning he found that they had gone; the maisonettes were finished. The scaffolding and the huts had gone; in their place was a desert of bald earth, tussocks, lumps of concrete and broken building bricks.

It was the only open space left on the estate. Tipper imagined they were going to build more houses eventually. That night he dreamed of Duncan Edwards again, but instead of wandering around the closed-in alleys and cul-de-sacs of the estate, Big Duncan was down by the maisonettes. He was kicking a football with Roger Byrne, across the open land where the builders' huts had been. But the open land was now a football stadium – grassed and pristine. The stands were filled with kids, and Duncan and Roger Byrne in their red United strips were waving to Tipper to come down and join them. Tipper woke in a sweat. It was three-thirty in the morning. He dressed without waking Morag and walked through the deserted estate to the newly completed maisonette blocks. He paced out the length of the deserted building site beside it. It was a hundred strides, and forty the other way. It was enough for a football pitch.

Tipper waited a month. The builders didn't come back. More people began moving on to the estate. On the land beside the maisonettes, grasses began to take root in the rubble and the bare earth mounds. Then one morning Tipper walked down on to the land with a spade and a crowbar. He took his jacket off, and began levering the first of the lumps of concrete out of the ground.

For three months he went down each day to work on the strip of land, clearing it of bricks, concrete slabs and girders abandoned by the builders, dragging them off the pitch he had marked out with pegs, and dumping them down in the gulley where the land dropped away. After that he started levelling the land spade by spade, barrow by barrow, working through the winter, often standing in mud, grinning his gummy grin.

The following spring he dug it over and seeded it. He got the seed from a businessman he was doing the odd job for. Ronnie Roots was impressed by a man who wanted paying in grass seed. To keep the birds off the seed until it sprouted, Tipper tied lines of rags across the pitch. When the birds grew used to that, Tipper borrowed the kite Morag had bought for Dorothy. He fastened strips of coloured paper all the way down the length of the string and fastened its end to his waist, then he ran up and down the sidelines, making the strips of paper flap and whistle to scare the birds off until dusk fell.

Barry Catlin had been watching him. Barry had an Alsatian called Paddy Crerand that he walked past the pitch every day, watching Tipper but not saying anything. It was the first dog Barry had on the estate. After Paddy Crerand died, Barry got another Alsatian – called Nobby Stiles. Then an Irish setter called George Best and then a collie called Brian Kidd, before he finally got the mongrel called Denis Law. Tipper heard him shouting for the dog one day and asked Barry if he was a Manchester United supporter. Barry Catlin in turn asked what Tipper had been doing.

Within a month the two of them were carrying dismantled goalposts from the Council pitches two miles away. Tipper assured Barry they were bought and paid for and they were only having to dig them out of the ground under cover of darkness because the Council groundsman was off sick. They marked Tipper's pitch out with a machine borrowed from the same Council groundsman. The day they marked the pitch out and erected the goalposts, kids from the slowly filling estate came down to see whose pitch it was and whether they could use it. It had taken Tipper a year and a half.

After that, nothing mattered. It was as if, unable to gauge the depth of things, frightened of floating away if Morag gave herself to Dorothy completely, Tipper Gill had dug his own foundations in the St Silas earth.

Anchored safely, a ship can weather any storm. And so Tipper weathered the fact that he had a daughter he could scarcely look in the eye; the way that the estate disintegrated around them like a cake left in the rain; the demands of Ronnie

Roots; the pass that his best friend made, drunk, one night at Morag; and the rise and fall of Councillor Roy Porrit. He weathered Morag falling a little in love with who Roy Porrit *might* have been, and the way her dreams for the estate threatened to overwhelm her and tear her from him. But always she drifted back to where his vessel lay, and, if he was never too sure why, he was at least grateful – the way the Busby Babes might have been grateful, having lost the ball, for the cover afforded them by Duncan Edwards and for a well-timed tackle to win possession back.

20

Whispers

The Big House closed down four months after Mr George's death on the final Founder's Day. It was sold along with the grounds to the golf club. An electrical fault in the wiring caused a fire two months later which gutted large parts of the building. With insurance not yet secured on the property, the golf-club committee abandoned the idea of converting the Big House into a new clubhouse because of the prohibitive cost. Work on converting the garden and the bottom field into a new eighteenth hole was abandoned at that point and the course remained as it had previously been. The golf club put the Big House up for sale again in 1977, but for a number of years no buyer came forward.

Rumours abounded that a hermit was living on the derelict property. When the Big House had closed, Goose had been found a flat in a sheltered-housing complex in the town, but he chose to spend most of his time in the derelict shell of his former home. He rejected all offers of an alternative lifestyle. He spent his remaining years trying to restore the gardens and the allotment to their former glory. He frequently slept over in the gutted remains of the Big House, and kept a dog for company and to keep the golf-club committee at bay in case they objected to his presence. For some years, the golf club forgot they even *owned* the Big House and its grounds. As for Goose, he kept a lamp lit in the window whenever he stopped there, in case the old fairground bear came by that way again.

In the midwinter of 1989 the reservoir up beyond the knoll froze over. When the water thawed in late February, Goose's body was found. He had gone walking on the frozen surface and had fallen through the paper-thin ice halfway across, somehow misjudging the weight it could bear. He was sixty-one.

Darius Whittle continued for some time to command the Council and everything else on the horizon. His daughter, sent to a private school and protected from men by her father, who knew how men were, fell for the ambitious and good-looking son of a pub barmaid. Matt Hoyle had the look of a medieval saint, hiding the talents of a gifted scoundrel. For his part, Darius reluctantly gave his new son-in-law a part to play in his business empire and in time brought him on to the Council.

When Darius had the first of his disabling strokes, his son-in-law quickly assumed control with the help of the smitten Whittle daughter. Within three years the remarkable Matt Hoyle brought Darius Whittle's empire to its knees – driving out the talent, reinvesting in outlandish schemes, corrupting everyone in sight, indulging in a string of women, and finally committing the one sin the helplessly watching Darius feared most, getting caught. Cut out of the will, Matt Hoyle turned up at Darius's funeral unwanted and unannounced to make a furious assault on his father-in-law's reputation. Investigations, both criminal and financial, were begun as a result of the allegations. People in the local corridors of power still smile when the name Darius Whittle crops up.

'Poor Darius,' they say, as if to emphasize that they at least never owed him any allegiance.

Every year, Walter took a fortnight's leave in December to play Father Christmas in a big department store. He gave his services for free, and he was acknowledged to be the best Father Christmas in the city. It must have seemed incongruous for a university professor to do such a thing, but everyone on the campus knew and nobody ribbed him for it. His colleagues and students were in awe of how good a Father Christmas he was.

It was a fairly open secret that Walter was gay, although he regarded his personal life as a private matter.

'It's just who I *am*, Noah,' he used to say.

His real passion remained astronomy ('That's where the *real* answers are, Noah,' he once confided), the subject on which he lectured at the university. He continued to play Father Christmas until the virus finally began to affect his appearance. He had told the department-store manager that he was HIV positive in 1991. She had fired him on the spot. Children complained, however, that his replacement wasn't like the *real* Father Christmas. They meant Walter.

To Walter's relief and gratitude, he was asked to return to the department store the following Christmas. He continued to be Santa for the next two years. He died in 1994. While he was in the hospice the manager took to visiting him every week; she was with him when he died. She still sees other AIDS patients in the hospice one evening a week as a volunteer visitor.

Megan and Jacob were married in 1975.

Jacob was employed by a subsidiary of an American corporation which promoted him several times and paid for him to work for an MBA in Manchester. He eventually set up his own business which continues to thrive. He has played golf with the same three friends every Sunday morning for eighteen years. Megan refers to it caustically as playtime. As a couple, they row furiously about politics, women's rights, eating meat – everything. They love each other madly.

Megan herself rose to become the director of a small charity in the North-West of England devoted to developing community businesses and co-operatives in inner cities. She was never averse to badgering Jacob's clients for donations or any other offers of help. She resigned when the first of her four children was due. She began a campaign from home to fund a local playgroup in their village and then helped to run it for eight years. Their children are grown now. Megan is at present a leading light in the National Pre-School Learning Alliance, and a local councillor. She has suffered an occasional fit, but her drugs keep the epilepsy largely in check.

She is shortly due to become a grandmother for the first time.

Gifford became an engineer at the nearby British Aerospace plant. He married, they had a son, and when the marriage began to go wrong, Gifford started to drink. He told Noah later that it was a way of steadying his nerves. Eventually his nerve broke and he disappeared. His wife divorced him a year later and subsequently remarried.

He resurfaced after three years. He found another job in the area and worked two evenings a week as an unqualified sessional worker in a local youth club to pay for the child maintenance he owed. He was introduced to rock-climbing ('A place where a man can *breathe*, Noah') by a co-worker.

Eventually, he decided to retrain as a full-time youth worker. He moved to Cumbria eight years ago to take up a job in an outdoor-pursuits centre.

He lives in a terraced cottage in Keswick and is now the director of the centre. He is reconciled with his son, Luke, who stays with him most weekends. Luke has become a renowned Lakeland rock climber and, to Gifford's great pleasure, has pioneered several new routes in his favourite Borrowdale Valley. These days, Gifford chooses to wait for him at the summit with the flask and sandwiches on any climb rated harder than 'severe'. He continues to attend weekly AA meetings in Carlisle. It is fourteen years since he last had a drink.

Solomon had been found at the age of four locked naked in a room emptied of everything except for a straw mattress. He arrived at the Big House in 1954 and was, like Gifford, one of the orphans still there when it closed. As a young man he worked his way through a number of jobs. He was in trouble with the police on several occasions and was on probation for a while. Twice, Noah had to bail him out. He had a mental breakdown at the age of twenty-six and spent eight months in a therapeutic community run by the Richmond Fellowship. It was after that that he learned to drive.

He began working for a long-distance haulier through a contact of Noah's, driving lorries to the Continent with heavy-metal music thundering in his cab. Two years ago Solomon was diagnosed as having a cancerous ulcer, having told no one about the pain for almost a year. He was operated on successfully. He wore a colostomy bag for a year after that until the procedure was successfully reversed. He now works for a parcel-delivery firm. He claims to have the most extensive heavy-metal CD collection in Lancashire. He has never married.

The others are all out there somewhere.

Sometimes Noah catches a glimpse of a face on a street or in a shop and he stands there wondering. Sometimes he sees a name in a newspaper – a christening, a suicide, a birthday. They are all out there. Sometimes at night Noah stands outside and wonders where they are, and wishes – as Goose once wished for the bear – that in the end they made it home, wherever that might be.

Noah was met by Flo in the reception area at the hospice. Flo took his hand and held it.

She told him that Sassy had died about half an hour ago. Flo was a big woman by then. She had been married twice and divorced twice and now lived on her own with a red setter and a German shepherd. They talked, as they had often done when he had been there visiting Sassy. She said to him that the jobs people did for the dying – feeding them, wiping the shit from between their legs – were greater acts of love than the romance of courtship, or the flowers and chocolates, or the sex. Flo had never had children. She'd never wanted them, she said. Her specialism had become the elderly. She had a particular skill with the dying. She was regarded with a kind of awe by the other staff for the miraculous touch she had with such people. She took Noah through to Sassy's room. They stood over the bed, looking down at Sassy's massively wrinkled face, the closed eyes, the small body empty of life.

'You should talk to her,' Flo said to Noah, sensing his

awkwardness. 'I always talk to them for an hour or so after their hearts stop beating.'

'Why?' Noah asked.

'I don't know,' Flo said quietly. 'I'm not religious or anything – Rachel knew that. But we all do it here. I tell the new nurses and the volunteers to do it. It feels right, that's all. As if they can still hear. As if they're still getting ready to leave.'

So while Flo stood silently beside him, Noah whispered to Sassy. He wasn't sure if she could hear him, but it didn't matter. Like Flo had said, it felt right. He didn't know what to say to make sense of the wreckage of her life. He didn't know much about anything, it seemed to him sometimes, but he talked anyway.

Turkey Street no longer led anywhere. It petered out into asphalt, and then grass.

Like Mr George's grandiose dream, Accrington Stanley too was gone. Peel Park Council School was still there. Small children ran around the yard in frenetic playtime circles, wrapped in winter coats. The stadium in which Stanley had played stood behind the school. Now there was only a field open on all sides. Two muddy schoolboy pitches ran widthways across it. The Len's Cooked Meat End was a grass bank; the other stands were long gone, including the one purchased from the Aldershot Tattoo which had finally bankrupted the club. The stadium had gradually fallen into disrepair. The main stand which had run alongside Turkey Street had been vandalized and wrecked long before it was demolished, as if for so long no one had *thought* to rip it down.

Noah wandered around for a while, then stood imagining – a middle-aged man alone in a field. He didn't stand on the pitch but to the side, where he imagined Mr George and the others had stood in 1937, watching with the bear Stanley's greatest triumph in the FA Cup, and where they had stood week after week, waiting for Stanley to win promotion, to become the team that Dunkiss always thought they deserved to be, were destined to become, ought to have been.

A raw wind blew in from Hameldon Hill. He pulled the collar of his coat up, stamped his feet. The only sounds up there above the town were the wind coming off the moors and the scraps of children's cries being blown like paper across the field from the schoolyard on Turkey Street.

Rachel and Noah were married the year after the Big House closed down. They were the last two. One year they decided to spend Christmas with Megan and Jacob, who were living in Lancaster at the time. It was snowing the evening they set off. Noah said he'd drive. Rachel was two months pregnant. He didn't know.

He never stammered again. He was in hospital for three weeks after the crash. His knee still gives him trouble in the winter.

At the funeral he had them play recordings of Duke Ellington's second *Sacred Concert*, and a Thelonius Monk tune she especially liked.

Rachel had always liked to leave scribbled notes or scraps of poems for him in special places. It remained her way of whispering. Sometimes they were messages; sometimes they were sentences she liked to hear spoken out loud. Every now and then he would discover one that had lain undiscovered while she was alive.

And how one can imagine oneself among them
I do not know;
It was all so unimaginably different
And all so long ago.

One day, he took the book of poems she'd had published down from the shelf. It was the first time he had looked at it since she had died. There was a kind of desperation in the act. When he opened it, a note fell out from between the pages: *You did not fail. You only succeeded quietly. Listen!*

He turned the note around in his hand. He sat trying to remember why she might have written such a thing. He tried to imagine which orphan's small crisis had led her to offer him this reassurance. He rummaged in Rachel's old record collection and put on a quiet Miles Davis tune. There was a coffee ring on the record sleeve. Goose had drawn a face inside it – two eyes and a grinning mouth.

Later in the evening, Noah played a more exuberant Ellington concert, full of joy and colour. He smiled at the memory of Rachel's expression as she listened to jazz. People from the Big House, Noah realized, would always be leaving him notes, reminders, signposts. They would always be whispering to him. There would always be Rachel's bitter-sweet music in his head, and Goose's antics; Dublin's Tiger Moth would always be the promise of a hum coming down the valley; and Mr George would always be arriving, always looking round, stepping down in Dounleavey's pristine borrowed jacket, a brilliant crushed carnation in his buttonhole and snow beginning to fall on the town, and his whole life (or so it would seem) would always lie before him.

21

Levelling the Score

Noah Brindle is in the yard of the Mustard Seed Centre in Lowell. His birthday passed quietly. He is fifty-two years old, with fine blue eyes, a long body that he carries inelegantly, long arms, heavy shoulders, a lack of definition. The yellow fisherman's sweater that Elly Pascoe mocks him for hangs on him. He is playing basketball with Josh Pascoe.

The two of them take turns in possession of the ball, one of them jinking lazily to slide past and win a clear shot at the hoop, the other blocking. Josh is the more agile. Almost as tall as Noah, he is slimmer, moves more easily around the court with the ball, and runs wider circles in his search for openings. There is a rhythm to Josh's movement with the ball that otherwise eludes the boy. The basketball organizes him, instils a tension and a discipline in his limbs. Moving like this around the court he seems more adult than child, except for the grin than breaks out foolishly on his face (Elly's face and yet not Elly's) when he breaks free of Noah's guard, swivels and shoots, and the ball is swallowed by the basket.

Noah moves with more economy, minding the difficult knee that is beginning to protest at the steady pounding on the tarmac of the court. Noah is content to be marked closely, to work with his back to the basket and to roll the close-marking Josh around him by tempting him into an interception and spinning the other way on his good leg.

Noah is breathing firmly now. The ball bounces once more off the backboard in the shadow of the old church and falls away. Josh jogs across to fetch it. With one hand, he works the ball up again from its diminishing bounce. He works a rhythm with the ball, hip high on the bounce – one, two, three, four. He is marshalling his forces once more, considering his options. He is waiting to make his move, somehow seeming simultaneously absorbed and unconcerned. And Noah, waiting too, feels a sudden, rising sense of place. Perhaps it is nothing more than physical exertion and commitment to the game, its immediacy, its universal present, but the feeling fills him nevertheless. It is the sense that the two of them are part of some single, seamless, co-ordinated motion – the two of them woven together into some larger fabric – that Noah feels but cannot explain. Noah nestles in tight again behind Josh's back, ready to mark him. His arms are stretched out, as if at any moment, instead of marking him, Noah might elect to embrace him.

Noah found the centre trashed two nights ago. He knew, even before Linde told him, that it was Melanie's brother levelling the score. All the internal windows were smashed, rooms were ransacked, filing cabinets emptied. The food co-op's weighing scales were covered in shit. Every one of Tipper Gill's football trophies, won by various St Silas teams over the years, had been broken with some diligence. The trophy cabinet they had been kept in had been toppled and smashed. Everything that could be dragged – playgroup trikes, kitchenware, records going back to 1972, Barry Catlin's immaculate files, photographs of playgroups, tenant committees and Tipper's junior football teams – had been piled up in the middle of the hall, doused with lighter fuel and set alight. Linde Wzinska saw the boy running from the building.

The fire brigade managed to save the shell of the centre. Graffiti had been sprayed on the office walls. The smoke had obscured most of it, but the crux of its message was still visible on Noah's office door.

'Tosser,' it said.

Everyone knew who had done it. Melanie's brother bragged about it down on the estate. He said Ronnie must be soft, keeping an eye out for that tosser in the community centre. He said why the fuck did it matter anyway if the fucking place was being shut down?

People guessed he'd been on something when he did it, and that retribution – on the orders of Ronnie Roots – would follow in due course. It was only a matter of time. Tipper, curious, dispassionate, imagined the youth falling from a landing, his dumb head striking the table a fraction of a second before his body hit the floor.

On the flat roof of the deserted maisonette block, Tipper Gill can see across the roof tops of the St Silas estate. The light in the sky is fading but Tipper can still see as far as Lowell's town centre and the early night lights of the distant houses on the high street. In the opposite direction he sees the land rising up beyond the houses towards the moors, and Haslingden.

The goalposts at one end of the roof are two hazard cones. Barry Catlin's goals at the other end are the two men's coats dropped on the bitumen. The roof is bordered by a small kerb a foot high before the sudden three-storey drop. Plastic skylight bubbles, aerials and ventilation stacks intrude on to the contrived football pitch up here in the sky.

The game being played up here by Tipper Gill and Barry Catlin has none of the languid rhythm of the basketball being played by Noah Brindle and Josh Pascoe in the yard of the Mustard Seed across town. Even with all the obstacles, and the roof's tarred and bitumened surface, Tipper has only one hurrying, mysteriously urgent speed. As for Barry Catlin, he has things on his mind that compel him to compete full-bloodedly. There has been another assault. A rape. The woman, in her fifties, is in a critical condition. Despite the fact that Nathan Ripley hanged himself, the police are saying the attack bears all the hallmarks of the earlier, less serious, ones on Olwen Sudders and two other women. The woman who has been raped had a note pushed through her door, made from letters cut from newspapers. She hadn't told the police, but they found it in her flat in the hours following the attack. She is on a ventilator. The police are searching for new leads, and Barry Catlin up on the roof of the empty maisonette block is clattering into tackles, running with the ball and shooting at Tipper's goal in the draining light. Only by looking closely at the scene – only by standing there on the flat roof sixty feet above the ground, with the two men engrossed in their frantic game – could you see that there is no ball.

Morag didn't talk much about the collapse of her dream. She felt she could cope with her own loss of face. She could put that down to a judgement on her rashness, on her loss of perspective. It was cause and effect. But her guilt over the loss of Tipper's football field – the last open space on the estate – was a greater burden. She agonized for weeks about what to do. There was nothing she could say to Tipper. One evening, when he'd come back from wherever he was spending his days these days, she had Dorothy present him with a carrier bag. He opened it and pulled out a red replica 1950s Manchester United football shirt, with short sleeves and a long, old-fashioned white V-neck – like the Busby Babes had worn.

Morag started to go to church again. She didn't attend the services but she called into the church to sit at the back when the place was empty. It was a time to *think*, she told herself. She went alone – with Dorothy. Not long after that she arranged for Dorothy to go to a day centre. Dorothy had gone to a sheltered workshop at the age of nineteen, when she'd finished at special school, but Morag removed her after discovering that one of the men at the centre had put his hand up her skirt. Morag had withdrawn her, and had learned to cope after that with having Dorothy with her all the time, and the kids on the estate singing 'I'm Jake the Peg' at them as they went by.

Dorothy was put forward by the day centre to join a supported employment programme. Morag had to be persuaded to give her permission. Eventually, Dorothy was offered a job in a tea shop two mornings a week. Morag had to help teach Dorothy how to catch the bus alone, and where to get off. After a few weeks, Morag went with Noah to visit the tea shop while Dorothy was there. She cried when Ted, the manager, said, 'Dorothy? Sure, she's through the back with the others on her break. Are you her mum?' In the kitchen, Dorothy was wearing a sweatshirt that said 'The Pantry', like the other staff. Ted told Morag that Dorothy had already decided what she was going to buy with her Christmas bonus.

*

Noah ambles back into defence again, breathing hard.

'You ready to surrender yet, old man?' Josh says.

'What's the score?' Noah asks.

'You're down about twelve.'

Hands on knees, Noah shakes his head. 'Still time to catch up.'

'Catch up? We'll be here till midnight!'

'*Play.*'

Josh shrugs, grins, begins to bounce the ball. They fall into the pattern of play again.

Last night, Noah received another telephone call. He had finished writing the last chapter. He had given it to Elly Pascoe to read.

'I don't know what to say, Brindle,' she had said. 'You never let me near those poems you were supposed to have written.'

She had taken the manuscript and glanced at the first page.

'Who was always arriving, Brindle?'

Noah, looking away from her, had shrugged.

'You'll read it?' he'd said, as she looked through the early pages.

'Yes.' Elly had looked hard at him, then smiled. 'Will there be a fee?'

The final scenes he had recently written were still playing in his head like a movie reel when the phone rang.

'Hello?'

'Is Joan there, please?'

'Joan?'

'I want to tell her something,' the voice on the end of the phone said. 'Can I talk to her?'

'There isn't a Joan,' Noah said quietly. 'Joan doesn't live here.'

The voice paused, as if the man was thinking for a moment. 'Would you tell her something for me?' he said. 'If you see her?'

'You want me to tell Joan something?'

'Yes. Please. If you see her, tell her I haven't had a drink in a month.'

'You want me to say that?'

'Yes,' the man said. 'Tell her that.'

'I'll tell her if I see her,' Noah said.

'You promise to tell her?'

'Sure,' Noah said. 'I promise.'

'Thanks.' The man sounded sober. He sounded relieved, as if he had finally pulled back from a precipice. 'I knew you would,' he said. 'I'll go now. Thanks.' And he put the phone down.

From where they are playing in the yard at the rear of the Mustard Seed, Noah Brindle and Josh Pascoe cannot see the front of the building where the women have been arriving in ones and twos. They cannot see the women leaving pebbles on the top porch step and then moving away. The Mustard Seed has been vacated; the sign attached to the front buttress of the former church says 'Sold'; the front doors are padlocked shut and boarded up.

It was Olwen Sudders' idea. Linde Wzinska had mentioned Noah's foolishness over the pebbles – how Linde herself had always carried pebbles in the pockets of her coat, how Noah had learned of this and had later confessed to imagining how *all* the women on the estate might carry pebbles around with them in this way. And so Olwen Sudders had written down what they should do, and Morag Gill had arranged for the women she

340

knew to leave pebbles on the steps of the Mustard Seed as a measure of their indebtedness both to the place and to Noah.

One pebble for each problem faced; one for each small dream realized.

Noah cannot see the line of women. He cannot yet see the pebbles on the steps growing in number as each woman quietly lays her pebbles down and leaves. He cannot yet see that the pile of pebbles, after an hour, covers the steps.

On the high roof of the maisonette block across town, Tipper Gill has taken a pass from Tommy Taylor in his own half. He slides it down the line to Eddie Coleman who is jockeyed aggressively infield by Barry Catlin in his flapping Al Capone suit, being careful not to go too near the edge of the flat roof. Tipper takes the return ball and plays it square to Duncan Edwards, running on for a one-two and collecting it inside Barry's half. The men in red shirts sweep forward. Roger Byrne is shouting for the ball on the far side, unmarked, and Tipper swings a long ball that's hard to follow in the deepening gloom of the evening and the ill-lit pitch. Tipper's team push forward, and so they go on, running hard, shouting for the ball, striving to keep possession, urging each other on as if they could play for ever up there, running more furiously, defending more frantically, growing more desperate, running closer and closer to the edge of the roof.

So it is that Josh Pascoe, on long, coltish legs, drives in one more time for the last assault on the basket – because Elly will have supper ready for them both by now – and fires a deep shot towards it. They hold their breath. It catches the rim, judders, then bounces out, incomplete, the ball still alive.

Instinctively, they both see the possibility, both knowing that the game is redefined in that instant. The first one to the ball can get the final rebound, and they both adjust their momentum for it.

Noah, moving more slowly as he strains to alter his direction in the air, reaches for the ball and pulls it into him. Josh is across, blocking him, stretching, but Noah swivels on his good leg, wrong-foots Josh, reaches up in slow motion and fires the ball.

In Noah Brindle's pocket there is a piece of paper, folded over twice and dog-eared. There are three things written on it, as Fred Wyke's wife had suggested. She'd said it was a reminder; a kind of map. Noah writes down three things every morning now and slips the piece of paper into his pocket. Sometimes the list changes, sometimes it doesn't.

Elly and Josh, Mr George, white-cell count are the three things written on the piece of paper in his pocket as Noah Brindle twists, reaches tall, and throws the ball from his big hands. The ball rides away from him and, as it approaches the basket, begins to fall sweetly in its casual arc.